NO TRACE

Barry Maitland
NO TRACE

A Brock and Kolla Mystery

St. Martin's Minotaur

NEW YORK

www.minotaurbooks.com

Library of Congress Cataloging-in-Publication Data

Maitland, Barry.
    No trace : a Brock and Kolla mystery / Barry Maitland.—1st U.S. ed.
        p. cm.
    ISBN-13: 978-0-312-35892-1
    ISBN-10: 0-312-35892-X
    1. Brock, David (Fictitious character)—Fiction. 2. Kolla, Kathy (Fictitious character)—Fiction. 3. Policewomen—Fiction. 4. Police—England—London—Fiction. 5. London (England)—Fiction. I. Title.

PR9619.3.M2635 N6 2006
823'.914—dc22

                                                                2006045082

First published in Australia by Allen & Unwin

First U.S. Edition: October 2006

10   9   8   7   6   5   4   3   2   1

FOR MARGARET,

and with thanks to Sam, Scott and Philip for inspiration

Before going down among you to pull out your decaying teeth, your
running ears, your tongues full of sores,
Before breaking your putrid bones . . .
Before tearing out your ugly sexual organ, incontinent and slimy . . .
Before all that,
We shall take a big antiseptic bath,
And we warn you
We are murderers.

EXTRACT FROM THE DADA MANIFESTO "TO THE PUBLIC",

SIGNED BY RIBEMONT-DESSAIGNES, PARIS, 1920

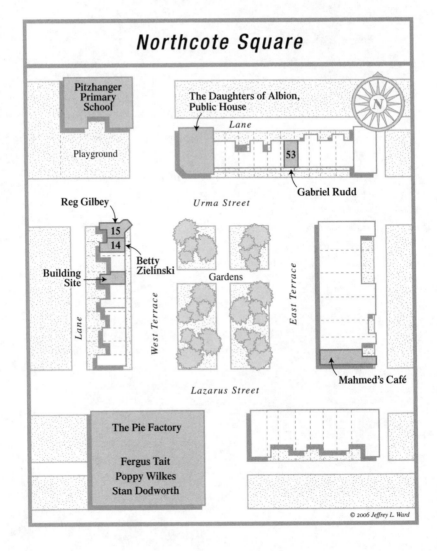

Northcote Square

Pitzhanger Primary School

Playground

The Daughters of Albion, Public House

Lane

53

Gabriel Rudd

Urma Street

Reg Gilbey

15

14

Betty Zielinski

Building Site

Gardens

Lane

West Terrace

East Terrace

Mahmed's Café

Lazarus Street

The Pie Factory

Fergus Tait
Poppy Wilkes
Stan Dodworth

N

© 2006 Jeffrey L. Ward

1

A CHILD'S CRY jolted Brock from sleep. He blinked awake, wondering if
it had been a dream. He held his breath, listening, then heard the almost
human bark of the fox that lived in the railway cutting beyond the lane.
That's all, he realised, only that. He heard the answering mournful horn
of an approaching train. There must be fog on the line, autumn arriving
in earnest at last.

Now he was aware of other sounds, the clicking of the central heating
pipes as they warmed, so it must be after five, which was when the timer
switched on. He turned his head to read the illuminated numbers of the
bedside clock. Five-fifteen. He would have preferred to lie for a while in
the dark, sensing the day approach, taking time to think about one or
two things. But there was so much to do, too much. He put on the light,
pulled on his dressing gown and slippers, and padded down to the
kitchen to put the kettle on.

Brock carried the mug of tea through to the living room and lit the
gas fire. On the table in front of him were three documents, all urgent.
He slipped on his reading glasses and heaved the first, a thick report,
onto his lap. Its title was *Stage 3 Restructuring of the Metropolitan Police Service: Discussion Paper*, and the words *Restricted Circulation*
were stamped across the top. The accompanying memo had urged its
importance, while his secretary, Dot, had heard from friends working at
10 Broadway, headquarters of New Scotland Yard, that Commander

Sharpe was apoplectic over it. Brock took a sip of tea and opened it reluctantly, scanning the index, then turning to the summary. Not much wiser, he skipped through 'Chapter 1: Cost and performance criteria for alternative models of decentralisation'.

He sighed and his attention strayed to the second item on the table, a letter, neat blue words on cream paper. He set the senior management report aside, picked up the letter and began to read it once again.

Dear David,

I have to put this in writing, because I haven't been able to find the words to say aloud . . .

He reached the end and sat lost in thought, feeling the drag of sadness inside him, the weight of time and loss. As if to emphasise this, his eyes moved to a small framed picture on the wall in front of him, a shabby little thing, a gift from a murderer. He remembered his first glimpse of it, long ago, above the mantelpiece of a house in Stepney as he kneeled on the floor with the body of Emily Crab, trying in vain to stop the flow of blood from her throat. Emily had ruined his suit but established his reputation on his first big murder case. Later, interviewing her husband, he had asked about the little picture, saying that it had looked to him like the work of the German artist Kurt Schwitters, whom he greatly admired. Walter Crab had been surprised and gratified by this recognition. He told Brock that during the war his mother had taken in a refugee, a man who had been hunted by the Gestapo from Germany to Norway, before escaping to London. The man was penniless, and Walter's mother had accepted the picture in lieu of a month's rent and board. When her friends saw it—an old bus ticket, a scrap of a newspaper headline and other fragments glued to a piece of cardboard—they laughed and told her she'd been had, and Walter had been mortified on his mother's account. Brock was the first person who had ever admired it, and yes, on the back was the signature *K. Schwitters,* and the title, *Merz 598a, London, 1943.* Then Walter confessed to Brock that he had murdered Emily and that the alibi provided by his sister was false. On the day that Crab was sentenced, Brock received a brown-paper parcel in the mail containing the Schwitters and a carefully written note from Walter, gifting him the picture in compensation for Brock's ruined suit. Ever since, Brock had regarded the little collage as an icon, a condensed statement of his own calling, gathering the discarded residue of people's lives and making out of it some kind of pattern and sense.

Brock folded the letter and tucked it into the management report to mark the place he'd reached, then turned his attention to the third document on the table, every page of which he'd memorised over the weekend. It was a file marked *Metropolitan Police, Case File Summary: Abductions of Aimee Jennifer Prentice and Lee Celine Hammond.* He turned to the pictures of the missing girls, although they were already imprinted in his mind; Aimee with a cheeky lopsided grin and Lee, dreamy and pensive, as if she could sense the onset of puberty inside her slight body.

Pinned to the cover of the report was the memo confirming the formation of a Major Enquiry Team, headed by Detective Chief Inspector David Brock, which would take control of the case as from 0800 hours on Monday October 13. Brock checked his watch. Two hours. Time to go.

2

KATHY DROVE SLOWLY down the clogged artery of Kingsland Road in Shoreditch, part of the stream of sullen Monday morning traffic splashing cold puddles over the legs of huddled bus queues. She could hear the howl of a police siren somewhere up ahead, and on the radio she picked up the first news reports of another missing girl, the third child abducted from her home in east London in recent weeks.

She made a turn into Lazarus Street and found herself hemmed between the dark brick walls of warehouses under conversion to offices, studio flats and uncertain investment opportunities. Two small girls burst out of a side alley, school bags bouncing on their shoulders, black faces bright with glee, and Kathy stopped to let them pass.

She was impatient. The call had come half an hour before, cancelling the first scheduled meeting of the new Major Enquiry Team and diverting personnel to Shoreditch, and she felt the anticipation itching inside her at the beginning of a new case. She checked the mirror to make sure the girls were clear of the back of the car and caught her own reflection. Serious eyes, official eyes. This is how you get to look in your thirties when you take your job too seriously, she thought. Her hair, very pale in the gloom of the dark street, fell almost to her eyes, and she remembered that she'd booked for a cut that afternoon. She'd have to cancel.

As she moved on she passed the end of a narrow service lane and saw two uniformed police examining a row of dustbins. Ahead she spotted a pulsing blue light at the point where the street opened into a square. The patrol car was parked outside a sandwich shop, Mahmed's Café, with two cops stooped talking to the driver, leaning against the car roof to ease the weight of their protective vests and loaded belts.

Kathy slowed and called across to them. 'Hi, DS Kolla, SO1. Northcote Square?'

'This is it.' The man, registering the initials of the Serious Crime Group unit, peered across at her. 'Better park down here, Sarge. The north end's chocker.'

As she rolled forward she saw what he meant, a jam of vehicles blocking the far end of the square. She hadn't been here before, and she had the impression of a rather forbidding place hidden away among the tangle of streets. The square was surrounded by buildings of mixed age and use, mostly in dark red brick, all severe and square-profiled against the grey sky. They overlooked a thickly treed central garden fenced by iron railings. Kathy pulled up beneath a no stopping sign and placed her Metropolitan Police Emergency notice on the dash. One of the uniforms came over to her.

'That's the house,' he said, pointing to a building at the other end of the square behind the densest crush of vehicles and people. Originally two storeys high and rather squat and plain, a further two floors of milky white glass had been added. 'Press have just arrived.'

'Thanks.'

She saw other uniformed men and women door-knocking and talking to staff arriving for work at offices on the east side of the square. Here on the south side, Lazarus Street, was an old industrial building with a sawtooth roof. Like most of the other older buildings in the area it showed signs of conversion. A large section of ground-floor brick wall had been replaced by frameless glass, through which Kathy could make out white linen on restaurant tables. Red neon letters attached to the parapet announced 'The Pie Factory'. Someone had sprayed a graffiti message in looping black letters on the brick wall beside the restaurant window: *same old shit*.

Kathy crossed to the pavement that snaked around the central gardens, her feet squelching on wet leaves dropped by the brooding trees. Bolted to the railings was a police notice, warning motorists that thieves were active in the area and giving the Crimestoppers' 0800 number. A logo identified Hackney Borough Police, the operational command unit for this area of the city. There was scaffolding up on part of West Terrace, which formed this side of the square, and some builders had stopped work to see what was going on. A man with a hard hat was leaning out of a windowless hole on the top floor of one of the buildings under reconstruction, passing observations down to his mates on the pavement below. Spotting Kathy, he paused in his commentary and the others turned to check out the blonde. One gave a desultory whistle and another called, 'Give us a smile, darling,' but the morning was too dull and their hearts weren't in it.

There was something of a melee at the top end of West Terrace, where traffic coming to the corner of the square was trying to work its way around stationary vehicles. She saw several cops trying to move people on, and when she reached the place Kathy realised that the problem was a school playground on the other side of the crossing, where small children were arriving with adults, all demanding to know what the police vehicles and press cameras were doing there.

Kathy turned along the north side, Urma Street, past a corner pub called The Daughters of Albion, and worked her way through the crowd standing outside number fifty-three. She showed her ID to a constable with a clipboard at the front door and he recorded her name.

'Scene of crime are working on this floor, Sarge. If you take the stairs, I think you'll find the others on the next level.'

The front door closed behind her. She was in an entrance hall leading to a corridor of open doors. Ahead, a man wearing white nylon overalls was backing out of a room with a video camera held to his eye. To her left, a flight of open-tread timber stairs rose towards the sound of voices. Kathy climbed the stairs and emerged into a large room that took up the whole floor, well lit with windows to both back and front. The building had been gutted, exposing bare brick walls and the underside of timber floor beams overhead from which industrial lamps were suspended. Kathy caught sight of very large grainy images hanging on the walls, of horses' heads with huge bulging eyes, like dramatic advertisements for a horror movie.

Kathy had never seen such a response to a crime scene. The place was crowded with police, as if half the Met had been called out. She spotted Brock's cropped white hair and beard among a cluster of large men in dark coats. She went over and he introduced her to a superintendent, head of Operations, and a DCI, head of Crime Investigations, both from the Borough Police. Then he drew her aside and said rapidly, 'I have a few things to sort out here, Kathy, then I want to speak to the father, Gabriel Rudd, over there.' He nodded towards a man sitting alone at a circular dining table, staring at a small TV on the table in front of him. 'Why not go and introduce yourself? I'll be with you in a minute. See if you can find somewhere quiet for us to talk to him.'

Kathy paused, struck by the man at the table, a solitary, motionless figure among all the bustle and noise filling the room. He had a startling mop of stark white curls and was wearing a black pinstriped suit without shirt or socks or shoes. The cut of the suit looked expensive. As she drew closer Kathy was surprised to see splashes of colour on its legs. His attention was completely focused on the screen, where a man with an Irish accent, red hair and large round glasses was being interviewed. '. . . A lovely fellow, and amazingly talented. And devoted to his little girl. He must be devastated . . .'

'Hello, Mr Rudd? I'm Detective Sergeant Kathy Kolla.'

He glanced up at her and said softly, 'Yes, saw you arrive.' He nodded back at the screen, which was now showing a view of the square outside and the crush of people at his front door. His face was lean and intelligent, Kathy thought, though very pale and drawn, with dark hollows around the eyes.

'I'm very sorry about your daughter.'

'Tracey,' he said. 'Her name's Tracey.'

'Right. I'm with the Major Enquiry Team led by DCI Brock . . .'

'Brock? Oh yes . . .' He looked vaguely in Brock's direction, then focused again on the small screen, which now showed a reporter talking into a microphone. ' . . . Turner Prize, and in the following year represented Britain at the Venice Biennale . . .' A news summary was tracking across the bottom of the screen: *Rapid police response to third child abduction in London borough.*

'Is there somewhere quieter we can talk?'

'What? Oh, right. I'll just record this on the other set.'

He stood up, very tall, easing himself through the gap between two bulky cops to get to a large flat-screen TV against the wall, and began working a remote. Brock arrived at Kathy's side.

'How are we doing?'

'He's just recording the TV coverage,' Kathy said. 'What's that on his legs, do you think?'

'He says it's paint. That's what he does. He's an artist, he paints.'

'In his best suit?'

Brock shrugged. 'Tracey Rudd, six years old, apparently taken from her bedroom at the back of the ground floor during the night. Mr Rudd rang triple nine an hour and a half ago, shortly after seven. You know about the other two cases of course. We'll have to postpone the briefing on them until we get on top of this one. Hackney Operational Command Unit are giving us facilities at Shoreditch police station and I've got Bren working with their search teams.' He gave her several names and phone numbers which she wrote down in her notebook as Gabriel Rudd returned.

'We can go up to the studio, if you like,' he said. He sounded distant, detached, as if all this wasn't really happening. They followed the slap of his bare feet on the timber steps up to a landing on the next floor. At the top, he opened a door and led them into his studio, suddenly empty and silent after the activity below. Kathy realised that this was the extension above the original building which she had seen from across the square, its white translucent end wall and ceiling producing a stunning luminous effect. The space was tall, with a ladder up to a gallery that stretched across one end. The lower sections of the walls were lined with white pinboard, and there were racks and trestles and pieces of equipment around the room, but not the easels and canvases that Kathy would have expected in an artist's studio, and as far as she could see no works in progress. The place looked like a cross between a mechanic's workshop and an art gallery, and there was a faint smell of acetate and paint thinner in the air.

They sat at a plywood table on stools like chrome tractor seats. A Macintosh computer and printer stood at the far end of the table, and Brock reached for an image that lay beside the machines and handed it to Kathy. It was of a pretty little girl with curly blonde hair, clutching a furry teddy bear.

'Mr Rudd had pictures of Tracey ready for us when we arrived, Kathy. When's her birthday, Mr Rudd?'

'Gabe, everyone calls me Gabe. She turned six in August, the tenth.'

'And you live here on your own, just the two of you?'

'That's right.' He blinked and rubbed his eyes, giving a little groan. It was the first sign of emotion that Kathy had seen, as if the TV downstairs had held reality in check.

'You said Tracey's mother's passed away. How long ago was that?'

'Jane died five years ago, when Trace was one.'

'That must have been difficult for you, bringing up a little girl on your own.'

He shrugged, dropped his eyes, sighed. 'Yeah, but well, you just have to cope, don't you?'

'What about close relatives, grandparents?'

'Yeah, Jane's parents, they . . . try to help.'

'I believe you said that Tracey stayed with them over the weekend, and they brought her back home yesterday about five in the afternoon, is that right?'

He nodded. Kathy thought she sensed some reserve at the mention of the grandparents.

'Have you called them this morning, Gabe?' she asked.

'No, not yet.'

'Maybe I should do that now, before they see it on TV. Can you give me their names and a number?'

He wrote on a pad.

'Anyone else? What about your parents?'

He shook his head. 'We don't keep in touch.'

Kathy moved away to the area beneath the gallery, where there was a sink and a microwave. She used her mobile phone to ring the number Rudd had given her. A man's voice, elderly and gruff, answered.

'Yes?'

'I'd like to speak to Mr Nolan, please.'

'This is Len Nolan speaking. Who's that?'

Kathy explained who she was and where she was calling from.

'What's happened?' The voice had hardened immediately, ready for the worst.

'I'm sorry to have to tell you that your granddaughter Tracey is missing, Mr Nolan. We're doing everything possible to locate her, and at this stage . . .'

'Where's her father?' the voice barked. 'Where's Gabriel?'

'He's here, Mr Nolan, helping us find her. He wanted you informed.'

'What's his story?'

'It appears she went missing some time during the night. You haven't heard from her, have you?'

'We dropped her there yesterday afternoon, just before five. We haven't heard anything since . . .' Kathy heard a woman's voice in the background, then a muffled conversation. 'We're on our way,' Len Nolan said.

'It might be better if you waited at home for now, where we can reach you.'

'We're coming,' he said firmly. 'I'll give you our mobile number so you can call us if there's any news.'

When Kathy returned to the table she found Gabriel Rudd explaining something technical about his picture of Tracey. '. . . to enhance the blue of the eyes, you see.'

'But they are that colour?' Brock asked.

Rudd considered. 'Pretty much, but I wanted to get the right balance with the flesh tones.'

He held the picture at arm's length, squinting at it. His mood had shifted, and again Kathy had the impression that a screen had been thrown up between him and the reality of what was happening.

Brock raised an eyebrow at her and she said, 'They haven't heard from Tracey. They insist on coming over here.'

Rudd winced. 'Oh no. I couldn't face them, not now.'

They lived in the outer western suburbs, apparently. Brock checked his watch and said, 'All right, we'll look after them when they arrive. Let's go over last night again, Gabe, step by step.'

Rudd ran a hand through his white hair, trying to collect his thoughts. 'There's not a lot to tell. Trace was tired when she got home. They always get her overexcited and give her too much to eat when she goes over there, and when she gets home she flakes out. She watched some TV and I gave her a bowl of cereal later, and afterwards she went to bed. I turned her light off about eight.'

'Apart from being tired, how did she seem?'

'Fine . . . normal. They'd taken her to the park near where they live, and she'd got her dress a bit muddy. She wanted me to put it in the wash.'

'Think back over your conversation. Did she mention anything that might help us? A stranger in the park?'

They worked slowly through everything Rudd could recall about his last hours with his daughter.

'So when did you last see her, exactly?'

'I put her light out at eight.'

'But after that, did you look in?'

'Oh . . . yes, of course. About ten, when I went to bed.'

'And are you certain she was there then?'

'Yes, yes.'

'Your bedroom's on the ground floor too, isn't it, but at the front, facing the square. You heard nothing during the night?'

'Nothing, not a thing. I woke up just before seven, got up to wake Trace for school, and found she wasn't in her room. I looked everywhere and couldn't find her. Her bedroom window was open. So then I phoned nine-nine-nine. I mean, with those two other cases . . .'

'Had you discussed those cases with Tracey?'

Rudd screwed his nose in thought. 'Don't think so.'

'Do you think she knew about them?'

'No idea.'

'Do you normally sleep soundly, Gabe?'

'No, not always.'

'Did you have much to drink last night?'

He looked vague. 'Yes, a bit. That might be why . . . Look, couldn't I be doing something? I mean, talking to the press, or something? Making an appeal for information?'

'Not yet. Where does Tracey go to school?'

'Right here in the square, Pitzhanger Primary.'

'Is she happy there?'

'Seems okay.'

'So there was nothing she was worried about happening today, a test or something?'

He shook his head. 'I don't think they have tests.'

The questions went on, without much result, Kathy felt, except a growing sense that the man didn't seem very knowledgeable about or interested in the details of his daughter's life. Rudd himself was becoming monosyllabic, and finally Brock snapped his notebook shut and straightened his back with a grunt. Kathy recognised the moment. Rudd looked up, thinking the interview over, but she knew better.

'I know your name of course, Gabe. You're famous,' Brock said.

Rudd shrugged carelessly.

'One of my colleagues downstairs was telling me that there are more artists to the square mile in this neighbourhood than anywhere else in Europe, and you're one of the stars. I think I've seen you on TV, "Parkinson", wasn't it?'

'Sure.'

'And you've exhibited at Tate Modern, yes?'

Rudd nodded. 'Couple of times.'

'And the Saatchi?'

'Yeah, yeah.' He sounded bored and mildly irritated by Brock's interest.

'I thought so. I recognised the horses' heads downstairs. That's one of your favourite themes, isn't it?'

'It used to be. I've moved on.'

'*Dead Puppies,* that was you, wasn't it?'

'Sure.'

'Of course, that was the thing on TV. Have you got an exhibition coming up?'

'I'm planning a show at The Pie Factory, the gallery across the square.'

Brock gazed idly round the room at the blank walls. 'Now that's famous too, isn't it, The Pie Factory? What's the name of the man who runs it?'

'Fergus Tait. He's my dealer.'

'Tait, yes of course. And he has a restaurant too, doesn't he?'

Rudd said, 'The Tait Gallery.'

Brock chuckled. 'The restaurant is called The Tait Gallery, and the art gallery is called The Pie Factory. He's a bit of a comedian, Mr Tait, eh?'

'He likes a laugh.'

'But sharp as a tack, no doubt. That was him on the TV downstairs just now, wasn't it? Talking to the media about Tracey. He was quick off the mark, wasn't he? How did that come about?'

Rudd's pale face coloured a little, his expression becoming stubborn. 'Fergus is more than just my dealer. He's a close personal friend, and I phoned him as soon as I'd called the police. I needed to talk to someone.'

'I suppose he handles your publicity and promotion, does he?'

'Yeah.'

'Well, from now on, Gabe, you let us handle it as far as Tracey's concerned. All right?'

Rudd shrugged. 'Sure.'

'And please make sure that Mr Tait understands that too, will you? Tracey's life may depend upon it. Understood?'

'Fair enough.'

'Good. Now is it possible that Tracey's disappearance could have something to do with your career or reputation? Have you had any unusual correspondence recently? Any odd phone calls or visitors?'

'No more than usual. Weird messages are often sent to the gallery or my Web site.'

'We'll need to check all those. There's also the possibility that Tracey's been taken for money, a ransom.'

'Is that what happened with the other girls?'

'No, but it's always possible that this is different. Just to be sure, we'll set up some special equipment on your phone, and I'll ask you to stay close to it for the next twenty-four hours. There'll be a police officer on the premises for all that time. Well, I think we can go back downstairs now.'

The horde on the floor below had vanished. Rudd went to the kitchen area to put on some coffee. 'I don't understand why they had to search the house,' he grumbled as he spooned out the powder.

'We always do, in cases like this,' Kathy said. 'You wouldn't believe the number of times a missing child has turned up asleep in a closet or beneath the stairs where they'd gone to play a game with their dolls.' Or bundled up in the freezer, or beneath the floorboards, Kathy thought. There's no place like home.

'I just feel so helpless,' Rudd said. 'I should be doing something.'

'Waiting is the worst of it,' Brock replied. 'But the best thing you can do is stay here with DS Kolla.'

At that moment there was a commotion from the floor below, a man calling out in protest, a woman's scream drowning him out, then footsteps crashing up the wooden stairs. A woman's head and shoulders burst into view, thick black hair streaked with grey, a black cloak flapping from her shoulders.

'The chief inspector!' she cried, looking wildly about. 'I must see him!'

Brock stepped forward, waving back the copper who had followed her.

'The scream!' she gasped. 'I heard the scream!'

Brock tried to calm her, but this only made her more agitated.

'You must listen!' she cried. 'I heard her, the missing child, last night!'

Then she noticed Gabriel Rudd for the first time and flew at him. He flinched, standing rigid as she grasped him, babbling, 'Poor boy! Poor boy! But I understand, you know I understand. My little girl, my own darling.'

Seeing the look of disgust on Rudd's face, Kathy stepped forward and, putting a firm arm around the woman's shoulders, drew her away. 'Let's sit down,' she said, 'and tell me everything. First your name.'

'Betty Zielinski, and I have vital information.'

She was a neighbour, she said, a long-time resident of Northcote Square, living at 14 West Terrace. She leaped to her feet and made them follow her to the window, where she showed them her place, a narrow brick-fronted terrace house almost at this end of the block and barely fifty yards away. They could see the builders working on the roofs of the buildings beyond. The jam of people and vehicles hadn't cleared from the square below, and faces turned up to look at them as they stood at the window.

'At five minutes past two last night I was woken by a scream,' the woman went on, her voice now dropping to a dramatic hush. 'A piercing scream. The scream of a female child.'

'I see. Where's your bedroom, Ms Zielinski?'

'At the back, on the first floor.'

'At the back?' Brock sounded doubtful.

'Yes . . . don't you see? He must have taken her away down the lane that runs behind our terrace. That way he wouldn't be seen in the square.'

'Are you quite certain about the time?'

'Yes, yes. I checked the alarm clock beside my bed. Five minutes past two.'

Kathy steered her back to a seat and asked her if she lived alone.

'I live with my family.'

'Did they hear anything?'

'I'm sure they must have.'

'What are their names?'

Betty Zielinski looked doubtfully at Kathy's hand poised over her notebook. 'You want all of their names?'

'How many are there?'

'Oh, hundreds and hundreds.'

Kathy looked into the big, wondering eyes and said, 'Maybe it would be best if I call and talk to them myself.'

'That would be a very good idea.'

They thanked her and she seemed satisfied as Kathy led her back towards the stairs. At the top she turned back to Gabriel Rudd and said, 'She knew, my dear. She told me. She was so brave.'

Rudd looked incredulous. 'Eh?'

'What did she tell you?' Brock said.

The woman turned her wild eyes to him. 'Secrets. Special children have the second sight, you know. And Tracey was a very special child.' Then she took to the stairs, her cloak flapping in her wake.

'Batty Betty,' Rudd said, shaking his head. He slumped in a chair, seeming unnerved by the visit. 'That's what they call her in the square. What she told you was rubbish. She has no family, she lives alone. The school kids in the playground call names after her and she complains to the teachers. Mad as a hatter.'

Kathy could imagine it, the children squealing with excitement at the mad lady in the black cloak, looking like a bat.

'You don't believe she heard something?' Brock asked.

'She probably dreamed it,' he said dismissively, and Brock, remembering his own awakening that morning, was inclined to agree. All the same, he had noticed how closely Rudd had listened to the woman, especially when she mentioned the scream.

'Did Tracey ever visit Ms Zielinski's house?' he asked.

'I don't know. Maybe.'

'You didn't mention that before. You said she goes to the café on the corner, but you didn't mention Zielinski. I think we'll check her house, just to be on the safe side.'

As Brock pulled out his phone Rudd got to his feet and wandered over to the window overlooking the square. He gazed down, then took something from his pocket and, opening the window latch, leaned out— too far out. Alarmed, Kathy hurried across to him. 'What are you doing?'

He stepped back and closed the window again. In his hand he held a small silver camera, and he was smiling. 'Taking pictures of them taking pictures of me taking pictures of them . . . Don't worry, I wasn't doing an Yves Klein.'

'Who?'

'The artist of the void,' Rudd said carelessly, and strolled away.

3

'THE WINDOW WASN'T locked.'

Brock and Kathy had left Rudd to drink his coffee and watch TV while they went downstairs to check the progress of the SOCO team in Tracey's room. The crime scene manager, a middle-aged woman with a cheerful smile, gave them a verbal report. As with the other two abductions, there were signs of forced entry to the girl's bedroom window. However, in this case, unlike the other two where force had been quite crudely applied, these traces were minimal. Scratches on the window latch suggested a tool with a sharp edge had been used to unfasten it from the outside, but a separate security lock was untouched, and appeared not to have been engaged.

'Not locked?' Brock said.

'That's right. It was latched but not locked.'

She'd noticed other differences between this and the earlier cases. With them, the girls' bedrooms had been visible from adjoining streets and there was some evidence that the abductor, having targeted his victim, had watched her house to identify her room. In this case, though, the window looked onto a back courtyard which was screened from the rear laneway by a garage and wall, so it would have been much more difficult for the intruder to have observed the window. The woman also pointed out that the other two cases were much closer to each other than to Northcote Square, and the girls were both older than Tracey by several years.

'So he's spreading his territory and becoming more organised,' Brock suggested. She conceded this possibility, but obviously remained unconvinced.

'Your profiler will have his own ideas,' she said. 'But I attended both the previous scenes and this one is noticeably neater and free of visible traces. There's no sign of disturbance in the room and no marks on the window surrounds.'

'How about the rest of the house?' Brock asked.

'Clean, very clean. Mr Rudd said he has a cleaner who comes on Friday mornings, and it doesn't look as if the place has had much use since then. You're aware that he put the washing machine on before we arrived?'

'What was in it? A dress of Tracey's? He mentioned her dress being muddy.'

'Yes, a red and yellow dress of hers, and her socks and pants. Also a complete set of his clothes—jeans, shirt, underwear, sweater and jacket.'

'A jacket?'

'Like a windcheater, washable.'

Clean seemed to be the operative word, Kathy thought, looking round Tracey's bedroom. It was as neat and Spartan as a motel room. There were no pictures on the wall, no toys on display, and the fabrics were plain and unpatterned.

'Anything else?' Brock asked the crime scene manager.

'No controlled drugs, but lots of medication—anti-depressants, anti-inflammatories, beta-blockers, sleeping pills, vitamins. We haven't touched his computers at this stage. He has four of them in the house. Are you going to access his emails?'

'Yes, though I imagine Tracey was a bit young to be talking to predators on the web.'

'Don't be too sure. Oh, one little thing. His alarm clock was set for six-fifteen, yet he didn't ring us till seven-oh-six.'

'Could have gone back to sleep.'

'Yes, or done a bit of cleaning before we arrived.'

'You'll take that suit he's wearing, will you? Check what those stains are on the legs.'

Kathy had one question. 'Does he dye his hair?'

The woman laughed. 'I asked him that. He said it went white almost overnight when his wife died.'

'How did she die, do we know?'

'He told me—suicide.'

'That's right,' Brock said. 'Those drawings of horses' heads on the wall, they're studies for an artwork he did after it happened. *The Night-Mare,* it was called, inspired by his wife's suicide. I remember it won a big prize a few years ago and got a lot of press coverage.'

'What about *Dead Puppies?*' Kathy asked.

Brock shook his head. 'You'd better ask him to explain that one himself.'

The SOCO said, 'Oh, was that him? Did he do *Dead Puppies?*'

There was a call from an officer at the back door. 'Sir? DCI Brock? Someone to see you, sir.'

The visitor was dressed like a young businessman, neat tie, smart suit, but even before he offered identification Brock had caught something in the way he looked around him at the crime-scene activity, familiar but detached, that had him pegged for a cop, and probably not regular CID.

'Special Branch?' Brock read his card, wondering what this could be about. 'What can I do for you?'

'A quiet word, sir?'

Brock took him upstairs to the living area and led him to the front window, at the far end from Gabriel Rudd, who was now joined by Kathy.

'I'm on protection duties, sir,' the Special Branch inspector said quietly to Brock. 'We—my charge and I—have been coming here to Northcote Square regularly now for eight months. We were following the news reports of your case on the radio on the way over. When we arrived and saw the crowds I thought I should let you know.'

'Really?' Brock was mystified. 'Can I ask who it is you're minding?'

The inspector leaned close to Brock and lowered his voice further. 'Sir Jack Beaufort, sir.'

'The judge? Why does he come here?'

The other man allowed himself a little smile. 'He's having his portrait painted. The artist's name is Gilbey, Reg Gilbey. Have you come across him?'

'No.'

'Well, he's apparently held in very high regard. The only problem is that he's bloody slow. Some days he works away there for a couple of hours and at the end of it I can't see any difference at all.'

'Where's his studio?'

'Number fifteen West Terrace.' The inspector pointed. 'The one on the corner, with the bay window.'

It was the end house on West Terrace, Brock saw, at the corner of the square opposite the playground of the primary school and next door to the house of Betty Zielinski. The bay window was a distinctive feature, projecting out from the first floor on the corner like an observation post, and crowned by a slate-roofed turret.

'That's where he paints, the room with the bay.'

'Why the protection?'

'The judge has had death threats.'

Brock could believe it. He knew Beaufort's reputation for tough sentencing and had seen him in action in the criminal courts, imperious and acerbic. 'Do you come at the same time each week?'

'No, we try to vary it. At first it was once a week, but more recently it's twice or three times, often first thing in the morning to keep his day clear.'

'Well, thanks for the advice. Of course, we'll be talking to Mr Gilbey.'

'The door-knockers have already been. He had nothing to tell them.'

'All the same . . .' Brock was thinking of Betty Zielinski's scream.

The inspector looked thoughtful. 'Did the little girl go to the school on the corner, by any chance?'

'Yes, she did. Why?'

'Only that I know he watches them in the playground from his bay window.'

'Gilbey? You've seen him?'

'Yes, you get a good all-round view from up there.'

'What's he like, this Gilbey?'

'In his seventies, I'd guess, dresses like a tramp, says very little.' He shrugged and checked his watch. 'Never know, he may have seen someone watching the place. Anyway, I should be getting back.'

They shook hands and Brock said, 'You'd better give me a number I can reach you on. My sergeant, DS Kolla, will be staying around here for a while. I'll give you her number.'

After the man had gone, Brock stood at the window for a moment contemplating the square. He felt as if he were on the stage at a public spectacle, with the mob down below and a judge in the royal box, observing his moves. He turned to speak to Kathy.

'I'm going over to Shoreditch station,' he said, and saw that Rudd was dressed now in sweater and jeans. The man blew his nose noisily with a large red handkerchief and Brock noticed moisture glistening around his eyes. 'Everything all right?'

Kathy nodded. Everyone was different, she thought; it was important to remember that. You barged into someone's home and bombarded them with questions, and expected certain reactions. If they didn't come, you began to make suppositions. But everyone was different. It had taken Rudd all this time to show real feeling about his daughter's disappearance. Kathy's question about the unlocked window had started the tears, quite suddenly. It was all his fault, he had blurted, not checking to see that the window was secure. And then his shoulders had shuddered, and he'd folded his arms over his head and begun to sob. She had caught some words: '. . . couldn't live with it, not again . . .'

She had assumed he was referring to the death of his wife, and for the first time she felt a real surge of pity for him. His stunt at the window, his careless manner and eccentric appearance, which had appeared silly and pretentious, now seemed only vulnerable and sad, and when he had finally pulled himself together and made some weak joke about something in his eye, his early behaviour seemed brave even, a show of defiance against fate.

Brock's voice, detached and sceptical, interrupted her thoughts. 'Stay close to him for a while, Kathy. Get him talking,' he said. 'Something doesn't feel right here. He says he's preparing for an exhibition, but there's no sign of any work. The place is empty. Then there's the medication. Maybe he's suffering from depression.'

When Brock had gone Gabe started telling Kathy about Tracey, what a happy and loving little thing she was, so sensible and responsible. Already, at six years old, she was looking after her own clothes, keeping her room so neat, always ready ahead of time—unlike her father, who left everything to the last minute.

'She gets that from her mother,' he said, rubbing his eyes. 'Jane was always organised, until . . .'

'That must have been terrible for you both, when she died.'

'Trace was only one. She doesn't remember. I'm not sure if she knows even now what actually happened. I've never told her. She accepts that her mother's gone to heaven, but she's never asked how she got there.'

'How did it happen?'

Gabe lifted his eyes to watch her reaction as he told her. 'She jumped off a bridge into the Regent's Canal, not half a mile from here.'

Kathy fell silent. She decided it probably wasn't a good time to ask him about *Dead Puppies*. 'I suppose your work would be a comfort.'

He raised his eyebrows as if the idea was bizarre. 'A comfort? You make it sound like a nice cup of tea. Is your work a *comfort?*'

'Yes,' she said. 'It is for most people, isn't it? Something outside of your personal life to concentrate on.' She had a sudden image of her flat, empty and cold since Leon had left.

'Why, isn't it going well, your personal life?'

Kathy blinked, as if he'd caught her out. 'What about yours?'

'I asked first,' he said, and narrowed his eyes, looking at her as if at something to draw. 'Let me guess, you split up with your boyfriend recently?'

He caught the flicker of surprise on Kathy's face and added, 'Doesn't take a genius.' His eyes travelled over her head and she felt even more annoyed to sense a blush in her cheek and an almost irresistible urge to run her hand through her hair.

'That's good,' he said, his voice soft and almost seductive. 'It'll make you sharp. That's what pain does. Those other cops who were here earlier didn't look as if they ever feel anything. I think if anyone'll find Trace, it'll be you.'

'Do you have a girlfriend?' Kathy asked evenly.

'I do have a friend actually, yes.' He didn't sound very enthusiastic.

'Have you spoken to her this morning?'

'Yeah. She'll probably be over later.'

The crowd in the street had dispersed, Kathy saw. Lights were on in all the windows of the office buildings on the east side of the square, and all the parking spaces along the kerbs around the central gardens were occupied. A small green Ford moved slowly along Urma Street and turned down East Terrace, obviously searching for a spot, and when a parked van ahead signalled it was leaving the Ford quickly manoeuvred into its space. A grey-haired couple emerged from the car and began striding purposefully towards Gabriel Rudd's front door. Kathy took the stairs down to the entrance hall and reached it just as the officer on duty there got up to answer the doorbell.

'Len and Bev Nolan,' the man said to the constable. 'We're the missing girl's grandparents. I spoke to someone on the phone . . .'

'That was me,' Kathy said, and introduced herself.

'Have there been any developments?' They both spoke together.

'I'm afraid not. Let's go upstairs where we can talk.'

When they reached the first floor Kathy found that Rudd had vanished, presumably upstairs to his studio.

'Where's Gabriel then?' Bev Nolan said, peering keenly around as if she expected to catch him hiding somewhere behind the furniture. Both she and her husband had lean features and trim figures. Their gestures were quick, and somehow communicated the impression of them being used to exercise and hard work. Recently retired, Kathy thought, perhaps still playing a sport.

'He must have gone upstairs,' Kathy said, 'but I'd like the chance to talk to you both, anyway.'

'I want to hear this from him,' Len Nolan said, threateningly.

'Please sit down,' Kathy insisted, and reluctantly they did. They sat silently, listening intently, as she told them what was known so far.

When she had finished, Len Nolan asked, 'But how did they get in without making a noise? That's what I can't understand. Tracey's bed is right next to the window. She'd have heard someone forcing the lock, surely, and cried out.'

'It appears that, unfortunately, the window wasn't locked.'

A growl of fury erupted from Len, and from his wife came a disbelieving cry, 'No!'

'That useless bastard!' Len fumed. He leaped to his feet and began pacing, unable to keep still. 'We warned them, didn't we, Bev? We said something like this would happen.'

'That's right, Len.'

'But would they listen? Would they?'

'No, Len.'

'Warned who?' Kathy broke in.

'The Social Services. We told 'em that he's irresponsible, unfit to be a parent. And that stupid woman told us that so were most fathers, but she couldn't do anything about it. By God, I'll have her bloody job for this.'

Len Nolan's face had become deep red by this stage, and Bev said anxiously, 'Yes, Len, but let's hear what Sergeant Kolla has to say. Come and sit down, love, please.'

'We even took legal advice.'

'About what?' Kathy said.

'About getting custody of Tracey, that's what!' Len snapped angrily. 'And she told us we wouldn't have a leg to stand on without evidence of abuse or neglect. I told her how he forgets to feed her, and lost her in the supermarket that day, and how he and his mates take drugs, and all she could say was . . .' and he put on a pathetic, whining voice, '. . ."Get some evidence, Mr Nolan. Get something a court will listen to." Yes, well, we've got that now, haven't we, but it's too bloody late!'

'Mr Nolan . . . Len,' Kathy said soothingly, 'please sit down and take me through this a step at a time. I need to know anything that might be relevant to Tracey's disappearance.'

'Yes, Len,' Bev said, patting the seat of his chair. 'Sit down, love, and tell the sergeant.'

'Oh Lord,' he said, rolling his eyes to heaven. 'Where to begin?'

But he did sit down again, and they told Kathy why they believed Gabriel Rudd to be a degenerate worm, as Len put it. No, they weren't saying he interfered with his daughter, or was deliberately cruel to her, although sometimes they almost wished he were, because then they could have made people act. What they were saying was that he was irresponsible, negligent and completely absorbed in himself.

'She has a nice home,' Kathy objected, 'clothes, food in the fridge. You should see the way some children live . . .'

'Yes, yes, but he simply doesn't care about her. It's mental cruelty, neglect. He doesn't speak to her for days on end. She's a poor little soul.'

As they talked, pouring out an endless list of niggling complaints about their son-in-law's inadequacies, Kathy sensed the big grievance that lurked unspoken in the background, and that had transformed disapproval of their son-in-law into outright hatred. Finally she put it to them.

'Do you blame him for your daughter's death?'

That brought them up short. They glanced at each other, uncertain how to answer the direct question. Then Bev Nolan said softly, 'Yes, I do,' and her husband, speechless for once, put his hand on hers and squeezed.

'Jane was never really well after Tracey was born. Post-partum depression, the doctors said. They gave her drugs and told Gabe he had to look after her, but he didn't. Quite the opposite in fact . . .'

'Totally,' Len jerked a nod of agreement.

'. . . left her to herself, went out with his friends, didn't help with the baby, in the night, and her so short of sleep . . .'

'We did what we could, of course, but *he* didn't like us coming round, made that plain as day. We had some rows, I can tell you.'

'He drove her to it,' Bev said decisively, 'as surely as if he'd pushed her into the canal himself.'

'And then he set about exploiting her death any way he could,' Len added. 'That was the sickest thing, the unforgivable thing, playing the tragic widower. He turned Jane's death into a public spectacle.'

'He sued the doctors—there was some question about the drugs they'd prescribed, and in the end they settled, though Gabriel wouldn't tell us how much for. And then he did that dreadful exhibition about her.'

'*The Night-Mare*. It won him that big prize. That's where this all came from . . .' Len waved a hand to indicate the house, '. . . from the court settlement and the art prize. He had nothing before that. Always broke when Jane was alive.'

As they lapsed into silence Kathy said quietly, 'But he does give you access to Tracey now?'

'She pesters him,' Bev said, 'until he lets her stay with us. Her room at our house has all the things she loves. Len has made her special furniture, and a dolls' house, and a farmyard.'

'But I suppose she has friends around here? At school?'

'No.' Len Nolan shook his head. 'She's not settled at that school. Oh, it's very *convenient*.' He made the word sound like an obscenity. 'Only a couple of doors away. Doesn't even have to collect her in the afternoon. But they give her a hard time. They know, you see.'

'Sorry?'

'The other kids, they know about her dad. *Dead Puppies*!' He turned away in disgust.

Kathy hesitated. 'What exactly is *Dead Puppies*?'

Bev said, 'Don't ask, Sergeant, please. Len's very fond of dogs.'

'Have they gone?' Gabe peered down the staircase from his studio.

'Yes,' Kathy said. 'You can come on down.'

'Hell,' he said, creeping down and slumping into a pink plastic sofa. 'I could do with a drink.'

As if to order, the doorbell rang. The duty policeman's head appeared over the rim of the floor. 'Two people, Sarge. Say they're friends of Mr Rudd. A Mr Tait and a Ms Wilkes.'

'Oh, thank Christ,' Gabe said, sitting upright.

'All right, let them up,' Kathy said, and immediately the couple burst into view.

'Gabe, Gabe,' the man cried. 'You poor old feller.'

'Oh, Jesus, Ferg,' Gabe sighed, jumping to his feet. 'You've no idea.'

Kathy recognised the newcomer as the man she'd seen on TV with the Irish accent. Though much shorter than Rudd, he caught him in a clinch and rocked him back and forward in his arms as his companion, a stocky dark-haired girl, put the bags she was carrying on the coffee table and turned to Kathy.

'You're with the police, are you? Are you looking after him?'

'Yes. DS Kathy Kolla.'

The woman scrutinised Kathy critically, as if wondering whether she was up to the job. 'I'm Poppy Wilkes, and that's Fergus Tait, Gabe's dealer. We saw the in-laws leaving and we thought he might need some moral support.'

'I kept out of their way,' Gabe said. 'They spoke to Kathy. I suppose they said it was all my fault.'

'Well, that's only to be expected.' Fergus Tait patted his shoulder. For a small man, he had a big presence. He wore a perfectly tailored black suit, dazzling white shirt and a large, green satin tie. His red hair was expertly layered, and his big round glasses gave his eyes a hypnotic stare. 'But we've brought you the antidote, old chum.' He reached into one of the plastic bags and drew out a bottle of vodka. 'Glasses, my love,' he said to Poppy, who seemed to know where to look. She returned with four tumblers and some plates.

'Ah . . .' Kathy began to object, but Fergus ignored her, pouring four drinks and picking one up. The other two followed suit. Fergus winked at Kathy. 'Won't you have a little drink with us, Sergeant? To the success of your hunt for little Tracey? We shan't tell on you.'

'I'd like Gabe to keep a clear head,' Kathy said.

'I can assure you that Gabe's head gets clearer with every one of these that he puts away, is that not right, boy?' He tipped the glass and swallowed in one gulp. The other two did the same, then Rudd sank back against the cushions and drew his long legs up to his chest.

'Oh Jesus,' he sighed. Poppy went to sit beside him and put her arms around him.

'They'll find her, Gabe,' she said, and from the way she looked at him Kathy guessed that this must be his 'friend'.

'You're feeling bad, of course you are.' Tait poured another drink. 'How else could you feel?'

'Helpless. I feel helpless.'

'You need something to eat,' Poppy Wilkes said briskly. 'We brought you some lunch from Mahmed's. Oh, Stan sends his love too, of course. He'd have come himself, but you know how he is with the pigs.' She shot a mischievous grin at Kathy. 'Come on, Gabe, have some food.'

'No, no, I couldn't.'

Poppy ignored his protests, unpacking Turkish bread and dips and cold meats and salads onto the plates. They looked good and Kathy suddenly felt hungry. Then she caught Tait watching her. He winked. 'Tuck in, Sergeant. There's plenty here.'

'Thanks. Maybe later.'

'What's going on out there?' Gabe asked, reaching forward to tear off a chunk of bread.

'They're searching the building site,' Poppy said. 'The builders have had to leave and they're really annoyed at the delay. So is Mahmed.'

'Why Mahmed?' Kathy asked.

'He owns the building. And most of the builders are his relatives.'

'Batty Betty barged in here. She claimed she heard a scream in the night.' Gabe was speaking with his mouth full, and Kathy noticed he was watching Poppy's reaction. 'Maybe that's why they're looking at the building site next door to her.'

'What time was that?' Poppy was making a sandwich.

'Five past two. She was very precise.'

Poppy shrugged. 'She probably saw little green men too.'

The drink had brought some colour to Gabe's face, and when he spoke again he was a little more voluble, his voice fluid. 'It's like a horrible dream, Trace disappearing like that, you've no idea. I still can't take it in, you know? I feel sick thinking about her out there somewhere . . .'

'What you need, old son, is something to occupy your mind while this is going on,' Fergus Tait said decisively. 'Work, that's what you need! Get down to some work.'

Gabe shook his head in protest. 'No way. I couldn't. Not while Trace . . .'

'That's exactly the right time. Do it for her. Better than sitting around chewing your nails.'

'I think he's right, Gabe,' Poppy said cautiously, as if she half-expected Gabe to round on her. But he just looked thoughtful.

'You've been promising me something for ages now,' Tait went on. 'So get off your backside and do it, will you? Art is pain, Gabriel, you know that. "Real pain for my real friends, champagne for my sham friends"—you know the old line. So show us your real pain. Remember *Night-Mare*, eh? Pure pain it was, and you can do it again.'

This seemed to be a common theme, Kathy thought, watching Gabe's bowed head as he took this in. Tait's enthusiasm was infectious, and Kathy noticed Gabe's right index finger begin to tap the side of his leg.

'I suppose I could try . . . maybe once they've found Trace . . .'

'No, no. Right now, boy, this very minute. I'll tell you what, I'll make things easy for you, I'll give you a deadline. I'll send out the invitations this very day to the opening of Gabriel Rudd's new one-man show at The Pie Factory on this Friday coming.'

'Friday!' Gabe looked incredulous 'Don't be daft, Ferg, that's only four days away.'

'Well, you'd better get moving then, hadn't you?'

'It's totally impossible, Ferg . . . Maybe in six months, a year . . .'

'No, Friday,' Tait insisted. 'I'm serious, deadly serious. The eyes of the world are on you, Gabe. Strike while the iron is steaming hot.'

Poppy, seeing that he really was in earnest, said, 'But my exhibition, Fergus. It's still got two weeks to run. Why don't we wait till then?'

'Sorry, love, I'll make it up to you. This has to happen now.'

Gabe stared at him. 'You're crazy.' But his mind was working, and it seemed to Kathy that there was a spark of excitement in his eyes. She wondered if it was Poppy's objection that had persuaded him.

'What'll we call the show?' Fergus asked. 'How about *Scream*, in ho-nour of Batty Betty? And Munch of course—we can put an image of his painting on the invitations.'

'Too corny,' Gabe said immediately. 'How about, *No Trace*?'

'Brilliant! That's it!' Fergus cried. 'I'll get the designer working on the invitations and posters right away.'

'But Poppy's right,' Gabe protested, though without much conviction, Kathy thought. 'Let's make it a month, three weeks at least. We'll know then . . .' he stopped, before adding in a whisper, '. . . about Trace.'

'That's exactly the point, Gabe, don't you see? We have to do this now, while it's front-page news. And it can only help police, with the publicity and all.'

'I'm not sure about that,' Kathy said. 'You'd better hold off any firm plans until I've got clearance.'

'You go ahead, Sergeant,' Fergus waved airily as he got to his feet. 'I have to go. Have you been to The Pie Factory yet?'

Kathy said no.

'Well, you must come over and see us. Poppy here has a fabulous show on at the moment, *The Loss of Many Little Things*—you'll love it. Are you coming, my dear?'

Poppy said she'd stay with Gabe for a while.

'Good idea,' Fergus said, heading for the stairs. 'Get a few ideas flowing for *No Trace*.'

Kathy started to protest, but he was already gone.

Poppy moved closer to Gabe and began talking to him in a low, insistent monotone. It was to do with his work, Kathy realised, picking up phrases, '. . . a narrative of pain . . . absence and loss . . .' but the tone was private, almost intimate, like a trainer psyching up a fighter for the ring. Gabe listened, stuffing food into his mouth. Kathy left them to it and went over to the window to ring Brock.

Brock was in the control centre that the borough operational command unit had established in the Shoreditch police station, the focus of a storm of activity. He listened to Kathy's report of Tait's plans to exploit, as she saw it, Tracey's disappearance.

'Publicity can only help at this stage,' he told her, and said he'd get the media unit to agree on some guidelines with the art dealer. 'Get over here for a team briefing at four, will you, Kathy? I'll send someone to sit with Rudd.' He sounded preoccupied.

All over London the mobilisation was in full swing, detectives tracking down previous offenders, uniforms knocking on doors, volunteers searching parks and wasteland, new technology cranked into action. Brock stared at the large plastic-covered street map of east London on the wall, on which coloured marks were constantly being added and erased to track progress on the ground. To one side, as if to encourage the searchers, were pinned the pictures of the three missing girls,

Aimee, Lee and Tracey. They depended on him now. The machine was in his hands. He was filled with a sudden overwhelming sense of inadequacy.

One of the computer operators said something and the supervising inspector replied, then turned to Brock as if expecting his comment.

'Sorry,' he said. 'What did you say?'

'Oh, just about the new data, sir—so much of it.'

They were all looking at him now, expectant, waiting for some word of insight or inspiration from the boss, and he felt at a loss, for he had nothing for them, not yet. 'This is how it goes,' he said, making his voice steady, confident. 'Until we get a finger on the pulse. We'll know when that happens.'

They seemed satisfied, nodding and turning back to their screens. The metaphor was wrong though, he thought, too gentle. He searched for something more visceral; *until I have something to get my teeth into.* His instinct was that the place to find it wasn't here, for all the Mission Control paraphernalia of computer screens and headsets and data charts; it was out there, on the street. He fought to suppress his frustration, picking up the latest copy of the log and forcing himself to read.

Gabriel Rudd was pacing up and down in agitation, muttering to himself. Having worked him up to this state, Poppy had left.

'You okay?' Kathy asked.

He stopped in his tracks and blinked at her. 'What? Oh, yeah.' He took a deep breath, trying to calm down. 'This is how it goes,' he said, flapping his hands in despair. 'Until something comes. An idea, something to get my teeth into.'

'Maybe this really isn't the best time, while you're worrying about Tracey.'

He frowned, as if he couldn't for the moment follow what she meant. 'Oh, Trace, yeah. No, Ferg's right. This is exactly the time to do it, while the pain's fresh.'

'Is it? I didn't really understand what he was saying about pain. Isn't art about, I don't know, beauty and making people feel good?'

He shook his head impatiently, as if he didn't want to get into some kind of childish debate. 'Science reassures, art is meant to disturb,' he muttered distractedly. 'A painter said that—Braque. I'm going upstairs to the studio, okay?'

Kathy went back to the window, wishing she'd been given something else to do. She didn't believe that there would be a ransom phone call, and she didn't think anyone else did either. Rudd needed a nursemaid rather than a detective in his house. Discounting their anger, Kathy suspected that the Nolans had pretty much summed Gabriel Rudd up—self-absorbed and neglectful. She checked her watch. The 'golden hour', that first chaotic period when the most important information was likely to be gathered, was long past. She felt a deceptive calm enveloping the house and the square, as if nothing had really happened. Maybe there would be news at the briefing.

4

THE LOCAL HEAD of Operations called the meeting to order. The room was packed, people squeezing into corners against filing cabinets and computer workstations. He gave a brisk history of the Critical Incident Procedures that had been followed since the disappearance of Aimee Prentice on the twenty-second of August, followed by that of Lee Hammond on the nineteenth of September, and now Tracey Rudd on the night of the twelfth of October. Then he introduced DCI Brock as head of the Major Enquiry Team that had assumed overall control. Brock thanked him and called for briefings from the leaders of the various teams.

The first was a uniformed inspector who had been coordinating the search teams. On a grid map he outlined the areas that had been covered by ground searches and house-to-house enquiries for each of the three abductions. In the case of Tracey Rudd, a number of premises in and around Northcote Square had been searched, including the house of Betty Zielinski, the neighbouring building site, and the grounds of both Pitzhanger Primary School and the complex of old buildings known as The Pie Factory. From there the search had expanded out towards the Regent's Canal to the north and Liverpool Street rail station to the south. Two detectives had also been out to the home of Tracey's grandparents in west London.

There had been some promising finds, but so far these had led nowhere. A plastic bag of children's clothing had been discovered beneath a hedge just two streets away from Northcote Square, but didn't match the description of clothes missing from Tracey's wardrobe. There were several reports of a young girl seen walking hand in hand with a man late on Sunday night, but before the time when Rudd had last checked on Tracey in her bedroom.

The next report came from the Rainbow Coordinator. When Kathy had first heard this term she'd imagined some benign social services program, but of course it was nothing of the kind. Operation Rainbow was the vast network of public and private security cameras that covered the city and were monitored by the Met. The local Rainbow Coordinator and her team had been searching this source for weeks, looking for vehicles and faces that might have been common to both of the first two crime scenes. Now they had a third area to trawl. So far they had come up with only one lead in the Northcote Square vicinity, a tantalising two-second clip of a pale child's face pressed against the front passenger window of a car crossing an intersection on Kingsland Road at two twenty-five a.m. The car resembled an early model Volvo saloon, possibly red or brown, its number indecipherable, and the team was searching for it now in the earlier tapes. The Rainbow team had also been working closely with SO5, the Child Protection unit, with their data on known offenders and their vehicles, and one of their officers reported next.

As Kathy listened to these reports, so professional and impersonal, she thought how remote they seemed from the plight of the three fragile faces pinned to the wall. Yet she knew that this was their best chance, the huge ponderous machine which most likely already had the name of the perpetrator somewhere in its maw, grinding away until it was revealed at last. But how long would that take? The voices were all so calm, Brock's most of all, whereas the sight of those three faces caused panic to flutter inside Kathy's chest.

Seeing the images together like that, their similarities—white, fair-haired, pretty—seemed compelling, and despite the reservations of the crime scene manager the indications remained overwhelming that the three cases formed a single series. They were discussing this now, and Brock called on the forensic psychologist assigned as profiler to the team to comment. Kathy hadn't seen him before, but she knew he'd had some impressive results recently. He noted the differences of age, location and MO between the new case and its predecessors, but pointed out how much publicity there had been after the second abduction, with information released about the means of entry through bedroom windows which had caused panic-buying of window locks and bars in the area. He speculated on the impact this would have had on the intruder, probably pushing him further afield, then turned to a map on which were marked numbered spots indicating home, school and other destinations for the first two girls, red for Aimee and yellow for Lee. A black circle had been inscribed around these spots.

'This is the magic circle,' the profiler said, with some deliberate dramatic effect. 'This is the abductor's zone of comfort. His base is somewhere inside that circle, I'm certain of it.' Then he pointed to a single green spot on Northcote Square, about half a mile outside the circle. 'He's been pushed out of his comfort zone.' He made a sweeping gesture with his hand across the map, spiralling out from the circle like the arm of a hurricane. 'We should look at possible linkages between the circle and the new location—bus and train links, routes to work, family connections . . .'

Brock nodded as if he'd already reached the same conclusion, and announced that one of his colleagues from SO1 would be taking charge of that line of inquiry. Kathy felt a stir of excitement. That was more like it, a real job at the heart of the case, from which she'd have access to anything she wanted. Then she heard Brock introduce DI Bren Gurney, and the big Cornishman stood forward so that they'd know his face. Stung with disappointment, Kathy heard Brock mention her name too, almost in passing, saying that she would remain close to Gabriel Rudd and make follow-up enquiries in Northcote Square.

It made sense, Kathy eventually conceded to herself, after she'd buried her disappointment. Bren was senior in rank and had already spent the day working with the other teams on this problem. But when she looked again at the photographs of the girls they seemed to be accusing her: 'Is this the best you can do for us?' Wherever they and their abductor were, it certainly wasn't Northcote Square.

Later, as the briefing drew to an end with questions, she made an effort to take her role seriously. She put up her hand and said, 'I wonder if we should look again at the circumstances of the death of Tracey's mother, Jane Rudd, five years ago.'

There was a moment's silence, and Kathy could see the puzzlement on faces trying to figure out the possible relevance. Then an older man across the room growled, 'I was the investigating officer at the time.'

'Fine,' Brock said quickly. 'Will you give DS Kolla a briefing after we've finished?'

The man nodded, watching Kathy through narrowed eyes. As the meeting broke up he came over to her and offered his hand. 'Bill Scott. Coffee?'

They found a quiet corner in the canteen and Scott said, 'Why are you interested in Jane Rudd's death?'

His manner was terse and not, Kathy sensed, sympathetic. She wondered if he'd felt threatened by her question in that gathering of his colleagues. 'It was only that several people have suggested a parallel between these two tragedies in Gabriel Rudd's life. I thought I should be aware of what happened.'

Scott screwed up his nose and sniffed suspiciously at his coffee cup before sipping. 'Don't see any parallel.'

'No, probably not,' Kathy said, and waited.

After a long silence Scott said, 'D'you think he's going to try to make money out of it again?'

'Rudd? Yes, probably. His dealer's encouraging him in that direction. Fergus Tait?'

'Don't know him. They mentioned Betty Zielinski. She's still around?'

'Yes. She knew Jane Rudd?'

Scott nodded. 'Neighbour. Off her trolley. Tried to take the kid after Jane died. Claimed she was hers. Completely nuts.'

'She tried to take Tracey?'

'Mmm.' Scott examined the look on Kathy's face. 'She didn't push Jane into the canal, if that's what you're thinking. Her movements were accounted for.'

'Right. What happened when she tried to take Tracey?'

'Got herself worked up. Quite hysterical. The grandparents had to step in. They took Tracey to live with them for a while till things settled down.'

'Was Tracey's father happy with that arrangement?'

'As far as I could tell. My impression was that he wasn't much bothered. More interested in his work, if you can call it that.'

'How did he react to his wife's suicide?'

Scott shrugged. 'He drank a lot. How do you know what's really going on inside someone's head?' He looked pointedly at his watch. 'Anything else?'

'No, I don't think so. Thanks, Bill.'

'Don't mention it.' Scott got to his feet, then added, 'I liked her, you know, Betty—mad as she was,' and marched off before Kathy could change her mind.

'Chief? The car's here for your evening prayers.'

Brock looked up at Bren who'd tapped on his door. He checked his watch and swore under his breath. He hadn't noticed the time and realised he was going to be late. He shoved a handful of papers into his briefcase and hurried out. The last thing he needed was a senior management meeting—dubbed morning or evening prayers, depending on the time of day—and especially this one, called specifically to discuss the report he hadn't read.

By the time he reached the conference room at the Yard the meeting was well advanced. Commander Sharpe scowled darkly at him as he took the empty seat next to Superintendent Dick Chivers. 'Cheery' Chivers, ever dour, was looking glummer than usual. Brock's heart sank as he looked around the table and saw that everyone else's copies of the report were decorated with dozens of place markers and stick-on notes of many colours, signifying the depth of their study. His own copy, entirely free of such embellishments, looked hideously naked apart from the letter tucked in at the end of chapter one. He made a mental note to get Dot to stick lots of things in for the future, and wondered where they all found the time. As he listened to them droning on he told himself that it was good to suffer these things from time to time, to remind himself just why he'd always refused promotion above detective chief inspector. He suffered less of this than any of them, and some no doubt spent their whole working lives in such meetings, pale termites in the ant heap of number ten Broadway.

By listening quietly, Brock was able to pick up much more from the exchanges around the table than he had from the impenetrable document. It seemed that some sort of power struggle was going on, though whether entirely within the police service or involving also the security services was not clear. The battlefield on this occasion was the ongoing allocation of responsibilities and resources between the centre—Scotland Yard—and the periphery—the thirty-three borough operational command units. The focus of this debate was Special Operations, and in particular the Major Enquiry Teams of SO1, to which they all belonged.

In essence, it was the opinion of Sharpe—always, in Brock's view, susceptible to conspiracy theories where his place in the organisation was concerned—that the Beaufort Committee would recommend that SO1 be shafted, sacrificed on some spurious altar of management theory.

'Did he say Beaufort?' Brock whispered to Chivers.

Cheery gave him a baleful look to see if he was joking, then reached to Brock's copy of the report and turned to the introduction. Listed were the names of the committee of inquiry headed by its chair, Sir John Beaufort. 'Jugular Jack,' Chivers snorted.

'Something, Brock?' Sharpe was leaning forward over his papers, beaming his piercing stare down the length of the conference table.

'Just that I happened to come across Beaufort today. He's got Special Branch protection, you know. He's been getting death threats.'

'Well, let's hope they come to something,' Sharpe said acidly. 'I suppose we can always consider that as a last resort. Murder is one thing we should be able to do reasonably well. No, Lillian, that's not to be minuted.' He allowed time for appreciative chortles around the table before moving to the next item on his long agenda.

5

IN THE FOLLOWING days the initial turbulent activity settled into a pattern. New faces became familiar, actions became routine and the hope of quick results faded into a dull frustration. The weather settled too, into the soggy monochrome of autumn; leaves fell in earnest from the trees and people reached automatically for warm coats as if summer had never been.

Kathy continued to visit Northcote Square each day, although no one seriously expected Gabriel Rudd to hear from his daughter's kidnapper. She became part of the background at 53 Urma Street, saying little but watching and listening in the hope of catching some reference that might be useful in the hunt for Tracey. She found that the enigma of Gabriel Rudd became no clearer to her. She attended a number of impassioned interviews he gave to radio, TV and press reporters in his house, in which he spoke agonisingly of his loss and pleaded with heart-wrenching conviction for his daughter's safe return. She also observed the careful way in which he positioned his interviewers and their photographers so that his studies for *The Night-Mare* always appeared to good effect in the background. She noticed that he encouraged certain styles of photograph of himself, in close close-up, or in apparent conversation with his work, and she was struck by his change of mood when the interviewers left, becoming brisk and focused on his preparations for the exhibition at The Pie Factory, which seemed to absorb all his attention. It was as if she were watching two quite separate movies spliced together, one of a shocking family tragedy and the other of the artist at work.

Kathy also learned a good deal about Rudd's creative process, which she found surprising. She had assumed that artists worked pretty much in isolation, applying their individual skills and inspiration to the material at hand, but it turned out that Rudd's work was fabricated by other people, a whole army of collaborators or subcontractors acting under his instructions. Some of them worked elsewhere, but many of them moved into 53 Urma Street and could be found in busy groups in the studio, or sprawled at meal breaks in the living room, or asleep in the bedrooms on the ground floor. When Kathy asked Rudd about this ('You mean you don't actually make your own works of art?') he laughed and gave her a rambling explanation of his fundamental challenge to the whole meaning of artistic authentication, which she didn't follow. 'I suppose you think this is dead easy, eh?' he challenged her. 'Wanking around dreaming up crazy ideas.'

'I was wondering how you know when you've got a good one, how you can tell a good idea from a less good one.'

'Interesting question. I just do. That's why I'm here, doing this. Sometimes it scares me rigid.'

His mood swung from garrulous to glum, and she was pretty sure that Poppy was bringing him drugs of some kind.

She liked the crew of assistants, who seemed a more light-hearted version of the police teams, industrious and painstaking and concerned with practical matters of obtaining things and making them work. They joked about Rudd's conceptual pretensions behind his back and ignored his tantrums when things weren't to his satisfaction, and it was from them that Kathy began to glean an idea of what he was preparing for the exhibition. It seemed to be a play on the word 'trace'— the missing girl Trace, lost without a trace, and the artwork itself in the form of tracings. These would be images and words transferred by various processes onto sheets of plastic tracing film used in draughting offices, with a pale milky texture which would give a shimmering, ghostly effect under certain kinds of light.

Each day at eleven a.m. Kathy got a phone call from Len Nolan, polite but firm, wanting to know of any progress. She imagined the two grandparents sitting together over their morning coffee, ticking off the points on a list, determined not to be ignored by the authorities. Kathy also did follow-up interviews around the square, and came to recognise the ebb and flow of the people who moved through it, and put faces and characters to some of the names on the list of residents. The first she visited was Betty Zielinski, who was a common sight in the central gardens, feeding the birds with bread scraps she collected from Mahmed's Café. At Kathy's suggestion, she was taken into Betty's home on West Terrace to meet her family, which turned out to be a fat black cat and a large collection of dolls, dozens in every room, each known by name and dressed eccentrically in clothes made by Betty on an old treadle sewing machine. Her sewing room was a chaotic jumble of homemade paper patterns and scraps of cloth. As she talked, Kathy tried to fathom her madness, if that's what it was; a strange mixture of what seemed like normal memory and sensible observations with disconcerting interpretations, as if Betty stubbornly refused to see the world the same way as everybody else. There was an element of deliberate calculation in some of this, Kathy thought, and one or two of the disjunctions bothered her.

'Tracey liked it here, with my little babies, in their mummy's house. She helped me choose materials for their dresses. She loved coming to her mummy's house.'

'Her mummy's house?' Kathy queried, wondering if she'd misheard. Betty gave a startled little laugh, absurdly girlish and playful for a sixty-two year old.

'We pretended that this was her mother's house,' Betty simpered, and Kathy remembered how she'd talked the previous day to Gabe about 'my own little girl, my own darling'.

'You knew Tracey's mother, didn't you?'

'Of course. I've lived here for almost forty years, longer than anyone else. Longer even than . . .' she cocked her head and whispered, '. . . the monster. Poor Jane. Such lovely long blonde hair. I was *so* jealous of her long blonde hair.'

'What monster, Betty?'

'Shhh! The children will hear you! They're terrified of him. The one next door, of course.' She nodded towards the wall to number fifteen, the portrait painter's house. 'Stolen!' she wailed suddenly. 'So many stolen children!'

'Reg Gilbey steals children?'

Again a look of surprise came over Betty's face, as if some unexpected shift had occurred inside her head. 'Oh dear me, no. My family took such a long time to get to sleep last night after all the excitement with the visitors. They simply wouldn't settle.'

'Which visitors were those?'

'Why, the policemen and women, looking for Tracey. They searched in every room, but I told them they'd never find her here.' Her eyes twinkled as if at the memory of a particularly exciting game of hide-and-seek. 'Thomas became so excited he wet his pants, and Geraldine was sick all over her brand-new dress.'

Kathy could imagine what the lads from Shoreditch had made of that.

From Betty's she went next door to see Reg Gilbey. She heard his old carpet slippers shuffling on the other side of the door before it opened. He peered at her through thick-framed glasses, sparse grey hair sticking in odd tufts from his head, and said, 'Yes?'

'I'm DS Kathy Kolla from the police, Mr Gilbey . . .'

'Not interested,' he said grumpily and made to close the door again.

She put out a hand and said, 'It won't take long. I can come back later, if you're busy.'

'I had two lots of coppers here yesterday.' He breathed whisky, and a musty smell leaked from the house. 'Can't tell you anything.'

'I was wondering if you might have noticed anything from that bay window of yours. You must get a good view of the school playground from there. Perhaps you saw . . .'

'If you're suggesting I spend my time watching the kiddies, you can clear off.'

He moved to slam the door in her face, and she quickly said, 'No, no. Look, I'm just doing my job. We all want to find her, don't we?'

He relented a little. 'Have a look if you want,' he said, then added gruffly, 'Won't do you any good.'

He closed the door behind her and led the way down the corridor and up the stairs, dropping the cat on the way. At the landing he showed her into the big front room with its corner bay window, and the smells changed from musty damp to a rich soup of ripe linseed oil and sharp turpentine. Paintings were stacked several deep all around the walls, mainly portraits and figures, some nude.

'Your work isn't like the artists of The Pie Factory, then,' Kathy said, making conversation as she went to the bay and checked the sightlines.

'That rubbish!' Gilbey scoffed. 'Those people can't draw and haven't got one original thought between them.'

'I suppose they do have original imaginations,' she suggested, noticing a canvas in the corner depicting the figures of children running in the playground below. So he did spend time watching them, she thought.

'No, no. That's all froth and show. What they do is steal an image from some famous artist—Goya, Munch, Van Gogh, Bacon, whoever—and recycle it in execrable workmanship and look clever, as if they're making some profound reference. They're just scavengers on the body of a great tradition, that's all they are.' He'd obviously made this speech many times before, but it still got him heated.

'Who does Gabriel Rudd steal from?' she asked.

'Henry Fuseli—now he *was* a painter. Others, too, I suppose.'

'And you've never noticed anyone hanging around the corner down there, watching the kids?'

He shook his head, and after a few more poisonous remarks about the decline of artistic standards he led her downstairs and showed her out.

The school was next. The headmistress of Pitzhanger Primary School was a confident, brisk woman of definite opinions. She had known a very different Tracey from the happy child Gabriel Rudd had described.

'We were concerned about her. She was withdrawn, found it hard to concentrate and didn't make friends. Sometimes she would hide rather than join the other children at play or in classes. She had a favourite place in the service yard, an old coal bunker, where we'd usually find her. I spoke to her father about it, and he insisted it was our fault, that the other children were bullying her, but that wasn't so. It's true that they'd heard about *Dead Puppies*—their parents told them—and that led to some teasing, but we soon put a stop to that. I believe there was some other problem. She seemed frightened.'

'Did her grandparents speak to you?'

'Yes, several times. They made it plain that they had a quarrel with Mr Rudd about his parenting, but I couldn't support any suspicions of abuse or mistreatment. She just seemed very insecure and uncommunicative. Her teacher was concerned about some drawings she did of so-called monsters, but Tracey said they were her dreams.'

'Do you still have the drawings?' Kathy asked, but the woman shook her head.

'I believe we gave them to her father.'

'I suppose the other officers asked you if you'd noticed anything unusual lately.'

'Yes. There's been nothing really—no break-ins or obvious strangers hanging around. I had words with the landlord of The Daughters of Albion across the street when he put chairs and tables out on the footpath at lunchtime in the fine weather, and some of his customers started calling out to the children in the playground. Builders from West Terrace, mainly.'

'I see. What about other locals? Reg Gilbey on the corner?'

'Oh, we see him up there quite often, staring down at us, waiting for inspiration I suppose. He's all right. He gave us one of his paintings for our fund-raising auction day. Quite extraordinarily generous of him, actually. It was just a little oil sketch of our chimneys . . .' She pointed up at the elaborate brick chimneys above the slate roof. 'It raised over five thousand.'

'Gosh. And Betty Zielinski?'

'Yes, she is a character. The children make up silly stories about her and call after her. We discourage it, of course, but they are fascinated and a little frightened by her.'

'She told me that Tracey was a particular friend of hers, and used to visit her house.'

'I'm surprised. I've seen her run from Betty when she's approached her on her way home from school. I'd say Betty was a rather unreliable witness. She does tend to fantasise.'

The Fikrets, the Turkish Cypriots who ran Mahmed's Café, were clearly a formidable clan, led by Mahmed Fikret and his wife Sonia. Mahmed and his son Yasher were usually to be found drinking coffee at one of the little tables in the shop, reading the *Economist* or the *Financial Times,* while the diminutive Sonia worked behind the counter, serving customers and yelling orders back to the kitchen in a piercing voice. The family had connections in several parts of the square, with a grandchild at the primary school, several nephews working on the building site, which, as Poppy had told Kathy, Mahmed owned, and a cousin working as a chef in Fergus Tait's upmarket restaurant, The Tait Gallery. 'We're art lovers too, you know,' Sonia told Kathy, pointing to a lurid print of a belly dancer on the wall. 'Yasher bought that one. He's got a good eye.'

On the fourth day of Tracey's disappearance, Thursday the sixteenth of October, Kathy bought a pita bread sandwich and tea in a polystyrene cup from Mahmed's and took them to the central gardens for her lunch. She found a seat and watched the activity around her. A steady trickle of people passed in front of 53 Urma Street, pausing and pointing to Tracey's home. Through the rapidly thinning canopy of leaves she caught a glimpse of Reg Gilbey in his corner turret, peering down at four builders walking along West Terrace towards the pub on the corner of Urma Street, followed soon after by a flock of girls from the typing pool of one of the offices on East Terrace, a man with a walking stick, two women with small dogs. Tourists of all ages, from teenage German backpackers to elderly Americans, passed by, drawn to the red neon letters above the gallery at The Pie Factory. She had resisted visiting it so far because she felt she should have more urgent things to do, but now she was at a loose end, marooned in this square while the real work was being done elsewhere. She would definitely speak to Brock about it. She finished her lunch, scattering crumbs for the sparrows, and made her way towards the gallery entrance.

Inside, in a pale grey foyer, she took a catalogue for Poppy Wilkes's exhibition, which described the artist as 'a ferociously gifted young British artist, one of the second wave of yBas following the pioneering generation of such international stars as Damien Hirst and Tracey Emin'. The first part of the exhibition was a video installation called *Dad's Car and Other Remote Sightings of Distant Kin,* and Kathy went into a square room, onto the ceiling and four walls of which black-and-white video films were being projected. When she reached the centre of the space, rotating to try to follow the different images, Kathy picked up a soft background soundtrack of sighs and moans and mysterious clicks. The films appeared unsynchronised and were difficult to follow, sometimes running in slow motion or frozen in a still or going suddenly blank, but there seemed to be certain recurring images: of an old car, a Jaguar perhaps, viewed from a low angle, door open; of various pieces of women's underwear in close-up draped across leather upholstery; of a woman's foot sticking out of a car window, jerking violently; of a cigarette burning in a car's ashtray. Kathy didn't stay long.

She moved on to another room containing a number of Poppy's highly naturalistic sculptures, dominated by half a dozen giant cherubs suspended from the ceiling. These winged figures had the extremely realistic features of a pretty child, disturbingly like Tracey Rudd, but magnified to larger than adult size, and of an unhealthy-looking mottled brown colour. The catalogue explained that the colouring had been made from blood donated by convicted murderers, after whom each cherub was named, as in *Cherub Maxwell, Cherub Henry* and so on. Another of the sculptures was called *Virgin Birth,* and the infant, again larger than life and very realistic, lay on the lap of the conventionalised drapery of a Madonna from which the figure itself had mysteriously vanished, leaving a void where the face should have been.

In one corner of the room were a few pieces by another sculptor, Stan Dodworth—presumably, Kathy thought, the Stan whom Poppy Wilkes had mentioned as having a problem with the pigs. According to the catalogue, Stan was a working-class lad from the north of England who had burst onto the London scene with his scandalous sculpture *Fag Thatcher,* a bust of the former prime minister made entirely from urine-stained cigarette butts retrieved from public toilets in northern mining towns. After the storm of controversy this and other similar pieces had provoked, Stan suffered a nervous breakdown and had only recently recovered sufficiently to expose his talent to public view in the exhibition *Body Parts,* from which these works had been taken. They comprised a series of withered limbs, like burnt driftwood, set up on plinths. Kathy resisted the temptation to spend twelve thousand pounds on a blackened hand.

One wall of the large exhibition area was glass, on the other side of which were the tables of The Tait Gallery restaurant, so that the diners could take in the exhibitions as they ate, while they in turn would appear as living sculptures, part of the show. Kathy could see the last lunch diners finishing their meals, and she and they smiled at each other through the glass.

'Look pleased with themselves, don't they?' a voice murmured in her ear.

She turned to find Poppy Wilkes.

'You didn't stay long in my video room,' Poppy said. 'Didn't you like my work?'

'I found it unsettling,' Kathy said, and then, seeing the scepticism in Poppy's eyes, added, 'My dad died in a car crash.'

'Really? Oh, wow.'

'He had a big old car like that—a Bentley. He drove it into a motorway bridge support.'

'Hell. An accident?'

'Probably not. He'd just gone bankrupt.'

Kathy had no idea why she was making this confession. She hadn't intended to, and she felt it to be completely out of character. And Poppy wasn't exactly the sort of person she'd want to confide in. It was almost as if the atmosphere of exhibitionism in this place had infected her.

'What about you? Was that your dad and his women?'

Poppy smiled. 'No. I'd like to say I had a tragic childhood, but it was just ordinary.'

'Is that what drives you to do this—to avoid being ordinary?'

'Ooh, that's a sharp one. What about you? What happened after your dad died?'

'Mum died, and I got on with my life.' Kathy was aware of Poppy appraising her, eyes half closed as if composing a camera shot. She decided she didn't want to be the subject of one of Poppy's artworks. 'You live here, don't you?'

'In this building, yes,' Poppy replied. 'Behind here there are workshops and a few small flats—bed-sits, really. When Fergus takes you on he gives you a room and workshop facilities and materials and exposure, and in return he owns your work. You get a percentage of anything he sells over an agreed amount. It's a way of getting started after art school. He's launched some good talent that way.'

'How about Stan?' Kathy nodded at the withered limbs. 'He's a bit older, isn't he?'

'Yes, he lives here too, trying to get back into the game. Fergus is helping him out. Actually he's over there, pretending to look at my *Virgin Birth*, but really he's watching us.'

Kathy saw a tough-looking character with shaved head and faded T-shirt and jeans in the far corner of the room.

'I'll introduce you, provided you don't let on you're a cop.'

'Why not?'

'He had a breakdown a few years back. He was a bit violent with someone who was harassing him and got himself arrested. The cops beat him up and put him into an asylum.'

If only it was that easy, Kathy thought, and followed Poppy.

'Hi, Stan. This is Kathy. She's interested in your stuff.'

Stan eyed her suspiciously.

'Yes,' Kathy lied. 'I was wondering how you get all those effects, of the veins and tendons and everything.'

Stan looked at his feet and grunted.

'He uses sandblasting and stuff, don't you, Stan?' Poppy prompted, but Stan remained silent.

'Where do you get your inspiration?' Kathy tried.

He slowly looked up to meet her eyes and said, 'Death,' then turned and walked away.

'He doesn't have Gabe's gift for self-promotion, does he?' Kathy said, and immediately felt a chill in Poppy's look, as if any criticism of Gabriel Rudd wasn't allowed.

'Stan's all right,' Poppy said. 'He's very serious about his work. It's very truthful. That's what we're all about, truthfulness.'

'Are you?'

'Yes. Stan, Gabe, me, we're all after the same thing, the truth, even when it hurts—especially when it hurts. You'll see it tomorrow in Gabe's show. You are coming, aren't you? We're setting it up in the morning.'

'Okay, yes. Although I feel I should learn a bit more about all of this.'

'There's lots of books. Fergus commissioned one on us. It's available at the desk outside.'

'Fine. Incidentally, is it just a coincidence that those faces on your cherubs look like Tracey?'

'No, she modelled for me. She has such an innocent face, just what I was after.'

Kathy picked up a copy of *Art of The Pie Factory* on her way out.

Later that evening, on her way back to Shoreditch station, Kathy noticed posters stuck on walls and taped to lamp posts calling for information about the missing Tracey Rudd, and at the same time advertising the *No Trace* exhibition. There was an image of Tracey on the posters, a poignant little sketch by her father, and each poster had been individually signed and numbered by Rudd.

Inside the police station the mood was flat, exhausted, and she mentally compared it to the buzz she'd left at Rudd's studio. Everyone here seemed drained, one officer actually asleep on folded arms on his desk. She asked if Brock was around and was told that he was in a meeting and should be back shortly. Anxious not to miss him, she went to wait in the corner where he had set up his work space. His desk was piled with reports, maps, memos and notes, his computer plastered with handwritten messages stuck to the screen so that he wouldn't miss them. As she sat down to wait, Kathy noticed a thick report lying next to her elbow. What attracted her attention was the end of a letter stuck between the pages. She recognised Suzanne Chambers' handwriting. Brock's friend Suzanne had taken care of her once when Kathy had been recovering from the violent end to a particularly harrowing case, and for this she would always be grateful. Suzanne lived with her two grandchildren fifty miles away in Battle, near the Sussex coast, but Kathy assumed she and Brock spoke regularly on the phone, and she wondered why Suzanne should need to write. Perhaps they've gone away somewhere, she thought. She leaned forward and twisted her head to read the address, but saw that it was that of the antique shop Suzanne owned on the high street.

Kathy looked back over her shoulder around the office. There was no sign of Brock and no one was paying any attention to her. She reached over and tugged the letter an inch further out of the report, and read:

Dear David,

I have to put this in writing, because I haven't been able to find the words . . .

A chill grew inside her as she reread the line. 'Oh no,' she murmured. 'They're splitting up.' She checked the room again, then tugged the bottom corner of the letter free of the report so that the final line on the page was revealed:

my future and ours. Before I had no choices, but now

Kathy took a deep breath, still not understanding. She decided there was nothing for it, and was reaching forward again when she heard Brock's voice behind her. 'That's not soon enough. Tell them to try harder,' he was calling to someone in the corridor. She slipped the letter back into the report and turned to face him. 'Hi,' she said and he gave a weary smile in return.

He listened to her patiently as she asked for a more active role in the investigation, then scratched at his beard before replying. 'I know how you feel, Kathy. This is a frustrating time for all of us. The reason I've kept you there is that the other two crime scenes are cold, but Northcote Square is different. It's in the news every day—Rudd's making sure of that. I'm hoping there may still be something to be got from it.'

He saw Kathy's puzzled look and went on. 'The man we're looking for is watching those broadcasts too. Have you thought that he may be tempted to pay another visit? Enjoy the circus he's created?'

She hadn't thought of that, although she realised she should have.

'We're monitoring the square with cameras, but that's not the same as a good pair of eyes on the ground. You may spot something. Stick it out till the end of the week, okay? Then we'll see. And in the meantime, talk to Bren. See if he's come up with anything that strikes a chord with you.'

She nodded, chastened, and he added, 'Missing children are the worst thing, Kathy. I know. We mustn't let it get to us.' They were silent for a moment, he thinking of the pictures of the girls that Kathy had pinned beside her desk both here at Shoreditch and in her regular office at Queen Anne's Gate, and she wondering if he was making false assumptions about her vulnerability.

'I'll talk to Bren,' she said, and turned away.

She found him, shoulders bowed, poring over a printed list, highlighting names with a green marker. A steady man, quietly spoken, he usually exuded confidence but now looked defeated.

'Hi, Bren.'

He lifted his head. 'Hi, Kathy. Got any goodies for us? We could do with something.'

'No progress?'

'Nothing to speak of.' He passed a hand over his eyes and yawned. He had three girls of his own, Kathy knew, and he had thrown himself into this case as if it were a personal quest. 'This is driving me crazy, Kathy. It really is.' He handed her an envelope with her name on it. 'We've all had one,' he said as she unsealed it to find an invitation to the opening of *No Trace*. 'Load of rubbish.'

'Brock suggested I sit down with you sometime and go through what you've turned up.'

'Good idea, I could do with a fresh brain. Tomorrow morning? Eight-ish?'

'I'll be here.'

She thought about Brock as she sat in the bright capsule of the underground train on the way back to Finchley Central, and about Gabriel Rudd, both running their teams, keeping them fed with ideas, dogged by the possibility of failure. She reached her station and tramped through the dark streets to her block of flats, where she took the lift to the twelfth floor. She was thankful now for the silence and peace of her flat, although at other times she dreaded the first sense of emptiness, of Leon gone. She microwaved a meal and sat by the window, the curtains open, looking out over the city. Brock's dilemma was a bit like Gabe's, she thought, a visual or conceptual one. How to recognise a good idea when a less good one might deflect the whole project and soak up crucial time and resources?

She took the book she'd bought at the gallery out of its paper bag. The cover was perfectly white, with the title spelled out in letters cut from newspapers, as in a ransom note. Inside, Fergus Tait's introduction to his vision of The Pie Factory read like an overenthusiastic advertisement for a new cosmetic, Kathy thought, but at least it was intelligible. When she reached the main text, written by a professor of media arts, she floundered. The first sentence ran:

> In the high art lite world in which the barely mediated procedures of Post-Minimalist convention reprise Modernist discourse in terms of docusoap myth, and what passes for British culture privileges a new ontological realm of narrative trite, the artistic production of The Pie Factory, the latest Britart powerhouse of London's Shoreditch/Hoxton (ShoHo) district, offers a stunning new avatar of the memorialising tendencies of the avant-garde.

She tried it again, a word at a time, but that didn't help, so she just looked at the pictures and resolved to try the web.

6

AS SHE WALKED from the tube to the police station the next morning, Kathy noticed that the posters she'd seen everywhere the previous night had disappeared. She mentioned this to the desk sergeant who said, didn't she know that those things were valuable? Apparently they were changing hands in the local pubs and market and on the internet for as much as two hundred pounds, some said, especially to foreigners. 'Well, they're works of art, aren't they? Signed original Gabriel Rudds.'

Bren looked as if he'd had little sleep the previous night. His breathing was shallow, his gaze bleary. Kathy had found him in the control room, in front of the big map. Two women working on their computers ignored them as Kathy and Bren sat together with mugs of coffee. The mugs came from a small tea-making alcove outside, and were stained and chipped from continuous use.

'I've been over this ground so often it's becoming a blur. We haven't been able to come up with any convincing connection between the profiler's magic circle and the site of the third abduction, Northcote Square. There's one little thing I keep coming back to, Kathy,' Bren said wearily. 'But I can't think straight any more, so maybe you can tell me if I'm just getting fixated or what.'

'Go on.'

Bren pointed to the red and yellow spots and the black circle. 'We've interviewed every single person inside that circle, some several times.

Nothing. Now Aimee and Lee went to school by bus, on different routes, from different stops. Their mums go to different shops and as far as we've been able to tell their paths may never have crossed . . . except there.' He rose and pressed a fingernail to a small cross. 'This is where Aimee caught her bus, and sometimes, not regularly, if Lee and her friends missed their usual bus home, they would take a different route that comes to this same stop. There's a row of shops there with a newsagent, where both girls have bought sweets. It's possible that they even stood together in the same queue at the counter.' He turned to Kathy with a look almost of appeal. 'That's the only place we've been able to find where their paths actually crossed.'

'Sounds significant.'

'But is it? I thought it might be, but we've turned up nothing.'

He looked ashen under the glare of the fluorescent lights. She said, 'Why don't we go there and you can show me.'

It was at the other end of the borough, and they decided to take a car.

The place was a nondescript section of street, busy with traffic and indistinguishable from any other. The abductor might have been passing, Bren thought, in a car perhaps or on foot, and first spotted the two girls here. At that moment, a red double-decker pulled up at the stop opposite the newsagent and Kathy looked up at several faces on the top deck gazing down at them.

'Or he might live around here.' Bren gestured to the row of houses across the street, and the windows of flats over the shops. 'But we've checked everyone in the immediate vicinity and found nothing. The shopkeepers haven't been able to help.'

The bus moved off and they crossed the street. Pictures of Aimee and Lee stared out at them from the window of the newsagent. When they reached the doorway they turned and looked back. Above the roofs of the houses opposite, the top two floors of a tall block of flats several streets away were now visible.

'What about them?' Kathy pointed.

Bren frowned. The fresh air had revived him a little. 'No, I don't think we've been up there.' He checked the map he'd brought. 'It's outside the magic circle.'

'Shall we take a look?'

Kathy directed Bren from the map, and they drew in at the base of a tall building on the Newman housing estate. They got into the lift and pressed the button for the topmost level. It was a graffiti-coated aluminium box, and Kathy made a comment about how Fergus Tait could probably sell it as an artwork. Bren didn't get it, and she said, 'Come to the gallery tonight. You'll see what I mean.'

'It's cut-up sheep and stuff like that, isn't it?'

'That sort of thing. Gabriel Rudd's famous.'

'Oh yes, I'd heard of him. He's the *Dead Puppies* guy, right? My girls saw him on TV and had nightmares for a week.'

The lift ground to a halt at level three and a woman got in. The lumpy shapes of curlers bulged beneath her headscarf. She looked them over.

'So what is *Dead Puppies*?' Kathy asked when the doors finally slid shut.

The woman spoke before Bren had a chance. '*Dead Puppies*? I can tell you that, love. I saw it on TV. This smart-arse cooked up some puppies and put them in tins, with labels and everything, and called them works of art. Some art gallery paid millions of taxpayers' money for just one.'

'Yuck,' Kathy said.

'Oh, it was much worse than that, love,' the woman continued, clearly relishing Kathy's reaction. 'He brought one of the tins with him on TV, and he had a tin-opener and a fork . . .'

'Oh no!'

'Oh yes. Tucked into it, he did. I was having my dinner at the time, but I couldn't finish it, I felt so ill.'

'It's true,' Bren confirmed.

'That's what they call art these days. Sick, if you ask me. You're coppers, aren't you?'

'Is it that obvious?'

'Yes, love, it is.'

They reached the top level and the woman got out ahead of them. They followed her around a corner and came out onto the access deck. A dozen residents were outside along its length, some chatting, others smoking or reading the paper in the afternoon sun.

'It's the Bill,' the woman called out so that everyone could hear, and they all immediately disappeared, front doors slamming.

'So much for the element of surprise,' Bren muttered.

The first door they tried was opened by a suspicious elderly man in shirtsleeves. His forearms looked strong and brown, with a tattoo of an anchor on each. Bren asked him his name, and how many people lived in his flat ('Just me') and the names and numbers of people living in the adjoining flats, then showed him pictures of the missing girls. As the man examined them they looked over his shoulder into the living room. Against the far window was a telescope.

'No, never seen 'em,' he said and made to close the door.

'That's a pretty powerful telescope, isn't it, sir?' Bren asked. 'Mind if I have a look?' He walked straight past the man, who took a moment to recover from his surprise.

'Oi!' he protested, and Kathy said quickly, 'He's a keen amateur astronomer. What do you look at?'

The man gave her an unpleasant glare. 'Birds.'

Bren looked into the eyepiece without touching the body of the telescope, then strolled slowly back, looking over the room and through the open bedroom door.

'Come on, get out,' the old man complained. 'While you're 'ere you should check out them next door. Dodgy, they are.'

'In what way?'

'All them strange kids.'

As they moved to the next front door, Bren said under his breath, 'That telescope was trained straight down on the bus stop outside the newsagents. I could see the girls' pictures in the shop window.'

The next door was opened a couple of inches by a young woman with a thin, pale face, whose eyes widened at the word 'police'. This time Kathy went through the routine, and at first the woman tried to respond, although her grasp of English obviously wasn't strong. As she examined the pictures a second woman called to her in a language Kathy didn't recognise, then a child gave a shriek and began crying.

'Where are you ladies from, miss?' Bren asked.

The question seemed to agitate the woman, who was suddenly unable to speak any English at all. More children were howling now.

'How many children do you have?' Kathy asked, trying to see past the woman. She caught a brief glimpse of the second woman with a small child under each arm.

'Babysitters!' the woman at the door suddenly burst out. 'Babysitters!' she repeated, and slammed the door shut.

'Well,' Kathy said, 'I reckon we're going to get enough leads up here to keep Shoreditch busy for weeks.'

There was no response to their knocks at the third door or the fourth. The fifth was opened by a young man in need of a shave. An odd smell, rather like that of a hospital, seeped out. Mr Abbott looked at the pictures and nodded.

'Yeah, I seen these on the telly. Can't help you though.' He spoke softly, as if not wanting to be overheard.

'You live alone, sir?'

'No, with me mum.'

'Perhaps she could help us.'

He shook his head. 'She's sick in bed. Has been for months. I have to look after her.'

'These two girls used the bus stop you can see from your window,' Kathy said. 'Do you mind if we come in and check how much of that street is visible from up here?' The man seemed keen to help and led them inside and over to the window, walking with a slight limp. He stood with his right leg braced stiff while Kathy and Bren made a show of examining the view. The bedroom was to one side, its curtains closed, the room in darkness. The chemical smell was stronger here.

'Your mother?' Kathy asked, whispering now, moving towards the door.

'Yeah, she's very poorly.' He followed and Kathy had a glimpse of grey hair against a pillow before he gently closed the door.

They moved on, flat after flat, each a glimpse of a moment in a life, a collection of short stories. At the end of it they returned to the ground.

'I'll put someone onto checking these,' Bren said, looking at his notes. 'Then I'll go home and get some kip. I'm all in. Thanks, Kathy.'

It would come to nothing, Kathy thought, but she agreed to look through the photo album of local suspects they'd put together in case she recognised anyone visiting Northcote Square, and Bren looked happier. 'Don't forget about tonight,' Kathy said. 'Why don't you bring Deanne? She would be interested. It's what she's studying, isn't it?'

Later that day, the report of Bren and Kathy's visit to the flats, together with the follow-up checks, reached Brock's desk. Of the residents on the top two floors, five had previous convictions—car theft, break and enter, assault. Brock noted further action against their names. There were also several discrepancies between the names that Bren and Kathy had gathered and those on the council rental roll. The flat with the pale-skinned 'babysitters' was rented to a Nigerian family, and another, occupied by four students, was in the name of an elderly grandmother. Such was the nature of intelligence. Brock initialled the cover sheet and moved on to the next file.

7

BREN'S WIFE, DEANNE, was very interested in attending the opening of *No Trace,* as it happened. She had been an art student herself for a while before marrying Bren, and was currently doing a part-time master's degree in art history. She was also a big fan of Gabriel Rudd. She arranged for her mother to look after the girls and arrived at Northcote Square with her husband just as Kathy joined the crowd converging on the entrance to The Pie Factory. It was a clear, dry night, and there was a party atmosphere in the square. Women in expensive Italian suede rubbed shoulders with young, arty girls in bright colours like parrots, men in suits and celebrity couples.

'That's what's-his-name and his girlfriend, isn't it?' Deanne whispered, pointing at faces familiar from the movies. 'God, I wish I'd got something more exciting to wear.'

'But how can you like *Dead Puppies*?' Kathy asked her.

'Oh, that was just about our hypocrisy towards animals—you know, eating some and idolising others as pets. He was just winding everybody up.'

'You mean it wasn't really puppy meat?'

'Oh, I think it would have to have been, don't you? For the point to work, I mean, and knowing Gabriel Rudd. And it was also about labelling and packaging, and about the idiocy of the art market. It was a pastiche of other famous art icons, of course—Warhol's Campbell's soup can, and Manzoni's excrement.'

'Pardon?' Kathy thought she'd misheard.

'In the sixties, this Italian artist made up cans of his own faeces, each one containing thirty grams, labelled and numbered. Of course we can't be sure that they do actually contain that, because they're far too valuable to open—they're worth tens of thousands each now.'

'So they made him rich?'

'Well, not really. He died soon after, at thirty, of cirrhosis.'

'That's ironic.'

'Yes, isn't it? But Gabriel Rudd certainly did all right out of his cans of puppy meat—after his TV appearance they were worth a bomb.'

They were almost at the door now, and Kathy pointed at the looping letters of the graffiti on the wall, '*same old shit*'. 'Appropriate.'

'Very,' Bren said heavily. Despite some sleep and a shower, he still seemed very ragged.

'It's a quote,' Deanne said. 'A New York artist from the eighties, Jean-Michel Basquiat, started out as a graffiti artist and signed his work "Samo", short for "same old shit".'

'So this is intentional, is it?' Kathy asked. 'You think Fergus Tait had it done?'

'Wouldn't be surprised. Basquiat died young too, at twenty-eight, of a drug overdose.'

'You know a lot about this stuff, don't you?'

Deanne smiled ruefully. 'Takes my mind off nappies.'

'We should hire you as a consultant. I'm lost.'

'You're not the only one,' Bren murmured.

They had reached the entrance desk, and exchanged their invitations for catalogues of *No Trace*. Inside they found that the main gallery had been cleared of Poppy's cherubs and the other work, and was now the setting for five pearly-grey banners, each about a yard wide, the full height from ceiling to floor. The subdued lighting was supplemented by ultraviolet lamps, making the banners shimmer like ghosts, and the images and text covering them appear at first like spiders' webs or wrinkles in ancient skin. The catalogue explained that each banner represented one day since the artist's daughter Tracey had disappeared, and there would be a new banner every day until she was found, even if it meant filling the whole gallery. The dominant image on banner number one was that used on the posters, Gabe's pencil sketch of Tracey's face, and looking around Kathy recognised other images too—the upturned faces of the press in the square photographed by Rudd leaning out of his window, chains of uniformed police searching a piece of waste ground, the face of a TV newscaster reading the evening news. The images seemed mainly to be derived from photographs, but processed and simplified to become grainy, abstract clouds of dots, so that they had to be stared at for some time before their meaning emerged.

'Rudd has a thing about Henry Fuseli, an eighteenth-century English painter,' Deanne said. 'His prize-winning picture *The Night-Mare* was based on a Fuseli painting of the same name. I think some of these scenes may be modelled on Fuseli's work too.' She pointed to a figure of Rudd himself crouching on the floor, like some kind of beast, and to an image on the first banner of a dark figure leading a small child by the hand into a dark tunnel.

'This is sick,' Bren said. He was looking around in disgust at the people chatting, drinking, idly studying the works. 'Hundreds of coppers are out there tonight busting a gut trying to find Tracey, and her father is in here supping champagne, exploiting the whole bloody thing, trying to make cash out of it.'

'Yes,' Kathy said. 'I think you're right.'

Deanne looked at Bren's face, tense, angry, and said gently, 'I know what you mean. It looks like that, but it's the business he's in. He's a celebrity. It wouldn't matter what he did, the papers would be full of him and Tracey. He's dealing with it in his own way, trying to make sense of it through his art.'

Kathy noticed that some of the other people in the gallery were looking pointedly at her and smiling and whispering to each other. She was about to ask Deanne what was wrong when she stopped short and stared in shock at the banner in front of her, number four. On it she saw her own face, staring back at her. 'Oh no.'

In the picture Gabriel Rudd was standing beside her, with an arm around her shoulder. She remembered the scene from the previous day in his studio, when she'd asked him something about his work, but she didn't remember anyone taking photographs. She was filled with embarrassment and then dismay, that her image should have been stolen and used in this way without her knowledge.

Bren and Deanne had seen it now, and were equally startled. Bren moved closer and read the title underneath; *Explaining Paintings to a Dead Cop,* it said.

'What!' He sounded incensed. 'What the bloody hell . . .!'

'It's a quote, Bren,' his wife said quickly. 'Joseph Beuys, *Explaining Paintings to a Dead Hare* . . .'

Her explanation didn't pacify him.

'I feel like an idiot,' Kathy said.

'I feel bloody angry,' Bren replied. 'Where is this creep?' He glared around, furious, and people nearby shrank away. Usually calm and self-contained, almost placid in his manner, he looked formidable now, all the frustration of the past five days concentrated in this outrage. They spotted Gabriel Rudd across the room, looking pale and tragic, wearing a suit that appeared as if it had been tailored from the same polymer material as the banners. He was talking to Fergus Tait and a circle of admirers, his white hair luminous beneath the lights.

Deanne said, 'I think you should leave it, Bren.'

'You two stay here,' he growled, and strode off across the room, the crowd parting before him. They watched him approach the group, saw Rudd's face turn in surprise as he broke in, then Tait was gesturing, Bren said something in reply, and Tait was abruptly still.

After several minutes, Gabriel Rudd turned and walked towards Kathy and Deanne, ignoring the congratulations of the people he passed, Bren at his shoulder.

'Kathy,' he said, 'your colleague here has explained how offended you are by my use of your image. I want to apologise, I meant no offence.' He was standing stiff and formal, his face even paler than usual. 'Artists are terrible magpies of other people's images, and I didn't think you'd mind. I know that you and your people are doing everything possible to find Trace, and the last thing I want to do is upset you, okay?'

Kathy had expected arrogance or defensiveness, but this almost painfully polite apology was disarming. 'Well, I wish you'd asked me.'

He nodded humbly. 'I'll fix it,' he said. Reaching into a pocket, he drew out a folding knife. People nearby strained to see what he was doing, then gasped in alarm as he raised the knife to the banner. With a smooth sweep of his arm he brought the blade scraping down across its surface, erasing part of the printed image. Then he did it again, and again, until Kathy's face was removed, leaving only a ghostly smudge. He shrugged at Kathy with a weak little smile and walked away. A buzz of excited conversation followed him.

Bren, Deanne and Kathy left soon after. They paused outside in the sudden cool of the square. A silvery fog had descended, blurring the streetlamps. Bren said, 'I overreacted, didn't I?'

'No, I'm grateful,' Kathy said.

Deanne slipped her arm through his and said, 'You blew Kathy's chances of immortality, darling. Now she knows how Mona Lisa felt, or all those nude models down the ages. At least she had her clothes on.' She shivered and looked at the black skeletons of the trees in the central garden silhouetted against the mist, and said, 'This is a rather sinister place, isn't it? Not a very cheerful spot for a little girl to grow up.'

A man was locking the gates of the garden, walking slowly around the railings, limping on a stick, and the sight of him brought a memory into Kathy's mind. 'You remember the bloke we spoke to at the flats this morning, Bren? The one with the sick mother? He had a limp, didn't he. Did you see if he had a walking stick in the flat?'

Bren thought. 'Yes, I saw one on the floor beside the armchair. An aluminium job, adjustable, with an elbow brace.'

Kathy visualised it, trying to tickle a memory into life. 'I'm sure I saw someone with a stick like that, here, in the last couple of days. A young man with a limp, but I didn't get a good look at him.'

'Well, those sticks aren't that uncommon. I think hospitals lend them out. Which leg had the limp?'

Kathy stared into the darkness of the gardens, remembering. 'The stick was in his right hand, so I suppose that was the bad leg.'

'Like the bloke this morning.' Bren pondered this, then said, 'Just a coincidence, I expect.' All the same, luck often did play its part in these cases—a comment overheard in a pub, a car pulled over for speeding with something suspicious in the back, perhaps a chance sighting of a limping man.

Then something else occurred to Bren. 'The bedroom window of the second girl, Lee, was fairly narrow. Forensics found threads of fabric from a pair of jeans snagged on the side of the frame, as if the man had knocked his knee or hip against it, climbing in.'

'The man's name was Abbott, wasn't it? Why don't we check if they've found out anything about him?'

Bren called in and was put through to the Data Manager.

'Abbott? Yes, I've got it. He's not known to us, Bren.'

Bren made a face, then the voice in his ear added, 'You got a bit mixed up with that one. You know how you said his mother was sick? Well, she's a lot worse than that.'

Kathy caught Bren's look as he rung off. 'What's wrong?'

He stared at Kathy. 'You remember Abbott's mother?'

'Yes?'

'Apparently she died three months ago.'

'But I saw her . . .' Kathy replayed the brief glimpse she'd had of pale hair on a pillow in dim light. 'Oh my God.'

Deanne, who hadn't been listening, was staring enviously through the windows at the diners in The Tait Gallery. 'I'm hungry,' she broke in. 'Where are we going to eat?' Then she saw her husband's face. 'Something's happened?' She said it with practised resignation. He explained.

'Oh well,' she said, 'they were bringing in finger food when we left. I'll go back in and wait for you. Maybe I'll get a chance to talk to Gabriel Rudd.' She kissed Bren on the cheek. 'Good luck. Be careful.'

'Be careful yourself,' Bren said. 'You might end up on one of his banners.'

As they approached the block of flats, Kathy looked up and counted the illuminated windows on the top floor. 'I think his light's on,' she said.

The lift seemed to take forever, and they were itching with impatience when they finally arrived. They hurried around the corner onto the access deck and stopped short; there ahead of them, backing out of his open doorway as if about to leave, was Abbott, juggling his walking stick and keys. He turned his head and for a frozen moment they stared at him and he stared back. Then, as they moved forward, he jumped with a strange lopsided skip back through his door and slammed it shut. As they ran towards it they heard the rattle of a chain. Bren hammered on the door, then stooped to the letterbox slot and bellowed, 'Open up, please, Mr Abbott. We have to talk to you.' There was no reply. Bren peered in and said, 'I can't see, the lights are off.'

'We have to get inside, Bren,' Kathy said, and pulled out her mobile.

While she called Shoreditch station, Bren moved back to the other side of the walkway and charged the door with a lowered shoulder. Kathy winced at the crash, but the door held. Bren backed off to try again. He had played for the Metropolitan Police rugby team, and he had the look on his face of someone charging an oncoming pack of forwards. The door burst open, then held on the chain. Bren used his boot to kick it clear.

As he went in, Kathy heard him cry, 'The window's open! He's gone out the bloody window!' She entered the darkened flat, feeling for the light switch. Ahead she saw the dark shape of Bren standing at an open window. She found the switch and the place flooded with light. At the same moment she became aware again of that hospital smell.

She ran to Bren's side, past the discarded stick on the floor. 'He jumped?'

'I don't think so.' Bren was leaning out, peering down into the darkness. 'I reckon that's him down there.' He was pointing to a dark shadow one floor beneath them and two bays along.

The façade of the building had projecting ledges and ribs of concrete, and Kathy could see how it would be possible to climb across it, if you had the nerve. Through the pounding in her own ears, she heard the murmur of traffic from fourteen floors below, and then something else—a grunt, a muffled curse.

Abbott had the nerve, perhaps, but he also had an injured leg. As her eyes adjusted, Kathy made out an arm reaching from the shadowy blob across a panel of pale concrete. Then the blob moved after it, slowly shifting towards the next bay of the wall.

'Abbott, there's no point to this,' Bren was shouting. 'Stay where you are.'

The warning seemed to galvanise the dark shape, which suddenly scrambled across its narrow ledge like a huge spider, reaching the next column, then crouching as if to lower itself down to the level below. There was another muffled snort, a cry, and suddenly the figure's legs seemed to fly out from beneath him and he was toppling, limbs flailing, out into the void. It took several seconds for him to scream, as if he couldn't quite take in what was happening to him. Then they heard a distant, piercing shriek, cut abruptly short.

Bren and Kathy were still for a moment, then he gasped, 'Ambulance,' and started working his phone. Kathy turned away, feeling giddy and sick. She wanted just to sit down, but there was something she had to do. She went inside the bedroom and opened the door. Gagging at the sour chemical smell that billowed out, she switched on the light.

There was the grey hair spread over the pillow, the motionless form of a small body beneath the blankets. Kathy stepped towards the bed, gently lifted the bedclothes away from the form. She saw a floral cotton nightdress, pink roses. She reached to the grey hair and stroked it away from the face, feeling cold, hard, wrinkled skin. The features were those of an old woman, sunken eye sockets, flesh shrivelled by illness and death.

Kathy forced herself to turn and walk steadily out, away from the smell, out onto the access deck, where she filled her lungs with the cold foggy air.

Brock arrived with the first patrol car. He met Bren in the car park at the foot of the block, where Abbott's body lay smashed on the ground. The ambulance arrived as they were searching him, and the driver baulked for a moment at the sight of them, two men like vultures in their black coats crouching over a scarlet mess. They found a wallet with a picture of his mother in the plastic window. Then they peeled off their gloves and took the lift up to level fourteen, where Kathy had remained to secure the scene, standing outside Abbott's door, talking to agitated neighbours.

The three of them entered the flat, and Bren and Kathy related to Brock exactly what had happened. Then they went through to the bedroom, and compared the face of the figure on the bed with that in Abbott's wallet.

'I think it is her, don't you?' Brock said, very calm, which Kathy found a comfort, for she was still feeling quite shaky. She watched him stroke the leathery old skin, then examine his fingertips. 'Makeup.'

'I thought it might have been one of the girls,' she said.

'Natural assumption,' he replied, yet she thought she heard a note of reserve. Was it a natural assumption, or had she just wanted to believe it too much? 'Three months dead . . .' Brock murmured. 'I wonder how he managed it.' He straightened up. 'So, why did he panic?'

'He had this startled, guilty look, as if he realised we knew something really bad,' Kathy said.

'This?' Brock nodded at the cadaver. 'Or something else? Let's take a look.'

They began searching the flat, Brock in the bedroom, the other two thankful to move out to the other rooms. Bren took the opportunity to ring Deanne's mobile. When she answered he could hear the shrieks of excited conversation in the background.

'I'm *fine*,' Deanne said, and sounded it. 'I've had *lots* of champagne and bits to eat, and I've been talking to these *fascinating* people. How are *you*?'

He told her what had happened.

'Oh that's terrible.' The playfulness evaporated from her voice. 'No sign of the girls?'

'No.'

'Darling, you can't carry all this by yourself.'

'Brock's here, and Kathy, and the others are on their way. Look, I think you're going to have to get yourself home. I'm sorry.'

'That's fine. Come as soon as you can. I love you.'

Bren ended the call, thinking how very fortunate he was that that was true.

8

THEY FOUND NOTHING in Abbott's flat before others moved in to take over the search. Now Kathy and Bren became the property of the duty inspector at Shoreditch as the first stage began of an official investigation into a death in connection with a police operation. Under questioning in separate rooms, their assumption of a link between Abbott and the missing girls began to seem increasingly doubtful. Kathy saw it in the sceptical gaze of her interrogators and heard it in her own voice, protesting too much. A man with a limp and a view of a bus stop. So what? She couldn't honestly say that she'd seen his face in the square.

Towards midnight there was a lull. Kathy sat drinking a cup of weak tea, expecting the worst. Her mind kept going back to that moment when they had turned the corner onto the access deck and confronted Abbott. Again and again the questioners had returned to that moment, and she had tried to recall and describe it so many times now that she no longer trusted her memory of it. She remembered the rush of excitement, and imagined that her body and face must have shown this, and that it would have been apparent to Abbott. But had he shown guilt before or after reading that signal? And was it really guilt or simply panic at seeing two psyched-up coppers bearing down on him? And what had then possessed him to climb out of his window? After that, her memory became bathed in an unreal light, spiderman toppling, arms windmilling, and the shrivelled little body in the bed. The whole sequence seemed so bizarre, so outlandish, that the steps that had led them there now seemed equally improbable.

She heard voices outside the door and assumed that new investigators had arrived, more senior and intimidating no doubt, and she braced herself. But when the door opened it was Brock who walked in, looking serious, an envelope in his hand.

'Some news, Kathy.' He sat opposite her, seeing the strain etched around her eyes. 'How are you?'

She gave him a tight smile. 'Okay. Did they find anything in his flat? Something about the girls?'

He shook his head. 'No, I'm afraid not. Clean as a whistle—apart from the little matter of dear old dead Mum.' Kathy felt nausea rise in her throat. 'However,' he opened the envelope and drew out some sheets of paper, 'we did find a memory card in his wallet, one of those little things they use in digital cameras. These are prints of the pictures it contained.'

She flicked through a series of street scenes—nothing incriminating, surely. She looked more carefully at the first, a pavement viewed from above, the space flattened by a zoom lens, and suddenly realised what it was. 'That's the bus stop, isn't it? And the newsagent. There are no posters of the girls in the window, so this must have been taken before . . .' There were children in the doorway, and she looked closer, trying to identify them. 'Could that be Aimee?'

Brock nodded. He reached forward and pointed to the second page. 'And that's Lee, we're almost certain.'

Almost certain. Kathy drew in a long breath. 'I could still be right then.' Relief began to trickle through her like some marvellous opiate. 'I could be right.'

'Yes. We've checked the angles and there's no doubt that they were taken from Abbott's window. But there's no camera in his flat. It's only a beginning, of course. But there's something there, I'm sure of it.'

Kathy thought of all that must follow; retracing Abbott's movements, tracking down his friends and acquaintances, searching for his hiding places. It would take time, and meanwhile the girls, if any of them were still alive, would be in a desperate state.

'I want to help,' she said.

'Not tonight. You're all in, and so is Bren. Get some sleep, then we'll see.'

'You look exhausted yourself.'

'Oh, I just plod on. One other thing may help you sleep better. One of Abbott's neighbours remembers him saying that he used to do wall-climbing as a sport, so his attempt to escape out the window wasn't quite as mad or panic-stricken as it seemed. He may even have tried it before.'

They got to their feet and Kathy went out to the lobby, where Bren was waiting for her. Before they went their separate ways he said, 'We were lucky, Kathy. Bloody lucky. If he hadn't had that thing in his wallet, they'd have made mincemeat of us.'

'I know,' she said, and pushed at the front door. Glancing back over her shoulder she saw Brock talking to two senior uniformed officers. They both nodded their heads and one of them glanced up at the clock on the wall. It was five past one in the morning. Kathy turned to ask Bren if he knew what was going on, but he was already striding away down the street. She looked back into the building but Brock and the others had gone, so she stepped out onto the pavement, pulling the collar of her coat up against the cold night air, and with the gust of chill wind she remembered the very first thing that had come into her head when she'd spotted Abbott. He had been on the point of locking his front door, on his way out, yet his clothing had seemed too light for the cold evening, and she'd thought he couldn't be going far. It had been the briefest of thoughts, barely formed, because then their eyes had locked and adrenaline had taken over. Kathy stopped dead, then turned and ran back into the station.

She found Brock in a corridor at the back, pulling on his coat, heading for the door to the rear car park. He looked surprised to see her.

'I thought you'd gone, Kathy.'

'I remembered something. I don't know why it escaped me. He wasn't dressed to go far. Suppose he was going to visit another flat in the same building? Suppose he climbed out the window to get to that other flat?'

Brock beamed at her and she realised that he'd got there ahead of her. He pulled open the door, and she saw a car waiting outside, engine idling. 'Want to come?' he asked. She squeezed into the back seat beside two uniformed men who were both talking on their phones. Brock got in the front, and the driver put the car into gear.

No one spoke until they reached the cordon below the block of flats, then Brock exchanged a few words with the two men before leading

Kathy past the barrier towards an unmarked white van. She saw the police tapes nearby, marking the place where Abbott had landed. There were no obvious signs of activity or alarm, but Kathy noticed groups of dark figures clustered in areas of shadow, some carrying weapons.

'Let's say,' Brock said, gazing up at the face of the building, breath misting, 'that the second flat is below the line of sight of the bus stop, so level twelve or lower. Abbott was heading down and to your right, looking from above, to our left from down here.' He pointed to an area of the façade. 'So they're starting there and working outwards. You and I just stay here and wait.' He tapped a knuckle on the back door of the van and after a moment it opened and they climbed in. A light came on and Kathy saw two people inside and the apparatus of a mobile command unit. A woman was crouched over a grid diagram on a table, marking names on the squares.

'Everyone's in position, sir,' a man with headphones said quietly to Brock.

'Then let's begin.'

The man spoke a few words into his mike and they sat back to wait. After four minutes the first report came in, and the woman put a cross through one of the grid squares. Two minutes later she marked a second cross, then a third. It made Kathy think of a game the boys used to play at school, Battleship, except now it was for real. She wondered if Gabriel Rudd could use it for his next banner. Would it become a work of art simply because Rudd, rather than an anonymous police officer, drew it? Kathy rubbed her face with both hands, feeling tired and slightly dizzy. Who cares, she thought, just let them find the girls.

After fifteen minutes the man with the headphones looked up. 'Something on level nine, sir. Flat 903. IC1 male refusing entry.'

The woman tapped a grid square. 'Flat in the name of Mrs Pamela Wylie.'

Brock and Kathy listened in silence to the low monotone of the reports. 'Entry gained . . . Occupant restrained . . . No sign of other occupants.' Then a pause and the man raised his eyes to meet Brock's. 'They've found something, sir,' he said, and Brock was out of the van and running towards the lifts, Kathy at his heels.

The body was stuffed into the back of a closet, hidden behind a suitcase and covered in a pile of old clothes. They recognised the pinched features of Lee, the second of the girls to disappear, and so pale and slack and still that they assumed she was dead until someone found a faint pulse and began CPR.

The occupant of the flat, Robert John Wylie according to the driver's licence in his wallet, was a large, fleshy man with quivering chins, a toad to Abbott's spider. He refused to say a word, and the detectives had to draw their own conclusions from what they could see. There was no sign of Mrs Wylie having lived there, and the flat looked as if it had become a den in which Wylie and Abbott could live out their obsessions. Unlike Abbott's flat, which had been neat and clean, this place was a mess of half-consumed tins, cartons, magazines and clothes, and the atmosphere was clammy and claustrophobic, tainted with a smell of burnt plastic that turned the stomach. There was a computer and its printer, still branded with the name of the school from which they had been stolen, and a digital camera. And there were pictures, hundreds of them.

A detective emerged from the kitchenette, calling for Brock. He was holding a small box in his gloved hand, and the smell of burnt plastic was stronger.

'What's that?' Brock asked.

'Found it in the microwave, sir. I think it's a computer hard drive. Looks like it's been cooked.'

The ambulance man laying Lee on the stretcher saw Kathy watching. He paused a moment and drew the blanket off the girl's left leg to show her. It was black, and Kathy gasped, 'What is it?'

'I've seen it before,' he said. 'With addicts. They use a butterfly syringe to draw the drug from soft capsules, then inject it. It causes blood clots but they keep doing it anyway and gangrene sets in. She'll lose the leg. At least.'

At that moment Wylie was being taken out of the flat. As he passed the unconscious girl on the stretcher he stopped and stared down at her, and at the same moment, as if there were some telepathic connection between them, her eyelids flickered open. She stared up, then her face convulsed in fear for a second before she lost consciousness again.

'Get him out of here,' Kathy snapped.

9

KATHY DIDN'T WAKE until noon the following day. As she surfaced slowly from a deep sleep she became aware of sunlight filtering through the blinds, and immediately her mind began spinning with memories of the previous night: a body falling into the void; the smell of burning plastic; Wylie's malignant stare; a blackened, gangrenous leg. She sat up abruptly and forced the images away. She might go for a swim, she thought, get her hair done, buy a pair of shoes, get in some food.

She noticed the trail of her discarded clothes on the floor. She still felt exhausted. The phone rang; she picked it up and heard Brock's voice.

'Didn't wake you, did I?'

'Mmm . . .' her mouth felt numb, not yet ready for speech. 'Not quite.'

'Sorry. Just wondered if you fancied brunch.'

Still slightly disoriented, Kathy wondered what kind of invitation this was.

'I'm meeting Bren in an hour,' he went on, 'at The Bride.'

'This is work?'

'Afraid so. Can you make it?'

'Of course.'

She rang off and got out of bed, opened the blinds, stretched and yawned at the window. It was a beautiful sunny day, white clouds scudding across a pale blue sky, a complete contrast with the drab grey days of the working week behind them. What did Brock want? Surely it was all but over now. Was it the questioning of Wylie? Or—her heart sank—breaking the news to relatives. Yes, that would be it. She should have realised he'd be needing help with that. She wondered how much sleep he'd had. It had been after three when he'd sent her home, but he'd still been working with the others through the material in the flat.

The Bride of Denmark was a myth, one of those unlikely accumulations that sometimes occur in the basements of old buildings in old cities. It didn't exist in the inventories of the assets of the Metropolitan Police because the occupants of the Queen Anne's Gate annex did their best to hide its existence, and because those few civil servants who had come across it considered it too difficult to deal with and had designated it 'miscellaneous'. In the years after the Second World War the former occupants of the building, architectural publishers, had gone about the ruined city like magpies, collecting fragments of old bombed-out pubs and reconstructing them in their basement as the eccentric Bride. The small rooms were crammed with salvaged fittings—the polished bar, the back-to-back pew seats, the mahogany shelving—and encrusted with rows of ancient cobwebby bottles, pewter mugs, porcelain spirit kegs, mirrors and animal trophies. A salmon gawped at an antelope's head, and the antlers of a moose met the unblinking gaze of a stuffed lion, or at least the front half of a lion, crouching among savannah grass in his glass case. The Bride was a refuge hidden beneath the annex, without phones, computers or office machines, a place where Brock retired to think.

Bren was already there when Kathy arrived, perched on a cane seat at the bar peeling plastic film from a plate of sandwiches. Brock, on the other side, was pouring coffee from a tall pot, and offered her a cup.

'Thanks,' she said, and sank onto a worn leather seat beneath the lion. 'Just what I need.'

'So as soon as I turn my back you two go and wrap the thing up,' Bren grunted, sounding peeved.

'I thought of something and went back . . .' Kathy began to explain, feeling awkward, but Bren waved a big hand. 'Brock explained. Well done, anyway.' He picked up a sandwich and took a bite, handed her the plate.

Brock came through the flap of the bar with a mug of coffee in his hand and sat beside Kathy. He smelled fresh from a shower and was wearing jeans and a thick knit pullover. 'Yes and no,' he said.

They both looked at him.

'The pictures they took tell it all as far as Aimee and Lee are concerned.' His voice was weary, as if the terrible images were a crushing burden. 'It's all there, even a photo of the place they buried Aimee when they'd finished with her. But there's nothing, not a thing, about Tracey. It doesn't look as if she was ever there.'

'What does Wylie have to say?' Bren asked.

'Not a word. Not a single word. He's been charged and he called a lawyer this morning, but he refuses to open his mouth to us.'

Kathy said, 'Do we know him?'

'Three convictions for possession and publication of indecent photographs, one involving children. Two fines and a two-month prison term. We're digging for more background.'

'The flat was rented in his wife's name,' Kathy said.

'Yes. We don't know where she is. Neighbours say they haven't seen her in months.'

He paused to let this sink in, then continued, 'The point is that we have Lee in intensive care and we know that Aimee is dead, but we have no more idea where Tracey is than we did last Monday morning. On the face of it, we have nothing to connect either Abbott or Wylie to her disappearance. And if that's the case, we're going to have to start all over again as far as she's concerned. Right from the beginning.' He took a deep breath, sat back against the padded seat and closed his eyes. 'So what are the alternatives?'

'But I saw Abbott in Northcote Square,' Kathy objected.

'You think you saw him. All you can really be sure of is that you remember a limping man.'

'You're suggesting it's no more than a coincidence?' Bren protested. 'That last night was a fluke?'

'I'm saying we should look at all the options.'

'A copycat?' Kathy said. There was silence for a moment, then she went on, 'The Tracey kidnapping is different from the other two in that her father is a celebrity. Maybe it's aimed at him.'

'Perhaps, but there's been no ransom, no threat. And why make it look like the other two cases?'

'To distract us from the obvious suspect,' Bren said.

'Who is?'

'Tracey's father,' Bren said immediately. 'Gabriel Rudd.'

Brock gave him a quizzical look. 'You've met him?'

'Last night. Kathy and Deanne and I went to the opening of his exhibition. He and I nearly came to blows.'

'Really?'

'Oh, one of his so-called artworks had a picture of Kathy and a caption that said she was dead.'

'What?'

'We persuaded him to remove it.'

Brock's eyebrows rose further. 'Rudd removed one of the artworks from his exhibition because you didn't like it?'

'Not exactly. He scraped Kathy's picture out.'

Brock stared at them both in astonishment. 'Has Rudd been giving you trouble, Kathy?'

'No. He apologised. He probably thought I'd be flattered. Perhaps I should have been.'

'Anyway,' Bren went on, 'what really got to me was that he was exploiting Tracey's disappearance for his own purposes. The whole thing has been turned into a circus for his benefit. It's been like that all week, his picture in every paper, every news report.'

'You're suggesting Rudd arranged his daughter's abduction to further his own career?'

Bren hesitated. 'It's not impossible, Brock. There are precedents.'

Brock shook his head. 'Some form of Munchausen by proxy, you mean? You know what a can of worms that is.'

'At least we should find out if he's ever done anything like this before.'

'We know he has,' Kathy said quietly, and Brock nodded and said, 'The Night-Mare.'

Bren looked puzzled and Kathy explained, 'After his wife Jane committed suicide, five years ago, he held an exhibition called The Night-Mare, inspired by her death. The main work won a big prize and he made a lot of money. Jane's parents, the Nolans, were incensed by it. When I talked to the case officer who looked into the suicide, DS Bill Scott, it sounded like a prequel to what's happening now, with the same cast of characters—Rudd, Tracey, the Nolans, Betty Zielinski.'

'There you are then,' Bren said.

'I've been wondering about it all week. Right from the start his reaction to Tracey's disappearance seemed ambiguous, and he has gone out of his way to make a public spectacle of it. I've also got the impression that his reputation has been fading recently, and he needed a boost like this. But on the other hand, I've found him weeping over a pair of Tracey's shoes when there was no one around to impress.

'There's also the fact that the publicity has really been generated by his dealer, Fergus Tait, and it was Tait who pushed Rudd into doing this exhibition. If you were to look at who's benefiting from all this, you'd logically have to consider Tait too.'

'Anyone else?'

'Well, there's the grandparents, Len and Bev Nolan. They say they've been worried for some time about Tracey's life with her father, and they explored trying to get custody, without success. They might have decided to take matters into their own hands.'

'We've been to their house in West Drayton, Kathy,' Brock said, 'and checked their story with the social services. They seem genuine.'

Bren shook his head doubtfully. 'And they told you about the custody business, did they? They didn't try to hide it?'

'That's true. I'm not saying you're wrong to have suspicions about Rudd, but maybe there's more to it. If Tracey's kidnapper wasn't the same as Aimee's and Lee's, then making it look as if it was would distract our attention away from Northcote Square, and I wonder if there are other secrets hidden there. For instance, both the grandparents and the headmistress of her school said that Tracey had become withdrawn and depressed in the past year. There may have been something going on in her life that we don't know about, that was leading up to her abduction.'

'An abuser?' Brock asked. 'Are there any other candidates in the square?'

'Too many. There's the painter Gilbey up in his turret, spying on the kids in the playground below; there are the builders who drink in the pub across the way and tease the kids; there's the mad woman, Betty, who's obsessed with stolen children; and there's the artist in Tait's stable who has a record of mental instability and violent behaviour and makes sculptures of body parts, and another who makes giant cherubs with Tracey's face and stains them with the blood of murderers.'

'Hell's teeth,' Bren groaned.

Brock sat up and stretched. 'We'll run more checks on them all,' he said, 'and meanwhile we'll get to work on Gabriel Rudd. So, where do we begin?' He took a bite of a sandwich and opened his notebook.

'Find out what he really did the night Tracey disappeared,' Kathy suggested. 'Watching TV alone all evening and going to bed at ten after tucking his daughter up never really struck me as likely. I'll bet some-one knows.'

'The grandparents say he takes drugs. Have you noticed anything?'

'Apart from the booze? Yes. When he gets really down, which happens several times a day, he gives Poppy a ring. She comes over and in no time he's buzzing with energy and optimism. I don't think it's because of her sunny personality. Maybe I should talk to her again.'

'Good,' Brock said. 'These aren't too bad.' He reached for a pile of sandwiches as if suddenly realising that he hadn't eaten for days, which was pretty much the case.

Kathy's mobile rang. She recognised Len Nolan's urgent voice and grimaced at the other two. 'We've just heard on the news,' he said. 'What's happening? Have you found her?'

Kathy took a deep breath and began to explain.

10

POPPY WILKES WAS wearing goggles and a mask as she worked, spraying paint in a fine mist over the bulging pink forms. As the paint landed, something miraculous happened to the surface, becoming a glistening sheen, glossy as a mirror. She made a last pass with the gun, then released the trigger and stepped back, pulling off her face protection.

'That's fantastic,' Kathy said from the edge of the room, hardly daring to move or speak for fear of stirring up a mote of dust to ruin the perfect surfaces.

'It's beautiful, isn't it—an American marine paint, expensive but beautiful.' Poppy knelt to switch off the motor and stood for a moment, a critical frown on her face, admiring the gigantic female bottom.

'Does it have a title?' Kathy asked.

'Mmm, I'm thinking of *My Mum's Weary Bum Has Seen It All*. What do you think?'

'I think I'm the wrong person to ask.'

'Oh, I don't know. Is this a social call?'

'No, it's official. Something's happened that I need to talk to you about.'

'Ah.' Poppy was abruptly still, her hand frozen in the action of shaking her hair out of a plastic cap. 'Let's go outside.'

She led Kathy through the jumble of benches and equipment that cluttered the workshop to a steel-framed glass door and out into a small courtyard, lit by the glow of the autumnal afternoon sun on brick walls.

Weeds poked between stone flagstones on the ground and old stone benches ringed the perimeter. It made Kathy think of a prison exercise yard. She sat down beside the artist.

'The women from the pie factory used to come out here for their breaks,' Poppy said. 'The benches are worn away by thousands of weary bums. Why do you want to speak to me?'

'I need your help. Last night we found one of the missing girls and arrested a man.'

'Oh, that's great! Was it Tracey?'

'I'm afraid not. The thing is, to find her we have to be very sure of our facts.'

'Yes, of course.'

'Especially about people's movements on the night Tracey disappeared.'

Poppy tugged a pack of cigarettes and a lighter out of a pocket of her overalls and took her time lighting up. She blew a narrow column of smoke into the cool air and said, 'I didn't see Tracey at all that weekend, or the night she was taken. I can't help you, I'm sorry.' She rubbed her nose with a thumb.

There was a theory that lying makes the nose tingle. The Pinocchio syndrome, it was called. Kathy wasn't sure she believed it, but Poppy certainly did seem to have an itchy nose.

'What about Gabe?'

'Yes, he bought me lunch on Sunday at the pub.'

'And did you see him later?'

'Don't think so. Can't remember, really. Ask him.'

'This is very, very important, Poppy. Tracey's life may depend on it. We need the truth now. Or was that just bullshit, that stuff you were telling me about truthfulness?'

Poppy took a long drag, sighing out the smoke. 'I did see Gabe that Sunday night. I didn't lie to anyone, 'cos nobody asked me that before. When he talked to you he was embarrassed, that's all. He was stoned that night, and I guess he didn't check on Tracey. He may have massaged his story a bit, to make himself look better. But it doesn't make any difference.'

'Tell me about Sunday night.'

'Gabe came over here about ten. He'd been drinking and he was bored. He had a bottle and he knocked on the door of my room.'

'He was on his own?'

'Yeah. He didn't say anything about Tracey. I didn't think to ask.'

'Go on.'

'Well, we talked, had a few drinks, then Stan looked in. He'd been drinking at the pub. About one or one-thirty, I'm not sure, they left together, and I went to bed.' Another puff, another scratch of the nose.

Kathy stared at her, waiting.

'That's all.'

'No it's not.'

Poppy frowned, then said, as if she'd forgotten, 'Oh, I did walk a little way with them, to get a bit of air before I went to bed. Down the lane behind West Terrace, then I turned back. We were a bit pissed, larking around. I squealed or something. I think that was what Betty heard, what she thought was a scream.'

'And Stan went on with Gabe, to his house?'

'What? Oh, no. He came back with me, to his own flat upstairs, near mine.'

This didn't sound right, Kathy thought. 'Come on, Poppy. And the rest.'

Poppy glared at her, suddenly angry. 'Christ, you're a pain, you know that?'

'Just tell me. You know you have to. You care about Tracey, don't you?'

'Yes, I do, but . . .'

'But what?'

'But I don't want to end up with my face cut, that's what.'

'Who would do that?'

Poppy took a deep breath, her hand dropped to her lap and finally she said, 'Yasher.'

'From the sandwich shop?'

'Yes. He's our dealer.'

'I thought Fergus Tait was.'

Poppy grinned briefly. 'Not art dealer—the other kind. He gets stuff for us—Gabe, mainly. About one o'clock Gabe decided he wanted some coke, so he gave Yasher a call. He wouldn't come here, to The Pie Factory, but he said he'd meet us in the buildings they're doing up on West Terrace. There's a room in the basement of one of the houses where the builders keep their tools. The three of us went down there, and Yasher sold Gabe some stuff, coke and something else—speed, I think. Gabe insisted we all try some of his coke, and for half an hour or so we had a bit of a party, the three of us and Yasher. Then I began to get tired and said I was going. Like I said, we fooled about a bit in the lane, Yasher pinned me to the wall, I screamed. It was just a bit of fun. Then I came back.'

'With Stan?'

'No. He wanted to stay a bit longer with the other two. I fell asleep as soon as I got into bed and I never heard him come back.'

Kathy sensed they'd passed the block that had held Poppy back before. Now she wanted to tell it all. 'I woke up on Monday morning with the phone ringing. It was Gabe. He'd passed out on his bed when he got home, he said, and he'd woken up and gone to get Tracey, and she wasn't there. He sounded confused, as if I might know where she was.'

'What time was this?'

'Quarter past six.'

The time Rudd's alarm had been set for, Kathy remembered.

'I said I'd go over and help. We searched the house, but there was no sign of her. I thought he must have got mixed up and that she was with her grandparents, but he insisted they'd brought her back the previous afternoon, only he had no idea where she was now. Tracey's window was open and the back gate unlocked, and in the end we decided he'd have to call the police. He gave me his drugs to keep for him over here, and we agreed not to mention anything about him being out the previous night, or me being there that morning. He seemed to be most worried about what Tracey's grandparents would make of it—he kept saying they'd crucify him. You know they wanted to get custody of Trace?'

Kathy nodded. 'Anything else?'

'That's about it. Only, I am serious about Yasher. He seems a charming sort of bloke, but he can be really mean if you cross him, and he's got some very ugly friends. They carry guns some of them. That stuff I told you about him selling drugs—I'm not going to put that on the record.'

'Okay, I'll do what I can to keep you out of it. Thanks for this, Poppy.'

'I'm glad I've told you now. I went along with Gabe at the time, but afterwards I didn't like keeping quiet about it. I hope it helps.'

'So do I. You are really fond of her, aren't you, Poppy?'

'Oh hell, yeah.' She stamped her cigarette out and began to rise to her feet. 'We were good mates.'

'And she was your model.'

Poppy smiled. 'Sure. She has a lovely face, real cute and innocent.'

'And her body as well? Your cherubs are very explicit —anatomically, I mean. She modelled for the bodies too, did she?'

Poppy arched an eyebrow, wary. 'Yeah, she did actually. There wasn't a problem with that. She was quite happy about it, and Gabe was always around.'

'Where did this happen, these modelling sessions?'

'Modelling sessions? Christ, you make it sound like . . . At Gabe's place.'

'Mostly, or always?'

'What are you getting at?'

'Did she ever come here, to this building?'

'Yes, she came here. She liked to see what we were doing.'

'Did she model for you here? Take her clothes off?'

'No! Well, maybe once.' Poppy turned to leave.

'Do you know where I can find Stan Dodworth, Poppy?'

'No, I don't. I haven't seen him today.'

The interview with Gabriel Rudd was more formal, conducted in a room at the Shoreditch police station. Rudd seemed fascinated by the whole process, peering up at the video camera, stroking the table he was invited to sit at, as if making mental notes for his work.

Brock, indicating Kathy at his side, said, 'You know DS Kolla, of course.'

Rudd gave a smug little smile and said, 'Oh yes, we've been practically living together the past week. Although I didn't realise until last night that she was an art critic. You two work closely together, do you?'

Again that supercilious smirk and a quick turn of the eyes to avoid Brock's sharp stare. Brock could understand Kathy's hesitation in summing him up. Rudd seemed to have developed the knack of appearing simultaneously aggressive and vulnerable, smart and gauche—though whether it was a case of cunning wrapped in innocence or the other way around, Brock wasn't too sure.

'We're going to record this interview, Mr Rudd, and I'm going to begin by cautioning you. You don't have to say anything, but it may harm your defence if . . .'

Rudd grinned. 'You really do say that, do you? Like on TV.'

Brock completed the caution and added, 'It's necessary because we need to be crystal clear on one or two things. You've been following the news, have you?'

'Oh, yeah, yeah.' Rudd's amusement abruptly evaporated. 'It really doesn't bother me.'

The two police stared at him in surprise.

'Oh, look, she's a spiteful bitch. Everyone knows she hates me.'

There was a moment of confusion before they realised that the 'news' he thought they were talking about was the first review of his exhibition, published in one of the morning papers. With a show of reluctance he pulled a folded page of newsprint out of the pocket of his leather jacket and tossed it across the table as if it soiled his fingers to touch it. Brock picked it up and quickly scanned the piece.

> Those remaining admirers of Gabriel Rudd's work who crowded to the opening of his new show at The Pie Factory last night must have been sadly disappointed. Not so much *No Trace* as *No Hope*. Hurriedly cobbled together, weak in concept, unimaginatively presented and short of ideas, it would have looked pretentious in a first-year art school exhibition. As a contender for the next Turner Prize, as some had anticipated, it doesn't rate a mention.

Brock handed the paper to Kathy and glanced at Rudd. His face was very pale, lips pressed tight, and he looked as if it did bother him a great deal.

'Actually, I was referring to news reports today of new developments in our investigations, Mr Rudd. That's why we wanted to speak to you.'

As Brock began to explain, Rudd looked first perplexed and then agitated. 'You arrested someone, is that what you're saying?' he interrupted.

'There'll be a press statement later today, but I can tell you that we believe we have found two men responsible for the abductions of Aimee and Lee. One of the men is under arrest, and the other died while trying to escape. We've found Lee alive, but it seems probable that Aimee was murdered some weeks ago.'

'My God!' Rudd sat stunned, eyes unfocused. 'Aimee . . . she was the first, wasn't she? But Lee is alive? So Trace must be too, yes?'

'I'm afraid we haven't been able to find any sign of Tracey so far. We're following up a number of leads, but at present there's nothing to connect her disappearance to these two men.'

'What? But that's impossible, surely? It must be them. Or . . . you mean there may be others? A ring? A network? Oh my God . . .'

'We're considering every possibility.' Brock opened a folder on the table in front of him and took out the two photographs that had just been delivered. 'Have you ever seen this man?' He slid the first picture across the table, and added, 'I'm showing Mr Rudd a photograph of Robert Wylie.'

Rudd showed no sign of recognition, nor with the second picture, of Abbott.

'Is that them?' He stared at the pictures with fascination, and when Brock made to put them away again he said, 'No! Wait, just so I'm sure,' and went on staring. 'Which one died?'

Brock pointed to Abbott.

'How? Did you shoot him?'

'He fell from a building. Have you ever visited the Newman estate in Bethnal Green?'

'No, no. I don't think I've ever heard of it. Is that where they lived?'

'We're still gathering information. What we now have to do is review every aspect of Tracey's case in the light of this new development. And I need you to help us by going back over what happened the night that Tracey disappeared. I want you to try to remember every detail you can, from the time Mr and Mrs Nolan returned Tracey to you on Sunday afternoon.'

Rudd met Brock's stare, eyes wide and innocent. 'Oh, right. Well . . . if you think that'll help.'

He began to repeat the story he had told them before, almost word for word, while the two detectives listened impassively. When he finished, Brock turned to Kathy and said, 'How would you rate that story, DS Kolla?'

Kathy gazed at Rudd and said, 'Well, to be honest, as an art critic, I'd have to say that it seems hurriedly cobbled together, weak in concept, unimaginatively presented and short of ideas.'

Rudd's pale face flushed pink. His mouth opened, but before he could speak Kathy went on, 'You didn't go to bed at ten that night, Gabe.'

Brock leaned forward and said, 'We know about your evening with Poppy Wilkes and Stan Dodworth; we know about your meeting with Yasher Fikret. Now I'm going to give you one last chance to tell us the truth before I arrest you for obstruction.'

The pink leached from Rudd's face, leaving it almost as white as his hair. 'Yasher? You know about Yasher?'

'From the beginning, Mr Rudd. Let's have it.'

Haltingly, the bravado gone, Rudd described much the same sequence of events that Poppy had related to Kathy—supplemented, at

Brock's insistence, with an impressive list of everything he'd smoked, drunk and taken during the course of the weekend.

'Why didn't you tell us this at the beginning?' Kathy said.

'I panicked. I knew I'd be in trouble. I'd left Trace alone for most of the night, and somebody had snatched her. Her grandparents would have murdered me. This was exactly the kind of thing they'd said would happen. They'd have tried for custody again. Christ, I might have gone to gaol, I don't know.'

'Hmm.' Brock, sceptical, scraped his beard with the end of his ballpoint. 'Bad things do seem to happen to the people around you, don't they? Whether by neglect or something worse.'

'What do you mean?'

'Your wife, Tracey's mother—did she die because you weren't around at the critical time? And was that just another unfortunate coincidence?'

'Jane had been depressed for months. They gave her the wrong drugs. You should read the coroner's . . .'

'Yes, I've read his report. No suicide note, no cry for help to her parents. She just walked out one night, leaving her toddler behind, and jumped in the canal. And you were out drinking with your mates that night too, weren't you? The parallels are striking.'

Rudd sagged, a hank of white hair flopping over his eyes. 'You think I don't know that?' he said softly. 'I'm not proud of it. That's why I wanted to keep quiet about Sunday night. I didn't see how it would make any difference to your investigation. They took Trace, whether or not I was there. Okay, I was useless as a father, I neglected her, but in the end it doesn't matter, does it? These . . .' he gestured at the photographs, '. . . these *monsters* just do what they want anyway.'

'There's another parallel with your wife's death, Gabe,' Kathy said. 'You told us before that Tracey was a happy child, but that isn't true, is it?'

'She's all right. She has her ups and downs, like anyone else.'

'Other people have described her as withdrawn and depressed, especially in the last few months.'

Rudd seemed genuinely surprised. 'That sounds like her grandparents talking, because if it is . . .'

'Other people,' Kathy repeated. 'Can you think of a reason why she might be unhappy?'

'Not at all.'

'They say she spoke of being afraid of a monster. That was the word you used just now, *monsters*. What was she talking about, do you know?'

'She didn't mention it to me. She had dreams, I suppose. Just dreams.'

'Dreams, you think. *Nightmares*. Like her mother.'

Rudd stared at Kathy for a moment, then turned his head away.

'And one other similarity,' Brock said. 'Both of these tragedies have happened at times when your career was in decline, and you've exploited both to get publicity and interest in your work.'

'Oh, come on, now you do sound like the Nolans. You'll be spouting garbage about Munchausen by proxy next.'

'You know about that, do you?'

'How could I avoid it? Len and Bev have been accusing me of it for years. To listen to them, they're the world's greatest experts on the subject. And this will only confirm it in their eyes. But I can't help that.' He sighed. 'Look, you can't honestly believe that I would deliberately do anything to Trace,' he gestured at the newspaper review, 'for the sake of this? I don't know you,' he said to Brock, 'but I've been watching her,' he nodded towards Kathy, 'and I reckon we're much the same.'

'How do you figure that out?' Kathy said.

'Everything I do, everything that happens to me, goes into my work. My work is everything. I am nothing else. We're all obsessive about our work, and I reckon that describes you too, doesn't it?'

Kathy leaned forward, holding his eye. 'I don't think I'm so *obsessive*,' she said, her voice quiet and dangerous, 'that I'd rent out my six-year-old daughter as a nude model.'

Rudd looked stunned for a moment, then began to splutter, 'Now look, that's rubbish! Who told you that?'

'The sculptures of giant cherubs on show at The Pie Factory last week were modelled on your daughter. Do you deny it?'

'They were *based* on her, yeah. Poppy needed a live model to work from and Trace was ideal. I didn't *rent* her out! It was a favour to a friend. Trace thought it was all a big giggle. She loved seeing what Poppy made of her. There's nothing wrong with it at all.'

'Nothing wrong? Your child's naked body was put on public exhibition at five times its actual size and you don't think there's anything wrong with that?'

There was silence for a long moment, then Brock said, 'Let's get back to facts, shall we? I'm interested in the time in the early hours of

Monday when you returned to your house. You said you were very intoxicated and can't be sure exactly how you got home.'

'Yeah, I was plastered.'

'You say you think Stan Dodworth or Yasher Fikret helped you home, or possibly both, but you can't remember. Have they both been in your home before?'

'Sure. They're friends.'

'Does either of them have a key?'

'No, they must have used mine.'

'Describe them to me, these friends.'

'Well, Stan is very quiet, very serious—*too* serious really. We tell him he should lighten up, but he's totally dedicated to his work.'

Kathy said, 'The Pie Factory Web site describes him as being obsessed with death.'

'In his work, yeah. It's his theme—in his work.'

'But you were telling us just now that there's no distinction between work and life for you people. What about Mr Fikret?'

'He's completely different from us, a practical sort of guy, no bullshit—a breath of fresh air, really.'

'Not that fresh, surely? He's a drug dealer, isn't he?'

'I never said that. Look, he knows people. Sometimes he can get hold of a little bit of something for us. As a favour for friends, that's all.'

'So,' Brock placed his hands flat on the table and stared at Rudd, 'At some time around three o'clock last Monday morning, you were taken home and dumped on your bed, paralytic, by one or both of a drug dealer and a man who has an obsession with death. And in the next room Tracey was possibly lying asleep. That's about the sum of it?'

Rudd's eyes slipped away from Brock's and an odd little expression, a grimace perhaps, touched his lips. 'Yasher Fikret is not interested in little girls, you can trust me on that. His tastes run somewhere else entirely.'

'What about Stan?'

Rudd took a little while to reply. 'To tell you the truth, I'm not sure what gets Stan's hormones buzzing. But you've got to understand, he's a very gentle guy. I know his interest—his aesthetic interest—might seem a bit morbid, but I'm sure . . .' he looked from one detective to the other, '. . . no, I'm positive he wouldn't do anything to hurt anyone. Really.'

11

IT WAS DARK as they waited in Brock's car for the team to assemble in the square, and a light rain began to fall. The large scarlet neon sign for The Pie Factory and the discreet little blue one for The Tait Gallery shimmered through the droplets on the windscreen. The radio crackled, a short burst of words, and they got out of the car and hurried towards the shelter of the building's entrance. Around them they heard the click of car doors and the soft thud of boots.

'Mr Tait here?' Brock said to the young woman at the desk. She was on the point of leaving for the evening and had a bored look that disappeared as she took in the uniforms assembling outside the door.

'I'll give him a buzz.'

Fergus Tait appeared, sporting a pair of rainbow-coloured braces that matched his bow tie. His smile froze, and the eyes behind the big glasses registered shock as he watched uniformed men crowding in behind Brock.

'Sorry for the intrusion, Mr Tait,' Brock said affably, as if they were a bunch of friends dropping in unannounced, 'but I have a warrant to search these premises. We'll be as quick as we can. I'll give you a copy of this paperwork and then I'd be glad if you'd act as our guide. We'd like to start with the rooms you let out to tenants.'

The service yard of The Pie Factory, accessible from the street and jammed with rubbish bins full of scrap materials and kitchen waste, had been thoroughly searched in the initial sweep of Northcote Square on the first day of the hunt for Tracey, but the check of the buildings had been more cursory. Packed into a city block, they looked deceptively compact from the outside, but inside formed a rambling maze. An agglomeration of cottages in the early 1800s that had gradually been extended, rationalised, rebuilt and modified over the years as its businesses grew, the result now was a warren of rooms large and small, corridors and lofts, storerooms and cellars.

'Maybe if you told me what you're after,' Tait protested as he led them towards a staircase at the end of a corridor running behind the main gallery.

'We understand Tracey Rudd used to visit here. Were you aware of that?'

'I've certainly seen her here with Poppy a number of times. And without her too, now you come to mention it. I do recall speaking to someone—was it Poppy? I don't remember—anyway, someone, about how a little girl like that shouldn't be wandering around the workshops with those machines.'

The stair dog-legged upward towards a skylight, then reached a landing giving onto another corridor.

'This way,' he puffed. 'We've had a bit of trouble with the fire authorities over the years, as you can imagine. Hence the emergency lights and fire doors and extinguishers and so on.'

'And fire-escape stairs?' Brock asked.

'Oh my, yes, several new escape stairs.'

'So there are plenty of ways for people to enter and leave the building unchecked?'

'Well, there's a measure of security, of course, but with the kitchen staff and the artists coming and going, and the whole place interconnected, it's sometimes difficult to be sure just who is here at any one time. At night we lock up, and the residents have their own keys to their separate entrance.'

'How many residents are there?'

'There are five bed-sits, with shared kitchen and bathrooms, though only four are occupied at present. Our semipermanent artists in residence are Poppy and Stan, and we also have two young artists who graduated from college this year and have a twelve-month tenancy while we see how they develop. The fifth room I like to keep free for visiting artists. Last month we had a lovely German boy, a vinyl fetishist. He did marvellous work, it made the hair stand up on the back of your neck.'

'Is that so.'

They turned into a broader corridor, and Tait pointed out utility rooms and a row of numbered doors bearing Yale locks. With a show of reluctance he knocked on them in turn and, getting no reply, opened each for a pair of officers to move in.

'There are only four doors here,' Brock said.

'Ah well, Stan's room is the fifth. It's up there.' He pointed to a steep little stair that closed the end of the corridor, leading up to the door of an attic room. 'He's the oldest, and has the most stuff, and his room's a bit bigger than the others. He has a lovely view from up there.'

'Let's take a look.'

Tait led the way up the stairs, knocked, cocked his head listening, then put his key in the lock. He swung the door open and reached inside for the light, then rocked back.

'Phoo, bit foetid in here. He needs some ventilation. Shall I open the window?'

'We'll do it, thanks.' Brock pulled on plastic gloves and crossed the room, opening the dormer window on the far side, while Kathy moved in behind him. The space was an irregular shape, jammed up into the pitch of the roof. Through one of the side walls they could hear the coo-ing of pigeons and the hiss of a water tank refilling. There was an open rack with clothes on hangers, books on the floor, and postcards and cut-tings stuck haphazardly on every surface.

'He does have a good view,' Brock said, looking out over a panorama of the square.

Behind him, Kathy said, 'What are these?'

Brock turned and saw her standing beside a table pushed into the an-gle of the sloping ceiling. It was piled high with what looked like with-ered human limbs.

'Oh, those!' Fergus Tait's voice sounded unnaturally loud and jocu-lar. He joined Kathy and picked up a leg. 'These would be from his last exhibition, *Body Parts*. Caused quite a stir.'

Now Kathy was pointing at the pictures on the wall, colour prints of photographs from newspapers and books and the internet showing car crashes, bodies being dug out of mass graves, executions, crime scenes, autopsies, abattoirs and butchers' shops. 'The girls must love getting in-vited back to this place,' Kathy said.

Tait gave a little giggle. 'I don't think he has any girlfriends right now, to tell the truth. He's much too taken up with his work.'

There was an old bed sheet hung across one side of the room with drawing pins. All three seemed to focus on it at the same moment. Brock went over and carefully drew it back. Behind, there was a small alcove in which, suspended on a chain, was the figure of an old woman, naked, body wasted and hunched in a foetal curl. Brushed by the sheet, it slowly began to rotate.

'Oh my,' Tait said. 'Now isn't she something! I haven't seen her before.'

'We have,' Brock said, and looked at Kathy, who was staring in shock at the figure. It was the old woman they'd found in the bed of Patrick Abbott's flat.

'These are not sculptures, are they?' Brock asked Tait.

The gallery owner hesitated. 'Well, I think I would say that they are, but I take it you mean that they're not carved or shaped in the normal way?'

Brock nodded. 'How does he make them?'

'They're made of bronzed plaster and fibreglass. From rubber moulds and casts.'

'Of real corpses.'

'Ye-es,' Tait said carefully. 'You'd have to ask him, you understand, but I think it would be fair to say that. It's what gives them their extraordinary truthfulness, their power. You know immediately that this isn't some prop from a movie or a waxworks show. This is the real thing, death, in all its terrible beauty.'

'Beauty?'

'Well, that's my opinion. I'm not normally a fan of the macabre, Chief Inspector, but I am moved by Stan's work. He faces unflinchingly what lies in wait for all of us.'

'And where does he find his subject matter, his body parts?'

'He has a source, so he tells me. Now he assures me, and I was insistent on this, that it isn't illegal, what he does. I didn't enquire too closely, but I gather he knows someone at a hospital with access to dead bodies. I'm sure Stan doesn't tamper with them, or cut them up or anything like that. I suppose he may, well, arrange them or whatever, like models, but he puts them back the way they were after he takes his cast. No one's the wiser—or sadder.'

Kathy was peering at some shelves on the wall behind the dangling figure in the alcove. On them there were hands, feet and a head. She reached out to touch one of the hands and felt a throb of revulsion. She touched another. 'These aren't plaster,' she said. 'They're soft.'

'They'll be rubber,' Tait said.

'I don't think so. In fact, I'm sure they're not.' She held one aged hand in hers, feeling the bones flex beneath the skin. She suppressed a surge of nausea as she picked up the same chemical smell that had been so strong in Abbott's mother's room.

Fergus Tait looked more closely, then gave a little sigh. 'Oh dear. Oh dear, oh dear. This is very naughty. I had no idea, none at all.'

'Where is he now, Mr Tait?'

'I really don't know. I haven't seen him since Gabe's show last night. But look, let me just say that, irregular as this may be, Stan is not a bad fellow. I want you to understand that. He's the gentlest of people, soft-spoken, polite, never a harsh word, loves animals and . . .' He hesitated.

'And children,' Brock finished the sentence for him.

'He's just completely caught up in his work.'

'Where does this obsession of his come from?' Kathy said. 'This thing he has about death?'

'Well, a lot of art is about death. Goya . . .'

'No, it's something personal, isn't it?'

'You may be right. I'm not altogether sure. He doesn't talk about it—not to me, anyway. There was some story of him being brought up by an elderly relative who died when he was a boy, but I'm not sure if that's the source of it.'

'He had a breakdown a few years ago, I believe?'

'About five years ago. He'd come down from the north, nobody knew him, and he produced this amazing stuff—dark, but very powerful. He did a very controversial sculpture of Margaret Thatcher and he was in-vited to exhibit in a group show with some other up-and-coming young artists. The work he exhibited was called *Bye, Bye, Princess*—you'll have heard of it?'

Kathy shook her head.

'You haven't? Well, it was a very realistic sculpture, a head and shoulders, presumably of Princess Di. The hair was the same character-istic style, and the lips and nose and one eye—it was definitely her—but the rest of her face was eaten away, it was very realistic, with maggots crawling in and out of the flesh. I mean they were *real* maggots, alive, breeding on some meat he'd put inside the skull, and they were dropping onto the floor and people were stepping on them—oh yes, it was quite disgusting. And this was just the year after Princess Di was killed, so you can imagine the tremendous fuss. I'm surprised you don't remember it. The press pursued him, but he wouldn't speak to them and that just drove them into a bigger frenzy. I mean, most of his contemporaries would have died for that kind of publicity, but he genuinely didn't want any of it.'

'When was this?'

'Let's see . . . Princess Di died in the summer of ninety-seven, right? So the exhibition would have been late ninety-eight.'

'Shortly after Jane Rudd died.'

'I suppose you're right. Anyway, he tried to hide from the reporters but they found him in his studio and there was this terrible scene. One of the reporters was hurt. Poor Stan, it was all too much. He was arrested, but the psychiatrists said he wasn't fit, and he was put away in a hospital. He did some marvellous work in there. When I saw it I offered to show it at The Pie Factory and give him a home here till he found his feet. That was a couple of years ago, and he's been here ever since.'

'You're a saint, Fergus,' Kathy said.

He looked serious. 'I'm a businessman, Kathy, and I look after my artists, because believe me, they need looking after. I can recognise talent, but I know I have to go gently with Stan. No fuss, next to no publicity, just a growing circle of admiring collectors of his work.'

'People buy these things?' Brock looked at the objects on the table in disgust.

'Oh indeed. Much sought after.'

'And you take a percentage, do you?'

'In the case of my artists in residence, I own the work they produce, and pay their board and a salary.'

'So you keep all of the proceeds of their sales?'

'At first. When they begin here it's a good deal for them, because their sales won't nearly cover my outgoings, but as they become better known the balance swings back, and eventually they become well enough established to fly the nest, as it were.'

'You pay for their production expenses, do you? Materials and the like?'

'Yes.'

'So it'll be your money he used to bribe his "source" in the hospital to give him, or lend him, his body parts.'

'Oh now!' Tait lifted his hands as if to show how clean they were. 'I know nothing about that.'

'Have you ever had a full-scale audit from the Inland Revenue? Our fraud people can be even more intrusive than that, I'm afraid.'

Tait coloured. 'That's a bit rough, Chief Inspector, threatening me like that. I'm trying to be cooperative, you know. I do perhaps recall Stan asking me for cash advances from time to time, for which no receipts were forthcoming. I didn't quibble. The amounts weren't large. More recently, as his sales have grown, he's been getting a share of the proceeds and is free to spend it as he pleases. As you see, he's a frugal man, dedicated to his work. I really wouldn't know what he spends his money on.'

Kathy, meanwhile, was looking around the room, thinking. There were no images of children, no sign that Tracey might have been there or had contact with Dodworth. But she imagined a small child visiting Poppy's room nearby and being intrigued by the attic room at the end of the corridor, climbing the stairway, opening the door, drawing back the curtain . . . Could that be Tracey's monster, the thing hanging in the alcove?

'Do you have a picture of Stan Dodworth?' Brock asked.

'Yes, there'll be one in the files in my office downstairs.'

'And I'd like to see where he worked, and any storerooms he would have had access to.'

Tait shrugged. 'You're the boss.'

As they turned to leave they heard a woman's voice raised in the corridor below, and as they came down the stairs they saw an officer backing out of one of the rooms, an angry Poppy following him.

'It's all right there, Poppy! Easy now!' Tait called out, as if trying to soothe a pony.

She turned and looked up at them, and her eyes narrowed as she saw Kathy. 'What the fuck do you think you're doing?'

'It's all right, Poppy,' Kathy said, hurrying forward. 'We have to do this. Let me explain.' She took the woman's arm and led her back into her room, followed by Brock.

The furniture in the small room was cheap, bare plywood wardrobe and shelves, utility bed, carpet squares on the floor. Across the end of the room, in front of a small window, a sheet of plywood formed a table covered with sketchbooks, sheets of paper, glass jars jammed with pencils, pens and brushes. The books on the shelves were all art books, tall volumes with names for titles, *Oldenburg, de Kooning, Gilbert and George*.

On a cork pinboard there were postcards and sketches, one of them a pencil portrait of Tracey.

'Have you ever seen this man?' Kathy showed her the picture of Abbott.

She seemed about to refuse even to look, but then relented, frowned. 'Why?'

'It's important.'

Poppy pursed her lips, then said quietly, 'Stan knows him. Why do you ask?'

'We believe he may have been involved in the disappearance of the girls. What about this second man?'

Poppy didn't recognise Wylie's picture. 'Are you sure about this?' she asked, suspicious. 'Why didn't you show me them before, when we talked downstairs?'

'We've only just got the pictures. What do you know of him?'

'I saw him here with Stan in the workshops a couple of times recently.'

'Before or after Tracey disappeared?'

Poppy screwed her nose, thinking. 'The first time was before, I think. It was a late afternoon, and it was sunny, so it couldn't have been last week, could it? I think the week before. They were in a huddle in the corner. I said hello but Stan didn't introduce him. That was like Stan, secretive. The second time was only a few days ago.'

'Do you know what they were doing?'

'Looking at the work, I assume. I thought he might have been a buyer. When I came in that first time they were at the bench where I'd been finishing off one of my figures. The bloke with Stan was laughing, like at a dirty joke. I thought he was touching my sculpture and I was going to say something, but they moved off to look at Stan's castings.'

'Was the figure modelled on Tracey?'

'I think so.'

'Naked?'

Poppy became very still, eyes unblinking.

'Did Stan know that it was based on Tracey?'

'I don't know . . . Yeah, he might have.'

'He knew Tracey, of course? He's seen her here and at Gabe's house?'

'Oh yes.'

As they were leaving, Kathy stopped in the doorway and turned back. 'I don't get it, Poppy. Your exhibition catalogue talks about your feminist principles and how you aim to expose the way men misuse images of women, but here you are manufacturing the images for them.'

Poppy looked subdued but defiant. 'That's what *Cherubs* was about; their nakedness, painted with the blood of murderers . . . I wanted men to ogle them, and then feel ashamed. I wanted to rub their noses in it.'

'Well, you certainly did that.'

12

BROCK AND KATHY left the team searching The Pie Factory and returned to the car. On the way back to Shoreditch they took a detour by way of the Newman estate. There were still a couple of detectives at the flats interviewing residents and visitors as they arrived, and a uniformed man stood at the entrance to the lift lobby. He recognised Brock and saluted as they approached.

'Evening,' Brock said. 'Any dramas?'

'Not really, sir. Quite a few rubbernecks, wondering what's going on.'

'Yes, it's them I was interested in. How long have you been here?'

'Since ten this morning, with a break early afternoon.'

'Wouldn't happen to have seen this bloke, would you?' Brock handed him the picture of Stan Dodworth that Tait had provided.

'Distinctive,' the constable murmured, and he was right—the face that stared from the picture was gaunt, head shaved and oddly tilted, eyes unnaturally wide. To Brock it seemed as if Dodworth had begun to resemble the death masks he collected.

'Yes, he was here. Late morning, perhaps eleven-thirty, standing out there in the car park near the taped area talking to some of the local kids. I'd begun asking the snoopers for their names, to discourage them apart from anything else, but he scarpered as soon as he saw me coming.' He opened his notebook to a list.

'Can I have a look?' Brock scanned the names, then stopped at one and showed it to Kathy. 'This one, Gabe Rudd. Remember him?'

'Let's see. Oh yes, the photographer with white hair. I thought at first he might be the press, taking all those pictures, but then I recognised the name, and he told me he was the father of the other missing girl. Wanted to know what was going on, he said, and take pictures of everything. Funny how people react, isn't it?'

Bren, working with the team checking on Wylie's and Abbott's backgrounds, had not yet visited the hospital where Abbott had been employed as a porter, but had made contact with the administration to obtain details of next of kin and had arranged a meeting with a staff manager later that evening. On the phone he gave Brock the name and number of the contact.

The woman met Brock and Kathy at the front desk and showed them to her office. 'Your colleague said that Mr Abbott had a fatal accident last night,' she said, 'but he didn't elaborate.'

'That's right. We had been hoping to interview him in connection with the disappearance of the three missing children you may have read about.'

The woman's face registered shock. 'Mr Abbott? Oh dear.' She stared at them for a moment, her mind elsewhere, working fast, then her eyes dropped to the file open on the desk in front of her. 'He worked in the wing that houses geriatrics, as well as the pathology and mortuary departments. Not the children's wing.' A note of relief. Abbott had been employed there for over two years and there were no complaints or disciplinary actions recorded against him.

'Was his mother, Mrs Eileen Abbott, ever a patient here by any chance?'

The woman was obviously puzzled by the question, but turned to her computer and began tapping. 'We did have an Eileen Abbott here recently. Age seventy-six. Yes, same home address. She died here last July, the twenty-fifth.'

'Cause of death?'

'Bronchial pneumonia. She was also suffering from advanced muscular dystrophy.'

'Do you have a record of how her body was disposed of?'

The manager scrolled through the record on her screen. 'It would have been prepared in the mortuary and then handed over to funeral directors of the next of kin's choosing for burial or cremation. Yes, here we are, Gill Brothers, a reputable local firm. Why?'

'We found Mrs Abbott's body last night, in Patrick Abbott's flat.'

The woman flinched. 'Surely not?' Her voice was a whisper.

'I'm afraid so. Any idea how that could be possible?'

'I can't imagine. It says here that Gill Brothers collected Mrs Abbott on the morning of the twenty-seventh. We know them well. I can't believe they could have lost her.'

'Why don't you give them a ring?' Brock suggested.

A couple of minutes later the manager replaced her phone, her face very pale. 'They checked their records. They say they never took her. There's no mention of an order on their files. But that's just impossible . . .' Her mind was working. 'Unless . . .'

'Yes?' Brock prompted.

'Unless he got into our computer and altered our records.' Her hand strayed to her keyboard and touched it gently, as if comforting a dear friend who had been violated. 'There will have to be an inquiry.'

'Of course. Meanwhile, do you have anything on a Stanley Dodworth? Did he ever work here, or check in as a patient?'

More tapping. 'Umm, not in our staff records . . . We have a patient listed, appendectomy, middle of last year.' She swung the monitor around to show Brock the details.

'That's him. I have his picture here. You wouldn't recognise him, I suppose?'

She shook her head. 'But then I wouldn't.'

'It's possible he came here more recently. I'd like to show it to people who worked in Patrick Abbott's area, and circulate it to your security.'

'Do you mind telling me why?'

'He was a friend of Abbott's, and we want to interview him, only he's disappeared. We think he used to visit Abbott here at the hospital, and it's just possible he might return here.'

'I should alert Mrs Siddons. She manages the staff on main desk. There's not much comes through our front doors that Mrs Siddons isn't aware of.'

'Would she be here now?'

She was. She came bustling into the office and immediately recognised the man in the photograph. 'That's Stan, one of our porters.'

'I'm afraid you're mistaken, Mrs Siddons. He's not one of ours.'

'He certainly is. I see him around a lot. With Pat Abbott usually.'

'But he doesn't work here.'

'Well, he wears one of our passes. I've seen it.'

Brock interrupted. 'I'd very much appreciate it if you'd take a copy of this picture for your staff, Mrs Siddons, and tell them to ring security immediately if you see him again. It seems he's been impersonating a hospital employee.'

When she left he turned to the manager and said, 'I think I'd better tell you what we think they were up to, and then I'd like to take a look at Abbott's work area, if you don't mind.'

By accident or design, the geriatric wards were connected directly by large, ponderous lifts to the pathology and mortuary areas beneath them. They found a number of workers in the basement who recognised Dodworth's photograph and who were convinced that he worked in some other department nearby. Sometimes he appeared in operating-theatre greens, they said, sometimes in overalls, sometimes in jeans and a T-shirt with a slogan, something about *cherish the frail*.

They were taken to Abbott's locker, where Brock signed a release for its contents—a pair of sneakers, several fat Stephen King paperbacks, a pair of glasses, an aluminium walking stick like the one he had in his flat, and, of most interest, a small diary. They spent some time sitting together at a table with a desk light, poring through its pages. It seemed to be a work diary, a record of shifts, overtime and leave. In addition, there were many entries of sequences of numbers and letters. It didn't take long to establish that the strings of digits were identification numbers for patients.

'I think he was keeping a record of what he was lending Stan,' Brock murmured. 'Probably didn't trust him to return the bits.'

'Like a lending library catalogue,' Kathy said. 'Maybe the letters refer to parts—'H' for head, 'RL' right leg . . .'

Brock was turning to the entries for the days on which the girls had been taken, and shook his head with disappointment. 'Nothing. Not a thing. I suppose it wasn't very likely.' He snapped the book shut and pushed it into his pocket. 'Come on. Enough of this.'

They returned to The Pie Factory to check on the progress of the search. Nothing of significance had been discovered and there was still no sign of Stan Dodworth. As they left, Kathy glanced back at the building. At one end, to the left, a tableau of elegant waiters and diners shone through the large plate-glass windows of the restaurant, like a scene from a play dropped absurdly, nakedly into the dark damp square. Between that and the locked gallery entrance was a smaller window with a view into the main gallery space, also lit up. Gabe Rudd's banners could just be glimpsed beyond a crew of people in there constructing some sort of structure behind the window. Banner number six, perhaps, Kathy thought. He certainly had plenty of material to work with.

'Edward Hopper,' Brock said. He, too, was looking at the diners mutely gossiping, laughing, raising glasses in a toast. 'Can I buy you dinner?'

'What, in there?' Kathy wondered if he'd checked the prices.

'No.' He chuckled. 'I was thinking more in terms of a little Greek place I noticed around the corner, not far away.'

'Sounds good.'

'I'll just call Bren and then we'll walk over. Some fresh air will do us good.'

They were lucky to get in, the Saturday night crowd boisterous, and were squeezed into a tight little corner at the back, between a stair and the door to the kitchens.

Brock eased his back against the bentwood chair and gave a long sigh. 'We're finished for the night, Kathy. Let's have a drink.' He ordered two large Scotches while they scanned the menu. 'It seems plain enough,' he said, as if it were spelled out there in the flamboyant hand-written script. 'Dodworth met Abbott when he was a patient at the hospital last year, and persuaded him to obtain body parts for him to make casts from, culminating in the whole corpse of Abbott's mother. I wonder if Dodworth met Wylie, and how much of Abbott's and Wylie's other activities he was aware of?'

'You'd have to assume he knew something. He obviously knew where they lived, and it looks as if he's trying to hide from us.'

'So one day Abbott visits Dodworth at The Pie Factory and sees the sculpture of a pretty child, and Stan tells him who she is. He and Wylie are on the lookout for victim number three . . .'

A waiter lit the candle in the centre of the red-and-white checked tablecloth and took their order.

'So Abbott and Wylie did take Tracey.'

'Looks very much that way, doesn't it? She was part of the series after all. So now it's down to legwork and manpower and luck, unless Wylie can be persuaded to tell us where she is.'

'Six days. It's too long. She's dead, isn't she?'

'Lee survived three weeks. Anyway, there's nothing we can do to speed the process, so tomorrow we'll have a well-earned day of rest, you and I, putting our feet up and reading more scathing reviews of Mr Rudd's masterpieces.'

'Will you be seeing Suzanne and the kids?' Kathy asked, feeling a squirm of guilt as she recalled the letter she'd partially read. She felt a sudden urge to scratch her nose.

Brock hesitated, and Kathy saw a frown pass over his face. 'Stewart and Miranda aren't with Suzanne any more, Kathy. I meant to tell you. Their mother came back.'

'What!' This was extraordinary news, and extraordinary too, that Brock hadn't mentioned it. Now Kathy thought she understood the reference to choices in Suzanne's letter. She had been looking after her two grandchildren for several years now, after her daughter had gone off with a new man who didn't want to be encumbered by her children. Having been abandoned by their mother, the kids had become extremely possessive of Suzanne, and although Kathy had got on well with them, she knew that they'd seen Brock as a threat and had given him a hard time.

'Permanently?' Kathy asked. 'Their mother's back for good?'

'Presumably.'

'Well . . . that's great, isn't it?' But Brock looked uneasy, and Kathy remembered her long-held suspicion that he actually found the arrangement convenient.

'Yes. But it'll take some adjustment for Suzanne.'

And for you, Kathy thought.

The waiter brought a mezze platter. Brock asked for another whisky, and poured a glass of wine for Kathy. She said, 'I must give Suzanne a ring. I haven't spoken to her for ages. How is she?'

She waited a long time before he replied. 'Fine. She's fine.'

The subject seemed closed, so she said, 'Can I have a look at that diary?'

He handed it to her, and she began to study the pages, working forward from the beginning. 'The codes are there right from the start of the year, so he was giving Stan stuff long before the business with the girls, before his mother died. When was that again?'

'July twenty-fifth,' Brock said absently, reaching for the dolmades.

She found the day, a Friday. Abbott had marked the place with a crude ballpoint outline of a cross. RIP was written across it. The diary was printed with little symbols to indicate the lunar phases, the twenty-fifth of July bearing the symbol of the new moon. Abbott had arranged his drawing on the page so that the arc of the new moon appeared at the top of the cross, like a symbol on a gravestone.

'And they took Aimee on the twenty-second of August,' Kathy said, turning to that date. As Brock had said, there was nothing to indicate its significance. But that day also carried the symbol of the new moon. She turned to the date of Lee's abduction, the nineteenth of September, and there it was again. She felt a tremor of excitement and also of disgust, as if she'd had a sudden glimpse inside Abbott's mind. Now Tracey's abduction, the twelfth of October. But there was nothing, no moon sign. Kathy frowned.

'Spot something?' Brock looked up from contemplation of his whisky glass. He felt the spirit soaking through him like a warm bath.

'I thought I'd found a pattern, but it doesn't work for Tracey.' She showed him the dates. 'The next new moon wasn't until the seventeenth of October, yesterday. Tracey was taken five days too soon.'

Brock shrugged, unconvinced. 'I wish I could think of something we could offer Wylie to get him to start talking.'

'I wonder . . .' Kathy began, then stopped.

'What?'

'I was just wondering if it's possible Abbott killed his mother too, in the hospital.'

Brock thought for a moment, then said, 'I think we're getting tired.'

13

THE NEXT MORNING Kathy walked down to the shops for some milk and the papers. It was cool but dry, a crisp breeze blowing leaves and wrappers down the empty street. When she got home she did as Brock had recommended, making toast and coffee and lying down on the sofa to read the reviews.

Was it unworthy to relish a savage review of someone else's work, especially someone you knew? The reviewer in the first paper she opened seemed to think it was:

> There are those in the art world who have been conducting a whispering campaign to the effect that, at thirty-three, Gabriel Rudd is burnt out and finished as a serious artist. Their *schadenfreude* was immensely piqued by the prospect of the critical failure of his new exhibition, *No Trace,* at The Pie Factory, and seemed confirmed by the first hurried review. Furtive cackling could be heard from certain Shoreditch studios as the champagne was uncorked. But they were wrong; the exhibition is a stunning success, the work breathtaking, and Rudd's reputation reaffirmed in spades.
>
> His subject is the recent abduction of his daughter Tracey (Trace), which has been so widely publicised in the past week. Rudd has transformed this tragic event into an immensely mov-

ing record of the anguish of a father's loss. Real-life tragedy seems to inspire him to heights of expression far beyond so much contemporary work, which merely apes human suffering with hollow gestures. Twice-bereft, he made a similarly evocative journey five years ago, after the loss of his young wife, in his celebrated exhibition *The Night-Mare*. *No Trace* is even better, more mature, more deeply felt.

The work comprises a series of ethereal hangings, each recording the events of a single day of Tracey's absence—the shock of discovery, the police hunt, the agony of waiting, the struggle to articulate pain. The ghostly quality of these tormented records is exquisite, like vapour trails of memory, elegant in their minimalism. We stare, we hold our breath, we say, here is Rothko at the dark midnight of the soul.

Rudd has promised to continue producing these works until Tracey is recovered, and while of course we fervently hope that this will soon occur, we cannot help but yearn for a gallery filled with such poignant expressions of the kind of contemporary tragedy that haunts us all.

'Well, well,' Kathy thought. She poured herself another cup, opened the second paper, and discovered an even more ecstatic review.

At his desk in Shoreditch police station, Brock put aside the same newspaper and thought about a more difficult problem. He hadn't yet answered Suzanne's letter, and the longer he left it the harder it became. The very idea of writing a letter seemed stiff and old-fashioned, as if they were living in an age before the telephone, when manners were more formal and correct. He wondered if that was her point, that setting things down on paper somehow made them more contractual and irrevocable. Not that there was anything unreasonable in what she had to say. Her life had arrived at a point which she hadn't expected; she was suddenly free of ties she'd assumed to be permanent and now she needed to reassess things. Everything.

He picked up the phone, and as he dialled a siren wailed outside like a premonition of winter. She answered on the first ring and he pictured her sitting in her bay window overlooking the high street. As soon as he heard her voice he felt the familiar tug.

'David! I've just been reading about Gabriel Rudd. He sounds outrageous.'

'How are you?'

'Missing you. You got my letter?'

'Yes. I've been thinking a lot about it.'

'I'm sorry, it must have been the last thing you needed with your new case starting at the same time. I know how busy you've been. I did ring you during the week, but you were in a meeting. I was put through to someone in Shoreditch and they said they'd give you the message. Did you get it?'

'No, I'm afraid not.'

'It just helped me to put everything down in black and white. I feel I have to sort things out.'

'I understand.'

'And it's not as if we haven't talked about it before. You remember, when you got beaten up in the street?'

'I wasn't beaten up, exactly.'

'You were attacked while you were making that arrest, and we agreed it was time you reassessed what you were doing, so that you weren't put in that kind of situation any more.'

He couldn't remember agreeing to any such thing, but he didn't argue.

'Anyway, I just think this has come at the right time,' she went on firmly. 'It's time to start again, for both of us.'

Brock couldn't decide whether it sounded more like an invitation or an order. He felt frustrated by the phone, unable to gauge the expression on her face, the set of her body. He sensed that she'd already moved on from the doubts expressed in her letter, and had already arrived at certain conclusions.

'You know things are impossible for us like this, David, hardly ever seeing each other, fitting our lives in around your job and my grandchildren. We put up with it because we had to, but we don't any more.'

'We need to talk these things through, Suzanne. We should make time, get away for a while, take a holiday,' he improvised soothingly. 'Soon, after this case is over.'

'Exactly!' Her enthusiasm caught him by surprise. 'You know who rang me the other night? Doug in Sydney—you remember? My sister Emily's husband. They're planning for her sixtieth birthday next month, and he thought how fantastic it would be if I turned up at the party, as a surprise. I haven't seen her for ten years. It seemed like a sign, coming out of the blue like that. I want us both to go, David.'

'That sounds wonderful,' he said cautiously. 'When is this?'

'In about three weeks. I thought we might make a proper trip of it, see the outback, take four or five weeks.'

'In three weeks? Oh.'

'Come on, David. Surely that gives you enough time to organise things at work so you can get away?'

'This is a major inquiry, Suzanne. A big one.' He knew he was sounding stubborn and obstructive, but he couldn't help it.

'They're always big ones.' Her voice was cool now. 'You work for a big organisation. They can handle it. I want us to do this, David. I think it's important, for both of us.'

'Yes, you're right. I'll have a look, see if it's possible.'

'Please. But don't take too long. The flights are heavily booked. I checked.'

Kathy felt edgy, unsettled, and went to a movie that afternoon, returning home at dusk. The phone was ringing as she opened the front door. She was surprised to hear the voice of Bren's wife, Deanne.

'Hi, Kathy.'

'Hi. Is everything all right?'

'Yes. Bren's gone back to work, but there was something I thought you might be interested in. You probably already know. Do you lot monitor Gabriel Rudd's Web site?'

'I'm not sure. I haven't seen it.'

'Well, you might find it interesting, and all the other sites about him and his work—there are hundreds of them. They've been going crazy lately, of course. But you should check out his official site, www.gaberudd.co. He's just updated it with a bulletin about his exhibition and his thoughts about everything. The thing I thought you should know is that he's claiming the police have treated him shamefully, like a criminal instead of a victim, and he's decided to refuse all further cooperation with them. He's going into retreat, apparently.'

'Retreat?'

'Yes, into his art. He says he needs to focus on that. And physically, he's retreating into a glass cube he's had built inside the main gallery of The Pie Factory, alongside his hangings. He's there now—there are pictures on his site of people looking in at him through the gallery window, and through the glass wall of the restaurant. He's the only one with a key and he's got a camp bed in there, and some kind of toilet, and electricity to run a fan and his computers. He says he'll only communicate through his computer. He's currently designing the next banner, and sending the images to his team. Oh . . .' Deanne hesitated, '. . .and he's got a badger in there with him too.'

'Did you say *badger*?'

'Yes, a live badger. He's called Dave, and he's currently hiding under a blanket. You know a brock is another word for a badger, don't you?'

Kathy groaned. 'Yes.'

'It's Joseph Beuys again, like he did to you.'

'How do you mean?'

'One of Beuys's art "actions" consisted in locking himself in a loft in New York with a live coyote. Rudd's quoting again.'

Kathy gave a sigh. 'Well, at least we know where he is. We can always go in there and pull him out.'

'Oh no, you couldn't do that!'

'Why not?'

'Oh, Kathy . . . This is sort of what my masters is about: relative values. In fact, I might use this as a case study. Society operates on a hierarchy of value systems, right? Religion was once at the top, but now it's way down, with royalty, say. Wealth is high up, and celebrity, and heritage and ethnicity, but at the very top is art. Art trumps everything else. You can blaspheme on TV, make jokes about the Queen, be obscene and poke fun at the rich and famous, but you can't afford to be seen as a philistine. You can't trash art, not really, not unless you're an artist yourself, in which case your trashing of art becomes art itself, which is okay. Gabriel Rudd in his glass box in the gallery is a work of art—he's said so. He's now part of the *No Trace* work. You can't possibly desecrate it. The whole world is watching.'

'So you're saying that the only way to get him out is to recruit an even bigger artist than him—this Beuys character, for example—into the Met and put him in uniform and give him an artistic sledgehammer.'

Deanne chuckled. 'He's dead, unfortunately. But I don't see it happening, do you?'

'No. Brock'll love this.'

'I know.'

'What about justice? Where does that come on your scale of values?

I mean, Stan Dodworth has been stealing corpses to make artworks out of them.'

'Oh, they all poked around in corpses, Leonardo, Rembrandt, Stubbs. That's all right. Body snatching wouldn't come close.'

'What about child murder? Suppose Dodworth has killed Tracey so as to make a sculpture out of her? What then?'

Deanne thought for a while. 'Mmm. Of course he'd have to face justice, but even then . . . I think the artistic recognition might outweigh the moral revulsion. Yes, it'd be a close call, but I think it would.'

'That's sick.'

'It's what you're up against. Is it possible that Dodworth did take Tracey?'

'It's possible, Deanne. Right now, anything's possible.'

The following morning Kathy went to see the performance in Northcote Square. Many others had had the same idea, lured by reports in the news. Office workers on their way to the City, parents dropping children at school, truck drivers unable to make deliveries to the building site because of the crowd blocking the corner of Lazarus Street and West Terrace, all strained for a glimpse through the window at the artist and, hopefully, his famous badger. In response to all this, the gallery was opening its doors early as Kathy arrived, and the good-humoured crush of spectators was syphoning inside to get a close-up view and maybe a quick photo to take back to friends.

Kathy joined the group outside the gallery window. She noticed a closed-circuit television camera mounted on the wall overhead, which she was sure hadn't been there before, and attached to it a small microphone. It seemed they were recording the reactions of the spectators.

'His hair really is *very* white, isn't it?' one young woman said, fingering her own blonde curls.

'But this isn't original, is it?' her friend said, and clutched the collar of her coat impatiently against the cold wind.

'What, his hair?'

'Him locking himself in the glass box. There was that other bloke.'

'Two others,' the first woman corrected.

'Well, what's the point then? If it's not original, what's the point?'

'I suppose the badger's original.'

'Yes, but you can't even see it, hiding under the blanket. Maybe there isn't a badger at all. Maybe they're just *saying* there's a badger.'

'Do you think he's going to go to the lavatory in front of everyone?'

'That I don't want to see. Come on, we're late.'

As they hurried away Kathy noticed a fresh graffiti message on the pavement, written in the same looping letters as the one on the wall further along. It read, '*this is art*'.

She joined the queue filing into the gallery. The girl at the desk had already run out of handouts for the exhibition and said more were on the way. She looked harassed, her face pink and slightly puffy, as if she'd woken up in the middle of a wild party. Her discomfort wasn't helped by a man claiming to be from the RSPCA, demanding to speak to someone in charge about the badger, asking where they'd got it and how it was being treated.

'I believe there is a vet on standby,' she fretted, but he wasn't to be put off.

'Get me the boss,' the man insisted stolidly. 'I can have this place shut down.'

'Oh, I don't think you can.'

Kathy passed through into the crowded gallery. The area around the glass cube was jammed, and she moved to a quieter corner where tables had been set up for three young female computer operators, all dressed identically in white caps and T-shirts with *Gabe's Team* written on the back. One of them looked up and gave Kathy a brief smile.

'Can I ask what you're doing?' Kathy asked.

'We're handling Gabe's Web site emails, all the messages coming in from around the world, thousands of them. We select interesting ones and publish them hourly.'

'Ah. I thought maybe you were part of the artwork.'

'Oh, but we are!' the girl said cheerfully. 'Gabe said so.'

'You've spoken to him?'

'Not verbally; he's refusing to speak to anyone. We report to him on our computers.'

Kathy turned back to the crowd around the glass cube and took advantage of a gap to work her way to the front. There was Gabe, white hair awry, crouched over a keyboard, ignoring the faces staring in at him all around. For a moment the whole scene was motionless, like a very realistic but improbable sculpture, then something caused a stir to one side, a hand pointed to the crumpled blanket at the artist's feet and someone said, 'I think it moved.'

On her way out Kathy saw that a new banner had been added. It was titled *He fell from a ledge on the thirteenth floor,* and showed a spread-eagled figure, wide-eyed with horror like a character from a cartoon strip, superimposed on a grainy photographic image of the block of flats at the Newman estate.

She hurried up West Terrace on her way to the morning briefing at Shoreditch station but was stopped short by a sharp little cry, 'Here!' She turned and saw Betty Zielinski's face peering up at her through the railings in front of her house. The woman was standing halfway down the steps leading to her basement door, and was clutching the cast-iron railings as if they were the bars of a cage, her face at pavement level.

'Hello, Betty. How are you?'

Betty pushed a crooked finger through the bars and wiggled it at Kathy to come closer. Feeling slightly ridiculous, Kathy approached and knelt.

'Have you caught him yet?'

'We caught two men, Betty. But we haven't found Tracey yet.'

'You haven't arrested *him,* though, have you?'

'Who?'

'The monster that took her.'

Kathy leaned closer to the bars. 'Why do you call him that?'

'That's what Tracey called him. I saw him that night, shiny black, like a lizard. After the scream.' She peered fearfully along the footpath to right and left.

'You saw him?'

Betty lifted her eyes to Kathy, the white globes wild and moist with tears. 'I watch him, you know, I know his secrets. It's not the first time he's taken a child.'

'I know, Betty. There were the other two girls. But what exactly did you see?'

'No! Not them. *Another* child taken *here* in the square.' Her voice was quavering, on the edge of hysteria.

'Here? What do you mean?'

Kathy's lack of understanding seemed to confuse and upset Betty more. She began to speak again. 'I know where she is!' she sobbed, 'Tra . . .' but then the words died abruptly in her throat. Staring past Kathy, a look of terror transformed her face.

'What's the matter?' Kathy said, then looked back over her shoulder to see Poppy and Yasher standing together, gazing at them from the other side of the street as if they'd just emerged through the gate in the garden railings. Yasher turned on his heel and started to stride away but Poppy remained, frowning.

Kathy turned back to speak again to Betty, only to find her gone. She caught a glimpse of her cloak in the dark opening of the basement door, and called out, 'Betty, hang on, let's talk.' But all she got in return was a frightened squawk and the slam of the door.

'What did she say?'

Kathy straightened to find Poppy at her back. 'I'm not sure. She was trying to tell me something . . .' She noticed a bruise on Poppy's cheek, a raw graze on the cheekbone.

'You don't want to take any notice of what she says. You think you're getting somewhere and then she flies off at a tangent. Everything gets mixed up in her head. She remembers someone from long ago and then's convinced she's just seen them. For a time she thought I was her daughter.'

'Yes, you're probably right.' Kathy looked at the dark figure marching down the street. 'Yasher doesn't look happy.'

'He's mad because your lot interviewed him yesterday and practically accused him of being a Turkish drug baron. He thinks someone in the square has been making trouble for him with the cops. I was trying to convince him it wasn't me.'

'Did he do that to your face?'

'I bumped into something in the workshop.' She paused, staring at the crowd milling outside the gallery, and her mouth turned down with distaste.

'It's quite a circus, isn't it?' Kathy said.

'Yeah. You were right, Gabe's got a talent for it.'

Kathy got the impression that the tribute wasn't altogether a compliment. Then Poppy abruptly said, 'Gotta go,' and hurried away.

Kathy checked her watch. She was running late for the briefing, but she had to find out what Betty had meant. It had sounded as if she was saying she knew where Tracey was. Kathy climbed the steps to her front door and called through the letterbox. 'Betty? It's me. The others have gone. Please come and talk to me.'

She listened but heard nothing and called out again. Still nothing.

She was on the point of giving up when the door opened suddenly in front of her. Betty stood there, wild-eyed, hair everywhere. 'There!' she said, and thrust something into Kathy's face. Kathy took a step back and reached for it. It was a small canvas on a wooden stretcher, unframed. The oil paint was thick and crudely applied, and Kathy felt it still slightly soft beneath her thumb. It was a rudimentary portrait of a human face, pink, with yellow hair and bright blue eyes.

'You see?' Betty laughed. 'She's still here with me.'

'Did she do this, Betty?' Kathy asked, but Betty only lifted an index finger to her lips.

'Sh! Secrets!' she whispered. She snatched back the picture and slammed the door shut.

14

THERE WERE SEVERAL badger jokes at the Monday morning briefing, talk of *badgering* witnesses and digging someone out of their *set,* which Brock tolerated. In fact, Kathy had the impression that he rather relished Rudd's little stunt. But the antics in Northcote Square were a sideshow, with the focus of the investigation fixed on trying to discover the place in which, they had to assume, Abbott and Wylie had hidden Tracey, and to find Stan Dodworth, who might have some idea where it was.

Bren summarised what was in progress; the visits to wall-climbing associates in Northampton and Southend, the search of letting agents' records for a rented storeroom, the examination of Rainbow camera footage across London for sightings of Wylie's white van on the night of Tracey's disappearance. The forensic reporting officer followed this with a summary of possible leads from the detritus of Wylie's flat: unmatched fibre samples, unlabelled keys, traces of chalky soil, photographs of unidentified places. An officer from SO5, the Child Protection unit, spoke of information gleaned from the computers of other known paedophiles that pointed to Abbott and Wylie, but the evidence was sketchy since the hard drive in the flat had been cooked and no other computer had been found. The psychologist profiler attempted to interpret the workings of the two men's minds.

Dodworth's disappearance was discussed. Tyneside police were currently checking his family and friends in the north. Someone suggested that if he knew of Tracey's hiding place he might have gone there to try to help her, but this seemed implausible. More likely, someone else suggested, he'd been in on it with Abbott and Wylie, and was currently trying to erase his tracks. There was an ominous silence in the room as people considered what this might mean for Tracey.

The task seemed daunting, and the cost of failure depressingly high, but Brock stirred them to action, loading them with tasks. Kathy's was to speak once again to Tracey's grandparents, in the hope that the girl might have said something to them during her weekend visits that had been overlooked.

She took her car onto the Hammersmith Flyover and steered for the M4. Traffic was heavy, with trucks thundering out to Heathrow and beyond, to Bristol and the West Country, buffeting her little Renault, and she was glad when the signs for the turnoff to West Drayton appeared. She had decided not to ring the Nolans in advance, hoping to catch them unprepared, but when she reached the crescent of shops near their home she came upon them unexpectedly as they emerged from the butcher. Kathy pulled in to the kerb and watched them stop to say a few words to a woman with a pair of fat corgis, wave to a couple loading groceries into their car, then continue past the off-licence, the Taj Mahal restaurant and Shirley's Hair Affair, to disappear into the newsagent. According to the A–Z their house was close by, and Kathy decided to wait for them there. She drove slowly through narrow suburban streets jammed with parked cars and found a space outside their number, one of a row of semis. Its paintwork was new, its windows sparkling in the weak autumn sunlight, and the little front lawn looked as if it had been groomed with nail scissors around the ornamental sundial centrepiece. Kathy didn't doubt that it would be aligned with precision.

After a few minutes she saw the Nolans with their shopping bags turn into the street. She waited until they were near before getting out of the car. They looked surprised, but Kathy had an odd feeling that they were expecting her.

'Is there news?' Bev asked.

'Nothing new, I'm afraid. I'd just like a few words, if you've got the time,' Kathy said.

'Of course,' Len said. 'As long as you're not hoping to catch us out, find Tracey hidden in the attic.'

'Len!' his wife scolded.

'Should I be looking there?' Kathy smiled.

'You wouldn't have much luck, but I thought our son-in-law might have put some such idea in your head. He's the one with the remarkable imagination after all, if the Sunday papers are to be believed.'

'Take no notice, Kathy,' Bev said. 'Is it all right to call you Kathy? Sergeant is so, well, *military*. Come inside and have a cup of coffee and tell us about any progress.' She stopped suddenly and sighed. 'Oh Len, we forgot the stamps from the post office.'

'Always forgetting something. Anyway,' Len said, getting in a last jab, 'there was no chance you'd catch us unawares. Enid across the street spotted you straight away and phoned us on the mobile to warn us there was a young woman waiting for us outside our house, and was it a relative or one of my mistresses? Nosy old bitch.'

The interior of the house was as immaculate as the exterior. Len took their coats and Bev showed Kathy through to a small sitting room over-looking the back garden. Through the French windows Kathy saw that the yard had been divided precisely down the middle, a vegetable garden on the left, flower beds on the right. A neat herringbone brick path formed the centre line, a frontier between utility and ornament.

While Bev made coffee, Kathy studied the framed photos on the mantelpiece—Tracey, Len and Bev, and a young woman, presumably their dead daughter, Jane. No Gabe.

'She looks like her mum, don't you reckon?' Len said from behind her. Kathy wasn't sure if he meant Jane or Tracey, but in fact it was true of them both. The particular twinkle in the eyes, the wide mouth, the fine blonde hair, were carried through the three generations, from Bev to Jane to Tracey, becoming, if anything, clearer and more pronounced.

'Yes.' Kathy had noticed framed drawings in both the hall and here in the lounge, pastel figure studies of ballet dancers. The signature, a discreet flourish, was *Jane Nolan*.

'She did those when she was still at school,' Len said, seeing her looking at them. 'Brilliant at drawing.'

'She got her talent from Len,' Bev said, coming in with a tray.

He took it from her and set it down. 'Rubbish. There's nothing artistic about me.'

'You know what I mean. He might show you his work later, if he's in the mood,' Bev said to Kathy. 'Sit down, dear.'

'You could say that art, or what passes for art these days, has been a curse on our family,' Len persisted, offering Kathy some homemade shortbread. 'Try a piece. There's more artistry in Bev's shortbread than you'll find in the whole of Tate Modern. Yes, Jane did some lovely things at school. But then she got a place in that art school, and they soon put a stop to that. You've got to be conceptual there, and ugly as you can make it. She tried to join in, but her heart wasn't in it.'

'Oh now, be fair, Len. She did well at first.' Bev was like a rudder, Kathy thought, making continual corrections to the wilder swings of Len's opinions. And because he knew he could rely on this, the two of them bound together, Len probably allowed his opinions to veer about more freely than if he were on his own.

'She wanted to fit in,' he said. 'If the teacher said, "Throw paint in the face of the bourgeois art-loving public!" she'd do it, just to fit in. But she knew there's got to be more to art than that.'

'Well, she couldn't very well forget, with you carrying on every time she came home.'

'I'm entitled to my opinions. Anyway, then she met Gabriel Rudd, hero of the Sunday supplements, and that was that. But that's not what you came about, is it, Kathy? I don't know why I'm rabbiting on. You've come about those men on the Newman estate, is that it?'

Kathy told them what more she could about Abbott's death and Wylie's arrest. 'But there's still no sign of Tracey, I'm afraid. We're following every lead we can, and we're going back over old ground just to make sure we haven't missed anything. That's why I'm here. I don't suppose Tracey ever mentioned those men's names to you, did she? Pat Abbott and Robert—maybe Rob—Wylie? These are their pictures.'

They passed them between them, Bev having to force herself to meet the men's eyes, even in reproduction. They shook their heads.

'There's an artist called Stan Dodworth who lives in The Pie Factory in Northcote Square. This is his picture.'

'Yes, we know him,' Len said. 'He's a friend of Gabe's. Why, is he mixed up in this?'

'We're not sure. Apparently he did know Abbott.'

The Nolans looked startled. 'Well! That's got to be more than a coincidence, hasn't it?'

'Yes.'

'What does he have to say for himself then?'

'Unfortunately he's disappeared, and we can't find him. His picture is going out to the media this morning.'

'You think he might know where Tracey is?' They both eased forward to the edge of their seats.

'It's a possibility that he may know something. That's why we're making every effort to find him. It's possible that Tracey may have visited his workshop in The Pie Factory. Did she ever speak about that?'

They shook their heads.

'Dodworth makes sculptures that are rather macabre, of bodies and body parts. Did Tracey mention having seen anything like that, a dead body or a monster?'

Bev pondered. 'I do remember something she said about a monster. I thought it was something she'd seen on TV.'

'Or a video,' Len declared. 'Some of the stuff Gabe let her watch would give anyone nightmares.'

There were moments in this conversation, Kathy felt, when she thought she saw glimmers of recognition or memory in their eyes, but it came to nothing. After another ten minutes of talk she finished her coffee and asked if she could see Tracey's room.

The bedroom was upstairs at the back of the house. From the window she could look out over the fenced backyards and the houses that ringed them tightly around the block. She was reminded of wagons protecting an encampment. There was little colour in the neat little gardens at present, but in the spring they would come alive with plum and apple and cherry blossom, and every new release of annuals that the gardening magazines and TV shows would be plugging.

Tracey's room couldn't have been more different from the one in her father's house. This one was full of colours and patterns, a perfect little girl's bedroom from *Good Housekeeping,* that made the other seem like some kind of experimental laboratory. In a corner was the farmyard Len had made, with flocks of little animals, and above it shelves were filled with dolls and books and frothy ornaments. Kathy could imagine Gabe Rudd's scorn.

There seemed nothing here to help Kathy. The childish drawings pinned to the wall showed a girl on a pony, a Christmas tree with a star, a house with a red pitched roof, but no monsters.

'Jane was born in that room,' Bev Nolan murmured when Kathy returned downstairs. 'And so was Tracey. Sometimes, when I'm alone in the house I think I hear them up there ... '

Len reached across to his wife's hand and gave a gentle squeeze.

'And I understand that Tracey lived with you here for a while after Jane died,' Kathy said.

'That's right, for over a year. Oh, she couldn't have stayed where she was. Gabriel had no idea how to feed her or change her nappies even. He'd left Jane to do all that. And then there was that mad woman always flying around, causing chaos. No, no, Tracey couldn't stay there.'

'And did Gabe agree to you taking her?'

'Oh yes!' Len broke in. 'He was delighted. Couldn't get rid of her fast enough.'

'So how did he come to change his mind and want her back?'

'Gradually things got better for him,' Len explained. 'He won that prize, got some money and became well known. He enjoyed the lime-light, playing the part of the tragic widower. Then one of the colour supplements did a story about Tracey, only they came and photographed her here, with no pictures of Gabriel, and he didn't like that one bit. Oh no. So he demanded her back, and we had to let her go, poor mite. She was just a publicity accessory, that's all she was. A bit of bait for the camera.'

They didn't know, of course, about the photographs in Wylie's flat, but the words chilled Kathy. 'So what's this you're going to show me?' she asked Len, wanting to move on.

'Oh . . .' he looked uncharacteristically sheepish, and his wife had to prompt him.

'Go on, Len. Show Kathy your shed.'

With an almost childlike show of resistance he relented and led her out of the kitchen to the garage. He opened its door and switched on a light to reveal an immaculate workshop. It seemed that Len Nolan's hobby was fine timber craftsmanship, and in particular the making of ex-quisite little boxes. He showed her his stock of exotic close-grained tim-ber slabs, his collection of superb Japanese saws and chisels. With hardly any prompting he explained the secrets of the nokogiri saws, with their fine hard teeth shaped to cut on the pull stroke rather than the push, thus allowing precision cuts with a much thinner blade than in Western saws.

'The blade's in *tension,* Kathy,' he said, 'rather than compression. So bloody simple! Now that is *true* art.'

He allowed her to handle the Dozuki fine-precision saw, the spineless Ryoba saw, the Azebiki plunge-cutting saw, and gaze upon the collec-tion of Shindo Dragon saws.

'Beautiful,' Kathy agreed, 'and so are your boxes, Len.' She admired the exquisite dovetails, all hand cut, the precise shaping of every part, the lustrous colour of the wood.

'I aspire to *craftsmanship,* Kathy,' he confided, 'not art. Craftsman-ship I can understand. Art leaves me for dead.'

Kathy drove away feeling dissatisfied, as if she'd missed something, or failed to ask the right question.

When she returned she was assigned to work with a joint team that had been set up with officers from the Paedophile Unit of SO5. She and five other detectives, in rotating pairs, were to work through a long list of names supplied by the unit—interviewing, checking and filing reports on the OTIS computer network. After three days she began to feel that the whole city was filled with the faces—bland, glib and sly—that she saw across the table in the interview rooms or staring back at her from her monitor. When she left work at night she saw them in the street and on the underground, and when she turned on the TV news they were there too, posing as politicians, priests and popular entertainers.

On the evening of the third day she was on the point of going home when she saw Brock outside in the corridor. He put his head around the door and, seeing no one else there, came in. The others that Kathy shared the room with had left for the night, and the place was strewn with the remains of another fruitless day, the frustration of dead ends and unproductive phone calls evidenced in balled and ripped-up paper and crushed drink cans.

'I've hardly seen you the last few days, Kathy,' he said, slumping into a chair. He looked exhausted, his eyes slightly unfocused as if from spending too long staring at a screen. 'How are you going?'

She shook her head. 'Getting nowhere. I've seen so many deviant males I'm beginning to believe there isn't any other kind. And they're all so bloody smug. They know we've got it wrong—this time, they really *are* innocent. Except that they're not, not in their minds, not in their imaginations.'

'Yes . . .' He put both hands to his face and rubbed, as if he might massage life back into his brain. 'That's really the worst of this, isn't it? That all this effort, all this pain, is caused by something so miserably dull, so unworthy—a nasty little obsession caused by a hormone imbalance, a brain defect, some emotional damage. A trivial malfunction, really, that's all we're dealing with.' He sighed. 'I should be used to it by now. So much crime is done for the most tedious of reasons. That's what'll finish me in the end, that the villains just aren't interesting enough.'

Kathy laughed, yet she felt uneasy. She'd never heard Brock talk about the end of his career before, even in jest. 'Are you packing up now?'

Brock shook his head. 'Can't. Look, I'll show you something.' She followed him down the corridor and into an empty room, where he waved her over to a monitor. The screen showed a huge crowd completely filling a city square. It took her a moment to recognise some of the surrounding buildings.

'That's Northcote Square, isn't it?'

'That's right. This is live, from a camera on the corner of Urma Street and East Terrace.'

Kathy looked more closely at the screen. The crowd was motionless. Many of them seemed to have white hair. 'What on earth is going on?'

'It's a flash mob, summoned by internet and SMS. They just appeared this evening, in support of Gabe Rudd. There was music earlier. Now they're watching their phones for instructions on the next phase. It's performance art. If it were summer, they'd have their clothes off by now.'

'Wow.'

'I need to be here, just in case something happens.'

'I don't mind staying, if you like.' Kathy felt a small prickle of embarrassment as she said it, as if they'd both just confessed that they had no one to go home for.

'No, it's late. Go home, get some sleep and come back refreshed for another day of deviant males. Nothing'll happen tonight.'

15

AS USUAL, TEVFIK Akif, second cousin to Yasher Fikret and site manager for the building work on West Terrace, was the first to arrive on site
that wet Thursday morning. It was still dark as he unlocked the gate
in the chain-link security fence along the back lane, and then the door of
the site hut in the compound formed from the cleared backyards of
the houses. He didn't remove his dripping raincoat because, having
switched on the lights and heater in the hut, it had become his habit
to go over to the basement room in number thirteen where they had
formed a kind of recreation room. There was electricity down there and
a sink, and they had installed a fridge, a microwave and a water boiler
for hot drinks. So he pulled on a pair of rubber boots, took a torch from
the shelf and made his way along the path of wooden duckboards that
crossed the mud and puddles of the yard to the back door of the old
brick building. He cursed as water from the broken gutter high above
splashed onto his neck and shoulders as he fumbled for the key of the
padlock securing the door, then swore again, louder, when the beam of
his torch revealed the hasp ripped out of the door frame. Some bastards
had broken in. He hesitated, then returned to the site hut and collected
the pickaxe handle he kept there for emergencies of this kind.

Returning to the back door, Akif pushed it open and flashed his torch
inside. There was no sound or sign of anyone. From the darkness of the
front of the house he heard the old sash windows rattle as a delivery

truck rumbled past in the square. There was nothing to steal here except down in the basement room. He went to the head of the stairs and found the light switch that the electrician had rigged up for them from the basement light. He switched it on and his heart leaped in his chest as he saw an unfamiliar shadow extending across the flagstones down there. Someone was waiting for him.

'I know you're down there!' he yelled in his fiercest voice. 'You come out now where I can see you!'

But the shadow of the figure remained motionless. Akif began to wonder if he was mistaken. Perhaps something the men had left propped in the middle of the room was casting that shadow. Holding the pickaxe handle in one hand and the torch in the other, he slowly descended the stairs. At first, the glare of the bare bulb blinded him, and all he could see was an indistinct shape. He froze—there was a man, a black shape against the light! Then his eyes adjusted and he registered the truth in a single shocking moment—it was not a man but a woman, completely naked, hanging by the neck from an iron hook in the ceiling.

Kathy ran through the rain towards the front of number thirteen, where a uniformed man was sheltering in the doorway beneath the scaffolding. Dawn was just beginning to glimmer through the upper branches of the trees in the square. She showed her card and was directed to the front room, there exchanging her raincoat and shoes for a white protective suit and rubber boots. Renovations hadn't got past the stripping-out stage in this house and the place had a desolate air, faded wallpaper peeling like skin from cracked plaster where shelving had been ripped away. She hurried down the hall to the doorway to the basement, where she could hear voices. A crime scene officer was coming up the stairs, and she stepped aside to let him pass.

'Not much room below,' he said.

She nodded and went down. Four people in white overalls were grouped together in the centre of the room, surrounded by an odd assortment of chairs and, over to one side, a packing case on top of which lay an abandoned deck of playing cards. She saw a microwave and a small fridge and an old sink, but it wasn't until two of the people moved apart that she saw the naked back of the hanging woman, her wrists tied together behind her with insulating tape.

One of the men adjusted the mask covering his nose and mouth. She recognised Brock and wondered how he always seemed to get to the crime scenes ahead of her.

'Come in, Kathy,' he said. His voice struck her as dulled, by the mask or something else—anger, perhaps. 'Recognise her?'

The others, a police doctor, the crime scene manager and a police photographer, made way for her as she walked around the body. There was a blindfold tied over the eyes, obscuring much of the face, but she recognised the thick grey and black hair, the chin. 'It's Betty, isn't it? Betty Zielinski.' Grey, shrivelled and abandoned, she looked older than in life. Her body seemed contorted by rheumatism, and afflicted by something else, too—covered in brown spots as if she'd contracted some strange form of chickenpox or been attacked by a swarm of bees. Her teeth were bared as if she was confronting an icy gale, or about to scream. Then another image came into Kathy's mind, of the cast of Abbott's mother suspended by a chain in Stan Dodworth's room. She felt outrage and shock. A little time ago this woman had spoken to her, laughed and cried. She remembered her last words: 'Sh! Secrets!'

'Not suicide?' Kathy said, trying to hold on to objective fact. Betty's feet were barely clear of the floor, her toes brushing the stone that was soaking wet beneath her. None of the chairs appeared to be in the right position to have been kicked away, unless something had been moved.

'No,' the doctor murmured. 'I think we can rule that out.'

'What are those brown spots?'

Brock pointed a gloved finger at a length of electrical lead lying on the floor. One end was plugged into the power board from which cables stretched to the appliances in the room. The other end had been taped to a length of wooden dowel used as a handle, and the insulation had been stripped back to expose the naked wire twisted into a stiff point.

'They electrocuted her?'

Brock nodded. 'Many times.'

An involuntary spasm of nausea rose in Kathy's throat. She turned away, tears of rage and pity welling in her eyes. She could hardly hear the doctor's next words because of the roaring in her ears.

'I'd say they deliberately wet her feet and the floor to earth her.'

Then the photographer said, 'Looks like someone's been here before me.' He was crouching by a small circular mark on the dirty surface of the old stone flags, and he pointed to two others forming a precise triangle.

'What's that?'

'Looks to me like the feet of a tripod. Could be a surveying instrument, I suppose, or a camera tripod.'

'You mean they may have taken pictures of her?'

'It's the right position, yes.'

There was silence as they took this in.

'She lived next door,' Brock said finally to the scene manager. 'I'd like to take a couple of your people in there with me. And you'll want to have a good look in the back garden. They seem to have forced an entry through the back door, but it's not clear how they got through the fence. Maybe over the wall from her yard.'

'Right.'

'Come on, Kathy,' Brock said grimly and led the way up the stairs. In one of the rooms above they found Tevfik Akif sitting on a pile of bricks, and had him repeat his story, then they collected two of the SOCO team and fresh protective gear so as to avoid the risk of cross-contamination with the house next door. They went out the back way, across the duckboard path to the rear lane, and into Betty's yard. Immediately they saw the broken pane of glass in her back door, which was unlocked.

The house was cold and very still, and a faint smell of fried onions hung in the air. While the two SOCO women went to work in the kitchen, Brock and Kathy moved on into the interior. The furniture was old and heavy and dark, like heirlooms from an earlier generation, and everywhere there were dolls, forlorn and abandoned, staring accusingly at the intruders. Nothing seemed disturbed downstairs, and they continued up to the bedroom floor. They found Betty's bedroom at the rear, facing onto the lane. The bedclothes were thrown back, an electric underblanket still switched on. There were pieces of a broken china vase in a corner, and a damp stain on a rug beside the bed.

They continued from room to room, but nothing else seemed disturbed. The victim had had a bath, it seemed, brushed her teeth and gone to bed. Then someone had broken into her house.

'Poor Betty,' Kathy breathed. 'She said she was afraid of a monster, just like Tracey.'

They opened the front door and were about to start searching the well leading down to the basement when they both noticed the looping letters of new graffiti on the footpath outside Betty's house: '*this is real*'. At the same moment, a belligerent voice barked at them from the neighbouring house.

'What d'you think you're up to?'

Reg Gilbey was standing at his open front door, peering at them suspiciously in the grey morning light. His eyes were bleary through the thick lenses of his glasses, his sparse grey hair sticking up in wispy clumps as if he'd only just got out of bed. He was wearing a heavy cardigan with frayed cuffs and his baggy trousers had been darned at the knee with a thread several shades too dark, as had his thick socks. In one hand he was cradling a fat black cat and in the other he held a lighted cigarette.

'Morning, Mr Gilbey,' Brock said. 'Remember us? Metropolitan Police, DCI Brock and DS Kolla.'

'What're you doing in Betty's place?'

'We'd like a word with you,' Brock replied.

As they came up Gilbey's steps Kathy said, 'That's Betty's cat, isn't it?'

'Yeah, woke me up this morning, mewing at the back door. Greedy tyke. What d'you want?' He backed reluctantly into his hallway as they followed him in.

'When did you last see Betty?' Brock asked.

Gilbey pondered, thought processes apparently sluggish. He cleared his throat with a rasping gurgle and Kathy caught a strong whiff of whisky along with the tar. 'Yesterday evening. Brought me a pie she'd baked. We ate it together with a glass of vino. Why? What's the matter?'

This unexpected glimpse of domestic harmony between the two neighbours surprised Kathy. 'I thought you two didn't get on,' she said.

'There was that big crowd in the square, all those weirdos. Made Betty nervous. Scared her cat. What's it to you, anyway?'

'I'm afraid we have bad news about Betty, Mr Gilbey. She's been found dead.'

Gilbey stared at her, then at Brock, face blank. 'Dead?' he said slowly, as if the word meant nothing to him. The cat sensed something and leaped abruptly from his arm. 'Betty?'

'Let's sit down in the kitchen,' Kathy said. She steered him towards the open door at the end of the hall where she could see a pine table and chairs. Along the way the cigarette dropped from his fingers and Brock, following behind, picked it up. He doused it in the kitchen sink, next to the remains of a home-baked cheese and onion pie and an empty bottle of wine, and ran a glass of water for the painter, who had removed his glasses to rub his eyes. The frames were old and worn, Kathy noticed, heavy plastic, like a museum piece from the 1960s. She wondered if Gilbey, presumably a successful and prosperous man, looked so resolutely down at heel by choice or through self-neglect.

'How did she go?' Gilbey grunted after taking a swallow of water, hand trembling. 'Was it her heart?'

'We're not sure at the moment exactly how she died.'

Gilbey picked up the evasion in Brock's answer and said sharply, 'She didn't hurt herself, did she?'

'No, she . . .'

But before Kathy could go on, Gilbey interrupted. 'Who found her then?'

'A builder. She was found in the basement of one of the houses they're doing up.'

Gilbey's brow wrinkled in astonishment.

'When did she leave you last night?'

'I don't know . . . ten, ten-thirty. When the crowd began to break up. But how . . .?'

'Was there anything specific about the crowd that bothered her? Did she mention anything?'

'Not really. They just made her nervous. When they began to drift away she said she'd go home and run a hot bath. How did she come to be in the building site, for God's sake? It's locked up at night, and she didn't get on with any of those men.'

'We're not sure at the moment. Did you hear anything unusual last night, after she left?'

'Well . . . yes, I did. Some time after midnight, getting on for one, I'd say, I was getting ready to turn in. Her bedroom is through the wall from mine. I heard a thump from next door, and I wondered about it. She could be a clumsy old cow, knocking things over. In the end I did nothing.'

'You know the layout of her house then?'

'Course I do, we've been neighbours for thirty-five years.'

Brock's phone rang and he listened for a moment, then murmured, 'Right, I'll be over in a minute.' He rang off and said, 'I'm going back to the scene, Kathy. You finish up here with Mr Gilbey, will you?'

He left by the back door while the old painter lit another cigarette with an unsteady hand.

'Do you want to lie down, Reg?' Kathy asked, wondering if she should get a doctor.

'No, I'm all right.'

'Is there anything else you can tell me that might help us?'

'How did she die then?' he asked.

'It seems she was hanged.'

'Oh, sweet Jesus.'

'Can you think of anyone who'd want to do that?'

He shook his head distractedly. 'She could be cantankerous, of course, accusing people of wanting to steal her things, stuff like that, but I never took it seriously.'

'Did she have anything particularly valuable?'

He pondered, taking a faltering drag on his cigarette. 'Never saw her wear jewellery, and she never had much cash. As far as I know, the only things of value that her husband left her apart from the house were his paintings. He'd been a bit of a collector, and his father before him.'

'And they were valuable?'

'The best English artists of the time: Ben Nicholson, Paul Nash, Sutherland, several Henry Moore drawings—stuff like that, all very solid, bought through reputable galleries. I know she's sold a few of them over the years. I'm not sure what's left.'

'Later on, when the scientific people have finished, I'd like you to come next door with me and have a look to see if you can spot anything missing.'

He shrugged. 'If you want.'

'So you've known Betty a long time?'

He seemed lost in thought for a while, then he stubbed out his cigarette and got stiffly to his feet. 'Come on, I'll show you something.'

He led her along the hall and began climbing the stairs, using the banister to help haul himself up. Kathy followed him up to the studio she'd visited before, recognising the smells of oil and pigment that seemed to impregnate the walls. Gilbey was searching through a rack of unframed canvases set up in a corner of the room. Finding the one he was after, he pulled it out, turning it towards the light for her to see. It was a large painting of a young nude woman, sitting in front of a window. Gilbey propped it up on a chair and stepped back, his eyes fixed on the face of the model. As she came closer, Kathy thought she recognised the large eyes and angular features, the central parting of long thick hair, jet black. The style of painting, with the paint densely applied in scoops and whorls of browns and white and black, was very different from the portrait of the judge standing nearby on its easel. Kathy assumed it must have been the work of another artist, but then she recognised the windows behind the seated model as those of the corner bay in this same room, with the trees of the central park beyond.

As if answering her unspoken question, Gilbey said, 'I painted differently then.' He gently touched the corrugated surface of the pigment with his fingertips. 'Laid it on thick, squeezed straight from the tube. I wanted to show the force of the material thing, the energy of its presence in the world, just as it was, without frills and tricks. The Kitchen Sink school, they called us in the fifties.'

In the corner of the painting Kathy noticed lettering, blunt and square: GILBEY 1969.

'Later I moved on. I became less interested in the material presence and more in the spirit of what lay behind it.' He sounded nostalgic, regretful, as if the texture of the paint against his hand had reminded him of an old friend. 'The paint became thinner, more calculated, as I tried to show the soul . . . but it's so bloody hard. I did this in one session, ten hours, and I knew I'd finished when I ran out of paint. Now . . .' He looked over his shoulder at the judge's portrait, 'Well, I've been doing that for eight months now, maybe seventy or eighty sessions, layer upon layer, and I still haven't captured the old goat, not really. I may never finish it.'

Comparing the two paintings, Kathy suddenly understood what he meant. The girl in the window had a real presence, but was flat and stylised, like a Byzantine icon, whereas the judge seemed to emerge out of the canvas as a human character in full, a man of judgement, intelligence and authority, yes, but also something else; crafty, predatory even, dangerous.

'She was the one who made me want to change,' Gilbey went on, and seeing the query on Kathy's face he explained, 'She was the first model I had who talked. Couldn't shut her up. Told me more than I wanted to know about her life, and Harry. Harry was her husband, owned the house next door. I wanted quiet to concentrate on the paint, but she had to talk, and gradually I came to realise that the person that the talking revealed was more interesting than the body I was trying to represent. Took me a long time to come to terms with that.' He turned back to examine the old painting, lost in memories. 'Resisted it until I began to see that my work was becoming just decorative, pattern-making. Then I had to start again, with sitters who would talk about themselves. And most of them will, with a bit of encouragement.' He nodded his head, thinking, talking more to himself than to Kathy. 'Reckon it's something to do with having to hold the same position all the time—frees the mind, like the psychiatrist's couch. The judge is a great talker, oh yes.' Gilbey gave a snort that sounded like contempt. 'Well, I knew his reputation, of course. A man of fine words and firm moral judgement. But why was he so strict with certain types of criminals; the sex offenders, the rapists and pederasts? Was it because he felt so deeply for their victims? Or was it because he understood what drives them only too well? Now how do you show that in a portrait?'

'He told you that?' Kathy asked.

Gilbey looked up sharply, as if he'd forgotten who he was talking to. 'What? No, no, of course not.'

He turned away, a stubborn set to his jaw, as if he'd said too much and wouldn't say any more. 'So Betty was your model all that time ago,' she tried, but he just grunted and refused to respond.

'I need you to help me, Reg. I need to understand her, how she came to be the way she was. Paint her portrait for me now, in words.'

She waited, and then he began to speak again, voice low. 'She was always like that, damaged goods. I don't know where Harry found her or when they came to the square, but her English was still very ropy when I first arrived in the late sixties. Harry was twenty years older than Betty, and he'd had an eventful war by all accounts, and was pretty damaged himself. Couldn't have sex with her, so she told me, after she'd been modelling for me for a while. Sounded like an invitation to me, so I obliged. Got her pregnant.'

Gilbey was speaking in a monotone, addressing himself to his portrait of Betty, stroking the surface of the paint like a lover.

'Harry scared me, to be honest. He got this odd look in his eye sometimes. I didn't fancy fronting up to him, or facing the complications that would follow. So I arranged for her to have an abortion. Practically frog-marched her to the place. Not like now. Backstreet knitting-needle stuff. Nasty . . . I was so self-centred, you see, I couldn't imagine what it was like. You've lost your whole family in Europe somewhere, and then you fall pregnant, life returns, new hope. And then you have it snatched away from you, like that.'

He sniffed, ran a hand absentmindedly across his head, making the tufts stand up more wildly than ever. 'Nearly did for her. Tried to kill herself twice. Then Harry died one bitter winter, of pneumonia, and Betty went into a kind of trance. I tried to help, but she wouldn't have me near her. Gradually she took on a role, Batty Betty, the mad woman of Northcote Square. She's gone on playing the part ever since, an actor in a long-running show, becoming more extravagant year by year. At least that's how I saw it, thinking of myself again, seeing it as a form of persecution of me, but maybe there was nothing voluntary about it.'

He fell silent, and Kathy became aware of sounds from beyond the window, of children's cries from the school playground. Gilbey heard them too, and said, 'Has this got something to do with the little girl . . .?'

'What do you think?'

'They knew each other. I used to see them talking together, through the school railings or out there in the park. They seemed drawn to each other, two lost souls.'

'Could Betty have known something about Tracey's disappearance, or seen something? Did she hint at anything to you?'

He frowned. 'I don't know. She liked to pretend she had secrets, it was part of her role . . .'

Then his concentration was broken by a loud rap on the door downstairs and a man's voice, harsh, imperious. 'Gilbey? I'm here. Where are you, man? Are you ready for me?'

Gilbey swore under his breath and Kathy heard footsteps, more than one pair, on the stairs. Then a tall, elderly man, hawk-nosed and severe in appearance, marched into the room.

'Ah, here you are,' the man said, and then, noticing Kathy, gave a stiff little nod of his head. 'Going to introduce me to the lady, Reg?'

'Sir Jack Beaufort, this is Detective Sergeant . . . I'm sorry, I can't remember.'

'Kathy Kolla,' she said.

'Hackney?'

'The Yard,' Kathy replied.

'Brock's crew? Aha.' Beaufort eyed her narrowly, then carelessly indicated his companion. 'You know DI Reeves, Special Branch?' Kathy recognised the man who'd come to see Brock on that first morning. She particularly noticed his eyes, watchful, but with an ironic glint, as if well used to Beaufort's antics. He nodded to her with a hint of a smile.

'I can't do it today, Judge,' Gilbey said. 'I'm sorry, I'll have to cancel.'

Beaufort looked from Kathy to Gilbey and back again, as if he suspected some kind of conspiracy in his courtroom. 'Nonsense. What's the matter?'

'I've just had some bad news. A friend of mine has died.'

'At our age that happens every week. Close?' Then he noticed the portrait of Betty against the wall. 'My God! I haven't seen that one before, Gilbey. You've been hiding her from me.' He moved closer, taking out a pair of narrow glasses and putting them on. 'Oh my! Sixty-nine, eh? Your best year, in my humble opinion. It's the same model as the *Woman in a Bath,* isn't it? Yes . . . yes . . .' He absorbed it, then barked, 'I'll have her. How much do you want?'

'She's not for sale.'

'We'll see. So who died?'

'My neighbour,' Gilbey muttered, staring at the floor, apparently intimidated by his client.

The boisterous mood seemed suddenly to desert Beaufort, and he became serious. 'Not the mad woman?'

'You know her?' Kathy said.

He took his time to turn his gaze to her and respond, as if to make the point that it was his habit to interrogate police officers and not the other way around. Then, at the last minute, he flashed what might have been intended as a disarming smile. 'Yes indeed. We've seen her in the street, haven't we, Reeves?'

'Sir.'

'She was being pursued by a flock of little girls, at a safe distance. What were they calling her?'

'Batty Betty, I think it was.'

'Yes. Were you *close* friends, Gilbey?' Then he stared again at the painting and realisation lit his face. 'It's her, isn't it? The *Woman in a Bath* was the lady next door, yes? How fascinating.' He turned to Kathy. 'And is this of interest to you, Sergeant?'

'Yes.' Kathy bit off the 'sir' that almost followed. 'It seems probable she was murdered.'

'Really!' Beaufort looked startled. 'But . . . why? Was it a robbery?'

'We're not sure at the moment.'

'But you people are looking into it, are you? Not the local division? So you think . . .'

'It's too soon to say, sir.'

'Well . . . yes, that is a shock for you, Gilbey. Northcote Square is becoming quite a hotbed of crime, it seems . . .' he regarded Kathy with a malicious glint in his eye, '. . . despite the heavy presence of Special Operations.'

Kathy caught the sarcastic tone and noticed a thoughtful frown cross the face of DI Reeves in the background.

'Well, anyway, I'm here now, Gilbey old chap. You need something to distract you, and our deadline is fast approaching, so let's get on with it, shall we?'

The way he spoke to the painter reminded Kathy of the way Tait had spoken to Gabriel Rudd that first morning, as to a distracted child needing to be brought into line. And Gilbey seemed to accept it, giving a resigned sigh and shuffling across to his easel while Beaufort draped himself on the chair placed by the window. It was the same place where Betty had sat almost thirty-five years before, Kathy thought. She also noticed that the pose Gilbey had given Beaufort had his head facing towards the window, although his eyes were turned back at the painter, as if the sitter had just been caught looking out at something—the children in the playground, perhaps.

'I will need to speak to Mr Gilbey again soon,' Kathy said. 'I'll call back at eleven.'

Beaufort said, 'Reeves, old chap, how about making us some coffee?' and the Special Branch inspector followed Kathy down the stairs.

'Talks to me like a bloody butler,' he said when they reached the kitchen. He seemed more amused than annoyed. 'Fancy a cup?'

'A quick one, thanks. He is a bit of a pain, isn't he? Is anyone really trying to kill him?'

'Hard to say, but we don't want anything to happen to him right now.' Kathy caught Reeves's glance at her, as if to see whether she'd followed the significance of the remark, but she hadn't and he went on, 'Did you ever see him in court?'

'No.'

'Worth reading his sentencing speeches. Venomous, they are—a pungent mix of sarcasm, self-righteous outrage and contempt. The barristers say they're an art form and should be published.'

Kathy smiled, thinking that his vocabulary was different from that of most coppers she met, and wondered if he was a reader. She noticed what looked like paperbacks in a carrier bag, and supposed he'd have plenty of time for that in his present job.

'I've no doubt that anyone on the receiving end of one of those must have spent a good part of their time inside dreaming of putting a bomb under his car, or something worse . . . You're thinking this woman's murder has something to do with the missing girl, are you?'

'Yes.'

'Must have.' Reeves poured boiling water into the mugs. 'Milk? Sugar?'

Kathy shook her head. He took a splash of milk.

'Smoke if you want,' he said. 'Reg does.'

'I don't.'

'Me neither.' Kathy had the feeling she was being assessed.

'They were setting up crime scene tapes closing the whole lane when we arrived.'

'She was found in the building site.'

'Really?' He thought about that, sipping from the mug. 'Have you seen how much they're selling those flats for?'

'No.'

'Four hundred k each, off the plan, four in each house. I wonder how much they offered the mad woman. Or Gilbey, come to that.'

'Mmm. Incidentally, did you tell Beaufort we're from Special Operations?'

'Didn't need to. He's come across Brock before. And then, of course, he has a particular interest.'

'What's that?'

Reeves lowered his voice. 'He's doing a review of SO for the Met. You didn't know? No, you and I are too lowly to be told—strictly senior management only at this stage. I only know because I saw documents he was reading in the car and he dropped a few hints. Could be radical. He murmured ominously about amputations.'

'Well, if he knows of Brock's reputation, he should be kind to us.'

'With Beaufort the opposite's more likely to be the case. That's something else he's famous for—puncturing other people's reputations.'

Kathy thought about the man upstairs and felt a sudden sympathy for the people who'd faced him in his court.

There was a roar from above. 'Reeves! Where's that bloody coffee? I can smell it! We're dying up here.'

'Promises, promises,' Reeves murmured, and got reluctantly to his feet. 'Funny thing . . . the morning after that bloke fell from the tower block, Saturday, his lordship had a session here. It was my day off and my offsider drove him. Afterwards he told me that Beaufort told him to drive here by way of the Newman estate, just to have a look.'

Another cry from above. 'Reeves! Put that damn woman down!'

The inspector winced and picked up three mugs. 'See you later.'

16

DR SUNDEEP MEHTA could usually be relied upon for a joke and a few wisecracks. When Brock and Kathy arrived at the autopsy room the pathologist was in the middle of a story about a man and a frog that he was relating to his unsmiling pathology technician and the bored photographer. For the benefit of the newcomers he quickly recapped, taking no notice of the grim looks on their faces.

'Man walking down street, frog stops him and asks him to buy it a drink, takes it to a bar, frog also starving, man buys it sandwich, frog says it's exhausted and could he give it a bed for the night? Man agrees, takes it home. Frog asks for goodnight kiss. Good Samaritan hides disgust, kisses frog, frog turns into beautiful princess. "And that, Your Honour, is how I came to be found in bed with an underage girl." Ha!'

Nobody laughed.

'Oh, come on you lot!' Dr Mehta protested. 'What's the matter with everyone this morning? Is it your dismal weather getting you down?'

'Where did you hear that one, Sundeep?' Brock growled. 'The Dirty Raincoat Club?'

'Ah, Brock, your other case, of course. How tactless of me. But still, if we can't laugh in the face of life's tragedies we have no business coming to a place like this. So, let's get to work.'

Betty was laid out on the table just as she had been found, hands bound and face blindfolded. Mehta removed the strip of cloth from around her head and set it aside for examination. Kathy confirmed the identification.

They photographed the corpse, turned it over and photographed it again. Mehta cut the tape from around the wrists, clipped nail and hair samples, and took a number of swabs. Then the technician washed the body and Mehta began a detailed examination. A mood of dispassionate routine established itself as he tonelessly described the injuries. He began with the head, noting a small contusion behind the left ear.

'Enough to knock her out?' Brock asked.

'Mmm, possibly.' The pathologist stroked the area, parting the strands of hair. 'We may see more when we look under the skin. It's not a big bump.'

He moved on to the throat, which had a broad band of bruising and discolouration.

'This is not a simple hanging,' he said. 'There are several overlapping rope marks. Notice the edges of the marks. No inflammation, no vital reaction. It looks as if she was hanged *after* she was dead.'

He peered more closely. 'Difficult to detect external signs of strangulation beneath these rope lesions. Signs of petechial haemorrhages here and here . . . Now, these marks . . .' He began to work his way over the body, peering closely at each of the small brown marks in turn. Then he asked for the plastic evidence pouch containing the electrical lead with the exposed wire, and placed it against several of the wounds. Finally, he straightened up and said, 'It's not easy to interpret electrical burns, you know, and we don't see them very often. Mostly domestic accidents, housewives poking about in the toaster with a fork, that sort of thing. There was one fascinating case I recall of attempted autoerotic stimulation by connecting a penile vibrator to a mains plug—what a silly man! But the direct application of an electrode to the body is more unusual than you might think. Certainly I've never seen anything like this before . . .'

'Come on, Sundeep,' Brock interrupted. 'You have a theory.'

The man smiled. 'A hypothesis, perhaps, yes. There is a characteristic mark for electrode burns . . .' He pointed to a burn on Betty's left breast. 'It comprises a central area of necrosis where contact occurred, surrounded by a ring of white, which in turn is circled by a halo of dilated blood vessels.'

Everyone moved in closer to see what he meant, and the photographer took a close-up picture.

'I can't see the halo,' Brock said, peering through the half-lens glasses on the end of his nose.

'Exactly. Now look at these other burns,' Mehta went on, pointing generally across the abdomen and legs. 'They all have the central brown burn, but none have the pink halo. Although I've never seen this before, it suggests to me that, as with the rope marks to the neck, there was no vital reaction. She was already dead.'

Kathy felt relief. She noticed the technician's eyes widen behind her clear plastic visor, showing more than professional interest for the first time.

'Why electrocute a dead body?' Brock said.

'Quite!' Mehta beamed. 'That's for you to puzzle out, I think, Brock.'

There was silence for a moment, then Kathy said, 'Would the electric shocks cause the body to convulse?'

'Of course.'

'I mean, even after death?'

'Yes, yes. Didn't your biology teacher at school show you the trick where you attach battery leads to a dead frog's leg to make it jump?'

Brock and Kathy exchanged a glance, both thinking the same thing.

Dr Mehta completed his external examination at the discoloured soles of Betty's feet, then took up a scalpel and moved back to her throat, where he began carefully slicing into the flesh. 'Yes, internal bruising, and both the hyoid bone and thyroid cartilage have fractures, which suggests manual strangulation,' he said. The technician moved in beside him with bone cutters to help open up the chest and remove the major organs. Kathy sat on a stool, barely paying attention to the famil-iar process while her mind returned to that room in the basement of the derelict house, trying to imagine what had been played out there.

Completing the routine of examining, weighing and slicing, Mehta was able to offer a closer approximation to the time of death. The cheese and onion pie Betty had eaten with Reg Gilbey around seven p.m. was found in the final stages of the small intestine, and this, to-gether with the state of rigor mortis and the body temperature, led him to believe that death had occurred at around one a.m. Cause of death was manual strangulation.

The doctor sat back onto a stool, bloody gloved hands dangling be-tween his knees. 'Is that enough for you, Brock?'

'Almost, Sundeep. Just let me be sure what we have. Betty has a bath and goes to bed around eleven p.m. About two hours later her neighbour hears noises from her house, perhaps the intruder. There is a scuffle in her bedroom, a vase is broken, perhaps she receives a blow to the head. Does he strangle her there?'

Mehta thought. 'Seems probable, doesn't it? There's no indication of a struggle when he took her next door, no significant bruising or abrasions.'

'That's right. He had to take her downstairs, out into the yard, haul her over the wall into the building site and carry her down into the basement. Why?'

'I've no idea. That's your job, old chap!'

'Humour me, Sundeep. I value your insight.'

The doctor gave a smug little smile and straightened in his seat. 'Well, to avoid being disturbed, I suppose? Perhaps he didn't want the neighbour to hear him, or people in the street to see a light—the basement next door had its window boarded up.'

Brock frowned, not altogether convinced. 'All right, let's say he wants time with the body undisturbed. So he takes her next door, and presumably he already knows of this place and how suitable it would be, and there he prepares, in effect, a torture chamber for the corpse. He binds her hands behind her with insulating tape. There was no sexual interference?'

'No signs of that. Perhaps he *thought* she was still alive and was hoping to get something from her. Information of some kind—where she kept her money and jewellery, perhaps.' With Brock's encouragement, Mehta was enjoying playing the detective.

'But why the camera?'

'If there was a camera. We don't really know that.'

'Well, he discovers that in fact she's dead. So he hangs her anyway and administers—how many was it?'

'Twenty-three.'

'Twenty-three shocks to her corpse. Can we infer anything about his state of mind? I mean, if those were stab wounds you'd be telling us he was in a frenzy, wouldn't you?'

'Maybe . . . it would depend on the depth and pattern of cuts. In this case, I don't see any evidence of a frenzied attack. Look at the pattern, Brock; not in a cluster, but rather evenly and thoughtfully distributed, wouldn't you say? Here to an elbow, there to the calf, the thigh. Almost like an experiment to test the reactions of different limbs.'

'And possibly photographing these reactions.'

'Exactly! One might almost say that he is a serious student of pathology.'

'Quite,' Brock murmured. 'Many thanks, Sundeep.'

'Stan Dodworth,' Kathy said as they emerged from the mortuary.

'That's what I thought.' Brock took a deep breath of the street air, trying to vent the smells from his lungs. 'As if he's started to make his own corpses.'

'Why would he pick Betty?'

'Because he likes older subjects, and he knew she lived alone, and conveniently next door to a place he knew he wouldn't be disturbed.'

'Yes, he was down in that cellar with Gabe and Poppy and Yasher just over a week ago.'

'That would mean he's still in the area. And now every solitary old person is at risk. We have to find him quickly, Kathy. We'd better have another talk to the people he was closest to in the square.'

Kathy checked her watch. 'I was going to take Reg Gilbey through Betty's house to see if he might notice anything.'

'You do that. I'll see you later at the station.'

Gilbey was in his kitchen, a glass of golden liquid on the table in front of him, a cigarette held in an unsteady hand. He looked as if he'd aged ten years in a week, grey skin, grey bristles on an unshaved cheek, bent shoulders. Kathy felt sorry for him, but then remembered Betty's words; 'I watch him you know, I know his secrets.' It seemed entirely possible that she had been referring to Gilbey, the neighbour with whom she shared a long and troubled history. Stan Dodworth wasn't the only one who might want to see Betty dead.

'Your sitter's gone?'

Gilbey gave an abrupt little nod. 'Couldn't do any painting, hand was shaking too much. Just seems to have hit me . . .' He reached for the tumbler of whisky and lowered his head to it so as to reduce the chances of it spilling in his trembling hand. He swallowed, gave a rasping cough. 'Wouldn't stop talking about her.'

'The judge?'

'Mmm. How well did Betty know the girl? Were they very close? Did she talk to me about the kidnapping?'

Good questions, Kathy thought, and wondered at Beaufort's curiosity. There had been something insistent about it, she remembered.

'What did you tell him?'

'Yes, of course Betty talked about it, we all did. But with Betty, you never knew what was real and what was fantasy. She was obsessed, you see, with the idea of the stolen child. Had been ever since . . . that business I told you about. So when the reports of the other missing girls appeared in the news, she got it all tangled up with her own fantasies, even before Tracey disappeared.'

'Do you feel able to come next door with me?'

'All right.' His eyes darted up to hers with an anxious look. 'You don't think those Turks could have done it, do you?'

'Why do you say that?'

'Only . . . well, they made no secret of wanting to buy her house, and she was always fighting with them about one thing or another—noise, mud in the lane, blocked drains, smells. I've heard her screaming at that Yasher character more than once . . .' His voice petered out. 'No, doesn't seem likely, does it?'

'Come on, let's take a look at her house.'

The SOCO team were finishing as they reached the back door. She led Gilbey slowly from room to room, trying to prompt his memory and taking notes as he identified this item or that. The dolls spooked him, watching with their blank smiles, and Kathy had to force his attention to the drawings and paintings. He pointed out a number that she'd hardly noticed on her previous visit, when she'd been concentrating on signs of disturbance. Some especially caught his eye. 'Oh yes,' he said as they came upon an abstract in a dark corner of the living room, 'William Scott, of course, I'd forgotten about this one.' She noted the unfamiliar names, checking the spelling: Wallis, not Wallace; Brangwyn not Brangwen. By the time they came to the last room, Betty's own bedroom, Kathy had listed a dozen original works of mid-twentieth century British art, which Reg assured her would together be worth well into six figures. They had also come across a similar number of empty picture hooks. He mentioned the details of those of the missing paintings he could remember. 'I helped her sell them, through my own dealer.'

'Fergus Tait?'

'Fergus Tait! Fergus Tat, more like. Certainly not, I wouldn't deal with that cowboy. My bloke's in Cork Street, in the West End.'

Gilbey was looking uneasily at Betty's bed, stripped of its sheets and pillowcases for laboratory analysis. He seemed very pale, and Kathy saw his eyelids flutter, his body begin to sway.

'Sit down, Reg,' she said, and quickly grabbed a chair into which he almost toppled.

'It's been a shock,' he whispered. 'I still can't believe it. Hanged, you say?'

'I think you need a doctor.'

'No, no. I need a drink. Take me home.'

Kathy looked at the colour returning to his cheeks and nodded. Then she said, 'What was the painting in this room?' She pointed at the empty hook on the wall beside the bed.

'I don't know. I've never been in here before.' He caught her watching him. 'And that's the honest truth.'

She took him back to his kitchen and got the name of his dealer in the West End, just in case. Then her phone rang, Brock on the line.

17

KATHY JOINED BROCK and Bren for their first formal interview regarding the murder of Betty Zielinski at Shoreditch, beginning with Yasher Fikret, as representative of the family companies that both owned the house in which Betty's body had been found and were carrying out the building renovations.

'What can I say,' Yasher said, making an expansive gesture with his hands, heavy gold rings glinting. 'I'm devastated, as a neighbour, as a friend, as a local businessman. My whole family is devastated. I speak for them all. When's the funeral, incidentally? We will want to show our respect with floral tributes etcetera etcetera. My mother is offering to cater, no charge.'

Yasher was smartly turned out in dark suit and thick silk tie, but his gestures and way of speaking suggested that the style of businessman he modelled himself on owed less to the *Financial Times* than to Hollywood, *The Godfather,* perhaps. But the suggestion of menace beneath the swagger was real enough, Kathy thought. She eyed the big gold rings and wondered if one of them had torn Poppy's cheek.

'That's very generous, I'm sure,' Bren said dryly. 'At present we're still trying to trace Ms Zielinski's next of kin. Do you know if she had a solicitor?'

'No idea.'

'You didn't have dealings with her, as an adjoining owner to your development?'

'Our lawyers may know. You want me to check?'

'Please.' Bren pushed the phone across the table, but Yasher ignored it, slipping an impressive little silver machine out of an inside pocket, unfolding it and pressing a few buttons.

'Allo, Tony?' Yasher drawled. 'You remember the owner of number fourteen West Terrace, next to the end of our block, Betty Zielinski? . . . Yeah, well she's been done in, mate, last night . . . I'm not kidding. I'm with the cops now. Listen . . .'

Bren and Brock waited impassively while the exchange continued. Yasher finally folded away his phone and said, 'Sorry, no. Never dealt with a solicitor, just Betty in person.' A slight pause, then, 'So you don't know the next of kin?'

'Not yet.'

Yasher looked thoughtful. 'Bad business.'

'Where were you last night, Mr Fikret?'

'Me? I was at home with my wife and little boy. After dinner I watched football on the sports channel till eleven, then I went to bed. My wife will confirm that.'

'How many people know about that cellar room in your property, where the men play cards?'

'Well . . . all the regular building gang, of course, plus most of the subcontractors—plumbers, electricians . . .'

'We'd like all their names. Anyone else?'

'You know about me taking some friends there, the night poor little Tracey disappeared. My *artist* friends.' He smiled as at a private joke.

'To sell them drugs, yes.'

Yasher held up his hands in protest. 'If you're going down that road, Mr Gurney, I'm saying nothing. I'm here to help . . .'

'The point is that whoever took Ms Zielinski down there knew it very well. They knew exactly what was down there—a live power supply, for instance.'

'They broke in; they didn't have a key,' Yasher said defensively.

'That doesn't necessarily follow. They knew how easy it was to break in with just a screwdriver through the hasp. No alarms, no guard dogs. Very poor security for a building site in that area, Mr Fikret.'

'That's the site manager's business, not mine.'

'The site manager tells us that you had your own arrangements for a dog and a security guard right up until last week.'

Yasher scowled truculently. 'As it happens, I'm in dispute with that company over a commercial matter. And I completely deny your allegations about drugs. If there were any there they had nothing to do with me. I resent your insulting . . .' He began to rise.

Brock broke in, voice mild, 'Please sit down, Mr Fikret. Tell us about your relationship with these artist friends. If it wasn't to sell them drugs, why did you go there the night Tracey disappeared?'

'It was their idea. They wanted to see what we were doing to the old building. I thought Gabe might be thinking of buying one of the flats for an investment. They're just neighbours, people I meet in the square. I don't pretend to understand what they're on about all the time, but I like their company, okay? That's the nice thing about living in this part of London—the culture you brush up against every day.' He gave a broad grin.

'But you're a bit of a collector yourself, aren't you?' Kathy said.

'Me?' Yasher looked astonished.

'That painting in the shop, your mother said you bought it.'

'Ah, that! Yes, I bought it down the market. That's real skill, that is. That's my taste, all right.'

'What do you think of your friends' work, Gabe and Stan and Poppy?'

'You want an honest answer? Don't tell them, please, but I can sum it up in two well-chosen words—total crap.' He saw the little smile cross Bren's face. 'Aha! You agree with me, Mr Gurney! Am I right?'

'When was the last time you saw Stan Dodworth?'

'Stan? That would be the night we went to the cellar that I told you about. Not since then. Why?'

'He's missing, Mr Fikret. Any idea where he might be?'

'No. I really don't know him that well.'

'And when was the last time you were in that basement?'

'Oh, I don't know . . . a couple of days ago. I seem to remember calling down there for some reason.' He gave another big toothy grin. 'Mr Brock, sir, let's be frank. If I was going to bump off the old lady, do you think I'd have left her for you to find on my own premises? The idea's crazy. If this has anything to do with me at all, it'd have to be someone wanting to embarrass me and my family, right?'

After he'd gone, Bren said reluctantly, 'He's right, Brock. He's not that stupid.'

'Actually, I think he's devious enough to do it this way just to put us off. But I don't think he's got the artistic talent.'

'Artistic talent?'

'Yes. The thing was staged, Bren. Artificial and composed, as if it was a commentary on something. I just wish I knew what.'

Listening to this, Kathy recalled Reg Gilbey's sneer that the young artists in the square didn't have an original thought between them, that everything was a reference to something else, and she wondered if Betty's killer might have been deliberately using some recognisable artistic image of death or suffering. The more she thought about it, the more plausible it seemed. What had been done to Betty surely had meaning, a message of some kind. If they could find the reference, perhaps they could find the killer. What images might inspire Stan Dodworth, for instance?

Bren looked sceptically at his boss. 'You don't think you've been seeing too much of this contemporary art lately, chief? It can get to you after a while.'

'Very true, Bren. And I've got a feeling there'll be more.'

Fergus Tait sat in the interview room at Shoreditch station, full of apologies. 'I feel mortified, Chief Inspector, but what can I do? I've pleaded with him, told him it's in his own best interests, but he'll have none of it. He simply refuses to come out of the cube.'

'It's his privilege to refuse to talk to us, Mr Tait, but it could compromise his position in the future. I do think he should be persuaded to get legal advice, at least.'

'Oh, he's had that all right.' Tait gave a coy smile. 'Advice from my lawyers is one of the services I provide my little stable of artists. Gabe spoke to them before he went into his retreat, and he was in touch with them by email again this morning. I believe he's quite clear about his situation, but if you wish, the lawyer will speak to you. And indeed, it's not as if Gabe's refusing to answer any questions you may have. It's just that he'll only do it by email. Can I also just say on his behalf that he has absolutely no information about this terrible event. He was in his cube all night, of course, and he saw and heard nothing. He's devastated, absolutely devastated, as we all are. I'm going to offer the gallery as a venue for the wake for the poor, dear soul. That way Gabe can be there too. But of course it'll depend on her family. Do you know who they are?'

'We haven't been able to trace them yet.'

'No trace, eh? Well, I'd be obliged if you'd let me know when you do. I seem to recall that the lady had one or two pictures I might be able to help them dispose of.'

'Just for the record, Mr Tait, is there any way we can verify that Mr Rudd remained in his cube all night? He's on camera, isn't he?'

'That's right. The eyes of the world were on him all night long. He's broadcast live on the internet.'

'What about you? What were your movements last night?'

'I ate with friends in our restaurant. My goodness, what a spectacle that was in the square. Did you see it? All those people. Anyway, I was there till we closed down, towards midnight. Then I went to bed in my flat at the back of The Pie Factory. I was there till eight this morning, but I'm afraid there were no cameras to back that up!' He chuckled.

'What about Stan Dodworth? Have you heard from him?'

'I'm afraid not. I did promise to let you know if I did, but there's been no word.'

Brock looked hard at him. 'I find that hard to believe. You were the one who rescued him from that institution, who brought him back down to London and gave him shelter and security, who protects him from unwanted publicity. Of course he'd get in touch with you.'

'Well, I assure you . . .'

Brock reached across to some papers that Bren had placed in front of him. 'At nine-oh-three p.m. on Saturday last you had a call to your private number in your flat. It lasted three seconds. It came from a public phone in a pub in Islington. Over the next ten minutes it was repeated five times, all for just a second or two. That would have been to your answering machine, I take it, no message left. Then at eleven-seventeen p.m. on the same night you got another call from a public phone, this time at St Pancras rail station. It lasted six minutes.'

Tait sat back as if he'd been slapped. 'You have my phone records?'

'This is a serious case. Anyone who obstructs our inquiries is going to find themselves in very deep water. Well?'

A faint glisten of sweat had appeared on Tait's forehead. 'It could have been anyone making that call.'

'Really?' Brock and Tait stared at each other for a moment, then Tait looked away.

'I get a lot of calls . . .'

'There are cameras in the concourse at St Pancras, Mr Tait.'

'Oh . . .' Tait swallowed, wiped his forehead. 'All right, I did speak to him, yes, that one time. That's all, I swear. It was that same evening you went through his room. He was agitated. He was telling me that he thought he would go away for a while, see his folks up north. I tried to persuade him to come back to the Factory, to have a talk with me first. He didn't seem to be listening, so I made a mistake . . . I told him you'd been into his room, and found the cast of the old lady and the other stuff. That really made him panic. He became hysterical, abusing me for letting you in. I begged him to calm down and come back, but he just hung up. I haven't heard from him since. I swear that's the truth.'

'Why did you lie to me?' Brock said softly.

'Like you said, Chief Inspector, I was trying to protect him. He's not a bad fellow, I'm sure of it. He couldn't have done this thing to Betty. I think he must have taken a train up north.'

'The camera shows him leaving the station. We don't think he ever caught that train.'

At that moment Tait's mobile phone sounded in his pocket, a cheerful rendering of 'Danny Boy', and for a second Tait seemed uncertain what to do. Then he snatched it out. 'Hello? . . . Not now, Trudy, I'm . . . What?' He listened in silence for a while, a look of consternation growing on his face, then he said, 'Hold on,' and looked up at Brock. 'That's one of the girls on Gabe's support team at the gallery. She says they've been going through his messages for the past twenty-four hours and there's one they want me to look at. It seems it contains pictures . . . terrible pictures, she says . . . of an old woman, naked, hanging by the neck, being tortured . . .'

One of the people inside the gallery unlocked the glass door as their car drew up and let them in. They had the impression of suspended animation, as if everyone there had been waiting motionless for them to arrive. Gabriel Rudd was standing against the wall of his cube, hands pressed to the glass, face as white as his hair. He still wasn't coming out, and there was something both bizarre and pathetic about his figure as he watched what was going on around him. People began to move, indicating the monitor that had opened up the attachments on the email message. The three police and Tait crowded behind the operator's chair as she clicked in the instructions. The screen went blank, then burst into motion, a movie clip lasting just a few lurid seconds, showing a figure wearing a full-length black cape, the face obscured, and holding an electric cable against the thigh of Betty's hanging figure, as she jerked violently on the end of the rope like a helpless puppet. There was no sound.

'Oh, dear God . . .' Fergus Tait breathed.

Three more brief clips followed, in each case with the exposed wires of the cable applied to a different part of the body.

Silence.

'That's the lot?' Brock asked.

The girl, pale, nodded.

'What about the email it was attached to?'

She showed him. A sender address, LSterne@kwikmail.co, no message, received at four-oh-three a.m.

'Who's L. Sterne?' Brock asked.

'We don't know who it is. We haven't had a message from that address before.'

Bren pulled out his phone and began to make a call while Brock turned to Tait. 'Where can we talk?'

He led Brock and Kathy through a doorway into the small gallery office, the walls lined with shelves of catalogues and books.

'This isn't very roomy . . .' Tait muttered, closing the door, looking distracted.

'Never mind,' Brock growled. 'Sit down. Now, what do you have to say?'

'It's him, isn't it? Stan.'

'Why do you say that?'

'Well . . . she looks like the figure in his room, suspended from the chain.'

'Anything else?'

Tait blinked rapidly. 'I . . . I don't know.'

'What does it mean, Fergus?' Brock insisted, leaning over the desk and glaring at him as if he wanted to tear the answer out of his throat. 'The hanging, the electrocution, what does it *signify*?'

'Perhaps . . . to make the body convulse, distort, like his sculptures.'

'Is that all?'

'Christ, I don't know.'

Brock stared at him, pondering, then came to a decision. From his pocket he took a photograph of the scene they had found in the basement, and handed it to Tait. 'When we found her this morning she was wearing a blindfold. What does that mean?'

'But there was no blindfold in the film.'

'Exactly. When he was finished he posed her for us to find, with a blindfold. Why? What does a blindfold mean to you?'

'I don't know, blind man's bluff, three blind mice, blind justice, love is blind, blind leading the blind . . .'

'What about in the world of art? Can you recall a blindfolded figure?'

'No . . . no, I can't.'

Brock straightened, his mouth tight with frustration. 'And you've no idea where he might be now?'

'None at all.'

Out in the gallery, Bren confirmed that a search was under way for the source of the email. 'And they've got the other artist, Poppy Wilkes, waiting for us at the station.'

Brock nodded. 'You finish up here, Bren. Kathy and I'll talk to her.'

Poppy said she hadn't heard the news about Betty. She had woken late after a restless, dream-filled night, seen the drizzle falling outside her window and stayed in her room, trying to work up an idea for a new version of the cherub sculpture. Then a woman police officer came knocking on her door, asking if she'd attend another interview, and she'd been taken directly to Shoreditch police station, where she'd been provided with a cup of tea while she waited. She seemed to sense their subdued mood as soon as Brock and Kathy walked in.

'Is it bad news?' she said, clutching her cardigan tightly at the front. 'You've found Tracey, haven't you?'

'No,' Kathy said, taking the lead while Brock sat off to one side. 'It's not Tracey, Poppy. Can you tell us when you last saw Betty?'

'Betty? I saw her in the square yesterday afternoon, I think. Yes. She seemed okay. Why, is something wrong?'

'Yes, I'm afraid so. Betty was found dead this morning. We believe she was murdered some time during the night.'

Both Yasher and Tait had described themselves as being 'devastated', meaning sympathetically upset, but in Poppy's case it didn't seem like an exaggeration. Her eyes, wide with shock, stared down unseeing at the table in front of her, and she seemed to withdraw into a state of paralysis.

'Poppy? Poppy?'

She finally registered Kathy's voice. 'Tell me,' she whispered. 'Tell me what happened.'

As Kathy told her everything, little shocks registered in her eyes with each new dreadful detail; the basement room, the hanging, the abuse of the body.

'Oh,' she said finally, then closed her eyes, gave a little gasp as if she herself were giving up the last breath in her lungs, and seemed about to pass out.

Kathy reached forward and touched her hand. 'Are you all right?'

'I'm sorry,' she apologised, taking a sip of water. 'I haven't been eating lately.'

That seemed true, Kathy thought. Even in the few days since she'd last seen her in the square, Poppy seemed to have lost weight and taken on an anaemic pallor. 'Would you like something now? I could get food sent up, a sandwich, or something hot . . .'

But Poppy shook her head, the thought of food making her gag. 'Do you know who did it?' she gasped.

'We're not certain. I'd like to show you a picture, Poppy. It's disturbing, so maybe we should wait for a bit.'

'It's all right. Show me.'

Kathy passed her the picture of Betty hanging in the basement room. She regarded it unblinking, for a full minute, then said flatly, 'You think Stan did it, don't you?'

'What do you think?'

'No, he didn't.'

Then an odd change came over Poppy. She suddenly seemed to notice the recording machine on the side table, its red light glowing, and then the eye of the camera suspended in the far corner of the room. She became agitated.

'Why do you say that?' Kathy asked.

'What? I don't know, maybe he did. I don't know anything.' She wiped the cold sweat on her face. 'I don't feel good. I want to go now. I think I may be sick.'

'I'll take you to the loo.' Kathy got to her feet and took hold of Poppy's arm, while Brock spoke to the machine again, halting the interview.

The toilets were empty, and Kathy was intrigued to see that Poppy checked this before she went to a washbasin and splashed water over her face.

Kathy moved close to her shoulder and spoke quietly. 'You had a reason for saying that Stan didn't do it, Poppy. What was it?'

She shook her head. 'No. I don't want to talk to you. I want someone else to see me out.'

'I want to help you, Poppy. You believe that, don't you?'

'But what if you can't?' She saw the disbelief on Kathy's face and blurted out, 'Betty *knew* something. Stan told me . . . the people who took Tracey, he told me, they have a friend, in the square. Someone who looks after them.' Then her body froze as the door to the toilets swung open and a uniformed woman came in. Poppy rushed abruptly past her and out into the corridor, Kathy on her heels. The main stairs lay ahead, and Poppy was down them and out into the front lobby before she caught up with her.

'Poppy!'

But Poppy didn't stop until they were out on the street and Kathy had hold of her arm.

'Let me go!' she yelled in a real state of panic, and a passer-by stared at the two of them. 'Leave me alone or I'll fucking scream!'

'Poppy, for God's sake, talk to me!'

She glared wild-eyed at Kathy. 'Don't you see? It's a warning *to* Stan, not *by* Stan!' Then she turned and ran off through the rain.

18

KATHY TOOK THE tube to Piccadilly Circus and began walking west down Piccadilly. The rain had eased to an irregular spit and umbrellas were being folded away. She passed the arched entrance to the forecourt of the Royal Academy where a large group was waiting to get into a new exhibition, then she turned into Burlington Arcade. The little shops lining the arcade were stuffed with luxury items—jewellery, clothing, travel paraphernalia and curious little accessories that might have been essential to the ladies and gentlemen of another age—and Kathy couldn't help thinking that, as desirable objects went, they could hardly be more different from the pieces that Stan Dodworth had to offer.

At the north end of the arcade she continued into Cork Street, lined with commercial art galleries. She spotted the sign for Adrian Schropp's and pushed the door into a brightly lit space displaying large hazy landscapes, painted, so the publicity said, by a well-known Norwegian artist. A young woman at the front desk pointed the way to stairs leading down to a basement, crammed with paintings in tall racks, at the back of which Kathy found the owner's office.

'Mr Schropp?' She tapped on the door, and a large man with plump pink features emerged with outstretched hand.

'Do come in. Grab a pew.' They settled themselves. His accent was an odd mixture of upper-class English and German. 'Vell, you seem to have your hands full over in Northcote Square, by all accounts. After you phoned I listened to the news on the radio. My goodness! Poor Mrs Zielinski!' Adrian Schropp's jowls trembled indignantly.

'Yes. As I said, Mr Gilbey thought you might be able to help me make sure that all of her artworks are accounted for.'

Schropp leaned forward conspiratorially. 'You think theft vas the motive? My God, the violence they use now!' He shuddered.

'Not necessarily, it's just something we have to check. It seems her paintings were her only valuables.'

He nodded vigorously. 'Mm, mm, that vas my impression too. I called in at her house several times during visits to Reg, vhen she vanted to sell something. Some of the furniture may be worth something, but so bulky! I tried to check my records . . .' He indicated papers pulled from the drawers of a filing cabinet. 'I'm not sure if I've found them all, but I can probably remember, anyvay. Do you vant to know vhat vas there or vhat I bought?'

'Both, if you can. I have a list of what's left there now, and Reg told me what he could remember.' She handed over the typed lists and he considered them.

'Ah, the Ben Nicholson, I'd forgotten that . . . Mm, mm, that looks pretty complete. Vait a minute, there vas a little Bacon, mm, very tasty.'

He smacked his lips appreciatively and Kathy was unsure if he was talking about food. 'Bacon?'

'Mm, Francis Bacon, a little study for one of his figures at the base of the crucifixion. I made her an offer for it the last time I vas there, to-wards the end of last year . . .' He rummaged through the papers. 'Here ve go, last December, she sold me a small Eric Ravilious vatercolour, but she never vent ahead vith the Bacon. Maybe she got a better offer.'

'She was in touch with other dealers then, was she?'

'I vasn't avare of any until that last time. I mean I vouldn't have minded if she had got a second opinion, of course, but I alvays offered her a fair price, and Reg told her not to bother.'

'But last December she said she had spoken to other dealers?'

'Yes, she said Fergus Tait had been around to have a look at her things, and had been quite interested in several of them.'

'Fergus Tait? I thought he was strictly contemporary.'

'Oh yes, but he vouldn't let an opportunity pass him by.' Schropp chuckled. 'Come to think of it, of all the things she had, the Bacon would be most up his street—rather bizarre, and vith a quite contempo-rary feel to it.'

'Could you describe it to me?'

'Mm, not easy. An oil sketch, roughly eighteen inches square, grey figure, orange background. The figure is strange, like a dog vith a long neck and a mouth instead of a head.'

'Thanks. Any others you can remember?'

'No, I'm pretty sure that's the lot.'

Kathy closed her notebook. 'Well, thanks very much for your help, Mr Schropp.'

'Adrian, please. Delighted to be of service. And how is Reg these days? I must call in again. I dare say these horrible events vill have shaken him up. You know the poor voman vas a model of his, years ago? I just hope it doesn't put him off that portrait he's doing. Have you seen it?'

'The judge? Yes, it looked pretty well finished to me.'

'I hope so. I vas the one who recommended Reg to Sir J. He'll never forgive me if the old rascal doesn't finish it in time for the exhibition at the National Portrait Gallery.'

'You know Sir Jack, then?'

'Oh yes, he's been a client for years. A great collector, and not just from me. He's even invested in some of Fergus Tait's monstrosities.' He led Kathy back to the stairs. 'Did you have a look at our show upstairs? Vonderfully atmospheric, aren't they? Perhaps I could interest you in one?'

Kathy smiled. 'That would be great, but I'd have to find a bigger place to live first.'

'Who are you interested in?' Schropp was being flirtatious.

Kathy wasn't sure, but the name that popped into her head was the one that Deanne and Reg Gilbey had said Gabe Rudd was obsessed by. 'Henry Fuseli?'

Schropp looked both surprised and impressed. 'Vell, that's a minority taste all right. You've been to the Royal Academy?' Seeing the puzzlement on Kathy's face he said, 'His Diploma Vork. Every painter elected to the Academy must give them a piece of their vork in exchange for the diploma, and these hundreds of vorks make up their permanent collection. Of course not all are on display, but you should take a look.'

Kathy did as he suggested on her way back to the tube station, passing up the great entrance flight of stairs to the lobby, where she was directed to the permanent collection. There she did finally find Fuseli's 1790 Diploma painting entitled *Thor Battering the Midgard Serpent,* depicting a muscular male figure on a boat, cloak flying, arm raised to strike a sea monster rising from the waves. Kathy thought it melodramatic and rather absurd.

Brock, meanwhile, had been called away to another senior management meeting. He was able to gauge the deepening crisis by the increasingly peremptory manner of Commander Sharpe's secretary, who gave the impression of holding him personally responsible for all the troubles her boss was enduring. On this occasion he seemed to be the first to arrive.

Sharpe waved him to a seat at the conference table. Once there would have been the offer of coffee, but such niceties had gone by the wayside.

'I asked you to come before the others, Brock. Couple of things we need to cover. First, what's the progress on Northcote Square?'

Brock gave him a brief summary, which only seemed to deepen his gloom.

'No progress, then. What about the email from the murderer? Can't you trace it?'

'It was sent from a twenty-four-hour internet café a few hundred yards away from the square. Nobody there has any recollection of the sender.'

Sharpe groaned. 'This murder couldn't have come at a worse time for us.'

'For us?' Brock queried.

'Of course. Northcote Square is turning into the biggest public entertainment since "Coronation Street", and this murder will make it bigger still. What the hell is going on? The place seems to be attracting homicidal maniacs like flies to a cow's arse. This Dodworth character, where the hell is he? And why the hell can't we get Wylie to talk?'

'I'm going to see him again as soon as we've finished.'

'Are you? Good. Look, I'm not blaming you, Brock. I know you're doing everything you can. But we're not looking good at precisely the moment when we need to look our best. I've just heard that the release of the Beaufort Committee recommendations is being brought forward. It certainly doesn't help that the man himself is on the spot, watching the whole mess unfold at first hand.'

Brock said nothing. Sharpe sat back, suddenly deflated. 'Strictly between us, Brock, I think the game's up. By the year's end you and I and the rest will have been put out to grass. I won't be saying so at our meeting, but that's what it amounts to. I want you to know that I'm going to recommend you for immediate promotion to Super. It would have happened long ago if you hadn't been so bloody precious about staying on the streets. At least you can step down on an enhanced pension.'

'Thank you,' Brock said without warmth. 'I appreciate the thought.'

The chill of the gaol, psychological rather than physical, gripped Brock as soon as he clipped on the pass and went through the barred internal security gates. He sat on the offered seat and waited while they brought out the prisoner. They had managed to fill in a little more of his background. Robert Wylie had lurked in the down-market end of the sex industry for years, the sometime proprietor of several adult bookshops with a special line in the back room, the publisher of cheap porn magazines using pirated images, the co-owner of a seedy brothel that had been closed down four times by the police in four different locations, and more recently an internet provider of suspect services. Over the years he had been the subject of numerous police inquiries, and a few successful prosecutions. Apparently he had learned from this the virtue of silence, and it seemed he wasn't about to change now. He sat down in front of Brock and regarded him with face blank while his solicitor drew a chair to his side.

Brock stared back for a while without speaking. The man looked out of place in prison clothes, not at all the hardened criminal, but soft and pasty-faced from too little exposure to the sun. He seemed to have some kind of impediment in his nose, so that he breathed with a slight wheeze through open mouth.

Brock began. 'We'd like to contact your wife. Can you tell me where she is?'

Wylie glanced sideways at his lawyer, who looked preoccupied and worried. Neither spoke.

'You're in an interesting position, Wylie,' Brock went on. 'I hope you appreciate it. This case is big. Have you been watching the TV coverage today? Do they give you access to the web?'

Brock gazed at Wylie's pudgy white fingers clasped loosely on the table, and tried not to think of the girls.

'I can understand how that might appeal, your moment of fame, but it's a dangerous game.' Brock caught a flicker in Wylie's eyes at the word dangerous. He wondered if he'd been getting trouble from the other inmates, and made a mental note to check. 'A clever lawyer might be able to persuade a court that Abbott led you astray—he certainly must have been strange. But that will count for nothing if you don't give us any help. That's the only leverage you've got. And with so much public attention on the case, it's only a matter of time before we discover everything for ourselves. Have you any idea of the number of people working on this? When we find Tracey, that's one less thing you have to trade; when we find Stan Dodworth, that's another. The information you've got has a very short shelf life, Wylie. Use it while you can.'

Brock sat back, realising it hadn't worked. The spark ignited by *dangerous* had faded. He waited in silence while Wylie's lawyer took a packet of cigarettes out of his pocket and began to strip off the cellophane. Brock shrugged and made to get up from his seat. Then Wylie spoke for the first time. 'No smoking please, Russell,' he admonished the solicitor with a wheeze. Then he leaned forward to Brock and muttered, 'What happened to the mad woman?'

'Did you know her?'

Wylie looked annoyed at this, but answered, 'I saw her around. Well?'

'We think Stan Dodworth killed her.'

Wylie pursed his fat lips as if in doubt, and Brock decided to tell him what had not been released to the press. 'Her body was mutilated. Electric shocks.'

Wylie drew back, startled.

Brock went on, 'You'll be judged by the people you mixed with, Wylie. And there's a rumour that you and Abbott had another friend in the square, apart from Dodworth.'

Wylie looked scornful but didn't reply.

'Where's Stan Dodworth?'

'No idea.'

'Where's Tracey Rudd?'

Wylie's eyes narrowed as if in calculation. Finally he muttered, 'Why don't you ask the judge?'

Brock was hardly sure he'd heard correctly, but before he could say anything more Wylie was on his feet, turning to the door behind him and slapping it with his pudgy fist.

Kathy was shown into Fergus Tait's office, but no sooner had she sat down in front of his desk than his phone rang.

'Oh, excuse me, they're going mad, I'd better take it,' he said, and launched into an animated conversation with someone about the latest developments. 'Your spies are quite right,' he said. 'The *No Trace* project will be entered for the Turner, and believe me, nothing else will come near it. Have you heard about today's banner? You must see it, a knockout, an absolute stunner. Every day it's becoming more spectacular . . .'

While he talked, Kathy examined the artworks on the walls—a large abstract painting, some blurry photographs which might have been stills from a video and, in pride of place on the wall behind Tait's director's chair, a small pyramid of cans bearing labels of frolicking puppies, mounted in a glass case.

Tait finally hung up. 'Sorry, Kathy, Channel Four. Now, what can I do for you?'

'I'm just trying to establish if there's anything missing from Mrs Zielinski's house, and in particular her paintings. I understand you may have bought some things from her, and I wondered if you could tell me what they were, for the purposes of elimination.'

'Ah, yes. Well, that's easy. There was only the one, a small study by Francis Bacon. I can find the receipt, if you like. As a matter of fact, I sold it not long ago, to someone you know.'

'Really?' Kathy thought he must have made a mistake.

'Yes, Sir Jack Beaufort, old Reg's sitter.'

'But . . . how did you know that I've met him?'

Tait chuckled, pleased at her confusion. 'Because he told me so, just the other night. He's a regular here at the restaurant. We always have a chat.'

'Ah, I see. Did he know that the painting came from Betty?'

Tait thought about that. 'I'm not sure. She certainly knew who I sold it to—I told her.'

The phone began to ring again and Kathy got to her feet. On her way out she looked in to the gallery, where four of Rudd's team were hanging the eleventh banner. They were watched closely by the hollow-eyed artist in his cube, like a Grand Prix champion watching his pit-stop crew in action. The new addition featured a twice life-size crimson image of Betty's corpse taken from the email attachment, the stark figure shocking in its contorted death pose, like a Gothic crucifixion. A cluster of press photographers was standing in front of it, mouths open.

Looking at the whole sequence of eleven hangings, Kathy could see elements tying them together that she hadn't recognised before. There was a thin meandering line, for instance, which began, unnoticed, in the top of the first banner, and then was continued in the next, gradually working its way across all eleven like the random trail of a worm or a spider. And there was also a sense of progression in the colour which she hadn't noticed. The first one had been entirely colourless, formed in shades of grey and black. Then the next had had a hint of blue, and after that, with each successive day, the colours had become stronger, as if the banners were coming alive.

Looking at the artist, an opposite process seemed to have been taking place, with the colour and substance leaching from him, leaving him each day leaner and more wraithlike. To Kathy it looked as if all his vitality were being transferred into his artwork.

While she was watching him, he suddenly turned his attention from his team to her, meeting her gaze. He gave her a little smile as if they shared some private knowledge, then turned away again.

Through the large restaurant windows she could see the waiters putting a final polish on the cutlery before the first diners arrived. She crossed the street to Mahmed's Café, not sure what kind of reception she might get. Sonia was there, of course, along with a young girl she introduced as her niece. She was formal but not unfriendly, and after she took Kathy's order for a black coffee she sent the girl to the kitchen and leaned confidentially over the counter.

'Have you caught the fiend?' she asked.

'I'm afraid not.'

'I know you can't talk about it, but you must believe that Yasher had nothing to do with this. He may have some shady friends, I dare say, but he'd never get mixed up in this sort of thing. It's beyond belief.'

'I hope you're right.'

'I am right. You know we've offered to cater for the funeral —no cost.'

'That's generous of you.'

'Ach, it's nothing. We're part of the community too, you know.'

'I know.'

'At a time like this we must work together. We are all connected.'

Kathy reflected on how true this was as she sat down with her coffee. Everyone in Northcote Square was connected to everyone else. Gabriel Rudd knew the sculptor Stan Dodworth, who knew Patrick Abbott, who had probably abducted Tracey Rudd; Betty Zielinski had been the model of Reg Gilbey, whose client Sir Jack Beaufort knew Fergus Tait, who had sold him a painting belonging to Betty Zielinski . . . And the police too, had been drawn into this web, for, according to DI Reeves, Beaufort was involved in some kind of inquiry into their future. She distrusted coincidences but she knew that real life was full of them, the appearance of false patterns when random events fall together. But sometimes the patterns were real and meant something. Somewhere in this, she felt, there was a pattern that would make sense of Tracey's disappearance and Betty's death. They just hadn't discovered it yet.

An enormous blood-red sun trembled on the western horizon like a tumour. It cast a baleful light over the City, gilding the flank of the Nat West Tower and turning the dome of St Paul's a petal pink. Brock gazed out through the glass balcony doors at the sunset for a moment longer, then turned back to examine the paintings. Each had its place, glowing beneath its own concealed spotlight, and Lady Beaufort had been particular about switching all the lights on before Brock entered the room, as if preparing her children for a visitor.

'My husband receives so many deputations from Scotland Yard these days,' she had said proudly. 'I wasn't able to contact him, I'm afraid, but I know he won't be long. He always lets me know if he's going to be delayed. I'm so sorry, but I've forgotten your name.'

'Detective Chief Inspector David Brock.'

'Well then, Detective Chief Inspector, would you mind if I leave you here on your own until Jack returns? I happen to be watching on the television the very last episode of a particularly engaging program, which I've been following for some years.'

'Please go ahead. I'll be fine.'

She had cocked her head just like her husband did, except that in her case the gesture was whimsical rather than interrogative. She was of the same narrow build as him, the same lined features and grizzled grey hair, but at half the scale, so that they seemed liked brother and sister.

The pictures were very good. If there was any criticism to be made of the collection it was that it lacked consistency. Thinking of the spare harshness of the man, Brock had expected some parallel in the paintings, all abstract expressionist, perhaps, or all of a certain period. But the paintings were of every style and philosophy, from Stanley Spencer to Roberto Matta, Bernard Buffet to Gilbert and George, as if the judge had been so greedy for the delights of twentieth-century art that he just hadn't been able to resist anything.

The paintings dominated the room, and the furniture seemed cowed by comparison. Brock knew the apartment building had not been long completed, and this was its most expensive unit, the rooftop penthouse, and the sofas and chairs had the air of refugees from some cosier suburban mansion.

'What are you doing here?' The voice cut into Brock's thoughts.

He turned to face the man, standing taut in the doorway, staring at him.

'I'm sorry, I phoned earlier, and your wife suggested this time. She's watching a TV program.'

'I'm not sure this is appropriate. If you've come to talk to me about the report . . .'

'No, no. I'm here in connection with the Tracey Rudd and Betty Zielinski inquiries.'

'I know nothing whatever about that.'

'This was hers, wasn't it?' Brock pointed to the Bacon painting. 'Betty Zielinski's?'

Beaufort seemed startled, and a new caution entered his voice. 'I believe that's true. I bought it from a dealer, Fergus Tait.' Then Beaufort's eyes narrowed with suspicion. 'Did Tait tell you this?'

'Did you ever talk to Mrs Zielinski about the painting?'

'No. I fail to see . . .'

'I'm interested in everything to do with Betty Zielinski, sir—who she knew, what she knew.' He paused, letting that register, then added, 'It would seem quite natural, inevitable even, that you would speak to the former owner of your painting when you've been visiting the house next door to her several times a week for the last eight months.'

'I didn't know the former owner lived next door to Reg Gilbey until today.'

'Well, she knew you had it.'

'Really?' His face set hard as if to an obtuse counsel whose claims didn't merit his consideration.

'So there's nothing you can tell me about Betty Zielinski that might assist my inquiries?'

'Nothing.'

'What about Stan Dodworth?'

'Who?'

'You don't know him? Stan Dodworth?'

'I think I recall the name . . .'

'He's one of Fergus Tait's artists.'

'Then I may have seen his work. Remind me.'

'*Body Parts.*'

'Oh yes, I remember. It was of no interest to me.'

Brock turned away, eyes scanning the walls as if searching for some clue. 'So you wouldn't have any idea where he is now?'

'No, I wouldn't. Why? What's he done?'

'He's disappeared.' Brock continued his contemplation of the paintings.

'And that has something to do with the crimes?'

Brock didn't answer.

Beaufort said, 'Have you any idea who killed Betty Zielinski?'

Brock said, 'Buffet went terribly out of fashion, didn't he? After being so popular. Do you think he's coming back?'

'If he is,' Sir Jack said acidly, 'then it's more than can be said of you, Chief Inspector. If you ever want to speak to me again, please make an appointment through my secretary to see me at my office, not at my home. Good-bye.'

As Brock strolled through the front door he heard the faint cry of Beaufort's wife, 'Is that you, Jack? There's someone waiting to see you in the living room. I can't remember his name.'

The phone was ringing when Brock opened his front door that night, and kept ringing until he climbed the stairs to the living room and picked it up.

'Hello?'

'Why don't you have an answering machine?'

'Must have switched it off. Who is this?'

'You know damn well who it is! Your mobile was switched off too.'

'Yes, sorry, sir.'

Commander Sharpe audibly controlled his irritation with a hissing intake of breath. 'Well, mine wasn't, and I've just had the deputy assistant commissioner, Special Operations, on the phone. His wasn't either, and he'd just had the assistant commissioner on his phone, who'd just had a call from the deputy commissioner on his. Tell me there's been some terrible misunderstanding, Brock. Tell me you didn't go to the home of Sir Jack Beaufort this evening.'

'I did.'

Silence, then a wondering voice. 'Why? Whatever possessed you?'

'We've been interviewing everyone who bought paintings from Betty Zielinski. He was one among several.'

'You behaved in a threatening manner.'

'No I didn't.'

'His wife was extremely upset.'

'Rubbish. Did he say that?'

'*Just listen.* If it weren't that he insisted otherwise, you'd have been suspended from this inquiry faster than a duck's fart. Dear God, I always thought you were reasonably intelligent! What on earth did you hope to achieve? Were you so desperate to retire? You have just done more than any single individual to end our chances of survival. *Congratulations.*'

The line clicked dead.

Almost immediately it began to ring again. This time it was Suzanne's voice. 'David? Thank goodness, I haven't been able to get through.'

'Are you all right?'

'Yes. I'm at the travel agent. Look, there are two seats left on a flight leaving two weeks tomorrow—the evening of Friday the seventh. They may be the last available.'

'Take them,' he said.

'You're sure?'

'Yes, we're going.'

19

THE FIRST SCHOOL parties arrived at The Pie Factory the following morning, Friday the twenty-fourth of October. As she came through the square after the morning briefing, Kathy saw the three coaches parked on West Terrace and the children in uniform forming queues at the entrance to the gallery. What surprised her were the distances they had come; judging by the company addresses on the coaches, they were from Birmingham, Bristol and Leicester. Curious, she followed one of the lines into the gallery. These were senior students, she saw, in well-organised study groups, with notebooks, cameras and sketchpads. The teachers were handing out study notes and question-and-answer sheets, and were carrying files of reference material. As they reached the gallery foyer, Kathy saw that Fergus Tait had set an entrance fee, which was new, and had lavish catalogues for sale, as well as *No Trace* and 'Gabriel' T-shirts that were selling fast.

The cluster of girls in front of Kathy were clearly excited by their first glimpse of the artist through the front window, and were talking about him in pop-star terms, text-messaging their friends with the news. When they got inside the girls hurried over to join the ranks of teenagers around the glass cube gawping in at Rudd, who ignored them, head down over his computer screen. Some of the girls were flirtatiously trying to attract his attention, while the boys hung back, smirking and muttering comments. One was on his knees, tapping the glass and calling,

'Dave, Dave.' Then teachers appeared, briskly separating the mob into manageable groups and leading them away.

Kathy went first to speak to the computer operators, who confirmed that there had been no further messages from LSterne and that they hadn't been able to find any earlier references to the name.

'This is quite a circus, isn't it?' Kathy said.

'Oh yes, and it's going to get worse. There are art societies and tourist groups booked in for the weekend, and more schools next week. It's becoming difficult to work, but that's all part of the deal, apparently. We are the artwork.' The woman laughed and returned to her keyboard.

Kathy moved over to the banners, curious to hear what was being said about them. A fierce grey-haired woman was challenging her group to interpret the images on the tenth banner. 'The badger, here at the bottom, what could that represent?'

Silence, a snigger from a gangling boy.

'Martin? What do you know about badgers?'

'They're extinct,' he offered.

'No they're not, they are endangered, which is relevant. What else?'

'They like the dark,' someone said.

'Fierce.'

'Secretive.'

'Vegetarian.'

'No,' the teacher corrected again. 'They do eat mice and young rabbits actually, as well as eggs and roots. They are in fact omnivorous, which could also be relevant. So we have endangered, nocturnal, fierce, secretive and omnivorous. So what could it be a symbol of?'

A willowy girl said, 'The spirit of the artist.'

'Excellent, Angela! The spirit of the artist!'

'She got that off the web,' someone muttered sourly.

'And also,' the willowy girl continued confidently, 'the badger's head is basically white, well, with black stripes. But white really, like . . .' she lowered her voice to a reverent hush, as if the artist on the other side of the room might be listening, 'Gabriel Rudd.'

'Ye-es,' the teacher said uncertainly.

'Which is a sign of shock and terror and loss . . . loss of life, loss of colour.'

'Ah yes.' Like many of her colleagues, the teacher was carrying a large loose-leaf file, Kathy noticed, subdivided into sections by coloured sheets. She thumbed through this for a moment, then said, 'Perhaps you should explain that, Angela.'

'Gabriel Rudd lost the colour in his hair after the tragic suicide of his wife, five years ago.'

'My dad says that's impossible,' someone objected, and Kathy had a sudden glimpse of the case being discussed over dinner tables and pub counters all over the country.

'But there was a precedent, wasn't there? Who remembers what I told you in class last week? Someone other than Angela.'

Silence, then a voice, '*The Night-Mare*, miss.'

'Which was . . .?'

'The picture he won the Turner Prize with.'

'Yes, but which was also . . .?'

'Based on a painting by someone else.'

'Called . . .?'

Silence.

'Henry . . .?'

Nobody remembered, and she was forced to complete the name herself. 'Fuseli, whose hair turned white as a result of a fever he caught in Rome, remember?'

'What about the murder, miss?' someone urged, and there was a general muttering of enthusiasm. The teacher relented, and they moved on to banner eleven.

'This has got everything, hasn't it?' a woman at Kathy's elbow said. 'Are you from Leicester?'

'No, London.'

'Ah. I'm from Bristol.'

'You must have had an early start this morning.'

'God, yes. But they've been pestering us for days, and with the murder yesterday . . . Our Head thought we should seize the moment. It's not every day the whole school's demanding to go on an art excursion. And it's perfect, really—being able to see the artist actually doing it, the work in progress, the workshops where the banners are being made, and hopefully a glimpse of the actual crime scenes, at least the outside of the houses. They even hope that they might catch sight of the murderer, lurking about in the square somewhere. I just feel sorry for the police— if they don't catch the bastard soon, they'll be branded as incompetent, and if they do, everyone'll be disappointed that the show will be over.'

'Yes. Tell me, what are those thick folders that you've got?'

'Our resource folders? They're mainly stuff we've got off the web. Have you seen his site? It's huge. Each section relates to one of the banners, about its symbolism, its references, its stylistic approach and so on. Of course, you don't know how true it is, because people are contributing from all over, both good and bad criticism.'

'Can I see what you've got on the first banner?'

The woman showed her. 'Anything in particular?'

'That image of the figure holding the child's hand.'

They thumbed through the pages, then the teacher said, 'Here it is. "On the lower left side is a haunting image of the lost child being led away by a sinister dark figure into a tunnel." That's all.'

'Nothing on the source of the image?'

'No, must be just the artist's imagination. Poor bloke.'

As Kathy turned to leave, the computer operator she'd spoken to earlier called out to her. 'Is your name Kathy? I've got an email for you.'

'For me?' Kathy read the page she was handed. It came from Gabriel Rudd and said, *Hi. Back again? Anything you want to know? Gabriel.*

Kathy looked back at the cube and saw him watching her, a little smile on his face. 'Can I reply?' she asked.

'Sure. You want to type it?'

'Just say, *Where's Stan Dodworth?*'

The reply came back after a few minutes. *Sorry, can't help.* She looked back at the cube, but a fresh horde of school children was blocking the view.

It was time to go, she knew, though she would have liked to stay. She was beginning to find Northcote Square addictive, but Brock had given her an assignment, and she had to return to Queen Anne's Gate to follow it up, because he was insistent that no one at Shoreditch should get wind of it. He'd remembered that she had a friend in Criminal Records, now the National Identification Service, didn't she? She told him that she did, Nicole Palmer, a good friend. And would Nicole Palmer do a favour for her, a discreet favour, possibly entailing unpaid overtime that Brock might repay in the form of theatre tickets or some liquid refreshment of some kind? It was quite possible, Kathy said, wondering why Brock wasn't using the numerous contacts he himself must have in the NIS. A computer check, but possibly, he wasn't sure, requiring a manual search—tedious, certainly. Theatre tickets *and* a case of bubbly. Maybe even a modest pre-theatre meal for two. What did Kathy think? Kathy asked who the target was. A certain judge, Brock said. He was interested to know if this man, let's call him Q, had ever presided over a trial or appeal involving any of the people of interest to them in their present investigations. But no one else must hear of Nicole's discreet inquiries, and above all there must be no mention of Brock or SO1. Definitely a pre-theatre meal as well, Kathy said, and not too modest.

The teacher's assessment of the significance of what was happening at Northcote Square seemed to be confirmed by the commentators in the Sunday papers two days later. What had started out for some as a self-indulgent exercise in dubious taste had now been transformed into a statement on art and life as significant as, according to one excited reviewer, Picasso's *Guernica,* or Andy Warhol's Marilyn Monroe paintings. There was speculation that, taken as a whole, *The No-Trace Project,* as people now seemed to be calling it, had become too big and too important even for the premier contemporary art prizes, such as the Turner Prize and the Beck's Futures award. Questions were being asked as to what should happen to the work when it was completed. There was speculation that Fergus Tait intended to auction the banners individually, something that would result in the whole set being fragmented and dispersed, number one to Los Angeles, perhaps, number two to Bilbao, and so on. This would surely be intolerable. There was call for a public subscription fund to keep the work together and in the UK, preferably at Tate Modern.

Kathy yawned as she read this and took another sip of the coffee she'd made. She was in her office at Queen Anne's Gate, where she came when she wasn't required at Shoreditch or elsewhere. Since that Monday morning two weeks ago when the case had begun she'd barely had a day off. It didn't seem right with Tracey still missing. She looked again at the girl's picture pinned to the screen behind her desk. Today she had been searching Gabriel Rudd's Web site for some clue as to the connections or references that Brock had suggested must lie in the style of Betty's murder. The trouble was that the material in the site really was as extensive as the teacher had said, and there were endless references to the work of other artists, from Giotto to Koons.

She needed help. She picked up the phone and rang Bren's home number. Deanne answered, the sound of children's voices in the background.

'Hi, Deanne, it's Kathy. Is this a bad time?'

'No, it's fine, Kathy. How are you? I'll get Bren.'

'It's you I wanted to speak to, if you've got five minutes.' She explained her problem.

'How about Fuseli?' Deanne said.

'Yes, you mentioned him before, but I can't find any references to him in connection with the work Gabe's doing at the moment. What made you suggest him? Didn't you say that the image of the little girl being led off by a stranger was his? Because there's no reference to that on the Web site.'

'Well . . .' Deanne hesitated. 'I just assumed it was Fuseli, because of the melodramatic style. I mentioned him because he inspired Rudd's last really successful show, *The Night-Mare,* and because he seemed to consciously model himself on Fuseli—brooding, eccentric, a bit violent and wild.'

'I heard someone mention that Fuseli's hair turned prematurely white, like Rudd's.'

'Really? I didn't know that. Well, there you are.'

'But I don't know that this has anything to do with Rudd's sources. It might be Stan Dodworth's that I should be looking at.'

'Oh . . . I'd have to think about that. Goya? Maybe Giacometti . . .'

'Oh dear.' Kathy groaned, feeling the ground sliding out from under her again.

'Tell you what,' Deanne said. 'I have to go to the university library this afternoon. Why don't I get some books for you to look at? That might give you some ideas. Are you free tonight? Come and have dinner with us and we can talk about it.'

After another fruitless day, the idea of spending the evening soaking in the warm tub of the Gurneys' domesticity seemed quite appealing, although Kathy almost changed her mind as she heard the sounds of squealing children through the front door. They were overtired and ready for bed, and after greeting the older two and handing over the colouring books she'd brought, Kathy kissed them goodnight and Bren coaxed them away. He was immensely patient and gentle with them, so huge and protective alongside their little figures that Kathy was touched with a sense of sadness and loss that she couldn't quite pin down.

Deanne was in the living room, about to feed the youngest girl, Rachel. At six months, Rachel was just beginning to appreciate her mother's fine art books, one of which she was trying to get into her mouth. Deanne whisked it away, wiped it with a kitchen towel and substituted her breast.

'Sorry, Kathy. You know how it is. There's a bottle of wine on the sideboard next to the books I got you. You can set the table if you feel like it. The stuff's on the tray. Dinner's nearly ready. How was your day?'

'Useless. I achieved nothing.' She began laying out the knives and forks.

'Oh dear. Mine was much the same.'

'Well, at least at the end of it you can say you filled a small stomach.'

Deanne gave her a curious look. 'Not envious, are you? Take her, she's yours. Let me have her back in a year or two.' She shifted the baby across to the other breast. 'I've been trying to think about your problem, but I couldn't come up with anything brilliant. I'm not sure I really understand what you're looking for.'

'Me neither. It's just that there were some odd things about the way the body of the murdered woman in the basement was treated.'

'Yes, I talked to Bren about that—the electric torture. It's disgusting. The only artistic allusions I could come up with were Andy Warhol's images of the electric chair, and a man called Leon Golub did some creepy paintings in the eighties of people being interrogated and burned with cigarette ends. Dodworth went to art school, didn't he? I suppose he'd have come across those. Was he a smoker?'

'I don't know.' Kathy thought back to the foetid atmosphere in his room, but couldn't recall the smell of tobacco smoke. 'I don't think so.'

'Well, maybe he substituted electric burns for cigarette burns.'

'There was the blindfold as well, that was put on after she was dead.'

'Yes, that *is* weird. That didn't ring any bells at all.'

Kathy finished setting the table and, picking up her glass of wine, came and sat opposite the mother and child.

'I'm sorry I never got in touch with you when you broke up with Leon,' Deanne said. 'I wanted to, but I didn't know what to say. I suppose I've forgotten what it's like. You were together for quite a while, weren't you?'

'He lived with me for six months.'

'I think that's a good way of putting it. More independent than saying you were living with him, or you were living together . . . So you've got over it?'

'Mm,' Kathy replied vaguely. Deanne was talking about it as if it were the subject of one of her master's assignments, something remote and academic that happened to other people. Seeing her there with her baby, her third baby, so pinkly fecund, Kathy hoped she would never have to make the sympathy call to her; *You've lost him, he's gone.*

'Well, try the books, anyway. You never know, something may strike a chord. It happens to me sometimes when I'm stuck for ideas—the pictures get my imagination going again. Maybe, when this case is over, you should take a holiday. You're looking tired.'

'Me? Not me. Hell, look at you and Bren. I don't have babies crying through the night.'

They both laughed.

Later, lying alone in her bed, Kathy thought about their conversation. They were about the same age, she and Deanne, and had known each other, through Bren, for some years, but tonight they had felt like strangers. She didn't mind being alone, she told herself, tucked up in a warm bed with a good book. Well, the book wasn't very gripping, as it happened—a thick biography of Henry Fuseli—and she was struggling to stay awake. She decided to focus on the illustrations, but didn't find them very inspiring either, scenes of posturing characters from mythology and Shakespeare . . . Feeling herself dozing, she sighed and turned to switch out the light, barely noticing the illustration in front of her as she closed the book, *Justice and Liberty Hanged, while Voltaire Rides Monster Humanity and Jean-Jacques Rousseau Takes his Measure.* It showed two eccentric eighteenth-century gentlemen, one sitting on the back of a crouching man and, in the background, not one but two figures hanging from a gallows, hands tied behind their backs, one of them blindfolded.

20

GABRIEL RUDD TOOK three sleeping pills that Sunday night, then switched off the lights inside his glass cube and lay down on the camp bed, wrapping the black duvet around him. The rest of the gallery lights had long been extinguished, and the last curious faces had disappeared from the gallery window. After a while, the tartan blanket on the floor began to stir and a nose emerged, sniffing the air. A head followed, white with two strong black stripes running back over the eyes to the ears, then finally, the coast being clear, the full yard-length of Dave the badger appeared. Following the clever nose, he made his way to the corner of the cube where two dishes had been set out for him, one containing Perrier water and the other an artfully arranged confection of egg, rabbit and fresh vegetables prepared by the Tait's second chef, another cousin of the Fikret family. Dave made short work of his meal, left a compensating deposit beside the empty plates and set off to explore his prison. Dave would have been able to see through the glass walls that another banner had been added since the previous night, making fourteen now in all, like ghosts suspended in the light seeping in through the window from the street. The latest one featured two huge mug shots, Abbott and Wylie. Gabriel Rudd heard Dave's snuffling progress, the soft scrape of his claws on the polished timber floor, just before sleep came.

The artist slept very soundly that night, on account of the pills. When he awoke, he blinked his eyes open briefly and was aware of the pale grey of dawn in the sky in the upper part of the gallery window, though the street lights were still on. He closed his eyes and pulled the duvet over his head again and, as he always did, examined whatever was in his brain for clues to his work for the day, a fragment of a dream, a pungent smell of animal droppings, a memory of getting up on winter mornings to go to school—any of these might spark a thought about the colour, texture or theme for the next banner. They were going well, he knew it in his gut, but he was conscious that as time went on people's interest might begin to fade, the number of hits on his Web site might begin to drop off. How long could he keep it going? What for number fifteen? Something vertical, something dark, something harsh, shocking. He opened his eyes and peered out at the phalanx of pale ghosts beyond the glass. One . . . two . . . three . . . *They work,* he thought, *they bloody well work! . . .* seven . . . eight . . . nine . . . *Nothing quite like this has ever been done before . . .* thirteen . . . fourteen . . . fifteen. He blinked and stared, for there it was, at the end of the line, number fifteen materialised—vertical, dark, and most definitely shocking. A suspended figure, motionless on the rope by which it was hanged from the roof truss. He thought they seemed familiar; the shaved head, the black T-shirt and jeans, the big clumsy feet.

At least, that was the way Gabriel Rudd later described it to the police. The shock of discovering Stan Dodworth hanging there in the gallery had driven him out of his glass cube for the first time in eight days. After checking that the body was real, he'd rushed out to the corridor that led to Fergus Tait's elegant apartment at the back of the building and hammered on the door, rousing Tait from his bed. The two of them had returned to the gallery, where Tait had rung triple-nine.

Brock was crouching beneath the dangling feet, carefully examining the floor and the chair standing nearby, when Kathy arrived. She took in the limp figure, the thoughtful expression frozen on the sallow face as if surprised that death wasn't quite what he'd expected, and she felt a sudden jolt of recognition—two hanged figures, one blindfolded, both with hands tied behind their backs, in this case with a loose cord.

Brock looked up, shook his head. 'I'd have said suicide this time, if it weren't for the tied wrists.' He spoke quietly, not wanting to be overheard by the others moving around nearby—the photographers setting up, and beyond them two men erecting a screen against the gallery window, across which a new graffiti message had appeared during the night, '*this too*'.

He straightened upright with a grunt and pointed at the man's throat. 'Nice clean rope burn, livid edge. Ah . . .' Brock's voice returned to normal volume as he saw the medical examiner arrive with a crime scene team. He went over to brief them while Kathy remained with Stan's body, studying the fingernails, the shoes, the knot that had been used to secure the free end of the rope to the leg of a nearby table loaded with computer equipment. Out of the corner of her eye she saw two men sitting together by the open door of the glass cube. Fergus Tait, in a green dressing gown and leather slippers, looked bemused; the other man, Gabriel Rudd, wore a long overcoat, feet bare, and was drawing in a sketchpad on his lap. They both looked up as Brock approached with one of the SOCO team, and again Kathy was startled to see how gaunt and hollow-eyed Rudd had become. They appeared surprised as Brock explained something to them and the officer began examining their clothing. Theatrically, Rudd placed his sketchbook on the floor and raised his hands to be checked and have fingernail scrapings taken. As Kathy went over to hear what they had to say she saw that the drawing he'd been making was of Stan.

'Did either of you touch the body?' Brock asked.

'I did,' Rudd said. 'I gave him a pinch just to make sure he wasn't one of his own sculptures. Funny, he seemed less real than they do. He was stone cold.'

'I touched him too,' Tait said. 'I thought I'd better try to find out if he was actually dead. I mean, there seemed little doubt, but I tried to find a pulse anyway, in the wrist, and then,' he gave a grimace, 'in the throat. Nothing. If I hadn't been so sure he was gone, I'd have cut him down, but I thought I'd better not. I mean, it's not a situation I'm used to dealing with.'

He sounded shaken, unlike Rudd, who had shifted his attention back to the corpse, narrowing his eyes, leaning his head from side to side as if mentally composing the image on a banner.

'How did you reach up to the throat?' Brock asked Tait.

'I stood on the chair. It was lying on its side beside his feet. I'm sorry, perhaps I shouldn't have touched it, but . . .'

'That's all right. Did either of you disturb anything else?'

They shook their heads.

'What about the cord around his wrists?'

'I don't think I touched it,' Rudd said, and Tait said, 'Oh, I probably did when I was looking for a pulse. That's what really shook me up—I mean, it couldn't have been suicide, could it?'

'And you have absolutely no recollection of any noise during the night?'

They shook their heads.

'One other thing before I let you get dressed,' Brock said. 'Who's spraying these messages on your building?'

'I've no idea,' Tait said. 'But he's a bloody pest. It's not just this building, several others in the square have been done over the past three or four months. "Property is theft" on the building site, adolescent stuff like that.'

Suddenly Rudd exclaimed and made a move towards the cube, but the SOCO put a restraining hand on his arm. 'Where's Dave?' Rudd said, and pointed at the tartan blanket lying flat on the floor. 'Where's my badger?'

Brock nodded to the officer to have a look. He made a quick search and shook his head. Dave, it seemed, had done a bunk.

Soon the photographers were finished and Dr Mehta arrived. The body was lowered onto a plastic sheet on the ground and the doctors conferred on body and air temperatures and the state of rigor. Mehta finally offered Brock a preliminary estimate of time of death—between two and five in the morning. 'I won't be sure until I get him on the table,' he added, 'but there's something odd about that cord on his wrists. It's quite loosely tied and I can't see any bruising underneath. It almost looks as if it was applied post-mortem.'

'Like Betty Zielinski's blindfold,' Brock said. 'And make sure they take care with his clothing and shoes, Sundeep. I'm very interested in where he's been for the past week.'

The body was removed along with everyone else except the SOCO team, which continued its painstaking search of the gallery and hallway outside. Elsewhere in The Pie Factory detectives were working from room to room, establishing who was present, and taking statements and swabs for aerosol paint traces on hands and clothes.

On the way back to the station, Kathy mentioned the engraving in the book Deanne had given her. 'I barely noticed it just before I fell asleep, but I registered the two hanging figures. Then I arrive here this morning and find a second hanging. It made me think.'

'Fuseli, you say?'

'Yes. You remember he was Rudd's inspiration for *The Night-Mare* after Rudd's wife died.'

'Mm, but still, it seems a bit obscure.'

'I wouldn't have made much of it if it hadn't been that one of the figures in the book was blindfolded—"Justice", I suppose—and they both had their hands tied behind their backs, as if they'd been executed.'

'Meaning?'

'If Rudd studied Fuseli's work, he might be expected to recognise the allusion. Poppy said that Betty's murder was a warning to Stan Dodworth, and maybe it was. Now Stan's death may be a warning to Gabriel Rudd. It's almost as if they're being stalked in turn, the artists in Northcote Square.'

'Betty wasn't an artist,' Brock objected, 'and we don't know that Stan was murdered.'

'Betty was an artist's model and someone tied Stan's wrists,' Kathy countered.

Brock obviously wasn't convinced, but he said, 'All right, why don't you discuss the two hanged figures with Rudd, see what he makes of it . . . Justice,' he pondered. 'Any word from your friend Nicole?'

'Not yet. She said it might take a few days if she couldn't do it openly.'

They reached the room at Shoreditch station where the team was assembling, and whiteboards and display panels were being cleaned off to make space for information on the new case. As the meeting progressed, Kathy began to understand Brock's reluctance to make much of the Fuseli illustration, for it soon became apparent that he had ideas of his own—ideas which, Kathy had to admit, made a lot more practical sense.

One thing that the hunt for Tracey had revealed was that Robert Wylie had a wide network of acquaintances, many of whom proved extremely reluctant to provide information about his business affairs to the police. He had an office in a run-down building on an industrial estate, and in it they had found a notebook of telephone numbers, some with a private four-letter code identifying their owners. It didn't take long to work out that this comprised the first four letters of their names written in reverse. Thus MMOS turned out to be disgraced vice squad detective Richard Sommersby, and OXID was an Inland Revenue tax inspector by the name of Jeffery Dixon, both of whom denied any knowledge of Wylie. Several phone numbers were believed to belong to serious criminals, members of crime syndicates, while many other names and numbers hadn't yet been deciphered.

As Brock and his detectives went over the recent events, it was clear that Brock saw this circle of Wylie's contacts as being related to his refusal to talk to the police. 'It's as if he knows he can expect help,' he said.

'He'd need divine intervention to get him out of the hole he's in,' someone suggested, but Bren had seen where Brock was going.

'You think they're getting rid of witnesses?'

'It's possible. Suppose Betty saw something. And suppose Stan Dodworth, through his association with Abbott, knew something.'

There was a sudden hush as they thought about that.

'If that was the way of it, it's just possible that Betty or Stan might have told someone else what they knew. Who would they be likely to tell, Kathy?'

Kathy thought. 'Betty knew Reg Gilbey well, and Stan was dependent on Fergus Tait, but I don't know if they were the sort of people they would confide a secret to. They were both pretty friendly with Poppy Wilkes.'

'Right. We'll speak to them all again. Of course, the same thing will have occurred to the killers. Maybe they persuaded Betty or Stan to tell them who else knew whatever they did.'

The team meeting was almost over, Brock giving a dutiful warning to make every effort to avoid antagonising Sir Jack Beaufort should he be encountered, when Kathy was asked to take an urgent phone call. It came from Poppy Wilkes.

'Can I see you?' the artist asked, her voice anxious.

'Yes. I'm at Shoreditch police station. Do you want to come here?'

'I'm with Gabe, at his house, and I don't want to leave him alone. Could you come to us?'

'He's left the gallery then, has he?'

'Yeah, it's not safe for him there now. *Please,* I wouldn't ask if it wasn't important.'

'That's all right, I'll come over straightaway.'

'Thanks, thanks . . .' There was a muffled thump, as if she'd dropped the phone.

It was only a ten-minute walk, but a patrol car was leaving as she stepped outside so she asked them to drop her off at Northcote Square. Traffic was heavy and as they crawled along the two officers chatted to her about the case.

'That Wylie bloke's a slippery customer,' the driver said. 'I pulled him over once, years ago, for going through a red light. I could tell something wasn't right about him, the way he was sweating. I got him to open his boot and it was full of dirty magazines, kiddie porn, you wouldn't believe. But he managed to wriggle out of it. Claimed he didn't know it was there. There was something else in the boot, too—a pair of handcuffs.'

'Straight up!' the other cop said. 'My missus has a friend whose cousin lives in that block in the Newman estate. She says everyone knew Abbott was weird. Is it right he worked in a mortuary?'

Kathy said yes.

'Only she said there was a rumour that he kept his mum's body in his flat after she died.'

'Don't quote me,' Kathy said, 'but yes, he did. We found it up there.'

'She says nobody knows much about Wylie though. Hardly ever saw him.'

They arrived at last at Northcote Square, to find it jammed with media and police vehicles.

'It didn't take them long to find out, did it?' Kathy said.

'It was on the eight o'clock news this morning,' the driver said. 'They quoted a spokesman for the gallery.'

Fergus Tait, Kathy thought, he never misses a trick.

She thanked them and ran across to 53 Urma Street and rang the bell. It was some time before the intercom beside the door crackled and a cautious female voice asked, 'Yes?'

'It's me, Poppy, Kathy Kolla from the police.'

'I'll come down and let you in,' the voice whispered. 'Wait a minute.'

She opened the door with a furtive look around the square, then led Kathy to the big living area upstairs where Gabe was sprawled out on one of the sofas, white curls against white leather. He lifted a hand in a lazy greeting and rearranged his long limbs to let Poppy sit by his side.

'It was my idea to come here,' Poppy said. 'Gabe thinks I'm overreacting, but I'm not. He's in danger, Kathy, I'm sure of it now, after what happened to Stan.'

'What makes you think that?' Kathy took a seat facing them. The room had a musty, unaired smell, and there was a pile of unwashed dishes on the kitchen bench top.

'Stan was killed more or less in front of Gabe. It's a warning that he's next.'

'Come on, Poppy,' Gabe said. 'That doesn't follow.'

'Whoever's doing this is insane,' Poppy insisted, becoming more agitated. 'They hate you—they took Tracey, didn't they? I think they hate all of us here in the square. I think it's a deliberate campaign against us, and you're the most famous, the most obvious target.'

'You mean it's an art critic?' Gabe laughed, but there was no humour in his voice.

'In a way, yes!' Poppy grabbed the sleeve of his shirt, sounding shrill. 'You can laugh, but you know there are thousands of people who hate what we do and the publicity we get for it. They say we just rip the public off, playing with pretentious ideas about life and death that we've got no right to. Well I think one of them's decided to make us face life and death for real, just like those messages on the walls say.'

Gabe looked at her with concern. 'But what about Betty?' he said soothingly. 'She wasn't one of us.'

'Yeah, I know.' Poppy hesitated, pulling away from his attempt to stroke her hair. 'But there is somebody who hates us *and* Betty.'

'Who's that?'

'Think about it, Gabe.'

He did, but clearly had no idea what she was talking about. She shot a quick glance at Kathy who also looked blank, then she said fiercely, 'Reg Gilbey.'

'Old Reg!' Gabe burst out laughing.

'You know Reg detests what we do! He says we're self-indulgent children who make a mockery of everything he loves and has devoted his life to—he used those very words to me once. He said we're poisoning the well that artists have been drinking from for thousands of years.'

'Did he really say that? That's rather good.' Gabe smiled to himself, turning the phrase over in his mind.

'He meant it too. And he also got seriously mad with Betty. I don't know why she couldn't stand him, but she did everything she could to get up his nose. She used to call him "the monster next door".'

'Yes, granted . . .' Gabe frowned, more serious now as he considered it. 'But still, old Reg? Anyway, how could he have tracked Stan down when nobody else could find him?'

'I wouldn't be surprised if he was hiding him all this time.' She turned to Kathy. 'Did you lot search Reg's house after Stan disappeared?'

'No, we had no reason to. But were they friends?'

'Not friends, no, but they did drink together sometimes in The Daughters of Albion. After he'd had a few Reg'd tease Stan, call him "my friend, Auguste" after Rodin, or "my old mate, Benvenuto"—as in Cellini, you know—or one of the other great sculptors. Stan would just take the joke and say "all right, Pablo" and let Reg buy him another drink. I used to wonder about it.'

'Look,' Kathy said, 'this really is just guesswork, isn't it? You don't have anything solid against Reg Gilbey, do you?'

'Maybe not,' Poppy conceded, 'but I still say Gabe's in danger.'

'Okay, I don't rule that out, or that you could be too, Poppy, come to that. Look at it another way. If Betty's and Stan's deaths are related to Tracey's abduction, could it be because they knew something that the abductor is trying to hide?'

'But you've caught him, haven't you?'

'We don't have any direct proof that the man we arrested, Robert Wylie, took Tracey.'

'And maybe there are others you haven't caught yet,' Gabe said, voice flat and forlorn. Poppy instinctively put out a hand to clutch his arm.

'That's right,' Kathy said. 'You told me, Poppy, that Stan had hinted to you that the people who took Tracey had a friend in the square, do you remember?'

Poppy nodded.

'Is there anything else that Stan or Betty said to either of you that could help us? I want you to think back over your conversations with them, especially in the last couple of months. Do it carefully, remembering each time, and writing down as much as you can remember. Will you do that? It could be important.'

Poppy nodded but Gabe looked doubtful.

'Yes, we will,' Poppy said. 'Won't we, Gabe?' She got a half-hearted nod. 'And in return, will you give us protection? I've tried to persuade Gabe to leave London, but he says he has to stay for the work.'

'You know I do, babe,' he murmured. 'This is the most important thing I've ever done.'

'I'll talk to my boss and see what can be arranged,' Kathy said. 'There is one other thing. It may not mean anything . . . Do you have a book about Henry Fuseli's work here, Gabe?'

He looked startled. 'What do you know about him?'

'Only that you used one of his paintings as inspiration for *The Night-Mare.*'

'You *have* been doing your homework, haven't you, Sergeant Kolla?'

There was something about the playful way he said this, almost flirtatious, that registered in Poppy's eyes. 'I'll get it,' she said sharply, and got to her feet. She pulled a thick volume from the bookshelves and brought it to Kathy, letting it drop on her lap. It wasn't the same book that Kathy had been looking at the previous night but if anything it seemed more comprehensive. She turned the pages of the early chapters until she found the picture, and was aware of Gabe's eyes on her all the time.

'There . . .' She handed the open book across to him. 'You see the two figures in the background, Justice and Liberty? Both have their hands tied behind their backs, and one is blindfolded. Like Betty and Stan.'

Gabe took a long look, then gave a low whistle. 'I'd forgotten this one. How did you find it?' He stared at Kathy.

'Just looking for clues.'

'Well, I'm amazed, Kathy, really,' Gabe said. 'That's inspired, it really is. But I always knew you were the bright one, didn't I? Do you remember, that first time we met? I told you the others were hopeless.' The respect and interest in Gabe's voice, together with what now looked like jealousy on Poppy's face, caught Kathy unawares, and she felt an embarrassing blush grow in her cheek.

'But how could this have anything to do with what happened?' Poppy's voice cut in. 'I mean, it's odd I suppose, but so what?'

'Don't be dumb, love.' Now it was Poppy's pale face that flushed at Gabe's words. 'You think someone might have arranged things as a message to me, Kathy?'

'Yes, that's what I thought.'

'Assuming that I'd be bright enough to remember my own sources, which it so happens I wasn't. Well, that is intriguing, isn't it? In fact it's bloody scary when you think about it, because frankly, I'm the only one around who's quoting from Fuseli. I should have spotted it straight away. I do thank you, Kathy. I really do.'

Kathy shrugged, avoiding his eyes. He was playing some game with Poppy, she felt sure, deliberately provoking her, and doing it very successfully.

But he was stroking the page of the book now, his thoughts moving on. 'I'll have to use this, Kathy, for the work, the next banner, you know that, don't you? And I will acknowledge you—not like the last time, but discreetly, so you aren't embarrassed. And when it's hanging in the big hall in Tate Modern, you'll be able to point it out to your friends. "See?" you'll say, "I helped make the first friggin' masterpiece of the twenty-first century."'

He laughed, and Poppy, unable to take any more of this, got to her feet and stomped off to the kitchen bench, where she began noisily loading the dishwasher.

21

BROCK AGREED TO Kathy's suggestion to place an armed police officer in Gabriel Rudd's house, at least for a day or two, and Fergus Tait put out a press and web statement saying that, in view of the dangerous events that had occurred in Northcote Square, he had insisted that the artist go into hiding at an undisclosed location where he could continue his work undisturbed. Poppy remained with him in the house.

Dr Mehta was in his office when Brock and Kathy arrived at the mortuary. While Kathy chatted to the photographer outside, the pathologist explained to Brock his tactics for survival in a work environment where everyone else was so much younger than he was.

'The vital thing is to give absolutely no indication that you were around in the sixties and seventies, Brock, otherwise you're finished. So when someone asks about something that happened then, you simply look blank, as if to say, "How should I know?" '

'I'll bear that in mind, Sundeep.'

'You do that, old chap. Even the early eighties is prehistory to some of the kids I work with now.'

Like the man himself in life, Stan Dodworth's remains were remarkable for having little to say. They bore no wounds or bruises, no signs of constraint apart from the single rope mark to the throat.

'I'd say it was a straightforward hanging suicide,' Dr Mehta concluded from his external examination, 'apart from two things. One, the cord tied around his wrists, almost certainly after death. And two, the dirt on his hands.'

'What about it?'

'There isn't any!' Mehta gave his comic magician's smile.

'How do you mean?' Brock asked patiently, well used to Mehta's ways.

'Just look at the rope he was hanged by. It's filthy, encrusted with a grey dust that I'll bet this month's salary is cement or plaster from a building site. It's come off on his neck and on his scalp, but there's none on his hands. I've taken swabs, but, unless somebody washed his hands afterwards, I'd say he never carried that rope, or rigged up the noose. I think someone else did that, and placed it around his neck.'

'You think he cooperated in this?'

'Well, there's no sign of coercion. None at all.'

'He was obsessed with death,' Kathy said quietly, almost to herself.

Later Mehta established that Stan had eaten a final meal of roast beef, peas and boiled potato approximately seven hours before his death. There were also traces of a grey putty or clay embedded in the soles of his shoes, which were sent off for analysis.

Within an hour, Yasher Fikret was complaining once again at having his building site closed down for another police search, which yielded nothing.

While that was going on, Kathy returned to 53 Urma Street, on the north side of the square. The uniformed cop who let her in had nothing to report. She went up to the living room where Poppy was reading a newspaper.

'Where's Gabe?' Kathy asked.

Poppy paused a moment before replying. 'Upstairs, in his studio.' She didn't sound happy to see Kathy, who had gone over to the kitchen, now clear of dirty dishes.

'Those things you were washing up, Poppy . . .'

'What about them?'

'Were they recently dirtied?'

'How should I know? Anyway, how could they be? No one's been here for a week.'

'Could you tell what the meal was?'

'What?' She looked at Kathy as if she were mad. 'No, I wasn't that interested, actually.'

Kathy was now examining the rubbish bin under the sink. 'Okay, thanks.' She smiled at Poppy and made for the stairs. 'See you later.'

In the dustbin in the backyard Kathy found week-old newspapers on top of plastic bags containing what was obviously old debris. She peeled off her gloves and made her way over to the lane behind West Terrace. Police were standing at the far end where the building site was being searched, but Kathy was interested in the dustbin standing beside Reg Gilbey's back gate. She lifted the lid and peered in at the plastic bag on top. Its neck was loosely tied, but through a hole she was able to see the packaging for a microwave dinner. She could just see an illustration, of potatoes, peas and sliced roast beef. She closed the lid and went down the lane to find a SOCO.

The call from the solicitor at the Crown Prosecution Service suggesting an urgent conference had left Brock puzzled, but he'd agreed to meet her during the lunchbreak of the trial she was involved in at the Old Bailey, at what she said was her favourite pub, The Seven Stars, just behind the Royal Courts of Justice. He found her perched at a narrow table against the window of the little pub, which was crowded. Some of the customers looked like lawyers and officials from the Law Courts, others like lecturers from the nearby London School of Economics.

Virginia Ashe was small, neat and ferociously bright. Through her narrow glasses she regarded Brock squeezing his way between the tables, and pronounced judgement as he eased into the chair. 'You look worn out.'

'Thanks. I see you're as indomitable as ever.'

'It must be this *awful* case of yours.' The relish with which she said it made him smile.

'Tell me you're not about to make it worse.'

'Order lunch first. The food here is fabulous. I think you need a square meal—try the steak and kidney pudding.'

'Fine.'

Virginia Ashe called, 'Roxy!' across the room, and from behind the bar an attractive dark-haired woman with bright lipstick looked her way. 'Yes, he will!' the solicitor cried, and the woman nodded and waved acknowledgement.

'Wylie's made a statement,' Ashe said, 'through his solicitor.'

Brock's fist clenched. 'When did this happen?'

'An hour ago. They phoned me from the office and gave me the gist. I'll have to give you a proper assessment, but I thought I should speak to you straight away. There'll be a copy of his statement waiting for you at Queen Anne's Gate—oh, wonderful!'

Roxy had appeared at their side with two glasses of cognac. 'She said you'd be needing this,' she murmured to Brock. 'Cheers, darlings.'

They lifted their glasses and Brock let the burn subside in his throat before speaking. 'Go on, Virginia.'

'He claims that he knows nothing about the abductions of Aimee and Lee, and had no idea that Abbott was using his wife's flat, although he had given Abbott a key to keep an eye on it for him.'

'What?' Brock was incredulous.

'Yes, I know. He claims he hadn't been there for several months. He was living in his office on an industrial estate, because of some dispute over the tenancy of the flat with the wife, though he admits he was paying the rent. He provides her current name and whereabouts. Apparently she's living with another man in the Midlands.'

'What was he doing in the flat when we caught him then?'

'He claims he went there because Abbott had phoned him earlier in the day and asked to meet him that evening for a drink.'

'Yes, we traced that call. Abbott made it soon after my people visited him the first time.'

'When he got to the estate he discovered that Abbott was dead. He went to his flat and found all that stuff inside, and claims he was as surprised as the police when you discovered Lee in the cupboard.'

'Rubbish. Why did he wait ten days to tell us this?'

'His statement doesn't explain that. No doubt they'll come up with something. Why did he?'

'Because the last person who could disprove it was found hanged last night.' Brock told her what had happened.

'My God. He was murdered?'

'Maybe, or assisted suicide.' Brock stared at his glass, surprised to see it empty. He had anticipated a number of possible strategies from Wylie to mitigate his guilt, but not outright denial. 'They must be confident they can pull it off.'

'Yes. I don't think I like this, Brock. There were no photographs of him with the girls, were there?'

'No, he was the photographer.'

'And the camera and computer equipment were stolen property and can't be linked to him.'

'Not so far.'

'And no change to Lee?'

'No, still in a coma. But we know she recognised him in that flat. Her eyes were only open for a few seconds, but she was terrified when she saw Wylie.'

'Yes, but that will work against us. If she regains consciousness and identifies him, they'll claim she's confusing the memory of having seen him that night.'

They were both silent for a time, thinking, then Virginia said, 'No, I don't like this. Why did they send his statement to us, and not to the police? It was my boss who phoned me about it. He told me to be very careful to get this one right. What did he mean? When I asked him, he made some lame remark about just doing my usual excellent job.'

Brock didn't reply. Finally he said, 'Have you come across a judge called Sir Jack Beaufort?'

'Jugular Jack? Yes, of course. Appeared before him a few times in my youth. Why?'

'Any rumours?'

'Only that he's got a savage tongue. What kind of rumours?'

'No, nothing, Virginia. Forget I mentioned it. So, where do we go from here?'

'You get us some hard evidence to pin Wylie down. Otherwise . . .' she shrugged, '. . . we're just not going to be able to proceed against him.'

Their food arrived, the best pub food in London, but Brock didn't taste a thing.

When he returned to Shoreditch he found the copy of Wylie's statement waiting for him. He summoned Bren urgently and sat down to study it. Bren was stunned by Brock's account of his meeting with the Crown Prosecutor.

'That's impossible! We found him in the flat, with the victim.'

Brock handed him Wylie's statement and watched his face fall as he read it.

'He can't get away with this. It's preposterous!'

'Virginia Ashe thinks he can.'

'His fingerprints were everywhere.'

'He says he had a good look around before we found him. He's thought it through, Bren. It does kind of fit with the evidence we have. We'll have to speak to his wife, of course, but presumably he's confident about what she'll say. What have we really got to tie Abbott and Wylie together, in that flat?'

'You think Dodworth saw them together?'

'That would explain the timing of this, wouldn't it?'

Bren pondered. 'We found the shop that supplied the batteries in the camera. The assistant thinks he might recognise Wylie.'

'That would help,' Brock said, but they both knew it was thin. 'There is one other avenue. Wylie claimed that Abbott must have destroyed his own hard drive in the microwave, but the smell of burnt plastic in the flat was fresh, and Wylie's own computer is missing, supposedly stolen.'

'Emails,' Bren said. 'Yes, we thought of that, but it didn't seem a priority to find out.'

'Until now . . .' Brock said.

Kathy was sitting in the central gardens of Northcote Square eating a sandwich bought from Sonia Fikret, whose mood had been markedly less accommodating than before, no doubt to indicate that the family's patience was running out over the continual police harassment at the building site. Kathy finished the sandwich and shook the crumbs from the paper bag. Immediately a sparrow swooped down to the gravel at her feet and began pecking.

'Ah, you miss Betty,' Kathy said. The gardens seemed bereft without her, the last of the leaves suddenly fallen as if in grief and the birds all gone except for this one scruffy little sparrow.

Her phone warbled in the pocket of her coat, and she wasn't surprised to hear the voice of Bev Nolan. She sounded older, a quaver in her voice.

'Kathy? I am sorry to bother you. I know you must be so busy. Do you have a moment?'

'Of course, Bev. How can I help?'

'I suppose I shouldn't ask, but we've just been so upset about these terrible things happening in Northcote Square. We only just heard on the news about Stan Dodworth. They mentioned suicide, is that right? I mean, did he leave a note? Did it have anything to do with little Tracey? Could he have . . .'

'I'm afraid there's not much I can tell you at the moment, Bev. We haven't found a confession, if that's what you were thinking, and we don't know if it has anything to do with Tracey, but you can be sure that we will get to the bottom of it.'

'Of course you will. We just . . .' She seemed lost for words. 'The poor man. He was always polite when we met him, but very quiet. I felt Tracey didn't . . . No, I shouldn't say that.'

'Go on,' Kathy coaxed.

'Tracey seemed very nervous around him. Maybe it was his manner. His appearance too, all dressed in black, his head shaved like a convict. But he wouldn't have killed himself because of Tracey, would he?'

She appeared to need reassurance on this. Kathy said, 'We've got no evidence of that, Bev.'

'I see, yes. Thank you, dear. I am sorry to have bothered you.'

'If we get any firm news about Tracey, I will phone you, I promise.'

Kathy rang off and saw that the sparrow had gone.

The laboratory liaison officer had encouraging news. The frozen dinner packet that Kathy had spotted in Reg Gilbey's dustbin had once contained a meal very close to, perhaps identical with, that found in Stan's stomach.

'Perhaps?' Brock pressed.

'They're doing chemical tests for additives, but even if they're identical, it won't prove that his food came from that particular packet. But we will be able to trace the shop where the packet came from.'

'Fingerprints? DNA?'

'No, we couldn't find either in the rubbish, I'm afraid. But there was a pear, half eaten, in the same plastic bag as the meal packet. They've made a cast of the teeth marks and the forensic odontologist over at London Hospital Medical College is preparing a mould to test against Dodworth's teeth. The trouble is, the pear was bitten into about forty-eight hours ago, and the flesh has lost some of its crispness. He's not sure if he'll be able to make a certain match.'

'Was there anything else in the bag containing the meal packet and the pear that we can definitely link to Reg Gilbey?'

The LO handed Brock the list of items: the plastic food tray from the meal, food scrapings, banana peel, stale bread, a wad of plastic film, a screwed-up paper bag, two crumpled beer cans. Brock shook his head, disappointed. 'He'll be able to claim anyone could have dropped it into his bin.'

'Fraid so.'

'Still, it should be enough for a search warrant.'

The timing was bad, no doubt about it. Bren's knock on the door was answered by DI Tom Reeves, whose eyebrows rose at the sight of all those police officers. Kathy realised what his presence meant, but she didn't have a chance to warn Bren as he and two others charged on up the stairs. After the others filed past Reeves, who held the door open for them like an ironic butler, Kathy said, 'I take it the judge is upstairs.'

At that moment there came a roar of anger from above, and Reeves said, 'Yes, I think we can assume that. Mind telling me what's going on?'

'We found some stuff in Reg's dustbin that links him to Dodworth, the bloke we were looking for who was found hanged this morning.'

Reeves looked puzzled. 'Meaning what, precisely?'

'That's what we're here to find out.'

'I take it your guvnor knows about this raid?'

'Of course.'

'I mean, he ordered it, right?'

'What are you getting at?'

'Kathy, a little bit of advice? Beaufort was steaming mad when I drove him over here. You know how shook up old Reg was after the woman next door was found. He's been refusing to get on with the judge's portrait, says his hands are shaking too much. Then this business in the gallery. It was all we could do to get him going today. But that wasn't the only thing making the judge see red. He was also mad about you lot, and especially your guvnor.'

'Why?'

'Because he thinks he's stuffing up this whole case . . .'

'No!'

'. . . and because of that stunt your guvnor pulled last week.' He saw the incomprehension on Kathy's face. 'You don't know about that? DCI Brock paid the judge a visit at his home last week and tried to intimidate him and his missus.'

'Oh come on, Tom, that's bullshit. Why would Brock do that?'

'Because he knows what Beaufort's got in store for SO1, and he's trying to use this case to get at him. That's why you're here now.'

'No, it's just an accident we came when you and the judge were here.'

'That's not the point, Kathy. By the time you're finished with Reg he won't be painting for weeks, and Sir Jack's moment of fame at the National Portrait Gallery will be stuffed. Listen, believe me or not, but do yourself a favour—get yourself off this case and distance yourself from Brock. He's finished.'

Kathy sat in the back seat with Reg Gilbey for the trip back to Shoreditch station. He looked stunned, hands trembling, and Kathy could believe Reeves's predictions about the effect on his painting.

'Don't worry, Reg,' she whispered. 'It won't take long, then you can get back and have a drop of Teachers.'

He shot her a panic-stricken look, his jaw clamped so tightly shut it looked as if his teeth might crack. Kathy wondered if they'd be taking a cast of them too.

When they got to the station Reg was led away to an interview room. Brock met Kathy at the door. 'Any problems?'

'Only that Sir Jack Beaufort was there, having a sitting for his portrait. He was mad with Bren for interrupting.'

Kathy knew every shade of expression on Brock's face, and recognised the neutral screen that seemed to slip across his eyes.

'Mm. Oh well.'

'His minder had a word with me. Apparently Sir Jack isn't happy with us. He told me that you paid the judge a visit last week.'

'Did he now? Well, let's get on, shall we? I think I'll do this with one of the Hackney lads, Kathy. You might like to observe, and tell us what you think.'

He left her standing in the corridor, puzzled. She turned back to the room with the monitors for recording the interviews and took a seat.

The Hackney detective was grim-faced as he led the questioning, while Brock was distant in his manner, as if he didn't much care what Reg had to say. The detective began with a formal caution. It was hard to tell if the painter understood; he looked as if he were about to be hauled away to the scaffold.

'Do you like fruit, Mr Gilbey?'

The absurdity of the question startled Reg out of his paralysis. The stare he gave the detective seemed to harden into focus. 'What?'

'Simple question. Do you like fruit?'

'Not particularly.'

'Apples, oranges, pears? When was the last time you had a piece of fruit?'

'Are you serious?'

'Perfectly. It's not a trick question. When was the last time you ate an apple or a pear, say?'

Reg turned to look at Brock, searching his face for some acknowledgement of the madness of this, but Brock just stared impassively back.

'Well?'

'I don't know. Not this week . . . Not last week. Why?'

'We found a half-eaten pear in your dustbin.'

Kathy could see the bewilderment grow on the painter's face. This is Kafka, it said, this is Lewis Carroll. 'Is that an offence now, then?'

'Who ate it?'

'I haven't the faintest idea. It wasn't me.' A bit of colour was returning to his cheeks, some spirit to his voice. 'Why, was it a *police* pear? Was it an *undercover* pear?'

Brock's voice broke in sharply. 'When did you last see Stan Dodworth, Mr Gilbey?'

'Stan?' Reg was bewildered again, trying to follow this jump. 'Stan? Not since he disappeared. The week before last . . .' His voice trailed off as he saw Brock shaking his head.

'No. Think very carefully before you answer. When did you last see Stan Dodworth? It was last night, wasn't it?'

'Last night? No, no. Who says so?'

Brock suddenly reached into his briefcase and produced the frozen meal packet inside a plastic pouch. 'You recognise this, don't you?'

To Kathy, watching Reg's image on the screen, it didn't look as if he did.

'No.'

'This was the last meal Stan Dodworth ate before he died last night. It was found in your backyard, in your dustbin, in the same plastic bag as the pear.'

Enlightenment seemed to come at last to Reg Gilbey. 'Ahhh . . .' he sighed, and sat back in his chair. 'You think . . . But you see, you've got it all wrong. I've never seen that before in my life, nor the pear. Someone must have put the bag in my bin, mustn't they?'

'Why would they do that?'

'To get rid of it, I suppose.'

'But why in *your* bin? No suggestions? Then we'll go back to the beginning and start again. Where did you buy the pear?'

Kathy watched Brock grind away at Gilbey for another forty minutes without result. As the time passed, and Reg realised that Brock genuinely didn't believe him, his confidence seemed to drain away again.

He became querulous and indignant, then more and more subdued, just shaking his head as he finally seemed to run out of words altogether.

It was at that point that Bren came into the room where Kathy was sitting. 'How's it going?' he said.

'Nothing. How about you?'

'No, we haven't found any sign of Dodworth in Gilbey's house. They're still collecting fibre samples, but there was nothing obvious. I'd better let the old man know.'

In the break that followed, Kathy continued watching the screen as Gilbey accepted a mug of tea and lifted it with both trembling hands to his mouth. She got up and found Brock and Bren, deep in conversation. 'Can I have a go?' she said.

They looked at her in surprise, then Brock shrugged and said, 'Be my guest, Kathy. Give him ten minutes to think about things first, eh?'

'Yes.'

She got herself a mug of tea and after a while took it in to the interview room with her, together with a uniformed woman officer, who remained by the door.

'I suppose you're going to be nice to me, are you?' Gilbey said.

'If I can.'

He heaved a deep sigh. 'That boss of yours isn't very nice, is he? I thought he seemed a decent bloke when I met him before.'

'Tracey's been missing for two weeks, Reg. DCI Brock'll do whatever's necessary to get her back.'

'Yes, yes, I know . . . It's just not very pleasant to be on the receiving end. It's not like on TV. I feel . . . gutted.' Another deep sigh. 'No chance of a smoke, I suppose?'

'I think this is a smoke-free workplace, Reg.'

'Gawd help us. Well, he's wrong about me hiding Stan.'

'Is he?'

'Anyone could have put that bag in my bin. Maybe the builders. Stan might have been hiding in one of their buildings.'

'We looked.'

'Yes, I suppose you did. I feel bad about Tracey too, you know.'

'She was a very pretty little girl, wasn't she?'

Reg looked wary. 'True.'

'Did you paint her at all?'

'I'm not Renoir. Pretty little girls aren't what I paint.'

'But you did paint the children in the playground, didn't you?'

'That's different, a pattern of shapes, light and shade.'

'That's probably what Renoir said.'

'Maybe he did, I wouldn't know. But if you're trying to suggest I'm a pervert, you're wrong.'

'Did she ever come to your house?'

Kathy caught a flicker of perturbation in Reg's eye that would never have registered on the monitor. He hesitated, and to Kathy's mind it seemed as if he was calculating the odds of getting away with something.

'Betty brought her up to my studio once. She wanted to show the girl that portrait I did of her as a young woman.'

'Did she stay long?'

'A while . . . She liked the smell and the feel of the oil paint I was using. Her father and those other so-called artist friends of his don't use oil paint any more. I gave her a brush and a small canvas to muck about on. A self-portrait, looking in the mirror, all blonde hair and blue eyes.'

Of course, Kathy thought, the little painting Betty had shown her. And now it occurred to her that she hadn't noticed it in Betty's house after her death.

'Did she come again?'

'Em, yes . . . she came one other time. That's all.'

'And was Betty there?'

Reg held Kathy's eye so steadily that she was certain he was about to lie. 'Yes.'

Kathy reached for her mug of tea, letting Reg study the puzzled look on her face. 'You couldn't be getting mixed up about that, could you, Reg? About Betty being there?'

'She was there,' he insisted, pressing his thumbnail so hard into a finger that the flesh went white.

Lying but also telling the truth, Kathy thought. 'For part of the time,' she prompted.

He looked startled. 'Ah . . . you may be right. I'm not sure.'

'When was this?'

'A couple of months ago. Look, you're barking up the wrong tree. It was all perfectly straightforward and innocent.'

'Then there's no need to be secretive, is there? I need to know all about that visit, Reg.'

'I'm not sure I can remember.' He was speaking more slowly, trying to give himself time.

'Yes you can,' Kathy said briskly. 'It was a weekday?'

'Um . . . yes.'

'Afternoon?'

'Yes.'

'Well, come on, there was a knock at the door . . .'

Reg was staring at Kathy as if she must be reading his mind. 'She was standing on the doorstep.'

'Alone.'

'Yes. She wanted to finish her self-portrait.'

'So you took her upstairs . . .'

'To the studio, yes. She sat down in front of the mirror and got on with her painting. It was a warm afternoon. The window was open, sun shining on the trees of the gardens . . .'

'She'd want your advice,' Kathy cut in gently. 'She'd want you to hold her hand, show her how to put the paint on.'

'No! She was quite confident, didn't need my help. I got on with my own work. We hardly exchanged a word.' Gilbey came to a stop.

'Go on, what happened then?'

'There was another ring at the front door. It was Sir Jack, for a sitting. His driver had dropped him off and gone to find a parking space. I took him upstairs and introduced him to Tracey, and he admired her painting.'

'What did he say, exactly?'

'I don't really remember. I think he said it was very lifelike.'

'Was she pleased at being praised?'

'Yes, of course. She was proud of it.'

'So she smiled and flashed her big blue eyes.'

'You make it sound indecent.'

'I'm just trying to get the picture. What happened then?'

'Em . . . the doorbell rang again. I thought it was Sir Jack's bodyguard, but it was Betty. She . . .' Reg hesitated, frowned.

'Come on, Reg.'

'Well, you know what she was like, flying off the handle for no reason. She'd been in the gardens, feeding her birds, and she'd seen Tracey up in my window. She blew her top, thought I'd kidnapped her or something. She marched in screaming blue murder and charged up the stairs.'

'So while this was going on, Sir Jack was upstairs alone with Tracey.'

'Yes.'

'What happened next?'

'Betty flew into the studio and grabbed Tracey. When I got there she had her arms around the girl, abusing Sir Jack. It took Tracey to calm her down. She told Betty she was fine, and showed her the painting she'd done, then she and Betty left. Tracey never came to my house again.'

'Why didn't you tell us about this before, Reg?'

'Why would I? It wouldn't help you find Tracey and it was just embarrassing for me. You were bound to put the worst construction on it, just as he said.'

'Who said?'

'Sir Jack. When we heard about Tracey being abducted, he suggested I'd be wise not to mention being alone in the house with her that day. He said he knew how the police mind works, and he was right, wasn't he?'

'Let me get this straight; Sir Jack Beaufort suggested that you lie to us.'

'Not lie, no! Just not mention Tracey's visit that day. I mean, it wasn't significant. But I didn't lie, and now you've asked me point-blank, well, I've told the truth, haven't I?'

'I hope so, Reg. You see, the way the police mind works, if a witness misleads you once, they're never really trustworthy again. Now, you and Sir Jack might keep quiet about being alone with Tracey, but what about Betty? Weren't you worried that she'd tell people?'

'I made it up to her, took her some flowers, and Tracey had reassured her.'

'All the same, she was a loose cannon, wasn't she? She used to call you "the monster next door".'

'People didn't take her seriously.'

'No, that's right. That was your salvation, wasn't it? All right, let's talk about Stan Dodworth.'

'I told you, I didn't shelter him. I didn't see him.' There was an edge of panic in his voice now as he realised that Kathy was leading him from one victim to the next.

'But you were good mates, weren't you? Drinking buddies.'

'No! You're wrong. We had nothing in common. I couldn't stand the man.'

'That's not what I hear, Reg. I hear you used to buy him drinks, have long conversations.'

'Look, I may have bought him the odd drink. He looked so bloody pathetic sitting there in The Daughters, talking to nobody, muttering to himself. When I've had a few I tend to be magnanimous—ask anybody.'

'So you met Stan regularly in the pub.'

'Not regularly, no. Frankly, there was no point. We had nothing in common. I hated his work and he had no conversation.'

'He must have talked about something. Didn't he tell you about his work, his methods?'

'Not really. I wasn't interested. Too grotesque for my taste.'

'Didn't he tell you where he got his models from?'

'Models?'

'For his sculptures.'

'No, can't say he did. Why, where did they come from?'

'From a mortuary.'

'Ugh.' Gilbey made a face of disgust.

'Rembrandt did that too, didn't he?'

'Rembrandt wasn't obsessed by death.'

'So Stan talked about death, did he?'

'A bit.' Then something struck Gilbey. He stared off into space, thinking.

'What is it?'

'I just remembered the last time I saw Stan. It was in The Daughters, a couple of nights after Tracey disappeared. He was particularly gloomy, even by his own low standards. He asked me if I thought children felt death more keenly, being newer to life.'

'What did you say to that?'

'I told him to bugger off. Look, I don't think I can take any more of this. I'm not feeling well. I want to stop now.'

'All right, Reg. If you think of anything else we might want to hear about, you'll let us know, won't you? Incidentally, what happened to Tracey's self-portrait?'

'Eh?' He thought for a moment and then said, 'Betty took it with her when she and Tracey left. She told me later that Tracey gave it to her as a present.'

'Well, it's not in Betty's house now.'

He shrugged. 'I don't know where it is.'

Afterwards Brock looked pleased. 'Well done, Kathy. You did well.'

'Thanks,' she smiled back but felt uneasy. 'What he said about the judge advising him to keep quiet . . . well, it doesn't really mean anything, does it? It's the sort of advice you might give a friend.'

'Yes, but it had the effect of protecting him as much as Reg, didn't it?'

When Brock had gone, Kathy said to Bren, 'He seems to have it in for the judge, doesn't he? I hope he knows what he's doing.'

'Judge or not, he's as accountable as everyone else.'

'Yes and no. You know this new review of Special Operations that's under way?'

Bren rolled his eyes. 'Another one?'

'Yes, and Sir Jack is the chair of the review committee.'

'Really? Brock never mentioned that to me.'

'No. We're not supposed to know. Senior management only.'

'And Brock knows?'

'Oh yes.'

'So . . . it's like the judge is investigating us while we're investigating him.'

'Mm.'

'Tricky.'

Kathy was working late that evening when the call came from Nicole Palmer. She listened carefully, taking notes, then thanked her and rang off. She thought for a moment, then tapped out Brock's home number.

'You owe someone some theatre tickets,' she said.

'Ah. Where are you?'

'Shoreditch.'

'Still? Can you talk?'

'Not really.'

'Have you eaten? I've got a nice steak here, if you're interested. Or I could come to you.'

'Steak sounds fine.'

It took her the best part of an hour by the time she'd caught the tube across the river, then waited for a connection on the surface electric rail at Elephant and Castle to continue south. She walked down the high street, almost deserted in the cold night, and turned into the arched entrance to a cobbled courtyard. A big old horse chestnut tree stood in the far corner, brown conker shells scattered on the ground beneath its branches, and beyond it the beginning of a lane, with a hedge on one side and a row of old brick houses on the other. Kathy rang the bell and after a moment Brock opened the door and ushered her in.

'I'm sorry,' Brock said when they reached the living room on the next floor, taking her coat, 'I should have come back up to town, or waited till tomorrow.'

'No, it's better done tonight, away from everybody. Unless your house is bugged.'

'I shouldn't think so.'

'Are you sure? He's got Special Branch protecting him, remember.'

Brock looked to see if she was serious, and saw she was. 'Well, that is a nasty thought.'

He watched her reach into her shoulder bag and pull out a folded sheet of paper, which she handed to him without a word. It read, 'Robert John Wylie appeared before Justice John Beaufort in May 1996 in the company of three other defendants on a variety of charges under the *Sexual Offences Act 1956,* the *Obscene Publications Act 1959* and the *Indecency with Children Act 1960.* The judge dismissed the case against Wylie. The other defendants went on to trial, were found guilty and received sentences of between three and six years. They are known to us as business associates of Wylie.'

Brock looked up with a grim smile. 'Well done, Kathy. Now, let's do something about that steak, shall we?'

22

BROCK WATCHED SEVERAL rooks burst cawing from the copse on the hilltop as three men appeared over the rise. They made their way steadily down the slope, towing their equipment behind them, untroubled by the fine rain. Coming to a stop, the leading figure, wearing a red tartan peaked cap, drew a weapon from his bag. It flashed through the air and for a moment all three men stared motionless at the sky. Then a white ball landed with a plop on the green in front of where Brock was sheltering, and came rapidly to a stop on the wet grass, barely a yard from the pin with its soggy red flag. A muted cheer went up from the distant group.

They noticed Brock watching them, of course, as they converged on the green, for they were all observant men, and when he moved out from beneath the eaves of the clubhouse to intercept them on the path they each gripped the handles of their clubs a little tighter, out of habit.

'Roy?' Brock asked, and the one with the red tartan cap peered at him more closely before exclaiming, 'Brock? Why yes, it's young David Brock!'

They all shook hands and proceeded together to the clubhouse door. Later, showered, changed and seated around a table in the bar, the three retired police officers seemed keen to hear about Brock's current case, but when he began to describe how it had turned into one of those difficult ones, a sticker, he sensed their interest fade to polite indifference.

'Frankly, I don't know how I ever had the time to work,' one said, and the others nodded sagely. 'I'm so busy, I just don't know where the time goes, the days, the months, the years . . . I've got six grandchildren now. Do you want to see their photos?'

'Roy,' another remonstrated, 'he hasn't got time for that; the man's working. Although I can't imagine why. You'll be entitled to your two-thirds pension aren't you, Brock? Why do you bother? There's another life out there.'

'Actually, I came about one of your cases, Roy,' Brock managed to get in.

'Course you did. Robert Wylie, right? You've finally got him for a big one. Knew it would happen eventually. Slippery customer. I almost had him in ninety-six.'

'That's the case I'm interested in. Before Justice Beaufort.'

'Old Jugular, that's right. He threw it out. I got the other three bastards though.'

'Was he right to throw it out?'

'Well, I didn't think so, of course, but the CPS had warned me. They really didn't want to proceed against him on the basis of what we had, but I was so revved up to get that slimy bastard—too keen, in retrospect.'

'So Beaufort acted fairly?'

The three golfers stared at Brock. 'That's an interesting question,' Roy said. 'Are you after Jugular Jack now?'

'I've got nothing specific, but Beaufort's appeared on the sidelines in this case—not really involved, you understand, but it did seem a coincidence, remembering your experience.'

'You've got a good memory,' Roy said, with a quizzical smile at Brock, 'because that case wouldn't be on Wylie's record, would it, what with him having got off scot-free?'

'I was hoping your memory would be pretty good too, Roy.'

'Well now . . . I do recall something one of my snouts said to me after that case. He said that he'd heard Wylie bragging that he'd had influence with the judge. I didn't believe it, and still don't. Not Jugular Jack, the scourge of scum like Wylie.'

'He didn't say what kind of influence?'

'No, nothing specific. One thing I will say, though—if you're after old Jugular, you might be well advised to check out your pension entitlements.'

'Thanks, Roy. Now, let me buy you gentlemen another shandy.'

Kathy had seen Brock like this before—secretive, unwilling to share what he was thinking or planning concerning the ex-judge. And because she had seen it before, she thought she knew the reason. It was protection, not for himself but for the rest of them, in case things went wrong. It was a measure of how risky he knew the enterprise to be, like a bomb-disposal expert ordering his colleagues out of range of the volatile thing he was probing. But it was a dangerous manoeuvre, separating himself from the support of the team, keeping them in the dark. She felt instinctively that it was wrong and wanted to circumvent it, which of course was precisely why Brock felt obliged to act the way he did. That morning, for example, with the press office clamouring on one phone and Commander Sharpe's office on the other, no one seemed to know where he'd gone, off on some mysterious trail apparent only to himself.

All she could do was try to find grist for his private mill—facts, observations, or failing that rumour and gossip. So she had come back to the source once again, Northcote Square, where everyone was connected to everyone else by invisible threads of history or loss, business or desire. On the north side, on Urma Street, she could see the light shining through the glass wall of Gabe's studio on the top floor, where he and Poppy had spent the night together in the foldout bed. She knew this because the duty sergeant had told her that their police bodyguard had said as much in his morning report. It must have been a great relief for them both after Gabe's idiotic vigil in the glass cube, Kathy thought with a touch of envy. If she turned one hundred and eighty degrees she could see the cube illuminated through the gallery window, with its untidy workstation and crumpled bed still as they were when abandoned twenty-four hours before, like a shrine for pilgrims, to judge by the queue waiting along the footpath outside.

But she planned to begin elsewhere, at Betty's house on West Terrace, for which she had signed out the keys. She started in the attic at the top of the house and worked carefully down through each room, each closet, each cupboard and drawer. She was looking for Tracey's self-portrait, and it took her two hours to work her way down to the basement floor. Along the way she had uncovered glimpses of Betty's life—a photograph of her husband, Harry, in army officer's uniform, an ancient West End theatre program for *Irma La Douce,* a snapshot of 'Helga's children at Broadstairs, 1963'—but no sign of what she was looking for.

She stepped out into the tiny sunken courtyard beneath the footpath on West Terrace, remembering that she hadn't searched the kitchen on the floor above, and climbed the stairs back up to the front door. As she opened it she glanced up at the projecting bay window beneath the turret on Reg Gilbey's house next door and saw a figure staring down at her. With a sense of apprehension she recognised the judge. She walked quickly into Betty's hall and closed the door behind her, wondering what excuse she could use to bump into DI Reeves again, who was no doubt sitting on the other side of the wall in Gilbey's kitchen at that moment, reading one of his books. She turned this over in her mind as she began searching the kitchen cupboards. Then the phone on the little mahogany table in Betty's hall began to ring, and when she picked it up she was startled to hear his voice.

'DS Kolla? It's Tom Reeves. I'm next door as it happens, with the judge, completing the session with Mr Gilbey that was interrupted yesterday. He wonders if you'd care to pop over for a cup of coffee in, say, half an hour?'

'Reg Gilbey?'

'No, Sir Jack Beaufort.'

'Oh . . . well, yes.'

She replaced the phone, astonished. For a moment she wondered if she should contact Brock, then decided against it.

Brock took his seat in the same prison interview room as before. Wylie and his solicitor came in, and he looked at them carefully as they took their seats, trying to interpret their moods. Unlike the lawyer, who seemed preoccupied and agitated, Wylie looked casual, sitting back in his chair, arms folded. But he was paler than the previous time, hair lank, eyes puffy, as if he wasn't sleeping so well, and there was the trace of what might have been a bruise on the side of his head.

The solicitor glanced anxiously at his watch and said, 'I was reluctant to agree to this meeting, Chief Inspector, given that my client will be released today, but he felt we should hear you out. You've read his statement, I take it? I really don't think there's anything we can add.'

'I'm sorry to hear that,' Brock said. 'I thought I should give Mr Wylie one last opportunity before we proceed to court.'

The lawyer frowned. 'To court? If you're thinking of pressing some lesser charge in the Magistrates' Court . . .'

'Magistrates' Court?' Brock looked at him as if he'd made some kind of legal gaffe. 'Murder and abduction have to be tried in the Crown Court, you know that.'

Now the lawyer was incredulous. 'Haven't you spoken to the Crown Prosecution Service? There's no possibility of you proceeding to committal on those charges.'

'Perhaps you misunderstood them. We're not talking about committal, we're talking about a notice of transfer to take the case directly to trial at the Crown Court without committal proceedings taking place. As you would know, we're entitled to do that where violence against children is involved and where, as in this case, a child victim is at risk from your client.' Brock gave him a patient smile. 'Maybe you'd like to explain the legal processes to Mr Wylie.'

'But . . .' The solicitor was perplexed but also wary. He knew Brock was no fool. He scanned his face and saw only confidence. 'You have no evidence. The CPS knows that. You can't go to trial.'

'Well, things are continuously developing, as you well know. Evidence is often buried in shifting sand.' He guessed the metaphor would register. Any lawyer representing Wylie would be painfully conscious of it. 'Mr Wylie's and Mr Abbott's email records, for instance . . .' He deliberately wasn't looking at Wylie as he said it, but he saw an involuntary twitch at the edge of his vision. 'They were lost along with their computers, of course . . .'

The solicitor glanced at his client, whose face was blank, then back at Brock. 'So?'

'But fortunately we can do something about that.'

'How?' Wylie couldn't help blurting out the question.

Brock turned to look at him as if for the first time. 'Microsoft keep servers in California which store information on all their email accounts around the world, including a copy of every email that passes through them.'

'You're joking,' Wylie said in disbelief.

His solicitor, who had obviously come across this before, said, 'You'll need a US court order. Have they agreed to release them to you?'

'It's in train. That's why there's been a delay in our proceeding. I'm afraid there's no question of bail, though.' Again he picked up a signal from Wylie, a clenching of fingers. 'As I said, we're convinced that the victim's welfare would be prejudiced.'

'You bastard.' Wylie stared at Brock, his face white, breathing becoming more laboured.

'I'd like some time alone with my client,' the solicitor said, fingering his watch again. 'Two or three minutes?'

'Be my guest,' Brock said. He got to his feet and knocked on the locked door.

Outside, he asked the prison officer to let him use a vacant interview room to make a confidential phone call. He got through to Virginia Ashe and explained what he was doing. She listened without interruption but with several sharp intakes of breath. When he had finished she made her points in the quick, decisive manner of hers.

'One, a notice of transfer has to be served on the court by the Director of Public Prosecutions.'

'You act for him. You can do it.'

'Not on something like this. I'd need approval, which I certainly won't get on the basis of what we currently know. Two, to be valid it must be served *before* the magistrates begin committal proceedings. Now you've disclosed your tactic, Wylie's legal representatives will press for those to begin.'

'You're the lawyer, Virginia. That's your field.'

She sighed. 'Three, since you've disclosed your subpoena for the emails, they will also fight to block their release. Do you know that they contain anything incriminating?'

'I didn't before, but I do now. It was written all over Wylie's face.'

'That's not evidence.'

'Microsoft refer requests from foreign police services to the FBI for approval. It'll be up to them. If there's the faintest hint of violence against children, I'm sure they'll be sympathetic.'

'But why did you warn Wylie of all this?'

'I want to panic him, Virginia. I want him to react before he knows for sure how we stand.'

'His solicitor will be straight onto us. My boss practically promised that Wylie could expect to be out of goal today.'

'That's why I'm ringing you now. I want you to stall them. Talk to Wylie's brief about shifting ground—the poor bloke looks as if he's balancing on a pile of shale. Just play for time. I think gaol is beginning to get to Mr Wylie.'

'I do hope you know what you're doing, Brock.'

'Of course I do, Virginia,' he said, sounding as confident as he could.

As he finished the call his mobile rang. It was Bren, his voice sounding unnatural, tight.

'Chief? We've just heard from the hospital. Lee passed away less than an hour ago.' Then he repeated himself as if he still couldn't come to terms with it. 'She's dead. She never regained consciousness.'

After thirty minutes Kathy rang the bell on Reg Gilbey's front door. It was opened by Tom Reeves. 'Hi.' He grinned at her, winked and nodded back with his head to indicate that they could be overheard. 'Come on in.'

Sir Jack Beaufort was waiting for her in Reg's dining room, sitting on one side of a polished pine dining table. The chair opposite him had been pulled out in preparation for her, and Kathy had the unnerving impression of a courtroom, the judge behind the bench and the witness— or was she the accused?—facing the court for interrogation.

Beaufort rose to his feet and offered his hand across the table, shaking hers briefly and indicating the vacant chair. 'Coffee, Sergeant?' he asked curtly.

'Thanks. Black, no sugar, please.'

'I know,' Reeves said, and left the room.

'He likes you,' Beaufort said. 'He speaks highly of you. That's what persuaded me to speak to you.' He cleared his throat, as if offering Kathy a chance to say something, but she remained silent. His gaze was steady and unblinking, and despite herself she felt intimidated.

'You look uncomfortable,' he said softly. 'Please don't be. I'm not a monster, you know. My colleagues used to call me "Jocular Jack" behind my back, on account of my sense of humour in court.'

'Really?'

'Yes, indeed. Reg Gilbey told me about your interview with him yesterday. He was quite upset about it.'

'I'm sorry.'

'We often forget, don't we, in our line of work, how distressing our ways can seem to the lay public when they experience for the first time what is commonplace to us?'

'I assure you that we complied with the rules laid down in PACE.'

Beaufort waved his hand dismissively. 'I never doubted it. But still, just the idea of being questioned like a criminal would be enough to throw someone like Reg into confusion.'

'He didn't seem confused to me.'

'He's desperately worried that he may have given the impression that he felt guilty, or had something to hide, about the encounter with the Rudd child that he described to you. As he said, I was there that afternoon, and I can assure you that there was absolutely nothing untoward about it. The little girl was perfectly happy and Reg behaved impeccably towards her. That's really what I wanted to tell you. Ah, Tom, well done. Biscuits too!'

Reeves came in with a tray, put it on the table between them and left again. Beaufort fussed over the milk and sugar, humming softly to himself as if content to have completed his business. Kathy watched him, pretty certain that he had not.

'Don't you find police work very stressful, Sergeant?' he asked conversationally.

'It can be, yes.'

'Especially a case like this. The thought of that missing child, the demands on you to come up with a result . . . I imagine the pressure must be almost overwhelming for the person leading the team, the senior investigating officer.'

Brock, Kathy thought, that's what this is about.

'You're SIO's getting on a bit too, for such a role, isn't he?'

'No, I don't think so. The important thing is his experience. That's what gives him the edge. It's what gives Special Operations the edge.'

Beaufort smiled. 'Very loyal, as you should be. But I must confess I'm not convinced. I'm pretty experienced too, at judging men and their patterns of behaviour under stress, and it's my humble opinion that your chief, and perhaps SO1 also, has been overstressed for too long. I would say that he is in the process of having a breakdown.' He held up his hand as Kathy started to protest. 'I know, it's none of my business, and I hope it won't go beyond these four walls. I'm just expressing a personal opinion, and perhaps offering a little insight for you to think about, because I know that, deserved or not, the team tends to be identified with the actions of its leader. Did you know that DCI Brock called at my house recently and behaved in a quite threatening way to my wife and myself?'

Kathy felt a jangle of anxiety.

'Of course, I know of his tremendous professional reputation,' Beaufort went on, 'and I imagine it was an action out of character, born of desperation, no doubt.'

He sipped fastidiously at his coffee and nibbled the corner of a biscuit. 'These are stale. Reg isn't a great one for housekeeping. Why he never married I can't imagine. Hm.' He laid the biscuit and cup to one side. 'There is one other thing that bothers me, Sergeant, and I don't mind if you do pass this on to DCI Brock, if you feel it relevant. The man Wylie you've arrested is known to me. He is an extremely devious and evil character, and I am quite sure he will try to exploit any weakness he perceives in those against him, including offering false information. I should hate to imagine that DCI Brock's opinion of Reg Gilbey, or of me for that matter, would be influenced by a character like that. Have committal proceedings begun?'

'Not yet.'

'Really?' He frowned. 'There's no doubt, I take it, about his guilt?'

'I shouldn't think so.'

'Then the sooner he's put away the better. Well now,' he brushed his fingers together and rose to his feet, 'it's been most pleasant talking to you, Sergeant. I'm obliged to you for giving me your time. Now I'd better return to the master upstairs. You've seen the portrait, haven't you? What do you think of it?'

'It's very strong.'

Beaufort seemed pleased with the reply.

'Did you ever see Tracey again,' Kathy asked, 'after that day she called here?'

'I believe I may have seen her in the square.' His voice had become cool. 'Why do you ask?'

'We ask everyone who may have seen her. Did you notice anyone watching her?'

'Ah, I see. No, I'm afraid I can't recall anything. I wasn't really looking, you see.'

'When would this have been?'

'I'm not sure. Two or three weeks before she disappeared? Now, if you'll excuse me, Tom will see you out.'

While he went back upstairs to the studio, Kathy looked in on Tom Reeves in the kitchen. He put down the book he was reading and closed the door quietly behind her. 'How did it go?'

'All right. I think I got the message.'

'Am I allowed to ask what it was?'

'Lay off Reg Gilbey and beware of my boss. The same message you gave me.'

'Not at his bidding.'

'He happened to mention that he saw Tracey Rudd a couple of times before she disappeared. Do you remember that?'

'No, I'm pretty sure I never saw her. Maybe he bumped into her at the gallery.'

'Why do you say that?'

'Well, I assume Rudd took his kid down there, and the judge calls in now and again.'

'Yes, the owner mentioned he has dinner in the restaurant.'

'And he checks out the exhibitions. He looked in there this morning, as a matter of fact.'

'What, with all those school kids?'

'Yeah.' Reeves laughed. 'He had some bone to pick with the owner. Seemed rather annoyed.'

'Do you know what about?'

'No idea. Why, are you spying on him?'

'Of course not. How's old Reg today?'

'He didn't seem too bad. From the bottles I found in his waste bin I'd say he had a boozy night and it must have restored his spirits. He was ready to get back to work this morning, at any rate.'

'I'd better get going.'

'Okay. You may not be seeing me much longer.'

'Oh. You moving on?'

'Yeah. This job's okay for overtime, but it's dead boring really.'

'What will you do?'

'Back to CID for a spell. Listen, you didn't think I was telling you that stuff because the judge told me to, did you? I mean, he did ask me to pump you about the case, but I said you wouldn't tell me anything anyway.'

'What did he want to know?'

'Oh, who your suspects were for the old lady's murder, and what the pathologist had to say about Dodworth's death.'

'Just out of idle curiosity, do you think?'

'No, he seemed more insistent than that. I assumed he was wanting to reassure Reg.'

'Hm. Well, I'd better go.'

'Listen, if I can help at all . . .' He suddenly seemed embarrassed, and shrugged. 'Whatever.'

Kathy smiled at him, realising she'd be sorry not to bump into him again. 'Thanks. I don't suppose you've come across anyone called L. Sterne, have you, Tom?'

'Lawrence Sterne,' he said immediately. 'Wrote *Tristram Shandy*.'

'When was that?'

'Oh, eighteenth century.'

Like Henry Fuseli, Kathy thought. But that couldn't be it.

'Why? Looking for something to read? Try this.' He handed her the book he'd been reading. She took it and saw from the cover that it was a crime thriller.

'It's good. I've just finished it. I was checking some of the early clues I'd missed.'

'Thanks. I'll try it, when I get some time. Better write your name in it, so I don't steal it.'

He grinned and wrote. Afterwards she saw he'd put his phone number as well as his name.

Brock looked up as the guard tapped on the door. 'Prisoner's ready to see you again, sir.'

'Thanks.' He followed the man down the corridor and waited while he unlocked the door to the interview room. Wylie was sitting alone, looking sullen and thoughtful.

'Where's your lawyer?' Brock asked. It was only on hearing the tightness in his own voice that he realised how much the news of Lee's death had shaken him. He looked down at the pale blob of Wylie's face and felt an overwhelming urge to bury his fist in it. Instead, he was obliged to wheedle and cajole and talk to this monster as if his needs and thoughts were really worthy of consideration.

'I sent Russell out to get some air. He needs to relax more. Sit down, I want to talk to you, off the record.'

Brock knew that he ought to stop this, walk out and calm down, but instead he took the seat. 'I'm listening.'

Wylie waved towards the tape recorder. 'I want that kept off.'

Brock nodded.

'The emails won't help you with the girls. They contain personal stuff, to do with business, that I don't want getting out. That's number one. Number two: I got slapped around last night; they told me it was just the beginning. I know who ordered it. I want out of here. I want the charges dropped or I want bail.'

Brock watched him become more agitated as he spoke, fidgeting with his fingers, tapping his foot beneath the table.

'And in return?'

Wylie leaned across the table and whispered, barely moving his lips, 'I'll give you the judge.'

'For what?'

'He took the girl, the third one, Tracey.'

Brock remained motionless, but inside his chest he felt his heart hammering unnaturally fast. 'Go on.'

Wylie shook his head. 'That's all I'll say. I've got pictures.'

'Who hit you?'

'I got bumped. It was a warning from him, of course. Christ, he killed the old woman, and now this other bloke.'

Brock sat back, wondering if the man's panic was genuine. He was inclined to think it was.

'Well?' Wylie demanded.

'I'll need a lot of convincing. I won't have you released, but I can move you away from here, to somewhere you'll be safe.'

Wylie chewed his lip. 'All right. Do it straightaway. My brief'll contact you after that.'

The girl at the entrance desk of the gallery was distracted by the winding snake of school students when Kathy arrived. 'Sorry,' Kathy said. 'I can see you've got your hands full. I want to see Mr Tait.'

'He's in his office, I think. Do you want me to ring . . .'

'Don't worry, I know where it is.' Kathy smiled brightly and continued past the scrum in the hall down the corridor that led to Fergus Tait's office. She knocked at the door, and Tait opened it. 'Ah, Sergeant, what can I do for you?'

'I'd like to have another look in Stan Dodworth's room, if that's all right.'

'Again? Your people were there yesterday. They have the key.'

'Oh, of course. I should have realised.'

'Not to worry. If you won't get me into trouble, I'll confess that I have a spare. You can use that.'

'Thanks.'

'Are you any closer to some answers, might I ask?'

'There's not a lot I can tell you.'

'Ah, only I paid a visit to Gabe this morning and he's in a bad way. He's worked himself up to such a pitch. I've never seen him so frayed, coming apart at the seams, pale as a ghost. Poppy's very worried about him.'

'I'll go and see them when I've finished here.'

'Today's will be the sixteenth banner. We're running out of space. Don't call me a cynical businessman if I say that it would be a great relief to everyone concerned if you could wind this thing up before too long.'

'We're doing our best.'

'Of course. I'll get you that key.'

While he searched in a drawer of his desk, Kathy said, 'I spoke to Sir Jack Beaufort just now. I believe he was in here earlier, wasn't he? Did you manage to sell him something?'

Tait raised his eyebrows. 'No chance of that. He was mad because I told you about selling him that painting of Betty's. Goodness knows why he was so upset. Told me in no uncertain terms not to gossip about him. Gossip! I ask you.'

'I don't suppose you've ever come across a little oil painting that Tracey Rudd did, have you? A self-portrait.'

Tait looked at her in surprise. 'Tracey? No, I've never heard of that.'

In Stan Dodworth's room she found that the gruesome contents that would be of interest to the coroner had been removed. There seemed little chance that the searchers would have overlooked a painting of a child's face, but Kathy searched anyway, without result. Later, she would check the inventory of items the police had removed, again without finding any reference to it.

23

'HE'S ON SOMETHING, no doubt about it. I'm Colin, by the way.' The officer closed the front door behind Kathy and turned to face her, speaking with voice lowered. He was wearing a protective vest over his uniform shirt and tie, and a 9-mm Browning was holstered on his right hip, yet he looked like a boy, barely old enough to be out of school. 'Doesn't look as if he's slept for days, and he's getting to the jumpy stage, I reckon. I told the lady we should get a doctor to check him, but she said he won't hear of it.'

'Has he been giving you any trouble?'

'No. He stays up on the top floor most of the time, working. At least he's safe up there.'

They climbed up the stairs to the main living floor, where Poppy was sitting by the big windows overlooking the square. 'Hi,' she said. 'I saw you coming.' Her voice sounded distant and vague.

'How are you?' Kathy asked.

'Oh . . . not bad. Bit tired.' She gazed blankly out at the skeletal branches in the gardens silhouetted against the grey sky.

Kathy wondered if this distraction was the result of a night in bed with Gabe, but then noticed the slightly uncoordinated hand movement as the magazine on Poppy's lap slid to the floor. 'Have you been taking medication, Poppy?'

'What?' Poppy slowly turned her head. 'Oh, Gabe gave me something to relax me, that's all. He says I'm too wound up after what's happened. God, you should see him! He's on three packs of fags a day now.'

'Has he been taking pills too?'

'I don't know. Probably. Can't blame him, can you? Poor Stan. Poor Betty. Poor Tracey.' A tear began to trickle down Poppy's pale cheek. 'Gabe says it's finished now, but it isn't, is it?'

'Why don't you lie down and get a bit of sleep?'

'Yes, I might do that.'

'Colin here will help you down the stairs while I talk to Gabe.'

'Right . . . Don't be cross with him about the pills, Kathy. He's doing the best he can. He doesn't show it much, about Trace and everything, but that's just his act.'

'Don't worry.'

Kathy watched the young constable take hold of Poppy's arm and help her to her feet. Her legs seemed rubbery and he had to support her to the stairs.

'Can you manage there, Colin?' Kathy asked, and he grinned and nodded. They disappeared and she took the stairs up to the studio. As she pushed open the door a cloud of cigarette smoke billowed out to meet her. Gabe was on his hands and knees on the floor. He was wearing a stained T-shirt and boxer shorts, bare feet, white curls all over his face, and looked like a shipwrecked soul crawling out of the sea. He lifted his head towards her and stared through red-rimmed eyes without a glimmer of recognition.

'Gabe? It's me, Kathy Kolla, from the police.'

'Oh . . . yeah.' He got laboriously to his feet and pushed the hair out of his eyes. His chest was heaving with quick, shallow breaths. 'Sorry, concentrating.'

Kathy saw that he had been crawling across a long roll of plastic, scribbling red pencil marks on what looked like a draft print of another banner.

'Yesterday's number fifteen. Liberty and Justice, remember?' His words were slightly slurred.

She saw the two figures dangling from a gibbet. 'Yes, I remember. How are you feeling?'

'On fire . . . drowning.'

'You should get some rest. I'm going to call a doctor to look at you.'

'NO!' The sudden violence of his shout made her start. 'I mean, no, please. Maybe tomorrow, but I haven't got time just now. When I've finished this I'll be able to sleep, then everything'll be fine.'

'You sure?'

'Really. Absolutely.' He reached for a mug of something and took a gulp, then for the pack of cigarettes beside it. 'They never found Dave, you know.' He blew smoke.

'Dave?'

'My little badger friend. He scarpered. Sensible bloke.'

'Oh, yes.'

'You think I'm paranoid, don't you? Well, you know what they say— just 'cause you're paranoid doesn't mean the bastards aren't out to get you.' He chuckled at his own joke.

'Why would anyone be out to get you?'

'See! You do think I'm paranoid. They'd be out to get me because I know too much.'

'What do you know?'

'Ah, that's the question.'

'Look, why don't I get you some food. I think you'd feel better.'

He waved a dismissive hand. 'I've eaten. Mrs Fikret brought us stuff.' He glared at an untouched plate of kebabs and vegetables on a table. 'Look, come over here, I wanna show you something you'll like. Come on.'

Kathy followed him over to the plastic on the floor and looked where he was pointing. Beneath the hanged figures was some text: *The Fate of Justice and Liberty, as revealed by KK.*

'There, is that discreet enough for you?'

'Yes, that's just fine, Gabe, thanks.'

'You see? You proved I wasn't being paranoid. It all means something.'

'I think I was wrong about that.' Kathy was regretting telling Gabe her bright idea. 'I'm sure it's just a coincidence.'

'No, no, no. There are no coincidences. Everything means something, if you can just figure it out.'

Later that afternoon, at Shoreditch, Brock called to speak to her. 'I've got a meeting arranged with Wylie's solicitor at six, Kathy. I was wondering if you'd be free to come along too. I may need a witness.'

'Yes, of course. I have to tell you one or two things.'

'Right. His office is south of the river. Can it wait until we drive down there?'

'Fine.' She thought he sounded keyed up.

On the journey she told him about her abortive search for Tracey's self-portrait. 'I just thought, if Stan stole it from Betty's house, and I could have found it among his possessions, it would have given us a firmer link from him to the killing.' She saw that Brock wasn't convinced, but when she mentioned the call to meet with Beaufort he immediately became interested.

'What did he want?'

'To warn us to be careful, I think.'

'Everybody's doing that,' Brock growled under his breath.

'He seemed to want me to pass on to you the idea that Wylie might try to sow suspicion in your mind about him. Is that possible?'

'Could be,' Brock said. 'We'll find out tonight.' Then he gave her an outline of his session with Wylie in the prison. Kathy thought Wylie's claims about the judge were preposterous, and said so.

'Let's wait and see, Kathy,' Brock said. 'Let's just wait and see.'

They stopped on the high street outside a Chinese takeaway. Half a dozen customers stood inside under a blaze of light, waiting for their orders. A nameplate on the doorway next to the shop said, *Russell Clifford, Solicitor*. They went inside and climbed a threadbare stair-carpet to the office above. Clifford's staff, if there were any, had apparently left for the night. He emerged from his room in shirtsleeves, looking as preoccupied as ever, and showed them to an interview room at the back. On the table lay a single large yellow envelope and a notepad.

'I'm acting on my client's instructions, of course,' he said. 'He's asked me to allow you to view the contents of this envelope, but not remove them.'

Brock stared at the envelope. It had a handwritten note on it: *Mr Wylie, Deposit A.*

'Do you know what it contains?' Brock asked.

'No.'

Brock reached for the envelope, unfastened the flap and looked inside. There were a number of photographs, which he shook carefully onto the table without touching. Kathy caught her breath as she made out the first—a picture of Tracey in her school uniform, standing in sunlight in a street. A tall man, Beaufort certainly, was bending to offer her something in his hand. Kathy recognised the corner of The Daughters of Albion in the background. Brock took out his pen and used it to slide the picture aside.

The second photograph showed Beaufort seated in a room. Tracey was sitting on his knee, an arm around his neck, face close to his cheek as if she'd just kissed it or whispered something in his ear. He looked rather surprised, but pleased, too. The light was very bright and clear, and there was no mistaking the two of them, although the background was out of focus. Tracey was wearing what looked like a dressing gown, too large for her, and one leg was exposed to the hip.

Kathy didn't want to see any more. She looked up at the lawyer who was staring fixedly at his framed certificate on the wall, as if using all his willpower to prevent his eyes dropping to the photos.

The third picture seemed to be taken in the same place, but now Tracey was naked. She was kneeling on a table with a fixed, faintly puzzled expression on her face and Beaufort, fully clothed as in the previous picture, was stroking her shoulder. The fourth was shot in a bedroom in poor light. A small naked girl lay beneath a large naked man. Again, Tracey and Beaufort.

Brock peered closely at each in turn for some time before speaking.

'You say you haven't seen these before, Mr Clifford?'

'That's right,' he said, eyes still fixed above their heads. 'Mr Wylie specifically asked me not to. I am simply instructed to make sure you don't remove any. There are four photographs, I understand.'

'No, that won't do. These appear to be material evidence relating to a major crime. I'll have to retain them.'

'But . . .' Clifford started to object, but Brock went on.

'And I want you to look at them so that you can identify them later in court, if asked.'

For a moment it seemed as if Clifford was debating trying to physically retrieve the pictures, then he subsided in his seat and allowed his eyes to drop. Brock turned the photos round, one by one, so that he could see them. With each, the solicitor's worried frown intensified.

'My God,' he whispered. 'That's Sir Jack Beaufort, isn't it?'

'And that's the missing girl, Tracey Rudd. You see why I have to have these, don't you?'

'Mm.' Clifford was chewing his bottom lip. Brock watched him, thinking how different he was to Virginia Ashe. The public prosecutor worked for the state, had a steady flow of work, lots of backup and a regular pay check, and could afford a wry air of clinical detachment. The defence solicitor, on the other hand, had a client who wasn't confiding in him, had a dodgy record and might not pay his bill at the end of the day. And there would be other calculations going through his head: his own legal position, his reputation within the profession.

'What exactly are your client's instructions, may I ask?' Brock prompted.

'I'm to seek your written guarantee that his and Patrick Abbott's email accounts will not be accessed, now or in the future. I am also to seek your assurance that you will support the dropping of all charges against Mr Wylie and his immediate release from detention. In return, he'll provide you with these pictures and other evidence he has relating to the same matter.'

'Do you know what form this other evidence takes?'

'No.'

'I assume you're holding it for him. Deposit B, presumably?'

'I really couldn't say.'

'When did he deposit these with you?'

'I . . . couldn't say.'

Brock rubbed a hand wearily across his eyes. 'Do you know whether your client took these pictures himself, or witnessed them being taken?'

The solicitor shook his head.

'Or what kind of camera was used?'

'No, I don't.'

Brock gathered the pictures, scooped them into the envelope and handed it to Kathy. 'I can't agree to anything on the basis of these. They're useless.'

'What do you mean?'

'They look to me like digital pictures. The courts won't accept them as evidence.'

'You think they've been fabricated?'

'I don't know. That's why your client will have to give us more, much more, before I can help him.'

The lawyer now looked very worried. 'There may be a problem. He mentioned to me that he had no faith in the police. He said—his phrase—that you were all in each other's pockets, and you might try to suppress his evidence and maintain his guilt in order to protect your friends. In which case, he said, he would have to find other ways to make use of it.'

'What do you think he meant by that?'

Clifford shrugged unhappily. 'Go public, perhaps?'

'There are other copies of these?'

'I don't know, but Mr Wylie is a very cautious man.'

'I think you'd better try to persuade him to give me what I need.'

'Yes, but he doesn't always take my advice.'

They bought takeaway downstairs and ate it in the car, still parked at the kerb. While they were eating the lights went off in the solicitor's office. A few seconds later they saw him exit the building and walk off into the night, stooped by the prospect of another visit to the gaol.

'What have you got on tonight?' Brock asked.

Kathy wiped her fingers and started the car. 'I thought I might do a spot of babysitting. Our artists, Gabe and Poppy, are in a pretty disturbed state, and I feel they know more than they've told us, but I couldn't get any sense out of them this afternoon.'

'Back to Northcote Square, eh? That place is getting to you, Kathy. They've got a minder, haven't they? Take a break. Have a night off. Catch a movie or something. Something light.'

'Yes . . . soon.'

She drove back by way of the Forensic Science Laboratories, where they dropped off the envelope with a note for someone Brock knew in the Photography Unit.

24

PC MCLEOD PEERED around the edge of the door, then released the chain and let Kathy in.

'Hi, Colin. You still here?'

'Yeah, my relief hasn't come yet.'

'How are the artists?'

'They ordered a pizza a couple of hours ago, but hardly touched it. Then they went up to the studio together. I heard them moving around and a bit of chat. Then he called down that they were having an early night and didn't want to be disturbed. That would be over half an hour ago.' He gave a yawn and led the way upstairs.

'Yes, I noticed there wasn't a light on in the studio.' Kathy smelled the pizza before she saw it, almost finished, on the coffee table with a can of soft drink. PC McLeod blushed. 'They said they didn't want it.'

Kathy smiled. 'So you're reading about art?' She nodded at a couple of books lying open on the seat.

'Yeah, it's interesting. I don't like to watch telly when I'm working in case I don't hear something. I was reading about Van Gogh. He only sold one painting in his whole life. How would that make you feel, eh? It'd be like being a copper and only making one arrest.' He eased his shoulders under the body armour.

'Heavy?'

'Yeah. By the end of the day you really feel it. I have to keep it on, even though there doesn't seem a lot of point, sitting in here.'

They heard a heavy thump on the floor above and both turned their eyes up to the ceiling, but heard nothing more.

'How's your day been then?' he enquired companionably.

'Bit frustrating, really.'

'Yeah, I know the feeling. Like having to make an arrest half an hour before the end of your shift.'

'How's that?'

'Well, you know you're going to be stuck for another five or six hours doing the processing. Try telling that to the missus.'

Another thump, more like a crash of something hitting the floor and breaking. McLeod rose to his feet. 'I thought I heard them having an argument earlier. I'd better check if everything's . . .'

A scream, piercing sharp. McLeod ran for the stairs, leaping up two steps at a time, Kathy following. He reached the landing at the top and grabbed the door handle. It didn't budge.

'Door's locked,' he panted, then loudly, 'Mr Rudd! You all right? Let us in, please.'

He stepped back a couple of paces and prepared to charge the door, but at that moment it was flung open. For a second, both he and Kathy were transfixed by the sight in front of them. A tall figure in black cloak and hood, a death's-head mask covering its face, stood before them. In its clenched hands it gripped the handle of a sword. As they began to recover their wits it gave an extraordinary roar and stepped forward, raising the sword high overhead. In front of her, Kathy saw McLeod fumbling for his pistol with one hand, then raising the other to protect his face as the blade began to arc down. For a horrified fraction of a second, she watched it flash through the air and across his body. He stumbled back against her, she put out a foot to brace herself and felt nothing but air, and together they crashed backwards down the length of the stairs.

He was on top of her, motionless. She struggled to push him off and looked back up the stairs. The door was closed again, the apparition gone, and for a moment she wondered if she'd imagined it. But the blood was real enough, lots of it. She hauled his body over onto its back and saw that his protective vest was slashed open, the armoured plates inside exposed. Blood was pumping from his upper left arm, and she grabbed it, feeling for the pressure point and gripping tight until the flow slowed to a seeping trickle. Then, with one hand she reached for the radio on his chest.

'Urgent assistance,' she panted, breathless. 'Urgent assistance. Officer hurt. Armed assailant. Five-three Urma Street. Suspects on.'

PC McLeod's eyes blinked open. 'Wha . . . What happened?'

'You're hurt, Colin. Can you move your right arm?'

He raised it. 'Yes.'

'Grip the pressure point. I've called for help. I need your gun. Do you understand?'

He nodded and she felt around his side, easing the pistol out of its holster. She got to her feet, working the Browning's slide, and pain shot through her left leg and shoulder on which she'd landed. It was as much as she could do to drag herself back up the stairs, holding the handrail with her right hand, gun in her left. At the top, she transferred it to her right hand and tried the door handle. Locked again. She aimed the muzzle at the base of the handle and pulled the trigger. There was a deafening crash, splintered plywood, then she pushed with her shoulder. The door opened and she stumbled inside, slipping on a pool of blood.

Gabe was on his back on the floor, blood all over him, Poppy curled on the bed nearby. A trail of things—the sword, the cloak, the mask—led beneath the overhanging gallery towards a panel of the wall which, inexplicably, was open to the night. Kathy went to Gabe's side and saw that his throat was cut, possibly with other wounds on his hands and body. There was no pressure to the blood that seeped from his throat wound, and when she felt for a pulse there was none. Kathy turned to Poppy and found that she was breathing normally, as if she were sound asleep. Then she heard the wail of the sirens, coming loud through the opening in the wall, and in a moment the pounding of boots on the stairs, men shouting.

'I'm fine, really,' she said, although she couldn't stop shaking, even after they'd wrapped a thick blanket around her shoulders. She was sitting propped against the wall with Brock and one of the Shoreditch detectives crouching beside her. 'How's Colin?'

'Who?'

'The bodyguard.'

'Don't worry, they're looking after him.'

'And Poppy?'

'They think she's been drugged. No wounds.'

She told them what had happened, every detail that she could remember. 'He must have got in through that door over there. I didn't even know it was there.'

'It's a fire escape onto the roof,' the detective explained to Brock, 'but he'd covered it with the pinboard that lines the rest of the walls, so you wouldn't notice it. It gives access onto the neighbouring roof and from there to a fire stair into the lane. There are footprints. We've got a dog on the way.'

'Gabe's dead, isn't he?' Kathy asked.

'Yes.'

She shuddered. 'I know it's what people always say, but it is like waking from a nightmare. The awful thing is, I feel I've had it before.'

She stared for a moment at the blank polymer strip of the next banner, which had been suspended against the wall not far from Gabe's body. At the top was the number sixteen, and beneath it the squiggle of black line that appeared on each of them. Below was a long blank space awaiting Gabe's inspiration. It was sprayed with his blood.

The detective's radio crackled. He listened, then said, 'They've found a pair of bloodstained shoes in a bin further down the lane. The dog's arrived.'

An ambulance officer came up. 'We've got transport for you, miss.'

They helped her to her feet. Her head was aching now, and she stumbled.

'I'll get a stretcher up here.'

'No, I'm okay.'

The square was filled with flashing lights once again, and on the way to the hospital they passed several road blocks and foot patrols.

25

SHE WOKE WITH a start. The room was in semi-darkness, some light reflected in through an open door. She had no idea where she was, and her mind was confused by an image, a dream or a memory, of a dark figure poised, arms upraised, and ready to strike. She turned her head towards the door and gave a cry as she saw him there, a dark shape rising against the light.

'It's all right, it's only me.' Brock's voice, gentle and reassuring. He was reaching to the wall above her head. There was a click and the bed light came on.

She tried to sit up, but a jolt of pain in her shoulder held her back. There was a dull ache in her head.

'Lie still. You're probably concussed. Nothing broken, only bruises.'

'Where am I?'

'Hospital. They're keeping you in overnight.'

There was a clock on the wall reading three-fifteen. 'You're still up?'

'I'm going to get a bit of sleep now. I just called in to see how you were.'

'Have you caught him?'

Brock shook his head. The assailant had vanished into the night, the dogs unable to pick up a scent from the place where they'd found the bloodstained shoes. 'He probably had some kind of transport waiting there.'

'What about Colin?'

'He's out of danger. He has a bad cut to his arm and he broke his leg on the fall down the stairs, but his vest saved him from the worst of it. Poppy's in here too, but she's not in any danger. She slept through the whole thing, doped to the eyeballs.'

'She was lucky.'

'Yes, I'll be interested to hear what she has to say for herself. Anyway, that's not your problem; you're on sick leave until the doctor says otherwise—two days' home rest at least. You took quite a fall.'

She began to form a protest but let it go. She felt very tired. Tomorrow she would see.

Among a pile of reports waiting for Brock at Shoreditch the next morning was a phone message from Wylie's solicitor, requesting an urgent meeting. It had been logged at nine thirty-five the previous evening, but in the turmoil at that time it hadn't been passed on to him. He put it to one side and concentrated on the various files that had been prepared for the new case; the action book, the policy file, and the preliminary forensic reports. When he'd digested these he went to talk to the action manager who was collating the various activities of the large number of people now involved. Like Brock, Bren Gurney had already returned to duty after a brief sleep and was now at the crime scene, where a new forensic team had taken over.

The crime scene manager was the same woman who had dealt with Tracey's disappearance seventeen days before. She met Brock as he arrived. 'First the child, then the father,' she said. 'This is really personal, isn't it? Obviously we're looking for connections.'

They were interrupted by the scream of a power saw. Brock watched as they cut away a section from the frame of the hidden fire-escape door. The door itself had already been removed.

'It'll be easier to examine the marks in the laboratory,' she said. 'We're removing the window and frame in Tracey's bedroom as well. We should have done that the first time around, but Mr Rudd objected.'

The studio had become a laboratory for the reconstruction of the crime, grided, measured and labelled with dozens of numbered plastic tabs marking the locations of key pieces of evidence. They were especially interested in the blood stains, which formed a dynamic record of the action that had occurred and where the players had been at each moment. In one part of the room they were calculating the angle at which a spray of elliptical blood spots had hit a wall so that a computer could calculate where the victim had been standing; in another they were tracking prints from a foot which had picked up blood from an arterial spurt on the floor. A man in goggles was spraying an area of floor with a chemical, fluorescin, and then examining it with a small UV light to find microscopic blood traces, while a second was recording their position with a laser survey instrument. It was rather as if they were deconstructing a Jackson Pollock action painting, Brock thought, rediscovering each gesture of the artist through the splatter marks he had made.

Bren appeared in the demolished doorway. He had been out on the roof, examining traces of blood left by the assailant's shoes. He waved to Brock and came over. 'Looks straightforward. The first crash Kathy and McLeod heard was probably him breaking through the door. The room was in darkness, but there was light from the square filtering through the big windows. Rudd wakes up, but he's been drinking and his reactions are slow. The second crash is when he and the intruder first make contact, and Rudd screams and is thrown to the floor. The intruder hears McLeod running up the stairs. He finds the light switch, waits till McLeod reaches the top, then opens the door and attacks. Then he re-locks the door and turns on Rudd, who is probably on his feet again, leaning against that table over there. That's the source of the first blood spray. Rudd falls, and things get messy, blood goes everywhere. The intruder retraces his steps, dropping his stuff along the way.

'That's the how,' Bren said, 'but why? What had Rudd learned or done to deserve this? And why do it in this bizarre way?'

'It's almost as if he wanted to frighten Rudd to death,' Brock said thoughtfully. 'And it makes the theory that Stan Dodworth killed Betty and then hanged himself look even more unlikely. I'm not sure what's going on, Bren, but we need to keep a close watch on Poppy—she's about the only one left who might be able to help us get to the bottom of this.'

'Right. Couple of other things, Chief. I don't know if it's going to be relevant, but they found this . . .' He led Brock to the far corner of the room, carefully skirting the taped-off areas of the floor, and pointed to a block of grey material wrapped in plastic. 'Modelling clay. There was some on the floor. I'm thinking of that grey putty they found on Dodworth's shoes.'

'Could be.'

'The other thing is that photo.' He pointed to a small colour snap pinned to the wall. They went over to examine it. It showed three people standing behind a seated woman with a child in her arms. The three were wearing paper party hats and silly grins. They were Gabriel Rudd, Stan Dodworth and Betty Zielinski. They all looked much younger, especially Rudd, whose curly hair, spilling out from below his hat, was brown.

Kathy still couldn't quite believe that Gabe was dead. She knew this disbelief was a measure of how vivid the other person had seemed in life, and it took her by surprise. Gabe hadn't really meant anything to her; if she'd been asked to sum him up, her account wouldn't have been flattering. He was as vain, self-centred and neglectful as his in-laws had claimed, and she thought his work pretentious. But there was a genuinely tragic dimension to Gabe which she hadn't met before. It didn't come from his health or his circumstances—that would have been normal and understandable. Instead it seemed to come from some inner sense of fate, as if he knew he was doomed. She'd resisted this idea from the beginning because it seemed such a cliché, the tragic artist. There were so many stories of premature death in modern art that Gabe's performance had seemed like a pose. But now he really was dead, and, looking back over the sixteen days that she'd known him, she felt that her scepticism had blinded her to what she was really witnessing—a rocket falling to Earth in a shower of sparks. It startled her to realise that she felt his death much more keenly than Betty's or Stan's, perhaps even (and she felt guilty at this) Tracey's. She wasn't quite sure why this was. Perhaps their tragedies had seemed stupid and ugly and unnecessary, whereas his was like a grander and more intense version of everyone's fate.

She had visited PC McLeod before she left the hospital. He was sitting up in bed, circling the names of horses in a copy of *Sporting Life* with his good hand, and seemed quite unperturbed by what had happened. He told her that he'd heard that Poppy had already been discharged into police custody, apparently oblivious to the mayhem that had happened around her. As Kathy sat waiting in the hospital lobby for the taxi her mobile phone rang. She winced to hear Len Nolan's voice. They had just heard the news report. Was it really true? Was Gabe really dead? Kathy could hardly bring herself to talk about it and asked him to ring Bren's number.

She was exhausted by the time she got back to her flat. Taking a couple of the pills the doctor had given her, she lay down on her bed, intending to rest for five minutes, and woke up three hours later. She struggled to sit upright, blinking gummed eyes against the glare of morning light in the uncurtained window. Her brain felt jangled by snatches of claustrophobic dreams, and she got up to make herself a cup of tea and a piece of toast, the only things she seemed to have in the cupboard. She flopped on the sofa, still unable to shake a dream image from her mind, something to do with a painting she thought. The art books Deanne had given her were piled beside the bed, and she searched through them for the biography of Henry Fuseli in which she had found the picture of the two hanged figures. She remembered how impressed Gabe had been by her discovery, and she wondered now if he had taken it as some kind of sign of his own fate. After the death of his wife he had been haunted by the image of one Fuseli painting, *The Night-Mare,* and now here was another. She wondered if it would have been better if she hadn't shown it to him. Gabe must have felt that Fuseli was speaking to him from the past.

She turned to the preface to check his dates, 1741 to 1825. So Fuseli himself had not died young. Throughout his life he had been a controversial figure apparently, seeing himself as a unique genius and shocking his contemporaries with images of witchcraft, sexually charged nude figures and melodramatic scenes trembling on the cusp between the sublime and the absurd. According to the introduction, Horace Walpole, author of the first Gothic novel, described one of his paintings as 'shockingly mad, madder than ever; quite mad'. Kathy could see why Gabe would have been interested in him. The description reminded her of the Fuseli painting she had seen in the Royal Academy, and the memory brought on a sudden feeling of anxiety, unexpectedly strong. She could barely visualise the painting now, and she turned the pages of the book to find it. When she did she realised with a jolt why the scene on the staircase of Gabe's house the previous night had seemed so familiar, like a half-remembered nightmare. For the figure of Thor, brightly lit and seen from below, weapon raised above his head to strike down upon the Midgard Serpent, was eerily reminiscent of the monstrous figure at the head of Gabe's staircase in the endless fraction of a second before he brought the sword down upon PC McLeod.

Kathy found that her heart was racing, her fingers causing the page to tremble. This was just a reaction to shock, she told herself. There were differences between the two images: the Fuseli figure was naked, although there was a cloak flying from his shoulders in the wind; also it was his left arm raised to strike, rather than the right, so that the picture was the mirror image of what she had witnessed in the flesh. And yet the resemblance was overwhelming. She forced herself to concentrate on the commentary in the book. The subject of Fuseli's painting for his membership of the Royal Academy was a scene from the ancient Icelandic saga *The Edda*—in which the hero Thor takes revenge upon the monstrous Midgard Serpent—and was intended to show the painter as a master of epic, sublime imagination. She assumed Gabe must have been to the Academy to see the original. He would certainly have known it in reproduction from his book. Had the murderer deliberately intended to use the Fuseli image to terrorise Gabe? The more she thought about it the more certain she was that the reference had been deliberate. She picked up her phone and called Brock's number.

He sounded preoccupied, and in her anxiety to explain her notion she felt she was gabbling. He listened in silence, then said, 'That's an interesting idea, Kathy. I'll pass it on to the profiler. You're still in hospital, are you?'

'No, I'm at home.'

'Really?' He sounded unhappy. 'Do you feel all right? Do you want someone to come and be with you?'

'No, no. I'm just taking it easy.'

'Yes, you do that. Forget about the case.'

But she found she couldn't, and the pain in her leg and shoulder only made her feel more restless. She closed her eyes but couldn't relax, and picked up the book again. A thought came to her, and she turned to the index at the back, running her eye down the names. And there she found 'Sterne, L.', the name on the email address that had sent the pictures of Betty's body. She turned to the entry and found that it was on the page following the engraving of the hanged figures. The text read:

> In the same year, 1767, a philosophical tract of baffling obscurity entitled *Remarks on the Writings and Conduct of J.J. Rousseau* was published anonymously in London. At first it was attributed to Lawrence Sterne, author of *Tristram Shandy*, but before long the real author was discovered to be 'one Fuseli, an Engraver'.

She lay her head back, trying to understand. It was as if the Fuseli book were a road map to the murders. What else might it contain? Then she had another idea. At the back of the book was an appendix with a comprehensive listing of every painting and drawing Fuseli was known to have done. It ran to thirty-four pages. She turned to the first page and began to work through it.

Morris Munns had been the acknowledged genius of the laboratory's Photography Unit for longer than anyone could remember. A stocky, balding cockney with thick-lensed glasses, he had helped Brock many times before, on one occasion conjuring an attacker's boot print from the deep bruising on a woman's body three months after the event.

'I made it a priority as soon as I realised what it was, of course,' he said, spreading the four photographs on the table between them. 'That little girl . . . the worst sort of case. Who took these, do we know?'

'They've come to us from the solicitor of the chief suspect, Robert Wylie.'

'Who you think also took the photographs we found in the flat, right?'

'That's right. One of the questions I have is whether they've been taken with the same camera.'

'Yes, I thought you'd ask that. These are all digital pictures, as were the ones in the flat. We have that camera, of course, which is lucky, because it has a small scratch on the optical zoom lens, that we've been able to relate to a faint distortion in the digital images. We reckon we can prove to a jury's satisfaction that that camera took the pictures you found in the flat.'

'And these?'

Morris pointed to the first three, with Tracey in the street and on Beaufort's knee, and Beaufort touching the naked child. 'I can make out the same effect on these three, yes, but not on the other one. They're also different in other ways. These three have been enhanced, I'd say, but I'm fairly sure they're genuine images, integral with their background. The shadows, the reflected light—I couldn't swear to it in court, but I'd say they're not fakes. But this one . . .' He picked up the remaining picture with disgust. 'Pure phoney, and not very good at that. The faces have been pasted onto a scene taken with another camera altogether. It's a con.'

'Thank you, Morris, that's helpful.'

'There's something else. I don't know if you've been able to identify the location of numbers two and three, have you? The girl on the old bloke's knee?'

'No, the backgrounds are out of focus.'

'Deliberately made to be, I'd say. Anyway, I've had a go at sharpening it up for you.' He produced new versions, in which the shadowy grid of lines in the background emerged as the frame of a large industrial window. Brock immediately recognised the big windows in the artists' workshops at The Pie Factory.

'Ah.'

'Mean something?'

'Yes, I think it does. You've been a great help, as always.' Brock gathered up the pictures.

'So the old bloke's involved too, is he?'

'Maybe. But it's hard to know what's fake and what's real these days, isn't it?'

'Picture number three is the clincher, I reckon, with the girl naked. I'd swear it's real. Who is he, anyway?'

'I'll tell you one day, Morris, but at the moment you don't want to know. Has anyone else seen these?'

'No, I dealt with it myself, like you said in your note.'

'Thanks. Let's keep it that way.'

When he got back to his car Brock called the solicitor, Russell Clifford, and made arrangements to meet him and his client. Wylie would be brought under escort to Shoreditch police station where the interview would be recorded and filmed. Then he called Bren.

Bren stared at the photographs in disbelief, then looked at Brock. There was a question written all over his face, but he wasn't going to put it into words.

'I'm sorry, Bren,' Brock said. 'I had to do this on my own. There are ramifications . . .'

'The review of Special Operations, you mean?'

'You know about that?'

'I've heard rumours. Beaufort is involved.'

'Yes, and I've been specifically ordered to leave him alone.'

'But you can't ignore evidence like this!'

'No, of course not, provided it's genuine. Morris Munns has had a look, and thinks these three may be genuine, and this one a fabrication.

But he can't swear to it. They could all be fakes. This may just be a ploy by Wylie to stop us looking at his emails.'

'That's what he wants to trade?'

Brock watched Bren turn this over, visibly uncomfortable as he weighed the options. 'Maybe . . . maybe you should cover your back. Get clearance from higher up. Talk to Sharpe.'

'If I do that without firm evidence, he'll stop me. It's just too difficult for them at this moment. Look, I've got Wylie being brought here for interview in half an hour. I want to get something solid out of him. I wouldn't mind some help, but I'll understand if you don't want to be involved at this stage.'

'Come off it, Brock, you know I'm in. How do you want to play it?'

They talked it through until the word came that Wylie and his solicitor had arrived. Bren got to his feet and Brock said, 'Let them wait for a while.'

Twenty minutes later Bren opened the door to the interview room and walked in alone. The two men seated at the table interrupted their argument and looked up at him in surprise.

'Mr Wylie?' Bren said, and gave a yawn. 'I'm DI Gurney, and you are . . .?'

'Russell Clifford, Mr Wylie's legal representative. Is DCI Brock coming? We've been waiting now for . . .'

'Sorry about that. There's a lot going on. DCI Brock may not be able to make it.'

'But he called me!' Clifford complained. 'He arranged this.'

'Did he? Well, he's very busy at the moment, another murder in the area. Most of us have been up half the night.'

'That's all very well . . .'

Wylie interrupted his solicitor. 'What murder?'

'In Northcote Square, another one of the artists there.' Bren paused, noting the alarm on Wylie's face. 'Anyway, I understand you want to give us some information, is that right?' He opened the file and scanned it as if he'd never seen it before, oblivious to the whispered conversation across the table. 'Oh, you're the gentleman with the lost emails. I heard about that.' Bren beamed happily at him. 'Shouldn't have much longer to wait now, sir. We're expecting them any day, you'll be glad to know.'

Wylie and Clifford stared at Bren as if at an imbecile. The solicitor recovered first. 'Look, we want to speak to DCI Brock, no one else. Please get him on his phone and tell him we're here.'

The amiable smile vanished from Bren's face and his voice took on an icy menace. 'You're not trying to tell me how to do my job, are you, sir? It so happens that it's quite likely that DCI Brock won't be dealing with you any more. I may be taking over his caseload, and I've got plenty more important things to do than sit around listening to your helpful suggestions. If you've got something to tell me then say it, otherwise get lost.'

The two appeared stunned, Wylie itching with the onset of panic. 'Has DCI Brock not briefed you about the evidence I gave him?'

'What evidence?'

'Photographs.' Wylie wheezed. He seemed to have trouble speaking.

Bren carelessly thumbed through the file. 'No photographs here. What were they of?'

Wylie dabbed his face with a handkerchief and Clifford broke in quickly. 'They were of a confidential nature, and . . .'

'Confidential?' Bren loaded the word with such scorn that the solicitor's mouth snapped shut. Then Bren leaned forward across the table and said suspiciously, 'He wasn't offering you some kind of deal, was he? He's ruffled a few feathers around here. Don't expect any favours from me.'

It was at that moment that Brock burst into the room. He appeared harassed and out of breath. 'Ah, DI Gurney . . .' He and Bren eyed each other mistrustfully. 'I didn't realise they were with you.'

'I thought you were otherwise engaged, sir.' He put unnecessary stress on the last word.

Wylie and Clifford looked from one to the other as if catching a glimpse of some chaotic office feud in which they had no bearings.

'No, no. I've got time for this.' Brock paused, then added unhappily, 'Ah, I see you've got the file. Well, I'll take over now.'

'I'd like to stay, sir.'

'You haven't been fully briefed.'

'All the more reason,' Bren insisted stolidly.

Brock took a deep breath as if summoning his last remaining strength. 'I'd like a few words with Mr Wylie alone first, Inspector. I'll call you when I'm ready to begin the formal interview.'

Bren looked angry, but got to his feet and slowly walked out of the room. Brock sat down in his place and leaned forward across the table to switch off the microphone. 'He can watch us,' he said quietly, 'but he can't hear us.'

'What the hell's going on?' Wylie said.

'There's nothing I can do for you. I can't stall the application for your emails, and they'll probably take you back to prison tonight.'

'Jesus.' Wylie went even paler. 'What about the pictures?'

'Useless. They're digital, aren't they? I've had one of our top experts look at them and he says they'd be useless in court. They're probably all fakes.'

'No! I . . . I *know* they're not.'

'The last one, with the two of them in bed, he says that's definitely a fake, not a very good one. The others he couldn't be so sure about, but if one's bad . . .'

'All right, that one maybe.' Wylie was talking very fast now, the words tumbling out. 'I can't rightly vouch for that one, but the others, I swear—I was there.'

'Where, exactly?'

'In the square, and in the gallery.'

'Tell me about it.'

'I was giving Pat Abbott a lift one day and he asked me to drop him off at the gallery to meet this sculptor friend he was doing business with. Beaufort was there—I recognised him. The sculptor and the owner were trying to get him to buy some of their stuff. Pat and I hung around in the back, waiting for them to finish, then Beaufort came into the next room. I could see him through the blind. Then the girl came in, and I took those pictures. They're real, believe me.'

Wylie was giving off an unpleasant odour as a sweat stain spread across his prison T-shirt. Brock eased his chair back into fresher air, brow furrowed as if struggling for a solution.

'So you knew Beaufort, did you?'

Wylie nodded, a sly look in his eyes. 'We go way back. He was a customer of mine, years ago.'

'A customer?'

'When I had the shop. Adult material, pictures of little girls, imported stuff.'

Brock said, 'People will find that hard to believe. Between you and him, whose word will they accept?'

'I can prove it.' He turned to his lawyer, who, looking unhappy, reached for his briefcase and drew out a yellow envelope which he handed to his client. Wylie glanced up at the camera watching them from the corner of the room and gestured to Brock to lean in closer. He drew two sheets from the envelope and slid them across. One was a photograph of two men on either side of a shop counter. They were viewed from a high angle and the quality was not good, like a grainy still from a security camera, but it was still possible to identify Wylie handing something, a magazine, to Beaufort. It was also possible to make out a title on the magazine, Tiny Tots. The second document was a photocopy of an eight-year-old credit card slip made out for 'goods' to the value of eight hundred pounds. The customer was John R. Beaufort, and the vendor Cupid's Arrow Adult Shop.

'That's a lot of dirty books.'

'Oh yes,' Wylie gave a nasty little smile. 'They were special.'

'Does Beaufort know you have this?'

'I sent him a copy a couple of years later, when I needed a favour.'

'And did he oblige?'

'Yes, a bit of bother with the law. He sorted it out. But now . . . now he knows I could be a problem for him, don't you see? That's why I'm helping you.'

'You're not serious about Beaufort killing the sculptor, Dodworth?'

'He wouldn't do it himself, but he had it done.'

'Why?'

'Because Dodworth set it up for him, with the little girl. He knew too much, just like I do.'

'What about the old woman?'

'She was there in the square that day, feeding the birds, when I took that picture of Beaufort and the girl. She saw them too, and she charged over and told him to leave her alone. She was crazy. I reckon she'd seen him at it before. And now there's another killing. Who was it this time?'

'The girl's father.' Brock watched Wylie's reaction carefully. He seemed genuinely shocked. 'He was attacked at home. It was very violent, I understand. DI Gurney's in charge.'

'But he's only an inspector. You're senior to him. You've got rank.'

'He's got friends, the support of people higher up. He's on the fast track, making a name for himself. I don't fancy your chances with him, Wylie. I don't think he'll lift a finger to help you.'

'You've got to save me.'

'Then you've got to give me the means. By themselves these bits of paper prove nothing and the photographs would be dismissed. What I need is you, on record, telling the story that goes with them. I need you to make a statement, to me and DI Gurney, on camera confirming that you took those photographs, describing the circumstances, just as you've told it to me.'

'It'd be my death warrant.'

'I'll look after you. Gurney and his friends won't be able to sweep it under the carpet if you go on the record with me present. Then I'll have something to work with.'

Wylie bit his lip, glanced at his solicitor. 'I'll have to think about it.'

'Don't take too long. Gurney won't wait.'

'And the emails? You'll stop them?'

'I can't promise. That's a chance you'll have to take.' Brock got to his feet. 'Five minutes, that's all you've got.' He turned and walked out.

He went to the monitoring room where Bren was watching Wylie and his lawyer on a screen. 'We should go on the stage,' Bren said. 'Do you think he'll agree?'

'That depends on how genuine he is about being afraid of the judge.'

'He looked pretty genuine to me.'

'Maybe, but he's still not telling us the whole story. He just happened to be at the gallery with a camera and caught Beaufort red-handed? I don't think so. If the pictures are genuine, then Beaufort was set up. The question is why, and who else was involved. But for the moment, all I want is for him to admit that he took those pictures, then I can tie him to the camera in his flat that he says he's never seen before.'

'Not to mention going for the judge,' Bren said. 'If Wylie goes on the record, you'll have no option but to act.'

'Yes, that too.'

On the screen they seemed to have reached a decision. They watched Clifford get to his feet and go over to the door, asking the guard outside for DCI Brock. When Brock arrived he said, 'My client agrees to do as you ask. He has to rely on your good faith to keep the other side of the bargain.' *Good faith* the phrase made Brock uncomfortable. There was no good faith on either side of this bargain. He said, 'I'll get DI Gurney.'

They resumed their double act, Brock coaxing, Bren feigning disbelief, but stopping short of anything that could be interpreted as outright deception on camera, and Wylie repeated the story he'd told Brock, complete with dates and times.

Kathy found what she'd been looking for on the twelfth page of the appendix, with the following entry:

Death Steals the Child at Midnight, 1792, oil on canvas, 47.6 x 35.4 cm, Soane Museum, London. Engraved by William Bromley (1769–1842). Imprint: Published 5th December 1802, by F.J. Du Roveray, London. Inscription (bottom left) Painted by H. Fuseli R.A. / (bottom right) Engraved by W. Bromley.

There was no illustration or description of the painting or the engraving copied from it, but the title was very evocative. Was this the picture that had inspired the image on Gabe's first banner?

Kathy closed the book and then her eyes. Perhaps she was becoming obsessive too, haunted by ghosts as Gabe had been.

26

DETECTIVE INSPECTOR TOM Reeves delivered Sir Jack Beaufort to the door of the Shoreditch police station precisely on time. The judge had said little on the journey, sitting rigidly upright, face as impassive as a Roman bust, hands crossed on the attaché case on his knees. He marched through the front door with the air of an inspecting general and was shown to the interview room with more careful deference than any of his predecessors along that route had ever received. Conscious of his own reputation as one of the country's sharpest legal brains, he had thought it superfluous to bring a legal representative.

Standing stiffly in the small room, Brock introduced himself and Bren as if they were all complete strangers, then recited the caution. They took their seats and all three of them, Brock, Bren and Sir Jack, drew small black notebooks out of their pockets at the same moment. Sir Jack unscrewed the cap of a Mont Blanc pen and began writing.

Brock said, 'I'm sorry to bring you here, sir, but there are a few things we need to clarify.'

If it was intended to be conciliatory it wasn't received as such. Beaufort raised cold eyes to Brock and said, 'I heard the news—the shocking news—this morning about Gabriel Rudd. Are you quite sure that this is the best use of your time and resources?'

Brock sensed the anger beneath the sarcasm, and saw it as his best hope. He replied with studied patience. 'As I said, I believe you can help us clarify one or two things.'

'I have two conditions. One, I want a copy of the recording of this interview.'

Brock said, 'Agreed.'

'Two,' Beaufort's tone became harsher, 'I want to know if you've cleared this with your superiors, and if so, what their names are.'

'Commander Sharpe has authorised this interview,' Brock replied, unperturbed. 'That's Sharpe with an *e*.'

'I see.' Beaufort wrote in his notebook. 'Very well, go on.' He had automatically assumed the role of presiding authority.

'I'd like you to tell us about each and every occasion on which you met or saw the missing girl, Tracey Rudd. I have a photograph of her here to help you.' Brock took an enlargement of Tracey's picture from his file and placed it on the table. For a moment the judge stared down at the bright blue eyes, the curly blonde hair, the shy smile, then he looked up.

'I saw her on the afternoon of the first of October, at the house of the painter Reg Gilbey, in Northcote Square. I believe Gilbey has already explained the circumstances to you, and I mentioned it again to one of your officers, Sergeant Kolla, yesterday. Do you want me to repeat it?'

'Yes please.'

Beaufort described the events just as Gilbey had done, emphasising the innocence of Gilbey's behaviour and the inappropriate intervention by Betty Zielinski. 'She really was very confused, you know,' he said. 'She seemed to have it in her mind that the girl was her child—she referred to her as "mine".'

'That was the first time you met Tracey? Did you see her again?'

'Yes, a couple of days later. According to my diary I had another sitting with Gilbey on the Friday, the third, so it was probably then. It was a pleasant sunny afternoon, and I took a stroll in the square after my sitting. The little girl was coming home from the school in the corner of the square there, and I said hello. We exchanged a few words.'

'Like what?'

'I really can't remember. Nothing of any substance. Just hello.'

'Anything else?'

'What do you mean?'

'Did anything else happen while you were talking to her?'

'I can't remember anything, no.'

'Take your time to think.'

'I don't need time to think,' Beaufort snapped, and for the first time he sounded defensive. He realised it too, and when Brock didn't say anything to fill the awkward silence that followed, he added, calm returning to his voice, 'There was nothing else I can recall.'

'All right, so that was the second time you met Tracey. And the third?'

'There was no third time.'

'Are you quite sure?'

Beaufort hesitated. 'I believe I may have glimpsed her once in the gallery, when I was with Fergus Tait.'

'Glimpsed? Did you speak to her?'

'No. I'm not even sure it was her.'

'Very well, now I'd like you to tell us about each of your meetings with Betty Zielinski.'

Beaufort gave an exasperated click of his tongue, a well-practised signal to dilatory counsel. 'Is that really necessary?'

'I'm afraid so.'

'To what end, Chief Inspector?' Beaufort demanded acidly, but Brock refused to be ruffled. 'We'll get to that,' he said, and the judge saw that he would have to comply. He had seen her twice, to his recollection, once in Gilbey's studio and once in the street, when she was being pursued by school children. Once again, Brock didn't challenge the judge's account, but asked him to go through the same process with Stan Dodworth, whom he remembered meeting a couple of times, in Fergus Tait's company, at The Pie Factory, when Tait had shown him Dodworth's work. 'But I wasn't interested. I haven't yet got to the point of regarding authentic art and bad taste as synonymous. After that appalling effort of his with the Princess Di sculpture, I was surprised that Tait bothered with him. He was obviously sick.'

'What about Gabriel Rudd?' Brock asked.

'I knew him by reputation, of course, after he won the Turner, and I have to say that of all Tait's stable Rudd is probably the only one I'd regard as having any talent. Tait tried to interest me in buying something of his too, but I thought him far too expensive—although in view of what's happened that was probably a mistake; I dare say his value has doubled overnight. Tait introduced him to me once, when I was having dinner with friends at the restaurant. Rudd was very drunk, and made a fool of himself.' Beaufort pointedly looked at his watch. 'Is that it?'

But Brock still had other names, other connections, which he wanted to explore. He showed Beaufort a photograph of Patrick Abbott. The judge stared at it without blinking. 'The face seems familiar, but I can't recall . . .'

'His name's Patrick Abbott.'

'Ah, the man who fell from that building. No, I don't believe he ever appeared in my court.'

'But you visited the place where he lived, didn't you?'

Beaufort looked startled. 'How . . .?' He recovered himself and his eyes narrowed, gazing more thoughtfully at Brock. 'I did drive past there after he fell, out of curiosity.'

'Were you ever there before?'

'No, I certainly was not. You're fishing, Chief Inspector, without a hook. I can't see the point.'

Brock produced another photograph.

'Ah.' The judge gave a grim smile. 'We finally get to the point. Robert John Wylie.'

'What can you tell me about him?'

'I'm sure you know more about him than I do. You've had him in custody for over a week now, haven't you? What has he been saying about me?'

'I'd like to hear your version.'

'He appeared before me five or six years ago with three other men on a variety of charges. Unfortunately the crown case against him was weak, and I was forced to dismiss it.'

'Had you ever met him before then?'

Beaufort and Brock stared at each other in silence for a moment. Then the judge said, 'He's told you so, has he? Yes, I see that he has. Very well.' He cleared his throat with the air of a boxer easing a muscle before the next round. 'Two years before he appeared in my court, I had occasion to do some business with Mr Wylie. I bought something from him.'

'What was it?'

'That's not relevant.'

'Oh, but it is,' Brock said softly. 'You know it is. How much did you pay?'

Beaufort's chin rose a little. 'Eight hundred pounds.'

'Wylie has made a statement that you bought obscene pictures of children.'

Beaufort flinched. The effort required to contain his anger was apparent in the taut muscles of his mouth. 'That is not true.'

'Maybe not, but the fact that Wylie places himself at risk of prosecution by making the statement lends it a certain credibility, wouldn't you say?'

'Robert Wylie is a devious and evil man who would say anything that suited his purposes. About a week ago, just after he was arrested, a solicitor by the name of Russell Clifford made an appointment to see me on what he described as a private matter. When he arrived he told me that he was acting for Wylie who, he said, had been arrested on serious charges, of which he was innocent. He told me that Wylie believed that, because of our past *association,* as he put it, I might be willing to exert my influence to put a stop to this miscarriage of justice. To help me in this, Wylie had asked him to give me an envelope. He claimed he didn't know what it contained. Inside were two photocopies, one of a photograph of me in Wylie's shop and the other of the credit card slip I'd signed that day . . .'

Beaufort paused as Brock placed the two copies in front of him.

'Yes, that's them. I returned the envelope to Clifford and told him that there was nothing I could or would do for his client, and that if he attempted to contact me again I would inform the police.'

Brock said, 'You'd seen these before, hadn't you?'

Beaufort looked stonily at him. 'Yes. The day before Wylie's trial began, five years ago, I received copies anonymously. It made absolutely no difference to my conduct of the trial, although Wylie may have believed otherwise.'

'You're saying that Wylie twice tried to blackmail you with these and that twice you failed to report it?'

'Yes. An error of judgement, perhaps, but not a crime.'

'An astonishing error of judgement for someone in your position,' Brock goaded gently. 'Almost beyond belief.'

'Don't presume to lecture *me* about judgement, sir!' Beaufort's anger finally burst into the open. 'I had very good reasons for my decision.'

'You were protecting a friend.'

The judge stiffened as if he'd been kicked. 'How . . . how did you know that?'

'Because I've heard it so often before. So have you. It's not very original.'

'But it's true. You don't believe me?'

'Go on.'

'A dear friend, who drank too much and behaved unwisely. Some embarrassing pictures fell into Wylie's hands. I got them back. That's what I paid him for.'

'And the name of this friend?'

'I can't tell you.'

'Of course not. And the pictures have now been destroyed, and all we're left with is an image of you and Wylie conferring over a copy of . . .' Brock peered at the photograph, '. . . *Tiny Tots.*'

'He pushed that into my hands . . .' Beaufort stopped abruptly and straightened in his seat as if he'd suddenly realised that he'd been betrayed. Brock could almost see the thoughts crystallising, some aphorism of the Iron Duke, perhaps, whom Beaufort increasingly resembled; *Never apologise, never explain.* 'I have nothing further to say,' he said stiffly. 'I am leaving now.'

'Well, that's up to you, but Mr Wylie has given us other material, much more graphic and incriminating. In fairness, I'd like to give you the chance to give us your point of view. Are you sure you don't want to call a solicitor?'

Beaufort looked shocked. 'What other material?'

In the same year that Henry Fuseli painted *Death Steals the Child at Midnight,* another star of eighteenth-century London culture, Sir John Soane, architect to the Bank of England, began the demolition and reconstruction of his terrace house at number twelve Lincoln's Inn Fields. This project, which was to continue for the rest of Soane's life and to expand into numbers thirteen and fourteen next door, involved the creation of a private treasure house to display his extraordinary collection of architectural fragments, antique objects, plaster casts, books and paintings. Near the end of his life he bequeathed the house to the nation by a private Act of Parliament which stipulated that its arrangements should be kept intact as at the time of his death.

Kathy arrived in the early afternoon, still feeling fragile, with a dull ache throbbing at the back of her head. Lincoln's Inn Fields was a grander version of Northcote Square, with the Fields forming a sizeable park in the centre, in one corner of which four lawyers from Lincoln's Inn were gamely thumping a ball around a tennis court. She found the museum in the centre of the north side and took the steps up to the front door of number thirteen. She was met in the hallway by a small, silver-haired woman who explained that entry was free but she might care to buy a guidebook. Kathy agreed, and said that she was looking for a particular painting in the collection.

'The best place to start would be the Picture Room,' the woman said. 'The guide there will help you. If it isn't there, he'll know where it is.' She pointed out the route on the map in the guidebook, and Kathy went through a door into the dining room and library, with its cunning mirrors set above the bookcases and behind objects to create an illusion of space. From there she passed through two small rooms, tall and narrow like the architect Soane himself, to reach the special chambers at the back of the house.

She found herself in what might have been an ancient vaulted crypt, crammed with urns and sculptures, and with fragments of classical buildings covering the walls. The light was ethereal, filtering down from above through yellow glass, and she felt as if she might have been transported back in time to Pompeii, perhaps, or ancient Rome. She heard a voice from an adjoining room, a cry of surprise, and made her way towards the sound. An elderly, impish man was pointing out features to a pair of visitors in a tall room filled with paintings. Kathy recognised some of the pictures from Hogarth's series, *The Rake's Progress*. Having finished his story, the man tugged at the wall panel, folding it back to reveal more paintings behind. This trick was duly met with cries of delight, and was repeated again and again as more ingenious folding panels were demonstrated.

When the other visitors finally drifted away, Kathy spoke to the guide.

'Ah, Fuseli, yes. Soane was a great admirer of the artists of the *terrible sublime*—John Martin, James Barry, Henry Fuseli, they're all here. Fuseli's *The Italian Count* is over there on the west wall. Now, let me see . . .' He went to a corner of the room and folded back a screen, then another, to reveal a dark painting of a man brooding over the body of a dead or sleeping woman. 'Recognise this one?' he asked.

Kathy said, 'It looks a little like *The Night-Mare*, doesn't it?'

'Yes indeed. That came two years later. This one is called *Ezzelin and Meduna*. Now . . .' He eased that screen away and there, on the final layer of the wall, was what Kathy was looking for.

'*Death Steals the Child at Midnight*. A gloomy little thing, hidden away at the back here. There seems to be a revival of interest in Fuseli.

I've never had anyone ask after this until this month, and now you're the second. Are you an artist too?'

'No, but I think that may have been someone I knew,' Kathy said.

'Ah, that would explain it.'

'Can you remember when that was?'

'Not long ago. I had last week and the week before off, so it would have been the week before that.'

'Are you quite sure?'

'Of course. I went down to Devon to stay with my sister.' He pulled a small diary from his pocket and turned the pages. 'I finished here on Friday the tenth, so your friend would have been here earlier that week. Why, is it important?'

'Actually it is. You see, he's dead now.'

'Oh, I'm so sorry.' The little man looked puzzled. 'But you said "he". The person who came here was a woman.'

'A woman? Can you remember what she looked like?'

'Rather stocky, dark hair, cropped short. She was wearing trousers, but I'm sure it was a woman. I know sometimes these days it's hard to tell. Oh dear, am I mistaken?'

'No, I know now who you mean. She's a friend of the man I meant. Can you remember anything she said?'

The man pondered. 'Yes, I do . . . She said she was doing research. She was interested in portrayals of a lost child. She said she'd seen a reference to the Fuseli but not found an illustration, and she asked if she might take a photograph for her records.' His look became anxious. 'My goodness, I wondered if it might be hers, but it's not yours, is it? The lost child?'

'Not mine, no. I'm with the police. We're trying to trace the movements of the man who died, and we thought he might have come here. And you're quite positive about the date she came? It couldn't have been yesterday or Monday of this week?'

'No, it was definitely before I went away. I'm absolutely certain of that.'

Kathy thanked him, took a note of his name and made her way back out into the square. The lawyers had abandoned their tennis on the Fields, returned to work perhaps behind the Tudor archway of Lincoln's Inn, or in the Royal Courts of Justice a couple of blocks to the south, beyond the little pub where Brock had met the CPS solicitor. Kathy wondered if Jugular Jack had ever practised here, thrashing his opponents in both law and tennis courts. She forced her mind back to what she had just learned, and took out her own diary, checking the dates again. The guide in the Picture Room had been a credible witness. If what he'd told her was true, Poppy Wilkes had been researching the theme of the missing child at least three days before Tracey disappeared.

Sir Jack Beaufort sat immobile, staring at the four photographs on the table. The anger had gone, leaving him seized by a terrible stillness.

'It's an awful thing,' he murmured at last, 'to become an unreliable witness. It renders you . . . infantile.' He made an effort and roused himself. 'Was he stalking me or her, do you suppose?'

Brock didn't answer, and Beaufort went on. 'This first one is as I told you. I met the girl by chance in the square, we recognised each other and said hello.'

'You appear to be giving her something.'

'I believe she showed me her watch and told me the time. I'd forgotten that.'

'Did Betty Zielinski see you?'

The judge stared into the distance. 'Yes, you're right. Unreliable again. She was there, feeding her birds. She shouted something at us, I don't know what exactly, and the girl took fright and ran off home.'

'Home? You knew where she lived?'

'Yes. Reg Gilbey had told me. As I said, I'd heard of her father.'

'What about the second picture?'

'In the gallery. I had lunch in the restaurant there one day after a sitting with Gilbey. I can tell you the date . . .' He took his time assembling a double-hinged pair of spectacles on his nose and peered at his diary. 'Thursday the ninth of this month.'

'Three days before Tracey disappeared.'

'If you say so. Tait sent over a complimentary bottle of wine, which I accepted. He wanted something, of course—to show me some new pieces in the gallery and hopefully persuade me to invest in them. So I let him take me around, and we met Dodworth, who just glared and looked suitably tortured. Tait saw that he wasn't getting anywhere, so he suggested I'd be interested in something another of his artists was completing in the workshops. We went through and there was no one there, just this extraordinarily lifelike sculpture of a naked child—Tracey Rudd. The artist was a woman—Wilkes, I think, is her name. We were examining it when Tait's secretary came in and said he had a call from New York or somewhere, and he asked me to take a seat and wait for him to return. I continued to look at the sculpture. It was quite uncanny, extremely disturbing in its realism, and, alone in that room, I found it impossible to resist touching it. There was a soft down of blonde hair on the skin of the arms, I recall. God knows how she did it. Anyway, that's what I'm doing in that photograph there, the naked child kneeling on the table. It's a statue, not the real thing, though you couldn't tell.'

'Poppy Wilkes's statues are always at the wrong scale,' Brock objected, 'very large or very small.'

'Not this one. That's what made it so unnerving. It was the little girl, exactly true to life. Tait jokingly called it "pornographic realism", and he was right. You felt intrusive, even unclean, just looking at it, so I left the damn thing alone and went and sat down as Tait had suggested. Then the most extraordinary thing happened. The child herself appeared in the doorway. I found I had to look back at the statue just to make sure it was still there. The girl was wearing a sort of dressing gown, as you see there, and she was hesitant, as if she had to do something and felt awkward about it. I said hello, and she suddenly rushed forward, hopped on my knee and planted a kiss on my cheek. I was dumbfounded. Then she jumped down again and rushed away. I hadn't the faintest idea what it was all about. I never understood it until now. Wylie must have put her up to it somehow.'

Brock let the silence hang for a moment, remembering Sundeep Mehta's joke about the man who met a frog in the street. 'Why didn't you mention this before when I asked you?'

Beaufort sighed. 'Embarrassed, I suppose. How could I explain it, without sounding guilty? Impossible not to say either too much or too little. I opted for too little.'

'As you say, Sir Jack—an unreliable witness. So what about this last photograph?'

The judge screwed his nose in disgust at the image of the man and the child on the bed. 'I have no idea how he did that, but it certainly isn't me. That's all I can tell you.' He gave a sudden start, then a shiver.

'Are you cold?' Brock asked, although the room was quite warm.

'No . . . I just had that feeling, you know, of someone walking over my grave. I've been rather naive, haven't I? I assumed just now that Wylie was behind all this, but perhaps he wasn't, at least, not on his own.'

'Abbott, do you mean?'

'No, I was thinking of someone else—Fergus Tait. Perhaps it was he who persuaded that child to come in to see me after he left for his alleged phone call.'

'Why would he do that?'

'I don't know—to persuade me to buy his damned artworks, I suppose. I've heard his business is in financial trouble. Perhaps Wylie suggested that I might be interested in the girl.'

Brock looked sceptical. 'Is there anything else you can tell us?'

'No, I can't think of anything else. You don't believe me, do you? Am I a suspect?'

'I'd like you to provide a DNA sample and fingerprints,' Brock said, and switched off the tape. Then he leaned forward and said softly, 'Give me the name of your friend, Sir Jack. The one you paid eight hundred pounds to protect. I need corroboration, otherwise I'll have no choice but to go on with this.'

'Sorry.' The judge looked bleak. 'Can't do that, I'm afraid.'

27

'YOU THINK HE'S been set up?' Bren spoke to Brock at his side, the two of them standing at the window looking down on the street where Sir Jack Beaufort was getting into the car that had just pulled up for him.

'Yes, but that doesn't mean he's innocent. I think Wylie knew there was a kernel of truth in what he was saying about Beaufort —enough to stop the judge making a fuss when Wylie tried to blackmail him. I don't know. He certainly seems genuinely afraid of Beaufort now.'

'We could have another go at Wylie.'

'I don't think he'll give us much more. No word on his emails?'

'Not yet. They expect a decision soon.' Bren checked his watch. 'But that isn't going to help us find Rudd's killer. Fifteen hours have gone by, and we still don't have a lead. I've got a meeting with squad leaders shortly, and we're going to have to make a decision about where to put our resources.'

'What's your thinking?'

'The three killings—Zielinski, Dodworth and Rudd—are connected.'

'Agreed.'

'But the killer isn't necessarily Tracey's abductor. That's most likely Wylie and Abbott.'

'Go on.'

'I think we've been mesmerised by the square for too long. I think we should be looking much further afield. I think we've got a serial killer attracted to Northcote Square by the publicity of Tracey's abduction.'

Brock nodded. 'Makes sense.' But he didn't sound convinced.

'I had some help,' Bren confessed. 'I spoke to our profiler. He's very excited by Rudd's murder and he's working flat out on a new profile—he hopes to be able to talk to us later this afternoon. The serial killer from outside is his idea. He thinks he could be coming from anywhere, maybe Europe or the States. Well, we know Rudd's publicity and Web site have turned this into an international spectacle.'

The phone on the desk behind them rang and Brock turned to pick it up. The operator said, 'I've got DS Kolla on line two, sir. Will you take it?'

'Of course.' Brock punched the button and said, 'Kathy! How are you feeling? Tucked up in bed?'

'I'm all right. No, I needed some air. Listen, do we know where Poppy is?'

'She's in the hospital, isn't she?'

'No, she left there this morning, apparently. I've phoned The Pie Factory, and they haven't seen her.'

'Hang on, I'll check with Bren.' But Bren didn't know and said he'd have to contact the local command unit who were supposed to be looking after her.

'Is it important, Kathy?' Brock asked.

'I think it may be. I'm going to the gallery now just to be sure she isn't there. Will you let me know if you find her?'

'Of course. I want to speak to Fergus Tait myself. I'll meet you there in twenty minutes.'

He rang off and watched Bren's face grow darker as he spoke to someone on the other phone. He rang off and turned to Brock. 'There's been a cock-up. The doctors discharged Poppy Wilkes at midday, and her escort brought her here to be interviewed about last night. She said she was hungry and he took her down to the canteen. While he was at the counter she walked out. No one's seen her since.'

'I want her found, Bren. Check taxis, bus routes, the tube station. I'm going to Northcote Square. Send a squad down there as well.'

There were crowds in the square. At the north end a small hill of flowers, bunches in cellophane, was growing against the railings of 53 Urma

Street, and tourists were taking pictures of the policeman on duty in the doorway. On West Terrace a smaller group clustered around a forlorn posy of violets tied to the railings outside number fourteen, and then the crowd swelled again towards Lazarus Street and The Pie Factory in the south. There were black T-shirts everywhere, emblazoned with a stark white graphic of Gabriel Rudd's face, curls rampant, which managed to evoke the iconic images of both Jimi Hendrix and Che Guevara. The mood was of subdued excitement, everyone conscious of the significance of this moment, which would undoubtedly figure in every future art history book.

Kathy eased her way around a TV camera crew unpacking their gear and saw Brock turn the corner into the square, then stop and stare at all the activity. They met up at the gallery entrance, pushing their way through the melee at the door and squeezing into the hall past the crush at the T-shirt counter. They heard Fergus Tait's voice coming from the side gallery and, looking past the reporters and photographers, saw him presenting a eulogy to Gabriel Rudd, complete with a PowerPoint display projected onto a screen.

They waited for him to finish, and he finally emerged, face flushed and triumphant. He saw the two police, motionless in the seething crowd.

'Ah, officers, how are you? Can it wait? I'm rather busy at the moment, as you see.'

'No, I'm afraid it can't,' Brock said. 'Maybe it'd be quieter at the station.'

'Oh no!' Tait said in alarm. 'I have to be here. I simply must.'

'Let's talk in your office then, and see where we go from there.'

Tait led the way, closing the door behind them.

'So how can I help you?'

Brock began by asking him if he had any information that would help them solve Rudd's murder.

'Absolutely not. I had no idea about it until I was woken by a phone call from a reporter I know at six this morning, and it's been absolute bedlam ever since. I haven't even been able to get away to see poor Poppy in the hospital yet. How is she?'

'She was discharged at midday, and hasn't been seen since. We were hoping you might be able to help us find her.'

'Disappeared! Dear Lord, not another!'

'There's no need for alarm at this stage. We just want to speak to her.'

'Well, I haven't seen her, but let me ask my staff.' He rang two internal numbers and drew a blank. 'No, no one's seen her here.'

'We'll check her room for ourselves, if you don't mind. What about her family?'

'I do have a number somewhere . . .' He flicked through a filofax on his desk. 'Yes, a brother—home and office numbers. Shall I try them?'

Brock nodded, but again Tait was unsuccessful; the brother hadn't heard from Poppy in weeks. 'That about exhausts my sources, I'm afraid, Chief Inspector, so if I can get on now . . .'

'I've got some other questions for you. Sir Jack Beaufort . . .' Brock paused, catching the sudden wariness that came over Tait, who touched his big satin tie—gold today—and cleared his throat. 'Yes, what about him?'

'You tried to interest him in buying a nude sculpture of Tracey, didn't you?'

Tait looked nervous. 'Em, may I ask who told you that?'

'He did.'

'Ah, well, I do recall showing him one of Poppy's pieces, but it wasn't Tracey, as such.'

'He said it was startlingly lifelike. Apparently you described it as pornographic realism, is that right?'

Tait flushed scarlet. 'Oh now, if I did it would just have been my little joke.' He laughed uncomfortably.

'What did Dodworth tell you about Sir Jack?'

'Only . . . only that he might be susceptible to that sort of piece.'

'Susceptible? That sounds like some kind of entrapment. What do you mean?'

'Not at all. I'm a businessman, Chief Inspector. I try to match the goods that I have for sale to the customers who come to me.'

'And the goods you had for sale included the little girl herself, yes?'

'What?'

'She was there that day. You sent her in to see Beaufort.'

'I most certainly did not,' Tait said, blustering with indignation. 'If she was there I wasn't aware of it, and I'm beginning to resent the drift of your questions. I'll have to ask you to go now.'

As they were leaving, Brock said, 'Sir Jack suggested that, with Gabriel Rudd dead, his prices would probably have doubled overnight. Was he right?'

'No, no,' Tait said, still ruffled. 'Not doubled—quadrupled. And nobody would have been more pleased than Gabe himself, poor fellow.'

'Where's that sculpture of his daughter now?'

'It was one of Poppy's, an early version of her cupids. She destroyed it because the true scale made it too . . . *literal*, I think that was her word. It was certainly unnerving.'

They reached the entrance hall. Through the glass wall to the main gallery they saw Gabe's banners above the heads of the crowd. The final, sixteenth one was in place, Kathy noticed—blank except for the spray of Gabe's own blood.

'They let you have that?' she asked, and Tait gave a grim smile.

'Art takes priority,' he said. 'We have to respect Gabe's intentions. Who knows, he may have given his life for this.'

'What's the point of that meandering line at the top of each one? What does it mean?'

'I don't know. It's like a little creature crawling from one to the next, leaving a wandering trail. It reminds me of that phrase of Paul Klee's, "I took my line for a walk". Gabe wouldn't explain it to me. He said every work of art had to have its unsolved mystery.'

Kathy frowned. She didn't like unsolved mysteries.

She managed to grab a late lunch of a sandwich and some painkillers in the station canteen before the team assembled for an expert briefing. The first specialist was the forensic psychologist, clearly keyed up. They had gathered in one of the larger meeting rooms, and the whole wall behind the speaker was covered by a huge map of Greater London.

The fascinating thing about this case, the profiler explained, was the way in which it inverted the usual pattern of serial crimes. The usual pattern was demonstrated by the abduction of the three girls, in which Abbott/Wylie had begun at locations within a safe distance of their home base, their comfort zone. Had they not been caught, they would have gradually worked further out into the surrounding city as their confidence grew, and, using the profiler's 'A4 rule' and its more sophisticated computer derivatives, the psychologist would eventually have been able to infer their starting point and lead the police to the Newman estate.

But in the case of the Zielinski/Dodworth/Rudd killings, the opposite had happened. The victims all lived in the same immediate area, and there was no way of inferring the killer's home base from these three deaths. Instead of picking victims at random points within the comfort zone, he was choosing them because of their association with this particular place and its current celebrity. *Celebrity* was the key. The effect of Gabriel Rudd's celebrity, enhanced by all the information about him in the media and on the web, was to draw a violent stalker to him. The traditional pattern was turned inside out. This type of celebrity stalking had been seen before, of course, but here it was taking a very sophisticated form. The murderer had done extensive research into his primary target, Gabriel Rudd, discovered his obsession with Henry Fuseli, and then used Fuseli's work to create a kind of ongoing drama, culminating in the tableau of Fuseli's masterwork, which DS Kolla had witnessed. The visual clues which DS Kolla had picked up (he gave her a quick little smile, which embarrassed Kathy) demonstrated just how elaborate was his thinking.

Kathy wasn't feeling at all well, her head and shoulder throbbing. She looked away to avoid further eye contact and focused on the London map behind him. It was colour coded—red for development, blue for water, green for open space, black for main roads—and with the preponderance of red it looked like an enormous chaotic bloodstain, as if the room had been the scene of a chainsaw massacre. Through the blood the pale blue ribbons of the Thames and other waterways looked like writhing snakes.

Kathy dragged her mind back to the briefing. She felt light-headed and wondered if perhaps she had returned to work too soon. The forensic psychologist was suggesting different ways in which the killer might be tracked down. He had probably done this before, perhaps not quite as ambitious or elaborate, but along the same lines—a celebrity group or family, perhaps, or a series of victims connected by some common celebrity activity like sport or the media. And he could have come from anywhere.

There was an uncomfortable silence, then Brock asked if the killer was likely to strike again in Northcote Square, and in particular whether Poppy Wilkes might be at risk. The psychologist thought not; Rudd had been the focus of the whole thing, he felt sure, and any further killing would be superfluous. Bren asked how they might recognise the perpetrator and the psychologist offered a sketch: craving attention yet shrinking from the spotlight, so an unhappy, neglected childhood relationship with his mother, and perhaps a physical blemish or handicap of some kind of which he is acutely conscious; very intelligent and organised but excited by violence, so perhaps a substantial academic and work history coupled with disruptive incidents.

Kathy said, 'You keep saying "he". Is there any reason to suppose it's a man?'

'No indeed, nor that there's only one individual involved. I was just using the singular male pronoun for convenience.'

There was something wrong with all this, Kathy knew, and it took her a moment to realise that she hadn't told them what she'd learned at the Soane Museum. Her head felt fuzzy, and before she could speak the psychologist had handed over to the laboratory reporting officer, RO in the jargon, the scientist with overall responsibility for managing the forensic examinations at the laboratory. He was describing progress on the crime-scene analysis, pinning up a series of photographs and computer-generated diagrams plotting bloodstains at the scene. From these he described the sequence of events that had occurred in the studio.

'We believe there was an initial struggle—the noises that DS Kolla and PC McLeod heard—during which Rudd received a blow to the head that probably incapacitated him. We believe that it was only after the assailant attacked PC McLeod that he returned to strike the fatal blow to Rudd's throat. One of the reasons for this is here . . .' He pointed to a photograph of a bloody shoeprint crossed by a splatter of bloodstains. 'The spray came after the footprint, so Rudd was still alive and pumping arterial blood as the killer made his escape to the door.'

'What about DNA?' Bren asked.

'Disappointing so far. We've only found Rudd's and Wilkes's DNA on the cloak, where it came in contact with them presumably, and the blood is all Rudd's as far as we can tell. The killer was very careful to avoid leaving traces—probably wore gloves and some kind of protective clothing beneath the cloak and mask. There were DNA traces on the abandoned shoes in the bin, but they don't match anything we have. We haven't found any discarded hairs or fibres. We had hopes for saliva traces inside the mouth opening of the mask, but there again it turned out to be Rudd's DNA—we think he must have spat at his assailant during the initial struggle.'

His words took Kathy back to the moment she had forced her way into the studio. Once again she felt her feet sliding on the bloodstained floor, and herself toppling . . .

'What happened?' She looked up in surprise. People were clustered around her, looking concerned, and she seemed to be sitting on the floor.

'You blacked out,' someone said, and then she heard Brock giving orders to get a doctor. Two men lifted her to her feet and began to move towards the door.

'I'm fine,' she protested, and heard Brock at her shoulder, 'I should never have let you come in today, Kathy.' She stopped objecting and let them lead her away.

Later that evening Brock received a message to proceed immediately to an urgent meeting with Commander Sharpe at New Scotland Yard. When he reached the office on the sixth floor he thought he detected a spark of interest beneath the chilly glare of Sharpe's secretary. She knocked on the connecting door and showed him straight in.

'Coffees, please, Lillian,' Sharpe barked. 'Sit.'

Brock did so.

'You look worried, Brock.'

'Oh, no. So many things to sort out.'

'Tell me. But you seem to have sorted out Sir Jack Beaufort. He's thrown in the towel.'

'What?'

'Couple of hours ago. Resigned from the review panel on personal grounds. The Beaufort Committee no longer has a chair.'

'That's interesting,' Brock said cautiously, trying to read Sharpe's mood.

'Interesting? It's spectacular! The whole building's buzzing like an upturned wasp's nest. You had a session with Beaufort this morning, didn't you? I'll need a full report; every fact, every suspicion, every innuendo.'

'Innuendo?'

'The man's a paedophile, isn't he?'

'I'm not sure that he is. I think Wylie set him up.'

'Come on, Brock, don't go soft on me now. You must have shaken him this morning. He knows the game's up. No smoke without fire.'

'In this case, there's lots of smoke and very little fire.'

'Well, we can hand him over to the tender mercies of the Child Protection Unit if you want him out of your hair. The important thing isn't him, though, it's his damned committee. We've got to make sure it's so tainted by this that they'll never dare to bring its recommendations into the light of day.'

The door opened and the secretary came in with a tray.

'What's this?' Sharpe asked.

'Your coffees, sir.'

'Bugger the coffee. We need a drink. Whisky for me. Brock?'

Brock nodded.

'Big ones, Lillian. And pour yourself one.'

While Brock was away, Bren made a last check of his emails for the night, giving a little start to see the letters FBI appear. The message was brief and impersonal. Approval had been given to release to the Metropolitan Police the contents of six hundred and seventy-two messages stored in the accounts of Patrick Abbott and Robert Wylie. A CD containing the material had been despatched by secure express mail. Bren sent an acknowledgement and thanks, knowing that he wouldn't sleep well that night.

28

KATHY BLINKED AWAKE and realised with relief that she was in her own bed. She'd had a dream about passing out in a team briefing held at a crime scene with enormous bloodstains on the walls. Then she heard a noise in the living room, a tap running, then stopping. Someone was there. A figure appeared in the bedroom doorway.

'Hi, how are you feeling?'

'Nicole? Is that you?' She couldn't remember what her friend from the National Identification Service was doing there.

'Yes. Brock asked me to come over. You've had a good sleep. Do you feel any better?'

Kathy sat up slowly. 'I think so, yes. I feel as if I've had a long rest. What time is it?'

Nicole checked her watch. 'Ten past ten.'

'I don't remember how I got here.'

'The doctor checked you out at Shoreditch and gave you a shot of something. They brought you home and Brock gave me a ring. He'd have stayed himself but he had things to do.'

'Have you had dinner?'

'Yes, and breakfast.'

'Breakfast?'

'It's Thursday morning. You slept for eighteen hours straight. I kipped on your sofa. I'll make us a cup of tea.'

As Kathy listened to the comforting sounds of Nicole outside at the kitchen sink she adjusted to what she'd just learned. It was frightening how little control you had when you could be switched on and off like a TV set. In her mind, the bloodstained wall and writhing blue snakes were more vivid and immediate than the smell of toast coming through the door. She closed her eyes and let the images fade.

Nicole returned with a tray and sat down on the edge of the bed. 'You've got a bit more colour in your face,' she said. 'I was worried about you. You looked so white.'

'I'm sorry, Nicole. I seem to be getting you to do me favours all the time.'

'That's what friends are for.'

'What about your work?'

'There's nothing urgent. I can stay as long as you need me.'

'Didn't Lloyd mind?'

'He's a copper too, remember.'

Kathy didn't know Nicole's latest partner well, but remembered that he was a detective in west London. All in the family.

'Incidentally, he knows someone you met recently. Special Branch, Tom Reeves.' Nicole raised a questioning eyebrow.

'Oh yes. I've bumped into him a few times,' Kathy said vaguely.

'Interesting?' Nicole persisted.

'I'm too ill to answer that.'

Nicole laughed. 'Only, he rang you this morning on your mobile. I answered it in case it was Brock. I hope that's okay.'

Kathy felt a small buzz of pleasure. 'That's fine. What did he want?'

'Didn't say. He seemed concerned about you. He left a number.'

'Thanks. Did Lloyd tell you anything about him?'

'He's single, that's the main thing. Lloyd said he seems a nice bloke, but he doesn't know him well. A bit of a dark horse. You know what Special Branch are like. Someone else rang your phone.' She checked her note on a piece of paper. 'Adrian Schropp.'

For a moment Kathy couldn't place the name, then she remembered the West End art dealer.

'He didn't leave a message either. Both Brock and DI Gurney phoned me as well, just to check how you were.'

'Did they say whether they've found a woman called Poppy Wilkes yet, by any chance?'

'They didn't say. There was a report about her on the news this morning. Police are appealing blah, blah, blah. We're nothing if not appealing. How's the toast?'

'Good. I'm really hungry.'

'I'd make you some more, but that's all there is. And it seems that was the only solid food you had in your flat.'

'Sorry. I wasn't expecting visitors.'

'I can see that. I might pop out and buy a few things.'

'There's money in my bag, wherever that is.'

While Nicole was out, Kathy washed her face and brushed her teeth. Looking at herself in the bathroom mirror she understood the concern she'd seen in her friend's face. She looked drained, the way her car battery sounded on cold mornings. Coupled with the empty fridge and generally unkempt state of her flat, it didn't need a detective to draw conclusions.

She had a drink of water and began using her phone, starting with Shoreditch, where she was put through to Bren. He was relieved to hear from her and sounded just a bit too sympathetic for her liking, as if she'd been relegated to the ranks of the fragile and infirm. They hadn't found Poppy yet; her face was in all the papers.

She got the answering service on DI Reeves's phone and left a quick message, then tried Adrian Schropp's number. The strange mixture of German consonants and plummy public-school vowels answered, sounding oddly evasive.

'I'm sorry, Sergeant Kolla, I rang you in error, really. It vas nothing.'

Kathy looked at Nicole's note, with his name, number and the time of the call, two hours before, and the comment, *Information for you.* 'I understand you have some information, Mr Schropp. What's it concerning?'

'As I say, an error. I saw the picture of that girl in the paper this morning, Poppy Vilkes, and thought I knew her. But I vas wrong. So sorry to bother you.' He hung up abruptly, leaving Kathy puzzled.

Nicole came back with four heavy carrier bags, and set about filling Kathy's shelves and refrigerator. 'We'll have a proper breakfast, bacon and eggs, and I've bought you some cutlets for your dinner, and salad and fruit . . .' Kathy watched, feeling guilty, guessing what was coming.

As they finished the bacon and eggs, Nicole said casually, 'You've been feeling low, haven't you, since you split up with Leon?'

'I'm not depressed.'

'Aren't you?' Nicole looked pointedly around the room, then at Kathy. 'When did you last get your hair done?'

'I had an appointment the day this case started, and I had to cancel. I haven't had time since.'

'You mean you haven't *made* time since. You can't just live through your work, Kathy. That's a trap.'

'I think about Leon sometimes, but mostly I think about that little girl we found, with the black leg.'

'What?'

Kathy explained, Nicole looking horrified. 'And I imagine Tracey going the same way while we've been trying to find her, the gangrene spreading . . .' She was suddenly startled to find her eyes filling with tears. Hell, she thought, maybe I am depressed.

Nicole put a hand on hers. 'You must find it lonely on your own up here, don't you?'

'Sometimes.' Kathy used her other hand to wipe her eyes. 'But not as lonely as living with someone whose mind is taken up with someone else. That's much worse, isn't it?'

'Look, I think you should go to your GP. There's lots of things they can give you now, to get you over a hump.'

'Thanks. Maybe I will.' She glanced at the time. 'I'm worried about you being away from work. I'm really fine now, if you want to get back.'

'Well, perhaps I should, if you're sure. I bought you the paper and a couple of magazines. Go back to bed and have a real rest today. I'll look in on the way home tonight.'

She was talking as if to an invalid, Kathy thought. She gave a suitably limp smile of thanks and saw Nicole to the door, then went to her bedroom and started getting dressed. Before leaving she spent a bit more time on her makeup than she'd been accustomed to lately, trying to manufacture a glow of health in her cheeks.

Adrian Schropp was talking to his assistant at the desk in the front room of the Cork Street gallery. On the walls around them the large, misty Norwegian landscapes glowed beneath the lights as if some revelation were about to emerge. Kathy hoped that it might serve as an inspiration to the fog in her own head.

Schropp looked up and tried to hide his surprise. 'Vy, Sergeant Kolla, how nice. Have you changed your mind about buying a fjord? Better hurry, they've nearly all gone.'

'Yes, I see the red spots. But it was your phone call I wanted to speak to you about, Mr Schropp.'

'But I thought I explained . . .' The dealer glanced at his assistant and said, 'Give me five minutes, darling.' He crooked a finger at Kathy and led her through to the rear gallery and a couple of seats set beside a coffee table piled with art magazines and catalogues.

'I'm sorry, Sergeant, as I said, it vas all a mistake. You've vasted your time.'

'Any information about Poppy Wilkes may be vital at this time, Mr Schropp. Please tell me what you had in mind and let me be the judge.'

Schropp sighed, looking uncomfortable. 'It really is important, is it?'

'Please.'

'Vell . . .' he began reluctantly, 'I recognised her face in the paper this morning. She came in here several years ago, vith an odd story. She'd been told she vas related to a painter who had done a portrait of Mick Jagger, years ago. She'd recently visited the National Portrait Gallery and had seen such a portrait there. The people there told her that the painting had been acquired through the Adrian Schropp Gallery, and that ve might be able to put her in touch vith the artist. I pointed out that there might be other portraits of the singer, but she vas convinced it vas this one. I saw no harm in it, and told her vhere the artist lived.' He hesitated. 'It vas Reg Gilbey. Vhen I saw the girl's picture this morning, I thought, that if Reg is her relative he may know vhere she has gone, to some other relative maybe, so I tried to ring him. Vhen I got no reply I rang you instead. Then I thought maybe that vas a stupid thing to do. Maybe the whole thing vas a mistake, and anyvay, it's up to Reg to get in touch vith you. I vouldn't like the old boy to think I vas *informing* on him.'

'You're quite right to tell me this, Mr Schropp. Reg may not have seen the papers.'

'Exactly!' Schropp seemed relieved. 'He's been rather vague lately. I think vhat's been happening in Northcote Square has affected him deeply.'

'Do you know of any relatives of his?'

He scratched an ear. 'I recall a couple of old dears who came to an opening once—sisters or cousins—but I don't know vhere they lived. You'd have to speak to Reg.'

The crowds were as dense in the square as before, and the floral tributes outside Gabriel Rudd's house had grown to a small meadow, extending out across Urma Street, which had now been closed to traffic because of the risk of accidents. People were moving among the flowers, taking photographs and stooping to read the messages. Although it was midday, the sky was so darkly overcast that the lights in the buildings shone almost as brightly as at night. From the street Kathy saw a light in the bay window of Reg Gilbey's studio. She pushed her way through the throng to the iron gate, went up the steps to his front door and rang the bell, hammering the brass lion-head knocker at the same time. There was no response. She returned to the street and went round the corner. Across the way, children in the school playground were pressed against the railings, pointing and waving to the crowds. She turned down the lane behind West Terrace and opened the gate into Gilbey's backyard. His kitchen door was unlocked, and she went inside. The house was silent, a faint smell of burnt cheese and cigarette smoke hanging in the air.

'Reg!' She listened for a reply, but there was nothing. She continued along the hall, seeing the mail spilled over the floor beneath the letterbox in the front door. She climbed the stairs and opened the door to the studio. Gilbey was sitting in the middle of the room, staring at his painting of Betty Zielinski as a young woman. Beyond him, the easel that had held the portrait of Sir Jack Beaufort was empty.

'Reg? Are you all right?'

The old painter stirred, turned his head and squinted at her through his thick-framed glasses. 'Poppy's not here,' he said, his voice weak. The flesh on his face seemed pinched and even more wizened than before.

'But she's been here,' Kathy said, guessing.

He gave a little nod. It seemed such an effort for him to speak that Kathy took a chair to his side and leaned close so that she wouldn't miss anything. 'Tell me about it,' she said softly.

'She screamed,' he said after a pause, eyes narrowed as if watching a replay inside his head. 'She just screamed. Never heard such a scream.' His voice faded away and with it his attention. Close to, his skin looked as thin as tissue paper. Kathy got to her feet and hurried downstairs to the kitchen, finding the cupboard where she remembered him keeping the whisky bottle. She found a glass and returned upstairs. He hadn't stirred an inch.

'Here, try this, Reg.'

The smell of the vapour under his nose roused him a little, but when he tried to take the glass his hand was trembling too much, and Kathy held it while he sipped. After a moment a little glow of pink blossomed in his cheek.

'Want a cup of tea?'

He shook his head. 'Another one of them.'

She refilled the glass, and his grip was steadier.

'You never told me you two were related,' Kathy said.

He shot her a sideways glance. 'How do you know that?'

'I'm the police, Reg. We get to know things.'

'Tell me what she's supposed to have done then.'

'That I don't know, but I do need to speak to her. So what happened exactly?'

He took another sip. 'Couple of years ago she turned up on my doorstep. Never seen her before. Claimed I was her natural father. I told her that was bollocks. I didn't know anyone by the name of Wilkes. She said that was the name of her adoptive parents, both now dead. Before she died, her mother'd told her she was adopted, and her real dad was a famous London painter, who'd done a portrait of Mick Jagger. Well, I had done one, but others had too, so I told her it was a case of mistaken identity.'

Gilbey emptied the second glass and handed it to Kathy, who took it but didn't refill it. 'Tell me the story first,' she said.

He grunted and fumbled in his pocket for his cigarettes, lit one and coughed. 'She wasn't convinced. She said she was an artist too, and it obviously ran in the blood. When I went on denying I had anything to do with her blood she seemed more sad than anything else. Anyway, she finally left. Then I discovered she'd got herself taken on by Tait as one of his tame artists at The Pie Factory. She didn't raise the matter of her paternity with me again, or mention it to anyone else, as far as I know, but sometimes I'd catch her looking up at my windows, or watching me in the supermarket, with a look in her eyes that said, *You know*. It got on my nerves. Eventually it occurred to me that Fergus Tait might have her date of birth for her national insurance or whatever. I thought I'd work out when she was conceived, and with luck I'd have been abroad at the time, or in hospital or something, and I'd be able to put the matter to rest.'

He sucked on his cigarette and took a deep breath. 'Tait did have the date. Trouble was, when I worked it out I found she must have been conceived around the same time as I got Betty pregnant, and that made me think. I thought back to that day I took Betty to get rid of the kid. She came out weeping and upset, but how did I know what had happened in there? Had she told them to keep the money and leave the baby alone? Soon after that, she went away to stay with a sister in Birmingham. She was away for months. Could she have had the baby and given it away? I didn't want to know, and I didn't raise it with Betty. The way she was about her lost baby she could have said anything, true or not.'

He hesitated, turning his attention back to the woman in the painting, her face bright and open, unclouded by dark dreams, sunlight spilling across her skin.

'Go on, Reg,' Kathy urged softly.

'Poppy came here this morning. She'd seen the pictures of herself in the papers, and she was rattled. She said she just wanted to know the truth—was I her dad? Well, this time I didn't deny it outright. I told her the story of Betty's baby and the coincidence of the dates. I said if she wanted we could have a test done. I thought she'd be pleased, but she just seemed shocked. I asked her where the Wilkeses came from, and when she said Birmingham I told her that's where Betty had gone, and she started screaming. I don't know why.'

'Reg, did she give you any idea of where she might be staying?'

'I did ask her when she first arrived but she wouldn't say. When she left I watched her cross the square, through the gardens, and head down East Terrace. Then I lost sight of her.'

'Okay. Is there anything else you can tell me?'

He looked fearfully at her and said, 'She knows who killed Betty, doesn't she? That's why she screamed. She knows who murdered her mother.' He closed his eyes as if to wipe away the thought, then turned to stare again at Betty's painting. 'When she came here it was almost as if she took the other woman's place,' he murmured.

Kathy hesitated. 'What?'

'The other woman, Gabriel Rudd's wife, can't remember her name now.'

'Jane? Tracey's mother?'

'That's it. They used to live at number thirteen, next to Betty, in the basement flat.'

'Who did?'

'The Rudds, when his wife was alive, before he bought that big place he's in now. They were broke then. You'd see them, out in the gardens together, Jane and Gabriel and the sculptor feller.'

'Stan Dodworth?'

'Yes, him. Big pals they were, the three of them. Betty loved them too, especially when Jane got pregnant with the little girl—Betty hovered around her all the time, living next door.'

'The Rudds used to live in the basement flat where Betty's body was found?' Kathy felt a prickle in the back of her neck.

'That's right.'

'How do you mean about Poppy taking Jane's place?'

'Well, they reminded me, the three of them. You'd see them together, just like it once was with the first wife. I thought Poppy might have ended up marrying the Rudd feller, to tell the truth.'

As she turned to go, Kathy said, 'What happened to the portrait of the judge?'

'Went to the framer this morning. Beaufort insisted. Last chance to get it into the exhibition.' Reg sounded defeated.

Once outside, Kathy phoned Shoreditch and was put through to Sergeant Scott. 'When you were investigating Jane Rudd's suicide, Bill, do you remember where they were living?'

'Yeah, in Northcote Square. Not where Rudd lives now. It was a small basement flat on West Terrace.'

'Next door to Betty Zielinski?'

'That's right.'

'The same basement where her body was found?'

There was a silence. 'I suppose it is. Is that significant?'

'I don't know.' Kathy hung up, wondering.

In a different office at Shoreditch, Bren was signing for the package that had just arrived. After the messenger left, he placed it on the desk in front of him and just stared at it. He remembered the feeling he'd had when the envelope with his O-level exam results had arrived in the post, years ago. You knew that no amount of wishing could change what was written inside and yet you hesitated, feeling that nothing was quite settled until you actually read it yourself. He wanted to get a coffee, but knew he shouldn't waste time. He ripped open the package, read the short covering letter, and slipped the CD into his computer.

Scrolling through the index of the six hundred and seventy-two messages, he found that the majority had come from Wylie's account and that most were either junk mail or exchanges with third parties. But there were about twenty messages between Abbott and Wylie. He selected the most recent one, dated a few days before Tracey disappeared.

From	pabbott@kwikmail.co
To	rjwylie@kwikmail.co
Time	10 October 7.38.23am
Subject	no subject

Bob, TOLD YOU! it's worse this morning, black up to her knee, this ones finished. Pat

Kathy crossed through the gardens to East Terrace on the other side of the square. As she approached the corner she could see that Mahmed's Café was doing a roaring trade. Schoolkids and tourists were queuing out onto the street alongside the office workers who normally bought their lunches here, and who were now looking quite put out. Through the window she saw that Sonia had brought in extra help—two more girls on the counter and several in the kitchen behind. She squeezed through the queue, getting dirty looks as she worked her way forward to the counter and the cash till where Sonia was stationed.

'Sonia?'

The woman looked up sharply. Maybe she was still annoyed with the police for harassing her son, or maybe it was something else. Kathy leaned close across the counter. 'Poppy Wilkes, have you seen her?'

If she'd been more sure of what was going on and where her duty lay, Sonia might have made a convincing show of ignorance, but Kathy saw her indecision.

'Come on, Sonia.'

'She was in a terrible state after what she'd been through. I felt sorry for her. I said she could stay with us for a few days.'

'Is she here now?'

'I'll go speak to her,' Sonia muttered, and Kathy said firmly, 'I'll come too.' She lifted the counter flap and followed Sonia through a door at the back of the kitchen into a cramped hall with a staircase. They climbed three floors, and by the time they reached the top the older woman was breathing heavily, one hand on the banister and the other pressing her knee.

'Wait,' she panted, and pulled a bunch of keys from a pocket beneath her apron. She tapped on one of the doors and, hearing nothing, fitted a key to the lock and opened it.

'Poppy . . .' she cooed, then stiffened and rushed into the room with a little scream, Kathy at her heels. Poppy was lying on a narrow bed, fully dressed in jeans and jumper and shoes, half a dozen foil capsule holders scattered on the floor beside her. Her pallor was frightening, and Sonia hesitated, but Kathy felt her body warm, and found a faint pulse ticking in her throat. She grabbed her phone and keyed in triple-nine.

29

BROCK LOOKED EXASPERATED. 'Kathy, I told you—I *ordered* you, to stay at home.'

'Just as well she didn't,' Bren said, putting down the phone. 'The hospital says Poppy's been stabilised. They give her fifty-fifty.'

'I should think the ambulance people must have wondered which one they were supposed to be treating. You look half-dead.'

'I'm okay,' Kathy said, though the frantic activity had left her feeling limp.

'I should send you home now,' Brock grumbled.

'You can't,' she said. 'Not till we sort this out.'

Brock conceded reluctantly. 'The forensic people should be here soon. Want something to eat?'

She shook her head. Bren offered her a file. 'This might help,' he said.

'What is it?'

'Transcripts of email correspondence between Abbott and Wylie. It arrived this morning.'

As she turned the pages she felt herself observing something like an ongoing domestic squabble between a married couple. Wylie was irritated at the way the girls were getting sick; he blamed Abbott for not looking after them properly, and for not stealing a better sedative from the pharmacy of the hospital where he worked. Abbott resented being scolded and complained that he was having to do all the chores. The callous banality was breathtaking and utterly incriminating. She finished the last message and looked bleakly at Brock and Bren. 'But no mention of Tracey.'

'No.'

'Brock . . .' Kathy hesitated; the past forty-eight hours was still confused in her mind and she wasn't sure how much she'd missed while she'd been out of action. 'I'm not convinced the profiler is right, about an outsider stalking the people in the square.'

'Go on.'

She saw Bren listening to her, ready to challenge what she was about to say. 'We've picked up some interesting leads, Kathy,' he said. 'Some of the messages on the flowers outside Rudd's house are pretty weird.'

'Okay, maybe there are stalkers out there, but Poppy was researching artworks about a missing child two days before Tracey disappeared.' She described her discovery at the Soane Museum. 'And now she tries to kill herself after hearing from Gilbey that Betty may have been her mother. Gilbey is convinced that she knows something about Betty's death.'

Brock nodded. 'I've been thinking the same thing. I've also been wondering about the way Poppy used Tracey as a model, and about the fact that both Wylie and the judge knew her work.'

Bren shrugged. 'Well, let's see what the evidence says. The others should be here by now.'

The forensic experts took their seats once more around the table in the large meeting room, this time including the pathologist, Dr Mehta. He sat next to Morris Munns, whom he knew and liked, and leaned over to whisper some remark that made Morris's shoulders shake with laughter. Kathy had hoped to get a seat that didn't place her facing the large bloodstained map of her nightmares again, but when she arrived she found that it was all that was available. She thought Sundeep Mehta scrutinised her with an almost clinical interest, as if measuring her up for his stainless-steel table, but then he gave her a friendly grin and she decided it was just her imagination.

Brock began. 'We've now found the missing woman, Poppy Wilkes, soon after she'd attempted suicide. She's currently in intensive care and may not survive. We've also learned that she seems to have had knowledge of Tracey Rudd's disappearance before it happened, and may be implicated in some way with the subsequent deaths of Zielinski,

Dodworth and Rudd. We need to reexamine the evidence in the light of this.'

There was a murmur of interest around the table. Brock went on, 'Let's start with the first death, Betty Zielinski's. Before she tried to kill herself today, Wilkes discovered that Zielinski may have been her natural mother. Her reaction to this information was apparently one of extreme distress, possibly indicating a sense of guilt over her death. Could she have been involved?'

The laboratory Reporting Officer cleared his throat, and Kathy sensed his resistance to Brock's argument. 'We found no fingerprints or traces of Wilkes's DNA at the scene, either in Zielinski's house or in the basement of 13 West Terrace. There were many different footprints inside number thirteen, most of them builders'.' He paused, thumbing through his file. He found the sheet he wanted and said, 'All right, the smallest size recorded was an eight. We should check her footwear, obviously. We can also confirm from their DNA whether Zielinski really was her mother, if that helps.' From his tone, he plainly didn't see how it would.

'Check Reg Gilbey from number fifteen too, would you? He may be the father.'

Kathy watched Dr Mehta, who was obviously intrigued by this, questioning the detective at his side. Her eyes strayed up to the map behind them. She saw that her imagination had exaggerated its menace; the red was more the colour of brick than of blood and, apart from the writhing Thames itself, the blue ribbons of waterways were nothing like snakes, but more like fine capillaries spreading out from it. There was one odd one that ran horizontally across the map, from somewhere above Heathrow in the west to meet the Thames at Limehouse in the east, not far from where they were sitting.

'Kathy,' Brock was saying, 'what about Dodworth? Do you have any insight into the relationship between him and Wilkes?'

'They lived near one another in The Pie Factory and they were both sculptors, using similar materials, so I suppose they spent time together in the workshops. She seemed protective when she found us searching Dodworth's room after he disappeared. I think there may have been quite a close bond there, although not as close as that between Wilkes and Rudd. Reg Gilbey told me that they were together a lot, the three of them, much as Dodworth, Rudd and his wife Jane had been when she was alive.'

'*Jules et Jim*,' Dr Mehta said, and then, realising he'd given himself away, added, 'I believe it was a popular movie, years ago, about two men and a girl—not that I was around then.' People were giving him quizzical looks, so he quickly went on, 'Wilkes surely couldn't have hanged Dodworth against his will. Are you suggesting that she may have persuaded him to kill himself?'

'Would that be consistent with what you found, Sundeep?'

'Well . . . I suppose it might. There were no signs of a struggle, but also no evidence that he had handled the rope.'

'And she had access to the building.'

'We have got one new result for Dodworth,' the RO said. 'We've traced the clay that was found in the grooves of his shoes. It was a modelling clay, and we had assumed that we'd find a match somewhere in the workshops of The Pie Factory, only we didn't. Instead we found it in Rudd's studio, as DI Gurney suspected. The deposits hadn't completely dried, and we estimate that Dodworth picked them up some time during the forty-eight hours before he was hanged.'

'Interesting.'

Brock glanced at Bren, who said, 'We did check Rudd's place on the Thursday that Betty was found, and there was no sign of Dodworth then. He must have gone there later.'

'But there's still no positive evidence that Wilkes was involved in his death,' the RO objected.

'No. But she was present at the third death, Gabriel Rudd's. Is it possible that she was the hooded figure that attacked DS Kolla and PC McLeod?'

'No,' the RO said firmly. 'There were no bloodstains on her at all. It would have been impossible for her to have killed Rudd without getting blood on her shoes . . .'

'Hang on,' Brock said. 'I didn't ask if she could have killed Rudd— that was going to be my next question. I asked if she could have been the hooded figure who appeared at the top of the stairs before Rudd was murdered.'

There was silence as they digested this. Kathy said, 'I thought the figure was taller than Poppy.'

'Could you have been mistaken?'

She saw the image in her mind, but she knew from experience how distorted witnesses' memories could be. 'We were looking from below, which exaggerated the perspective. Yes, I suppose it's possible I'm mistaken.'

'You're suggesting Wilkes was cooperating with the third person, the killer?' The Reporting Officer was openly sceptical.

'I'm just trying to establish what possibilities are compatible with the forensic evidence. Is this a possibility?'

Reluctantly they agreed that it might be.

'All right,' Brock continued, 'let's consider another possibility, that there was no third person. Could Wilkes have killed Rudd, then dumped the bloodstained shoes while Kathy and PC McLeod were recovering at the foot of the stairs, then returned in a pair of fresh shoes, taken sedatives and feigned unconsciousness. Is this compatible with the evidence?'

'No, Brock,' Bren spoke up. 'There wasn't enough time for her to do all that before Kathy broke in. We did test runs for each of the stages of the action. It just doesn't work that way.'

'All right,' Brock persisted. 'Suppose she dumped the shoes *before* she attacked PC McLeod and killed Rudd.'

'But the shoes were bloodstained.'

'Rudd had a cut on his arm, didn't he, Sundeep?'

Mehta was looking keenly at Brock. 'Indeed.'

'Could Poppy have incapacitated Rudd—he had drunk a lot remember, and he had a bruise to the head—and made that cut first, staining the shoes, and laying a false trail out into the lane. Then she returned, went through the charade with the disguise and made the noises to attract Kathy and McLeod up the stairs to witness the intruder before killing Rudd.'

There was silence as the others considered this. From their expressions, they were more impressed by its ingenuity than its probability.

'It would explain the blood splash that we found overlapping the footprint,' the RO conceded, 'but it would mean that Wilkes carried out the final assault on Rudd without getting a drop of blood on her second pair of shoes. I just don't think that's possible.'

'All the same,' Brock insisted, 'I'd appreciate it if you'd have another look at the bloodstain evidence, just to be sure.'

Reluctantly he agreed.

'Thank you.' Brock turned to the forensic psychologist, who had said nothing so far. 'What about motive?'

The man scratched his ear. 'Well, I'm having some trouble with this line of thinking, I must confess. It isn't the direction I was pursuing at all, as you know. But the idea of the killings being "within the family", so to speak—if we can think of the community of Northcote Square as a family—has appeal. And the close relationship between the three artists is intriguing. You're thinking of jealousy, perhaps? But what has it got to do with the disappearance of Tracey Rudd?'

'I was thinking along the lines of Poppy punishing the others for neglecting Tracey, or even conniving in her abduction.' Even as she put the ideas into words Kathy realised how bizarre they sounded.

'One step at a time,' Brock said. 'Let's establish the forensic options, and hope that Poppy regains consciousness.'

As the meeting broke up, Dr Mehta came over to speak to Kathy. 'How's my favourite lady detective?' he murmured, with a jokey leer. 'I was watching you, you know. You're not well. If you don't look after yourself, you'll end up on my table, and you wouldn't like that.'

'No, I wouldn't,' she said, managing a smile despite his apparent enthusiasm for the idea. She was preoccupied. She'd been looking at that odd blue line on the map again, and was convinced that she'd seen it somewhere before. Then Brock interrupted her thoughts.

'I wanted to show you something, Kathy,' he said, and produced a copy of the photograph they'd found in Rudd's studio. 'Have you seen this before?'

She took in the faces, especially that of the pale woman holding the baby. She looked ill, a strained smile forced onto her face, very different from the buoyant young woman whose pictures Kathy had seen at West Drayton. 'That's Jane Rudd,' she said. 'Must be Tracey's birthday, just before she died. She doesn't look well, does she? No, I haven't seen it before. Where did you get it?'

'It was pinned to the wall of Rudd's studio.'

Kathy was puzzled. 'Whereabouts?'

Brock described the place, not far from the hidden exit door and in plain view.

'I'm positive it wasn't there before the attack,' Kathy said. 'I spoke to Gabe in his studio on Tuesday afternoon before we went to see Wylie's lawyer, and I'm sure it wasn't there then. Gabe must have pinned it up after I left.'

'His prints aren't on it,' Brock mused. 'And I wonder who was behind the camera?'

Kathy was staring again at the face of Jane Rudd, noticing the cut of the hair, the big eyes. 'She looks a bit like Princess Di, doesn't she? It was soon after this that Stan did his shocking sculpture *Bye Bye Princess* and had his breakdown. I wonder if the "princess" could have been Jane rather than Di. Maybe he was in love with her.'

The face on the pillow looked drained of life, dark hollows around her closed eyes made more stark by the whiteness of her face, but the monitor beside the bed insisted that she was alive. Although there were two other police at hand to avoid losing Poppy for a second time, Kathy stayed on, hour after hour, wanting to be the first person Poppy saw when—if—she opened her eyes. To keep her mind occupied, she studied a sheaf of printouts from the official Gabriel Rudd Web site and a London A–Z. Several times she fell asleep, and finally, jerking awake in her chair, she decided to have a wash and get a coffee and something to eat.

When she returned twenty minutes later, she saw the armed cop outside Poppy's room talking with a dark-coated man she didn't at first recognise. He was holding a bunch of flowers and as she got closer Kathy recognised Reg Gilbey's voice, arguing with the guard to let him see his daughter and at the same time trying to see past him through the open door. Perhaps the sound of Gilbey's voice triggered some reaction in Poppy's brain, for they suddenly heard a plaintive call from inside the room, 'Reg? Reg?'

Kathy nodded to the guard and took Gilbey's arm, steering him in towards the bed, where a nurse was checking the drip. Poppy was staring up with wild, unfocused eyes.

'Gabe's dead, isn't he?' she asked hoarsely. 'It's not a dream?'

The old man murmured a reply. 'Yes. I'm sorry, girl, he's gone.'

Poppy sobbed. 'It's all so awful. I didn't understand. Everything's ruined.'

Then she stared up at Gilbey and her voice dropped to a whisper. 'I should never have come to the square.'

'I'm glad you did,' the old man replied. 'I'm very glad you did.'

Poppy's eyes closed, and the life seemed to drain out of her again. The nurse checked her and said, 'She's all right. I think she's going to be fine. But you'd best be going now.'

Kathy led Reg away, taking him down to her car to give him a lift home. Along the way he said, 'She was telling the truth, wasn't she, about not understanding what was happening? She wasn't involved, was she?'

Kathy kept worrying at that thought after she'd dropped him in Northcote Square, and also at another possibility that was throbbing in her head. As she drove back through the dark streets, she began to wonder if she too, had been infected by the dark fantasies of Henry Fuseli.

30

THE LABORATORY RO cleared his throat, rather smugly, Kathy thought.

'We've done a thorough reanalysis of the blood patterns,' he said, 'and there's absolutely no possibility that Poppy Wilkes could have cut Rudd's throat and got herself back to the bed where we found her without getting blood on her shoes and leaving footprints in the bloodstains. Sorry, Brock.'

Brock shrugged. 'Thanks for trying.'

'We also compared the DNA of Reg Gilbey, Betty Zielinski and Poppy Wilkes, as you requested,' the RO continued, conciliatory. 'You were right, are related. Poppy Wilkes is their daughter.'

He paused to take a sheaf of photographs from his folder and passed them round. 'One other result. The analysis of the marks left by the tool on the doorjamb. It was a chisel with a half-inch wide blade, and the marks are identical to those left on the door to the basement where Zielinski was found, and on her back door, and also on Tracey's window.'

Brock examined the pictures, some taken through a stereo microscope. 'What about Aimee's and Lee's windows?'

'No, those were different. Actually, he didn't manage to open the studio door. That would have been quite difficult with a chisel. It looks as if he was trying and Rudd heard him and opened the door to see what was going on.'

'Does anyone else have something new?' Brock asked.

No one spoke, and after a pregnant silence people began to gather their papers. Kathy felt a knot of anxiety tighten inside her. Although she'd been wrestling with it half the night, she didn't feel confident about what she had to say in front of this group of highly qualified scientists. She would have preferred to have discussed it first with Brock or Bren, but hadn't had the chance.

'There is one thing,' she said, 'though I don't know exactly what it means.' She took up her file of Rudd's Web site images and got to her feet, aware of everyone watching her as she walked to the big map on the wall. Her hand was unsteady as she pinned the sheets in sequence along the base of the map. There were sixteen in all, and she was acutely aware of their silence as she worked her way slowly to the end.

'These are the sixteen banners that Gabriel Rudd made, the last one incomplete at his death. You'll see that each one has a thin, irregular line across the top.' She pointed them out. 'No one seems to know what they signify. But if you look at the map of London, you'll see what I think is the answer.' She pointed at the odd blue line stretching across the map above the sequence of images. Her audience frowned at it, then one by one they made little sounds of surprise and interest.

'This is the Grand Union Canal, which comes down from the north, from Birmingham, past Watford, and enters the London area here.' She pointed to the large coloured map. 'On the first of his strips, Rudd begins the line of the canal at West Drayton, where it turns eastward. This happens to be where Tracey's grandparents live, and where Tracey's mother Jane was born and grew up. In the following strips he traces its route across north London, around Ealing to Kensal Town, where Jane and Gabriel Rudd shared a flat when they were art students together. The canal goes on to Little Venice and turns into the Regent's Canal around Regent's Park, then runs through Camden Lock and Kings Cross. Rudd's final strip takes the canal as far as Shoreditch, close to us here.'

'Where Jane died,' Brock said thoughtfully.

'Yes, it finishes exactly where she drowned.'

The forensic psychologist was peering keenly at the blue line. 'Jane's lifeline,' he suggested. 'Her journey through life.'

'Perhaps,' Kathy said. 'The thing is, if the line does mean something like that, then Rudd calculated its length.'

They looked puzzled.

'I mean, he cut it up into sixteen sections, one for each banner, and when he reached the end he died. As if he planned the whole thing. I'm wondering if this is his suicide note.'

Several voices broke out in protest, but not Brock's, Kathy noticed. He was looking at her thoughtfully, nodding approval.

She let the hubbub die down, then continued, 'If you took the scenario that Brock suggested yesterday, and substituted Rudd for Poppy, laying the false trail with the bloody shoes, then returning to stage his own murder, would that be feasible?'

The scientist frowned. 'But why?'

'I'm not sure about motive. But in terms of the evidence, remember that odd DNA trace of Rudd's on the mask, as well as the blood spray over the top of the footprint, both compatible with what I've just described. What about the wounds, Dr Mehta? Could they be self-inflicted?'

The pathologist spread the autopsy photographs on the table and pointed to close-ups of the throat wound. 'Suicides with a blade usually make a few initial tentative cuts before they summon up confidence for the fatal slash. This is not like that—it's clean, decisive and, though not very deep, it was certainly effective. But yes, it could have been self-inflicted.'

'His fingerprints weren't on the sword hilt,' someone argued.

'But there was a handkerchief lying on the floor,' Kathy said. 'He could have used that.'

'What about the chisel? It wasn't found in the studio.'

'The marks on the door could have been made earlier,' Brock suggested. 'I think the crucial test would be the bloodstains on the cloak. If there were a third person he would have been wearing the cloak when Rudd was struck, whereas if Rudd killed himself he probably would have already composed the scene, laying out the cloak on the floor, before he made the final cut.'

The RO was examining his file, turning over computer diagrams of the blood traces. 'It's true that there was almost no blood on the floor beneath the cloak,' he said. 'I don't know, we'd have to look at these again.'

'There's one other thing,' Kathy went on. 'Jane wasn't the only one born in West Drayton. Her parents told me that Tracey was born there, too. So this might be Tracey's lifeline as much as Jane's. I'm wondering . . .' Kathy hesitated before saying the thing that most troubled her, 'I'm wondering if he's telling us where Tracey is.'

'Oh no.' Bren groaned as he understood what Kathy was saying. 'In the canal, following her mother?'

Kathy stood at the parapet of the bridge from which Jane Rudd had jumped, watching the divers working in the dark waters below. It was all conjecture, she told herself, for she really didn't want to believe that Gabriel Rudd was capable of this, but the sight of the shiny black-rubber figures bursting to the surface reminded her of Fuseli's image of the Midgard Serpent. The symbolism seemed all too appropriate. After a while, the men reported that they could find no trace of a child's body in the area of the bridge, and proposed to extend their search to the east. They warned that after nineteen days it could have been moved by slow currents, or been caught up by a passing houseboat and carried miles away.

At midday on that Friday they were called from the canalside search by a message from the hospital, where Poppy's doctor had pronounced her sufficiently recovered to undertake a first short interview with the police. Clutching the bedcover tightly with the hand that didn't have the drip, she told them that she had no recollection of the evening of Gabe's murder after the pizza was delivered, and that she had no new information at all about the deaths of Stan Dodworth or Betty Zielinski. When Kathy began to probe her about whether she knew that Stan had visited Gabe's studio while he was on the run, she became emotional and began to cry, and the doctor insisted on her being left alone. He would be keeping her in hospital for at least another night, he said.

As they were leaving, Brock had a call from Morris Munns. He had something interesting to show them, he said. Dave the badger had blown Gabriel Rudd's story.

It was the poetic justice of the thing that especially appealed to Morris—Gabriel Rudd undone by his own joke at Brock's expense. Munns' section had previously scanned the twenty-four hour camera coverage of Rudd in his glass cube which had been broadcast on the web, especially for the periods during his fourth and eighth nights, when Betty Zielinski and Stan Dodworth had died, and had found nothing suspicious. But after listening to Kathy's bizarre theory at the morning meeting, Morris had taken another look. During the periods of darkness, the lighting level was too low to make out much detail, but it would certainly have been possible to see if Rudd had got out of bed and left his cube. Also, the distinctive white stripes on the face of the badger were clearly visible.

During the eight nights he had been in the cube with Rudd, Dave had adopted a routine. The first night he had had some difficulty coming to terms with the glass walls which prevented him from going out into the gallery, and he had made a frustrated attempt to dig through the timber flooring. But once he'd recognised his boundaries he seemed to settle down, and in the succeeding nights he followed a regular pattern— emerging from his hide an hour or so after the lights went out, roaming around the cube, eating the food left for him, drinking and defecating, exploring some more, and then retiring again well before dawn. Of course there were variations in his movements from night to night, but by careful plotting of Dave's white stripes on a grid, and precise timing of each shift of position, Morris Munns had been able to establish that for certain periods during nights four, five, seven and eight, Dave's movements were precisely the same as during periods from earlier nights.

'They're fakes,' he told Brock gleefully. 'They're recordings of earlier scenes that've been patched into the live transmission.'

'Could Rudd have done that from inside his cube?' Brock asked.

'Absolutely. He had all he needed in there with him. His computer controlled the camera, and he could have switched the film on and off while he was still in his bed. So we don't know where he was at the times Zielinski and Dodworth died, nor on a couple of nights in between.'

'I think we can make a fair guess,' Brock said.

Later that afternoon, Kathy's mobile rang. It was Tom Reeves.

'Hi,' he said. 'How are you now?'

'I'm feeling a bit better, thanks.'

'Good. You've heard about Beaufort stepping down, I suppose?'

'Yes.'

'And I've been taken off his detail, which means there's no more risk of a conflict of interest.'

'How do you mean?'

'Between your job and mine. So that leaves me free to ask you if you'd like to go out for a drink or something.'

Kathy smiled to herself. 'Oh, well . . . thanks, Tom. Though I did go out with a Special Branch man once, and it didn't work.'

'What happened?'

'They changed his identity, and he disappeared without a word.'

He laughed. 'Still, you don't sound too resistant to the idea of one date, by way of a preliminary investigation.'

'You can tell that, can you?'

'I think so. How about tomorrow night, Saturday?'

She hesitated. 'I'm still tied up in this case. Maybe next week, I'm not sure. Can I call you?'

'That's a brush-off, isn't it?'

'No, really.'

'Well, can I ask you for a favour anyway? It's about the judge's wife, Maisie.'

'Is she really called Lady Maisie?'

'That's right. She's okay, a bit vague when she takes too many of her little pills. She asked me to help her. She wants to have a private word with your boss, Brock, but not at the station. I thought you might be able to arrange it for her.'

'And my reward is a date with you?'

'No, no.' He sounded embarrassed.

'When does she want to do this?'

'Soon. Right now, if you can fix it. I can bring her straight over.'

'Hang on.'

She saw Brock in the corridor, talking to Bren, and she went and spoke to him. He raised an eyebrow then said, 'Make it the exhibition at the National Portrait Gallery in half an hour.' Then he added under his breath, 'As long as she's not armed.'

Half an hour later he was standing in front of Reg Gilbey's portrait of Sir Jack Beaufort, described in the exhibition catalogue as a leading figure of the British legal establishment and a noted collector of twentieth-century British art. The painting had a powerful presence, and Brock was struck by the contrast between the frailty of the artist, whom people might dismiss as a boozy old codger, and the strength of the work, as if the discipline of a lifetime had a momentum of its own, carrying him through.

He became aware of someone at his side and, turning, recognised

Lady Beaufort. Her hat and silk scarf gave her an almost jaunty air, off-set by slightly sinister tinted glasses. She gazed vaguely at the portrait as if uncertain whether she knew who it was, then murmured, 'Thank you so much for agreeing to see me, Chief Inspector. Jack hasn't told me much of what's been going on, but I think I can interpret him quite well by now. He announced the other day that he was getting tired of his work commitments and wanted to take me on a cruise, and I realised right away that things must be very bad, very bad indeed. Jack has never willingly taken a holiday in his life, and detests cruises. Of course, he refused to elaborate, but fortunately he keeps a personal diary, which he doesn't know I read. From that I gathered that he has been going through a form of purgatory recently, in which you appear to have been the principal tormentor.'

She paused and looked around the gallery room, which at that moment was empty apart from themselves. 'Is it little girls?' she asked, gazing steadily up into Brock's face. 'Is that the problem?'

'Yes.'

'I assumed so. It's something that's always troubled him. I remember not long after we were married confronting him with some pictures which I'd found in his study. He was mortified, literally sick with shame. I must confess I've often found it difficult to fathom what goes on in men's minds, but I am absolutely certain that that is where Jack has kept this particular demon of his—in his mind. He would never, never do anything shameful in that way.'

'How can you be sure?'

'I know him, Chief Inspector. I know him better than you or anyone else does. That's what I wanted to tell you. I realise that it may not be a very satisfactory thing for you, a wife's endorsement of her husband, but in this case it's the most dependable thing you can have.'

She turned back to consider her husband's portrait. 'It's caught him rather well, hasn't it? His weaknesses as well as his strengths, Moloch as well as Solomon.'

'Didn't Moloch demand children as sacrifices?' Brock said.

Lady Beaufort gave an embarrassed flutter of her hand. 'Oh, well I've probably mixed him up with somebody else.'

'Your husband told me that he became involved with a man called Robert Wylie in order to help a friend whom Wylie was trying to blackmail. Have you any idea who the friend might be? It might help your husband if the friend could confirm the story.'

'Didn't Jack tell you? Well, well, how gallant of him.' Brock caught the stress on the word "gallant". A group came into the room, and Brock and Lady Maisie drew back into a corner as the people clustered in front of Beaufort's portrait.

'It's a Gilbey, isn't it?' one said, peering at the title panel. 'Yes. I've always loved this guy. Do you remember his Mick Jagger? He hasn't really lost it, has he? A bit more blurry, like Monet in his old age, his eyesight going.'

'I don't think Jack would be altogether happy that they call it a Gilbey, rather than a Beaufort, as if he's coincidental, like a bunch of flowers or a bowl of fruit.' Lady Maisie allowed herself a little smile. 'The friend was my sister—my younger sister. When Jack and I first went out she was a sweet, spoilt little girl of ten. Jack adored her, like everyone else. Well, perhaps not quite like everyone else. Anyway, later she became bored with being spoilt all the time and took to drink in a big way, and got into various kinds of trouble. Jack pulled strings for her a couple of times. She's a reformed character now, so one is led to believe, married to a lovely man in the City. I'm not sure if she'd confirm Jack's story or not. It might be an interesting test.'

There had been an edge to her voice throughout this account, and while he believed her, Brock wondered what else there might be to the story. Did the little sister know something about Beaufort that he wouldn't want her to bring up?

Lady Maisie glanced at her watch. 'I really must go now. There are so many last-minute arrangements to be made. I'm so glad we've had this little chat, Chief Inspector. I feel I shall be able to relax now, while we're away.'

She pursed her lips into a smile. They were orange, not quite right with the crimson scarf, and Brock wondered if she was colour-blind.

31

THE NEXT MORNING they picked Poppy up at the hospital and took her back to Shoreditch station. Some colour had returned to her face, and though she still looked exhausted, a little of her old cheek had reasserted itself. 'Got a fag?' she demanded as she sat down. 'Can't talk without a fag.'

After a search was mounted in the front office, a packet of Benson and Hedges was requisitioned from a reluctant constable and the interview resumed. Kathy decided Poppy was robust enough to take some hard questions.

'Okay now?'

'Yeah, yeah, fire away.' Poppy casually lifted her chin and drew on the cigarette.

'Just so you know, we checked your DNA. Betty Zielinski was your birth mother.'

The thin column of blue smoke quivered. 'Yeah,' Poppy said after a pause, 'I know.'

'When did you find out?'

'When Reg spoke to me. Yesterday was it? God, it feels like weeks ago.'

'Did you suspect it before?'

'No, of course I didn't. What, that old bag?' She shook her head in disgust, as if someone had swindled her out of small change.

'And the DNA confirmed that Reg was your father too. But you've been sure of that for some time, haven't you? Is that why you dumped that rubbish of Stan's in Reg's bin and told me to look there? Were you trying to punish him for denying you?'

But Poppy wasn't yet ready to make admissions of this kind, and Kathy took a different line.

'Reg said you were very upset when he told you about Betty. So upset you ran back to Mahmed's and tried to kill yourself. Why was that?'

Poppy seemed to shrink a little in her chair, as if fending off some terrible memory. She didn't reply.

Kathy leaned forward and spoke gently. 'We know. We worked it out for ourselves, Poppy. It was Gabe, wasn't it? You realised that your boyfriend had killed your mother.'

Poppy flinched but kept herself under control, biting her lip as if at a spring tightening inside her. 'He didn't. He was in that glass cube.'

'We've found out how he was able to leave the cube without being seen on camera, just as he did later, when Stan died. Were you there, Poppy, when Stan was hanged?'

Poppy glared at her, mouth tight. 'God, you're so fuckin' sanctimonious, aren't you? So pleased with yourself. *Were you there, Poppy?* like a fuckin' primary school teacher. Gabe was so right about you!'

Brock broke in, 'That's not going to help, Poppy . . .' but Kathy had seen the glint of tears in Poppy's eyes, and she said gently, 'It's okay, I think it already has.'

Poppy stared at her for a moment, and then the tears began to flow.

They sat in silence while Poppy sobbed, head bowed, then Kathy nodded to the uniformed woman constable who was standing by the door. She came forward and put an arm around Poppy's shoulders, took a packet of tissues from her pocket and said, 'It's all right, love. Can I get you something, a nice cup of tea?'

Somehow the uniform and the platitude had a calming effect. Poppy sniffed, nodded her head and wiped her nose. Then she took a deep breath and lit a new cigarette from the stub of the old one. 'No, I wasn't there,' she said, voice subdued to a whisper. 'I had no idea that was going to happen.'

'Just tell us what you know,' Kathy said.

She had seen Stan Dodworth on the morning after Betty was murdered, Poppy explained, though she didn't know about the murder at the time. He had returned briefly to his room at The Pie Factory, and he was so jumpy and wired that she'd thought he'd taken drugs. Something had happened, he said, something really scary and exciting. He said he had to go away for a while, and made her promise not to tell anyone she'd seen him. She'd stayed in her room after that until the police came to get her to be interviewed, and only then did she learn about Betty being killed. She was terrified that Stan had been involved, but decided to say nothing until she'd had a chance to speak to Gabe, which she did later that day, on his mobile. He told her to keep quiet and wait to hear further from him.

She was surprised when Gabe came to her room later that night, after everyone was asleep. He told her he had a way of slipping out of the cube without being seen in the dark, and together they went across the square to Gabe's house, where Stan was waiting for them. Gabe explained that the police thought Stan had something to do with Betty's murder, and they had to help him because he had no one else to turn to. He was going to hide at Gabe's until things quietened down, and Gabe wanted Poppy to keep an eye on him, get him food and pass him messages. Apparently the police had already visited Gabe's house, looking for Stan, who'd hidden outside on the roof until they left. Stan seemed very low, and Gabe was trying to keep his spirits up.

Later, at the weekend, Stan told her that Gabe had been visiting him again at night. Stan was lively now, almost too lively, and Poppy was worried that he might do something stupid like go out into the street. He'd been making little clay maquettes for sculptures in Gabe's studio, and he said he felt inspired to do something really awesome. That night he died.

The next day she was very upset when she heard the news. She couldn't believe Stan had committed suicide, and when she eventually got Gabe alone in his house again she told him how he couldn't have killed himself when he was planning to do a really special work. Then Gabe said something weird. He said, didn't she realise that's exactly what he had done?

'He wouldn't explain what that was supposed to mean.' Poppy was oblivious to them now, telling the story as if arguing with herself, trying to make sense of it. Her fingers flew between the cigarette packet, her mouth and the ashtray, flicking, tapping, scratching. 'He changed the subject. Didn't I ever get fed up, pushing the same tired old rubbish, spouting the same pretentious garbage, *playing* at being an artist, showing off like a kid with a drum? I told him I took it seriously, what I did, and he laughed. He said we were just playing with other people's second-hand toys, that we made these gestures about life and death and violence and stuff, like we were really angry and profound, but nobody believed us and nobody gave a toss. People just wanted a bit of a laugh. We had less meaning than the ads on TV. Far, far less than some demented madman who strapped a bomb under his coat and got on a bus.'

Poppy paused as the constable came in with her tea. 'He really meant it. He scared me. I said that wasn't so, that people really were interested in his work, that *No Trace* was pulling bigger crowds than Manchester United. He said that was because people realised it was true, it was real. It wasn't just another artist wanker pulling down his pants to shock the bourgeoisie. Trace really had gone, Betty really was dead, so was Stan, and so . . . He didn't finish the sentence, and that was when I first realised that he was behind the whole thing. The idea was so terrible that I couldn't really take it in. Betty and Stan had died for Gabe's artwork. He'd killed them so that he and his work would be more famous. He'd used them like disposable models.'

'Did he actually admit this to you?'

Poppy shook her head. 'I didn't dare ask him, but I didn't have to. It was written all over his face. He *knew* what had happened. He'd known all along. He'd planned it and carried it out. I didn't want to believe it, especially about Betty. Why did he have to do that to Betty?'

She blinked and looked up suddenly, as if thinking she'd said too much and wanted to retract, but Kathy said, 'It's okay, Poppy, we worked it out for ourselves. He staged his own death too, didn't he?'

'I found the sword in a drawer. I couldn't bring myself to ask what it was for. I think I half-believed it was for me, but I still stayed with him. I wouldn't be telling you now except that I believe he wanted people to know. All his heroes killed themselves—Van Gogh, Mishima, Pollock. Art validated by death, death validated by art. He said *No Trace* was the biggest thing in his life, and I suppose he thought this would make it even bigger. Well, it has, hasn't it?'

'Yes,' Kathy said. 'It has.' She watched Poppy reach for another cigarette, hand shaking. The air was blue, but no one dared break Poppy's concentration by moving to open a window or switch on the fan. 'Tell me about Tracey.'

'I've dreaded you asking me that. I don't know what happened to her. That's the truth.'

'But Gabe did, didn't he?'

Poppy hesitated, then gave a little nod. 'He didn't say so, but he had this calm about him when I asked him. He said I didn't need to worry, he was sure she was happy wherever she was.'

'When was this?'

'When we saw that man's picture in the papers, the one who fell from the building, and they said the police had wanted to talk to him about the other missing girls. I knew he was a friend of Stan's, and when I asked Stan about it he told me he'd warned Gabe about the man being interested in Trace. I told Gabe we should tell the police but he said to wait, and Stan was worried that he'd get in trouble if it came out he knew the man, because he was using him to get into the mortuary at the hospital.'

'What was the monster that frightened Tracey?'

'I think it was the cast of the old woman that Stan had in his room. Trace was scared of Stan's room, but fascinated too. I'd catch them whispering together sometimes, and he'd say they were telling about secrets. Of course he'd known her since she was a baby, and she looked up to him as a kind of uncle. He could get her to do things she wouldn't do for anybody else, like recite a poem in public, stuff like that.'

'What about kiss a strange man on the cheek?' Kathy told her of the episode that Beaufort had described, and Poppy looked shocked.

'Yeah, I think he could have got her to do that. I remember she was modelling for me one day and she disappeared for a while. She was wearing that dressing gown. But why would Stan make her do it?'

'As a favour to his friend Abbott?'

'Maybe.' She gave a shiver.

'But you'd been doing research into pictures of missing children before Trace disappeared, hadn't you, Poppy? At the Soane Museum?'

Poppy was startled. 'Yes . . . how did you know that? Gabe asked me to do it and get a photo if I could. We'd been reading reports about the hunt for the first two girls and he thought it might be a subject for a work.'

'Why didn't he go himself?'

'He said people would recognise him, with his white hair.'

'And this would have been after Stan had warned him about his friend Abbott taking an interest in Tracey?'

'Maybe, yes, I suppose so. But . . . I'm sure Gabe would never have been involved in Tracey's disappearance. She was . . .' for a moment Poppy seemed lost for an appropriate word, '. . . important to him.'

'But not as important as *No Trace,* the first masterpiece of the twenty-first century.'

'Oh God.' Poppy lowered her face onto her arms and began to weep silently.

Kathy got up and opened the window, wondering what it was that Gabe had said about her that was so right.

As they waited for the experts to arrive that afternoon, Bren, who'd been going over the tape of Poppy's interview again, said to Kathy, 'I've got to hand it to you. I thought your theory was barmy, but Morris and the Wilkes woman have shown you were spot on. Rudd must have been off his head.'

'Obsessed, I suppose,' Kathy replied. She still felt numb after the session with Poppy. Her question, 'Why did he have to do that to Betty?' kept coming back to her. And then there was the question of Tracey. She replayed mental images of Gabe—drunk, sober, gleeful, morose—and wondered how he had been able to hide so thoroughly the cruelty that must have lain inside.

This time, the laboratory reporting officer came accompanied by re-inforcements—two scientific officers, and a technician who connected their laptop to a projector and set up a screen. Brock began by sum-marising what they had now learned, and the lab team listened impas-sively. Then the RO spoke.

'What we've tried to do is track the blood particles backward in time, from the last spot to the first, then reverse the sequence to get a picture of what happened.' The technician switched on the equipment and the screen was filled by the image of a framework representing Rudd's studio, with outlines of furniture and his figure placed inside it. A sequence of images followed, like stills from a cartoon film, with red arcing lines projecting from Rudd's figure as it gradually changed position, turning and falling, and an irregular pattern of red spots spread outward on the floor around.

'It would need more work if we had to take this to court,' the RO said, 'but we're confident that the basic sequence is right.'

He paused, then nodded to the technician who pressed more buttons. The sequence began again from the beginning, but this time there was a second outline figure in the room, and as it moved towards Rudd and then away again, they saw how the figure blocked and interfered with the spray of red blood tracks. The reason for the irregular pattern on the floor now became clear. 'There was someone else in that room,' the RO said. 'It just doesn't work without them.'

There was total silence, and then Brock opened his file and drew out the copy of the birthday party photograph they'd found pinned on the studio wall. He stared at it for a long moment, then said, as if musing to himself, 'The unmatched DNA on the shoes we found in the bin outside . . . Did you try to match it with Tracey's?'

'Tracey?' They stared at him in surprise, and then Kathy realised what he meant, and something occurred to her, something she'd been trying to recall.

'The dolls' house,' she said, and then, her mind racing, 'I should have checked the phone calls.' Finally she asked, 'Have you got anything on the chisel, apart from its width?'

The RO checked his papers. 'Yes, it seems it's an unusual type, hollow ground on the underside of the blade. Japanese probably.'

32

KATHY GOT UP early the next morning, hours before sunrise, and drove into Shoreditch to join the others. There she exchanged her car in the police station compound for an unmarked observation van and headed west. She found a parking spot in the silent suburban street as dawn broke, and slipped into the back of the van to wait. After a while the smells of a suburb stirring awake on a cold Sunday morning began to percolate into her hiding place—coffee, frying bacon, the exhaust of a car. Later she watched an old orange Volvo turn out of the side road and she got behind the wheel to follow it and a trail of other cars heading for church.

When she finally arrived at the Nolans' house they were still reading the Sunday papers over the remains of their breakfast. They seemed embarrassed to be caught out in this state, and Bev started clearing dishes.

'I'd like to speak to you both together, if that's all right,' Kathy said, and led the way to the sitting room overlooking the back garden, the Nolans following reluctantly. Through the French windows they could see a thrush with a snail in its beak, trying to crack its shell on the brick path.

'It's about Gabe, of course?' Bev said, still flustered. 'We weren't sure whether to ring you again. What a shocking thing.'

'Have you caught someone?' Len asked, still not inviting Kathy to sit.

'I think we're getting close.'

'Really? Well, thank goodness. A maniac, I suppose? A stalker?' Len put an arm around his wife's shoulder as if to protect her from this, but she pulled away, glancing uneasily out at the garden. 'Look,' Len continued, 'I don't mean to be rude, Kathy, but this isn't a very convenient moment for us. You really should have phoned. Could we do this another time?'

'Sorry,' Kathy said. 'Do you mind if we sit down?'

'Of course. Where are our manners? I'm forgetting myself,' Bev said. Her voice sounded strained. 'I think we could all do with a nice cup of coffee, don't you?'

As she bustled out, Len said, 'She's still in shock, Kathy. We both are. Let's hope you do clear this up soon. But we really didn't expect to see you on a Sunday morning.'

'I understand, Len,' Kathy said getting up and moving to the door.

'No, don't worry . . .' Len called after her, but Kathy was already out of the room. She found Bev in the kitchen, pressing the buttons on a phone. She stopped and looked up guiltily when she saw Kathy, who came to her side and gently lifted the phone to see the number on the display.

'Yes, they're probably back from church now. Come on, Bev, it's time to talk.' Bev seemed to have shrunk a little as Kathy led her back into the sitting room.

'That's the Lovells' house over there, isn't it?' Kathy nodded at the back of another house directly behind their garden, identical to the Nolans' and all the others surrounding the block. 'They must be good neighbours. You phoned them the last time I came here. It was the first thing you did as soon as Enid across the street rang you on your mobile to tell you I was waiting for you. And then you rang them again as soon as I left.'

'You've been tapping our phones?' Len said, aghast.

'I checked last night, after I remembered something.'

'What was that?'

'When we first met you told me you'd made Tracey a dolls' house and a farmyard. I saw the farm upstairs in her old room, but where's the dolls' house?'

They looked stunned. 'Did we tell you that?' Len said. 'I don't remember.'

'So where is it?'

Len's face flushed red. 'You tap our phones and come here on a Sunday morning to ask us about dolls' houses? What's got into you people?'

'I see you've put a gate in your back fence since I was here last, so you don't even have to go out onto the street to visit the Lovells. That's handy. Oh . . .'

They followed her gaze, staring through the window at a small hand reaching over the top of the gate and fumbling with the latch. Bev took a sharp breath as if she were about to cry out. The gate swung open and a small girl dressed in Sunday best, with a smart tan coat and polished shoes, stepped into the Nolans' garden. She had dark brown hair, cut short, but Kathy recognised the features straight away. She'd been staring at them across her desk for the past three weeks. She felt a sudden sense of lightness, as if a dull weight had been lifted from her heart.

'How long have you known?' Len said.

'Not long.'

They watched the small figure come down the path between the vegetable and flower gardens, under the clothes line, to the kitchen door, then heard the voice, 'Grandma! Grandpa!'

Len roused himself. 'In here, cherub.'

Kathy looked at him, but there was no sign of irony. They seemed unaware of the reference. In fact, they both looked grey and defeated, barely aware of anything, and the little girl sensed it as soon as she came into the room.

'Are you all right, Grandma?' she said. 'Who's this?'

'Yes, dear. This is . . . a friend of ours.'

'Oh.' The little girl looked frankly at Kathy. 'What's your name?'

'Kathy. What's yours?'

'Tra . . . Lucy,' she corrected herself. 'Lucy Lovell. I live at thirty-six Nightingale Crescent with my great-aunt and uncle.'

'Do you like that?'

'Oh yes. When I'm seven I'm going to join the junior school orchestra.'

'I see. And where do you keep the dolls' house that your grandpa made for you?'

'In my other bedroom, of course. Grandpa's going to build an extension for it, aren't you, Grandpa, for my Christmas?'

'Yes, cherub,' Len said faintly.

'If you're busy with Kathy, can I watch cartoons on TV?'

'Of course.'

They watched her leave, and Kathy said, 'She seems happy.'

'Yes,' Bev said, an edge of resistance entering her voice. 'She's changed, even in three weeks. She's so much happier.'

'Took to it like a duck to water,' Len said.

'What have you told the school?'

'That the Lovells have taken in the daughter of their nephew, whose marriage has broken down. It's a common story, our generation having to step in to pick up the pieces. The school sees it all the time, didn't doubt us for a minute. We provided some paperwork.'

'And the Lovells were happy to go along with this?'

'They understood. We'd have done the same for them. It was only to be until you stopped looking for Tracey, then she'd have moved back in with us.'

'What about Gabe?'

'What about him? It was his idea.'

'*His* idea?'

'That's right. We'd been fighting with him over Tracey for years, and finally he came up with this. He admitted she was at risk staying with him—there were some dodgy characters in the square, apparently, and those other little girls had gone missing. So he said we could have her.'

'But why didn't he just transfer guardianship to you? Why the secrecy?'

'This was the only way he would do it. It was this or nothing. We had no choice,' Bev said, a note of desperation in her voice.

Len said, 'The question is, what are you going to do now?'

'There are lots of questions to be answered,' she said, and their attention was suddenly diverted to another movement in the garden. Brock was coming through the gate, and at the same moment the front doorbell chimed. 'Why don't you let those people in while I go and fetch Tracey?'

The television noise was coming from her bedroom upstairs. Kathy tapped on the door and a little voice said, 'Come in.'

'I just wanted to say hello, Tracey.'

'Hello.' The girl was stretched out on her stomach on the bed and didn't turn away from the screen, where some children were painting with their fingers on a wall.

'You are happy here, aren't you, Tracey?'

'Oh yes. Aren't they stupid? They think they're being like artists but they're just making a mess. My daddy's a real artist, and so am I.'

'Are you?'

'Oh yes. Look, I'll show you.'

She suddenly ducked forward and reached under the bed, pulling out a small canvas. 'I did this with real brushes. It's a picture of me with yellow hair.' She handed it to Kathy.

'So it is. It's very good. Betty showed me one just like this.'

'This is it! I gave it to Betty as a present when I left, but Grandpa got it back for me.' Tracey suddenly cocked her head. 'What is that noise? Who are those people?'

'They're friends of mine. They want to have a look around the house while we all go for a car ride together. You'd better put your coat back on again, because it's still cold outside.'

Kathy looked out the window into the street. Across the way, Enid and several other neighbours were standing at their front doors watching the police vehicles arriving, and people in white plastic overalls making their way to the Nolans' front door. Enid had a phone to her ear, alerting the neighbourhood.

33

BY THE FOLLOWING morning the physical evidence had become overwhelming. In Len Nolan's workshop they had found a set of Japanese Iyoroi brand chisels with hollow ground backs. Upon laboratory examination one had been established beyond doubt as the implement which had caused the marks at the various crime scenes. It had traces of blood on the handle which matched Gabe Rudd's, and his blood had also been found on a pair of gloves in a toolbox in the workshop. Len Nolan's DNA had been found to match the unknown DNA on the bloodstained shoes found in the bin near Rudd's house. This was the DNA which the lab had found, on Brock's prompting, to belong to a close blood relative of Tracey Rudd.

The Nolans responded to these damning facts with a strange mixture of self-justification and denial, Len full of bluster and Bev quietly insistent. Yes, they had hidden Tracey and lied to the police, but no, they were neither criminals nor murderers. Len Nolan freely admitted that the chisel was his, and even showed Brock the little mark which he had branded on the handle in case it was ever stolen. The gloves and shoes were also his, he conceded, and Bev could recall the shops where he'd bought them. Len also acknowledged that he had only one key for his workshop, the one on the key ring they had found in his pocket.

But when it came to linking these things to the murders in Northcote Square, they protested their total innocence. They vehemently denied any involvement and could offer no explanation. When asked about Tracey's self-portrait, removed presumably from Betty's house at the time of her murder, Len could only say that he had found it on their doorstep one morning, wrapped in a plastic bag. They hadn't told Tracey that Betty, or Stan, or her father were dead.

The contrast between willing cooperation in some things, and total denial in others, began to worry Brock and made him wonder if the couple was suffering from some kind of psychological condition. A psychiatrist was brought in to examine them and spoke of obscure cases of dissociative fugue and multiple personality disorder in which couples had been involved, experiencing periods of shared amnesia.

When shown the photograph of the Christmas party, Len agreed that he had been the photographer, and they found the space in their family album from which it had been removed. When they looked at the picture both Len and Bev became wistful. Prompted by Kathy, Bev volunteered that it was the last time they saw their daughter smile. Within a few weeks she would be dragged from the waters of the canal. Kathy pointed to the three people standing behind Jane and her baby, and Bev offered the opinion that all three of them, in their different ways, had contributed to Jane's despair—Gabe by his neglect, Betty by her mad claims upon her child, and Stan by his morbid preoccupation with death.

'So you'd say they were responsible for Jane's death, would you, Bev?' Kathy suggested, and Bev agreed that she would, apparently without any recognition that she was talking about three murder victims.

'There's a lot more work to be done,' Brock said unhappily, sinking back into the armchair in Commander Sharpe's office. 'We'll have to pick away at every detail to be sure we've got it right.'

'But still,' Sharpe said, stroking the cover of Brock's report appreciatively, 'an excellent piece of detective work.'

'I've spent hours locked up with those two over the past days, and I still can't get inside their heads. I can't . . .' he groped for the word, '. . . see it.'

'Oh, come on. Do you have children, Brock? I should know.'

'A son. He's in Canada now, I believe. We've lost touch.'

'Well, I have a daughter. She's intelligent, ambitious and beautiful, and holds down a responsible job in the City. She married a deadbeat who gets up at noon and spends his day between the pub and the betting shop. He hasn't driven her to suicide yet, but even so there have been many times when I wanted to slit his damn throat. And let me tell you that a million parents and grandparents in the same situation would have paid for my defence. I'm not sure that I followed all the mumbo jumbo in the shrink's report, but I can understand the Nolans perfectly, and let's face it, the physical evidence is irrefutable. It's a great result, Brock. Five murders solved, including Wylie for Aimee Prentice and Lee Hammond, and, best of all, Beaufort's dead.'

'Dead?' Brock sat upright.

'The committee, not the man. As of midday today the Beaufort Committee was suspended, consigned to limbo, relegated to the outer darkness. Nobody wants to hear about it.' He paused, clearing his throat in a way that made Brock look up. 'Which means, unfortunately, that your promotion to super is best left in abeyance at this stage. Much as we appreciate the work of you and your excellent team, we mustn't appear to be crowing, you understand?'

'All right,' Brock said, 'but my sergeant, Kathy Kolla, is long overdue for a move up to inspector. She passed the exams ages ago. I'd like something to be done about that.'

'Blockages in our personnel profile,' Sharpe nodded, as if regretting a medical problem. 'I'll see what I can do. She'll probably have to move to another unit, though.'

'No.'

'No? Oh, very well. Leave it with me. There's another matter. You probably know that at least one well-known reporter has got wind of you interviewing Beaufort at Shoreditch—somebody at the station probably tipped him off. They sniff scandal, Brock, and they're going to be after you, very soon, and we'd like to avoid that. Sir Jack has had the good sense to go abroad. And I was recently reminded—no, reprimanded—by Human Resources, or whatever they call themselves this week, that I've allowed you to accumulate an intolerable amount of untaken leave.' Sharpe aimed his most piercing look at Brock. 'Time for a holiday,' he said firmly.

'Yes,' Brock said. 'I've been thinking that myself.'

Sharpe, who had clearly been anticipating resistance, looked surprised. 'Good. When?'

'Tomorrow, actually.'

'Better still! Somewhere far away, I hope?'

'Australia.'

Sharpe leapt to his feet and shook Brock's hand as if to seal the matter before Brock could change his mind.

34

HE DROVE DOWN to Battle that evening and spent the night with Suzanne. The house seemed unnaturally still without the children, making Brock feel slightly self-conscious, as if they were starting a new relationship. He saw how much work Suzanne had put into preparing for the trip—new clothes, gifts for her family, the house readied, bags packed, documents assembled, arrangements for the stopover in Singapore, detailed instructions for her assistant on running the shop—while he had done nothing, barely having checked that his passport was current.

The next morning they drove up to London to collect Brock's things in preparation for their departure that evening. As they went through his house he realised how disorganised it was. Despite his protests, Suzanne helped with the piles of washing, ironing and clearing up, vetting his packing. 'It's spring there remember, David,' she said, and somehow the words brought home to him what a step they were taking.

They broke off for a last English pub lunch at The Bishop's Mitre in the high street, and as he supped his pint he was aware of Suzanne scrutinising him gravely with her intelligent grey eyes. 'What's wrong?' he asked.

'You're still thinking about work, aren't you?'

'Yes.'

'They're a bit like me, aren't they, the Nolans?' she said. 'Stepping in to protect their grandchildren. You've thought of that haven't you?'

'Of course.'

'And you're still not absolutely sure that they did those murders.'

'No.'

'I could, if I had to.'

He looked at her and smiled. 'No, not like that. And the point is, they didn't have to.'

'Oh well,' she put her hand on his, 'they'll still be here when we get back, won't they?'

'That's true.'

'It feels odd, the prospect of seeing Emily again,' Suzanne said. 'I mean, I'm very fond of her, and we were close when we were children, but she was the classic older sister, always in charge, always manipulating things to suit herself. It was a relief to get out from under her shadow. We'll have to watch she doesn't completely take over when we get there. She's probably organised every minute.'

When they got back to the house Suzanne decided to lie down for an hour while Brock finished clearing up. There was a pile of documents relating to the case that he planned to drop off at Shoreditch on the way to the airport, and as he gathered them up he came again upon the photograph of Tracey's first birthday party. It was this that had really convinced him about the Nolans' guilt. Here was everyone, all the victims, gathered together in a single moment captured by—who else but the murderer? There was a psychological aptness, a completeness about it that had seemed irresistible, crowned by the defiance of that final act of pinning it to the wall of Gabe's studio.

But what disturbed Brock was how poorly the Nolans had lived up to the vicious bravado of that gesture. Their defence had been naive and unprepared, without cunning or manipulation. That word reminded Brock of Suzanne's description of her sister, pulling strings in the background. He put the photograph aside and saw another picture beneath it, a print of the Fuseli etching that Kathy had copied to him. In the background were the two figures hanging from the gibbet, and in the foreground the two philosophers, one riding on the back of crouching humanity. Visual clues, if you could only decipher them; the case had been full of them.

When Suzanne saw him later that afternoon she found him keyed-up and distracted, ramming the last of his papers into a briefcase, and she put it down to the imminent journey. She felt the same way herself; things would settle down once they were on the move.

'Shall I make us a cup of tea?' she asked.

'We should go,' he said. 'I want to make an extra call on the way.'

It was growing dark when they loaded the last bag, locked Brock's house and set off towards Shoreditch where he'd arranged for Kathy to drive them to the airport and bring back his car.

He crossed the river on London Bridge and continued north along Bishopsgate and Shoreditch Street before turning off into a maze of narrow lanes and emerging into Northcote Square. He parked outside the glass doors of The Pie Factory and said, 'Won't be a minute.'

Fergus Tait was standing talking to the girls of 'Gabe's Team'. They all turned to Brock as he came in.

'Can I have a word?' he said.

'Of course, Chief Inspector,' Tait beamed through his big glasses.

'In private.'

'Follow me.'

The women watched them curiously as Tait led him away to his office.

Tait waved to a seat, eyeing Brock's clothes, the light windcheater and cotton drills, the polo shirt. 'You look as if you're off-duty, Mr Brock.'

'I'm just leaving on holiday, actually.'

'Somewhere warm by the look of it.'

'Yes. I'm on the way to the airport, but I thought I'd stop by. There was something I wanted to tell you.'

'Can I offer you a drink? I find I always need one before a flight. Whisky?'

'Thanks.'

Tait poured two glasses and handed one to Brock. 'Cheers. Is it about the case? Your people have kept me pretty well informed, I think. I must say I was as staggered as everyone else when they told me about the Nolans.' He shook his head to emphasise his amazement. 'What a shock.'

'But not bad for business, I suppose?'

Tait grinned. 'By no means. If I told you what one of these was worth now . . .' He indicated the puppy cans in the glass case behind him. 'Well, let's just say that it's a good bit more than the price of your holiday, wherever you're going, first class. But you know, I was talking about this to one of our customers in the restaurant last night, and they pointed out that a few years ago the Nolans would probably have got away with it. It was the science that caught them, was it not? The DNA and the laboratory analysis. No offence to you, of course, Chief Inspector, but police work is science now, isn't it?'

'Actually that's what I came to tell you, that the science was wrong. I don't believe the Nolans did kill Betty and Stan and Gabe.'

'What?' The affable smile vanished from Tait's face. 'You've got new evidence?'

'No, not a thing. Just a feeling.'

'Well . . . I don't follow.'

'It's a matter of interpretation and feel. Art rather than science. The science may say the Nolans are guilty, but the art says they're not.'

Tait gave a guffaw. 'Oh, come on. What on Earth do you mean?'

'You're in the art business. Don't you get presented with work like that? Your head says it should be okay, but you know it doesn't really feel right.'

'Maybe you should tell me what doesn't feel right about it, then.'

'First of all, Gabe knew what was going on. He was involved in it, right to the end, but with somebody else. You remember the etching? There are two people observing the hanging of Justice and Liberty—Voltaire and Rousseau, the two students of "monster humanity". And there were two people involved in the deaths that happened here, in the square—Gabe and a partner, a controlling partner.'

'Len Nolan,' Tait said. 'He admitted that they were in it together.'

'He admitted the removal of Tracey, yes, but not the murders. I don't believe that Gabe planned them at all, but he got drawn into it, couldn't stop it. From the way Poppy described him, I'd say he was both appalled and fascinated by them, until finally he became the last victim.'

'You're not suggesting that Poppy was this mysterious partner, then?'

'No, no. The thing about the killings—especially Betty's, but the others too—was their callousness, their deliberation, their cruelty. The Nolans simply weren't like that. Neither was Poppy, nor Gabe. In the end, that's why I couldn't believe the science.'

'I see. Well, who is this amazing specimen of monster humanity then, Mr Brock? Don't keep me in suspense.'

'I think it's you, Fergus.'

There was a moment's silence, and then Tait chuckled. 'What is this, some kind of entrapment scheme? Do you expect me to blurt out a confession, like the villain in a cheap novel? Are you wearing a tape recorder or something?'

'No; no tape recorders, no witnesses, no evidence. I simply wanted you to know.'

'Well . . .' Tait put his hands behind his head and rocked back in his chair, examining Brock's face. 'I'm not sure whether I should feel affronted or flattered. You'd better tell me what I did, exactly.'

'I imagine it might have begun quite casually. Maybe Stan had been telling Gabe about his friend Pat Abbott's interest in Tracey, and Gabe said something about wishing sometimes that he didn't have Tracey on his hands. Then you might have made a joke about what a publicity coup it would be for him if she became the next missing child—Jane's suicide all over again. And just out of idle curiosity perhaps, over a few drinks, the two of you speculated on how it could be done—without hurting Tracey, of course; in fact, really, in her best interests. Then Gabe put this to the Nolans, and realised that they would go along with it, and with your encouragement he decided to go ahead. Am I warm?'

'Fascinating. But why should I have been involved? Surely Gabe could have done all that on his own?'

'I don't think he had the nerve. I think he needed to be organised and pushed.'

'I see. So what happened then?'

'I think you discovered that Tracey had spoken to Betty before she went away. She gave her the self-portrait as a memento, and you couldn't be sure what she'd told her. The publicity was working wonderfully well, and Gabe's exhibition opening was a huge success, but you must have realised just how disastrous it would be if we began to take Betty's wild hints seriously and the truth came out. Apart from any criminal proceedings we might bring, both Gabe and your gallery would be utterly discredited, his work valueless.

'Did you tell Gabe that you'd only intended to question Betty about what Tracey had told her, and her death was an accident? At any rate, you convinced him that you'd had to make it look as if Stan had done it in order to cover your tracks, and that meant that Stan had to die too. I imagine that wasn't too hard after you told Stan that the police would put him back in the asylum when we caught him. Did Gabe work on him too, or did you do that alone? I think a joint campaign, myself. The great compensation for Gabe was that all this was providing incredible material for his *No Trace* project in the gallery. That would have eased his conscience no end, especially when you pointed out that there really was no alternative.

'But there was another problem, both practical and aesthetic. How the hell were you going to bring *No Trace* to a convincing, satisfying conclusion? You couldn't have the police finding Tracey, but you also couldn't have the whole thing dragging on for ever. I think Gabe had been thinking about this from the start. He planned sixteen banners, at the end of which he would expose his in-laws and get Tracey back, to everyone's relief, denying the Nolan's claims that he'd been involved in Tracey's abduction. Better still, with the two killings in the square you and Gabe could now stage a failed murder attempt, against him, with watertight clues pointing to the Nolans.

'That was all right as far as it went, but from your point of view it didn't really go far enough. It left Gabe alive to expose you one day if the fancy took him, and it didn't have the necessary climactic force. The punters want real drama, real tragedy, real pain, isn't that right? They don't want Van Gogh *pretending* to commit suicide, they want the real thing. They don't want Modigliani recovering from his drugs and TB, they want the tragic corpse, and the distraught pregnant mistress throwing herself out of the window after him.

'And that's really what this has all been about, isn't it? The price of *Dead Puppies*. Gabe Rudd and Stan Dodworth weren't making enough money for you any more, so you decided to enhance the market, give the punters what they really want.'

Tait had become very still, his eyes narrowed in thought.

'You're not saying much,' Brock said, draining his glass. 'Are you thinking of the killings? The moments of death? You enjoyed those, didn't you?'

'I don't find this conversation very amusing any more,' Tait murmured. 'If you've finished what you had to say, you'd better go.'

'Right. There is one thing I can't work out—how you got the photograph from the Nolans' house, and the things from Len's workshop. He swears there's only the one key.'

Tait gave a grim little smile. 'Well, for your peace of mind I could suggest a hypothetical answer. Len Nolan once made the mistake of lending Gabe his car to ferry Tracey somewhere. While he was at it,

Gabe had copies made of the other keys on the ring, the ones to the Nolans' house. He thought they might come in useful if things between him and the Nolans got nasty.'

'I see.' Brock got to his feet. 'I'm not going to let this go, Fergus. You know that, don't you?'

'Good luck, Chief Inspector. And can I say that if this little visit was intended to rattle me, it was a waste of time. You see, I know I'm smarter than you are. I won't be losing one minute of sleep over you. Enjoy your holiday, won't you.'

Tait stepped into the outer office and then stopped short. Beyond him Brock saw one of Gabe's computer girls standing by the photocopier behind the door. She was clutching a sheaf of paper to her chest as if for protection. She stared hard at Tait then spun on her heel and ran out. As Brock passed the door to the gallery he saw her with the other two girls, deep in whispered conversation.

'That took a long time,' Suzanne said as he got into the car.

'Yes, I'm sorry, it took longer than I thought. I had to get one or two things off my chest.'

'That's all right. I went into the gallery to see the show. I've been reading about it, of course, but I suppose seeing it in the flesh brought it home to me how big this thing has been. I think it's taken more out of you than you've been prepared to admit.'

'You may be right.' He stared into the darkness of Northcote Square gardens.

'What is it?' She was staring hard at him now, trying to make out his expression.

'I'm sorry, Suzanne,' he said softly. 'But I can't go. I thought I could, but I can't.'

'Don't,' she replied, surprising herself with her self-control, almost as if she'd known all along that this would happen. 'Don't do this to me, David.'

'I'm sorry,' he repeated.

'Is it me? Aren't I interesting enough company?'

'Of course not.'

'Well what then? You've found the little girl. Surely you don't love the Met that much? The hours? The heartache?' She couldn't hold back the bitterness in her voice now. 'It's a job, David, like any other. It's not your life.'

'It's my case,' he said, as if that was all that could be said. 'I can't leave now.'

He started the car and drove to Shoreditch station.

When Kathy and Bren saw him in the office their smiles faded.

'What's wrong, Chief?' Bren said. 'You feel all right?'

'I've just been to see Fergus Tait,' Brock said, and told them what had happened.

'He admitted it?' They both looked stunned.

'No, but he wanted me to know I was right. He's rather proud of himself.'

'Hell.' Bren sank slowly into a chair. 'We'll get to work on it while you're away. He must have made mistakes. We'll find something.'

'So Deanne was wrong,' Kathy said. 'She said art was the highest value, beating everything else, but Tait has proved that in the end, money trumps art.'

'Sir?' A woman had put her head round the door. 'Sorry to interrupt, but I'm monitoring Gabriel Rudd's Web site and something's just come up. I thought you might be interested.'

They followed her to her computer and saw the message in bold letters:

URGENT

ALL FRIENDS OF GABE RUDD WHO ARE ABLE ARE ASKED TO COME IMMEDIATELY TO THE GALLERY ENTRANCE IN NORTHCOTE SQUARE. WE HAVE IMPORTANT NEW INFOR-MATION REGARDING GABE'S DEATH

'They don't say what the information is,' the woman said.

Brock read the message again. 'It's possible that one of Rudd's computer operators overheard some of my conversation with Tait.'

'Blimey. You think they're organising a protest or something?'

'Or a lynching. Is the camera operating in the square?'

They went to the monitor and saw that already a small crowd had gathered at the gallery entrance. It was lit up by the headlights of cars circling the square, and knots of people were hurrying in from all directions. It was impossible to gauge the mood.

'That was quick,' Bren said. 'Do you think we should send a patrol car down?'

'Better inform the duty inspector,' Brock answered, but then Kathy pointed to a figure standing in the gallery doorway.

'Is that Tait? Can we get in closer?'

Bren worked the control panel and the camera zoomed in. It was Tait, they saw. He was waving, but not in panic, more as a celebrity might to his fans.

'He looks full of himself,' Bren said. 'Maybe it was he who put the notice on the web, trying to get his spoke in before we do.'

'Yes, you could be right.'

'What time's your flight, Brock?' Kathy asked. 'Shouldn't we be on our way? Don't worry about this. We can handle it.'

'I'm not leaving, Kathy. I'm going to stay.'

They looked stunned for a moment, then both began to protest, speaking at once, but he held up his hand and said, 'I'll drive Suzanne to the airport, then I'll be back.' He turned and walked quickly away before they could say any more. Kathy wanted to go after him, but Bren persuaded her to leave it.

'Let them sort it out,' he said. 'We could have a riot on our hands here.'

He pointed at the camera monitor, where it seemed that half of Northcote Square was now filled with people, a crowd seething like a single organism, amorphous and unsettled.

Brock returned a couple of hours later, looking sombre. He found Bren at the monitor.

'What's happening?'

'It's still a bit confused. Kathy's gone to the square to try to get a better idea.'

'What does she say?'

'It seems you were right about Gabe's computer girls. They've summoned the crowd.'

'What for? What are they telling them?'

'Well . . . pretty much what you told us. That the police know Gabe was murdered by Fergus Tait and not the Nolans, but they can't prove it. Tait came out to try to calm them down and protest his innocence but apparently that didn't go down too well and now he's back inside again, holed up in his office. We're sending a couple of cars down.'

35

KATHY HAD WORKED her way down West Terrace towards the gallery entrance, but there the crush was so dense that she was halted about thirty yards away. The people around her were all young, finishing their day's work when the messages started coming in. They had poured off the commuter trains and buses, out of the nearby tube stations and pubs, and made their way to Northcote Square. At first it had just been a bit of a lark, and everyone was cheerful and intrigued, the atmosphere rather chaotic. But Kathy had sensed a gradual change. As the stories about Fergus Tait began to circulate, the laughter died away, and the mood became sombre. Kathy realised that they really had seen Gabe as a star, a tragic hero. The crowd was also becoming organised, although it was difficult to see exactly how this was happening. Messages would filter through about the aims of the gathering and how they should behave, but it wasn't clear where they were coming from—the group closest to the gallery entrance, Kathy assumed, yet it seemed that people were receiving text-messaged instructions from all over London. An enterprising TV news crew had managed to set up a camera at the top of the scaffolding on Yasher's construction site, and was now broadcasting live.

'So what are they after?' Bren asked over the phone.

'They're describing it as a vigil,' Kathy replied. 'It seems peaceful enough at the moment, but I think we should be careful about sending in the storm troopers. There's so many people here now that a panic would cause a disaster.'

After four uniformed officers were stopped, politely but firmly, at the edge of the crowd now occupying streets all around Northcote Square, the Borough Commander agreed with his Head of Operations that a softly-softly approach should be adopted. Ambulances, a fire tender and a number of unmarked police vehicles were standing by, and uniformed police were attempting to turn new arrivals away. A call was made to the Public Order Operational Command Unit and an expert was on his way from 'Riot City', the Public Order Training Centre at Hounslow Heath.

Despite the alarming growth in numbers, the crowd remained calm, almost motionless, and the police were somewhat reassured by a second notice on Rudd's Web site, which announced the formation of the 'Vigil for Gabe', a nonviolent demonstration of support for the dead artist. Its aims were to honour his memory and seek justice for his murder.

'There really was no need for you to interrupt your holiday, Brock,' the Borough Commander said. 'The best thing we can do is pray for rain.'

Brock got Kathy on the phone. 'Are you sure you're all right?' he asked. He thought he had spotted her on the monitor, one pale head among thousands. It made him think of a sea of wild flowers, swayed by the wind.

'A bit cold, otherwise fine. I wish I'd brought my big coat and some thick socks. What's the forecast?'

'Heavy frost.'

'There's a rumour that coffee is on its way. I get the impression that they're planning on a long wait.'

'For what?'

'Nobody's sure. Brock, what about Suzanne?'

There was silence for a moment, then, 'She's gone on.'

There was nothing Kathy could find to say.

Dawn seeped like icewater into the sky. Kathy thought she'd never felt so cold or stiff. All around her people were groaning and stretching and rubbing frozen body parts. Strangers had huddled together in dark clumps to share their warmth, and she had found herself against the garden railings with half a dozen young women from the post office. There had been movement throughout the night, with some leaving and others taking their places, but the overall numbers didn't seem to have diminished. At one point she'd been tempted to seek shelter with Reg Gilbey, whose lights had been on for most of the night. She saw his windows illuminated now, and then his front door opened and the old man himself appeared, precariously balancing a tray of paper cups from which steam rose into the morning air. The same thing was happening all around the square—from the building site, from Mahmed's Café and The Daughters of Albion—but not from The Pie Factory, which was shrouded in darkness.

Kathy's mobile rang, Brock's voice. 'Still with us?'

'Just about.' The phone was freezing against her cheek. She stood up and gave a wave towards the parapet where she knew the camera was mounted.

'Your chums have been busy during the night.'

'Have they?'

'They've put more information on the web, and we've been monitoring thousands of messages of support from all around the world. They've announced that they want a complete and voluntary confession from Tait, and apparently you're all going to stay there until he gives it. They've established a liaison committee with the Hackney police and they assure us they intend their actions to be nonviolent. They've also proclaimed that *Vigil for Gabe* is an artwork, somewhere between a happening and an installation, and any interference from the authorities will be regarded as cultural vandalism. A number of impressive names and organisations from the art world support their position, and they plan to submit an application to the Arts Council for funding, and to the Tate for the next Turner Prize, in conjunction with *No Trace.*'

'Tricky.'

'Yes. And I'm ordering you to return to the Shoreditch canteen for debriefing over a hot breakfast.'

'If you insist.'

They'd been busy in other ways too. While Kathy was in the canteen a call came through for Brock from Fergus Tait, his first contact since the occupation of Northcote Square had begun. 'They've cut off my bloody electricity and phone lines. I'm freezing in here. You've got to come and get me out.'

'I'll pass on your request, Mr Tait, but you've got to appreciate that it's a very difficult situation. We don't want to provoke a riot.'

'I don't care what you provoke, they're going to kill me.'

'We've had no indication of that. Have they threatened you?'

'They won't let me leave! They've even locked off the restaurant and kitchens—I've got no food and I'm bloody starving.'

'Why don't you just give them what they want?'

'Don't be bloody stupid.'

'Better not waste your phone battery, Mr Tait. Goodbye.'

The Pie Factory Siege, as the press named it, continued through that day and on into its second night. There was another call from Tait as dusk fell. His voice was rambling and confused, and it appeared he had finished the last dregs for the liquor cabinet in his office. He was very hungry, he said, and he was frightened they would come for him in the night. He was burning paper for light and heat, and Brock warned him to be careful of causing a fire. Did he have water? The mains had been turned off, he said, but there was still a trickle coming through the tap in the toilet. He refused to discuss a confession. 'I didn't go through all that to have the rewards snatched from me now,' he barked angrily, and hung up.

Soon afterwards Bren answered a phone call for Brock. 'Someone saying he's a concerned citizen. Won't give a name, but it sounds to me like a Turkish Cypriot trying to imitate Tony Soprano. He's offering to solve the impasse by going in and persuading Mr Tait to confess.' Brock took the phone and thanked the anonymous caller, but declined his kind offer.

A crisis meeting of combined authorities was held later that evening. There were fears about public health and safety issues, traffic disruption and public order, as well as bad publicity. The fire brigade was especially concerned about the risks of a conflagration in the old buildings, with their stores of flammable liquids in the workshops and kitchens. And then there was the problem of Fergus Tait. If he could be extracted, the whole situation would be defused—but how could this be done? The spokespersons for *Vigil* were adamant that no police or other authorities would be allowed through, and several plainclothes officers had been caught and ejected before they could reach The Pie Factory. Plans were prepared for a helicopter-borne rescue from the air, but the crowd had anticipated them, and people now covered the roof, like a human blanket smothering Tait.

Tait called Brock again at dawn on the third day, sounding exhausted and disoriented. He wanted to speak to Brock face-to-face, he said. Brock agreed to see what he could do. The liaison committee was consulted, and after some debate it was agreed that Brock could go in alone, without food. If he was taken hostage, they said, that was too bad.

A car dropped him at the edge of the crowd, which parted before him as he approached. It was an eerie experience, walking through the muffled streets in the dim grey light, as if a whole quarter of the city had been taken over by an army of silent ghosts. He reached the gallery entrance of The Pie Factory, feeling hundreds of eyes on him as one of the crowd came forward and unlocked the glass door.

'He's in the gallery,' the man said. 'We can see him through the window.'

'Thanks.'

Brock stepped into the gloom of the interior, hearing the lock snap behind him. 'Tait?' he called, but there was no reply. When he got to the doorway to the gallery he saw the pale figure sprawled beneath Gabe's final, sixteenth banner, his back propped against the wall, chin down on his chest.

For a moment he thought Yasher Fikrit must have got to him after all, but then the head lifted and Tait said, 'Ah, Mr Brock, you made it. Do come in.' His attempt at jauntiness was betrayed by his voice, as frail as an old man's. Brock went over and lowered himself to sit beside him.

'Did you bring anything to eat?' Tait asked querulously. 'Anything hot? I'm so bloody cold.'

'I'm afraid not. They wouldn't allow it.'

'Bloody Nazis!' he spat, then the fight faded out of him again. 'It's very lonely in here, you know. You've no idea. After three nights in here, you know what lonely means.'

It had only been two, but Brock didn't correct him.

'It used to be full of life, this place. Full of people, my friends, people who liked and needed me. But then I got greedy and destroyed it all. Now it's just full of ghosts . . .' He waved a hand up at the banners, then at the faces through the window. 'I've become an exhibit in my own gallery, a still life. *Nature morte* is the French term. Very appropriate, don't you think? Dead nature, that's what I am now.'

He stared for a moment at the faces outside. 'They'll never go away, will they? Doesn't matter where I go or what I do, they'll be there, peering in through the windows, staring across the aisle of the aeroplane, saying, "There he is. There's the man who killed Gabriel Rudd." The waiter who serves my meal, the man who drives my taxi, the barber who cuts my hair, they'll all look at me in that same way. There'll be no peace, no forgiveness. Unless I confess. Maybe then.'

'Yes, Fergus. Maybe then.'

'I'll give them what they want, Mr Brock. Just set it up, will you? I don't want to stay here any longer.'

Brock helped him to his feet, and Tait made one final attempt at bravado. 'You never know, there may be scope for an art dealer in gaol. There could be a big market for prison art, don't you think?'

36

THE WHOLE OF the previous forty-eight hours now seemed like a surreal dream, Brock thought, a piece of Dadaist experimental theatre. The bar was filled with coppers from the Major Enquiry Team, drinking and joking with a particular intensity, as if to reassure themselves that the world hadn't gone completely mad and there were still a few normal folk around.

Emboldened by her Scotch, Kathy said, 'Have you tried calling her?'

He frowned, looking at his watch. 'It's probably the middle of the night over there.'

'You should tell her what's happened. She'll understand.'

'Hmm.' He bit his lip, not at all sure about that. He still got a lump in his throat when he remembered the way she'd disappeared through the passengers-only gate, without a backward look. It was a memory he'd replayed many times over the past couple of days and nights.

'Anyway,' he said, changing the subject, 'Deanne's hypothesis proved right after all; art triumphed over Mammon.'

'That's true.' She turned as the door of the bar opened, and smiled as she recognised Tom Reeves. He caught sight of her and grinned back, and she thought how nice he looked, dark hair swept back, face flushed with colour from the cold.

'Do you remember Tom?' she said to Brock, who looked up in surprise.

'Oh, yes, of course. How are you, Tom?'

'Great. Congratulations, sir. Fantastic result.'

His enthusiasm was genuine, Kathy saw, probably enhanced by wonder at Brock's durability.

'What will you have to drink?'

'Let me,' Brock said, and went over to the bar.

'You must be exhausted,' Tom said to Kathy, scrutinising her face as if for signs of damage. 'Are you hungry?'

'Ravenous. Is this our date, then?'

He nodded.

'Well, I should warn you, I spent last night lying on a pavement and I didn't get much sleep. I may just flake out.'

'That's fine, but I warn you, that excuse only works once,' he said, and Kathy laughed, suddenly happy to be alive.

Brock returned, catching the flush on Kathy's cheek. 'Well, don't think me rude,' he said, 'but I'll be pushing off. Have a good night.'

He picked up the brown-paper parcel and made for the door, looking forward to a long bath and a warm bed, and, in the morning, hanging a second picture on his living room wall, next to the Schwitters. It was a present from a little girl now reunited with her grandparents, against whom, Brock felt confident, Virginia Ashe would shortly agree to drop further proceedings.